Miles

The House of Bannerman, book 1

by Melissa R. L. Simonin

© 2014

Miles

The House of Bannerman, book 1

written by Melissa R. L. Simonin

copyright 2014 by Melissa R. L. Simonin

Dedicated to...
Mom, for all of the support and encouragement and hours upon hours of proof-reading you've spent on "Miles;" to Dad, for your feedback and encouragement; to my husband, Brad, who has been very under-standing of the late hours spent by this writer and at being woke up in the middle of the night and expected to listen and answer "how does this sound?" and to my daughter, Emily.

This book is also dedicated to Chip, my own chocolate Lab pal, dearly loved and dearly missed in spite of the many years that have passed. May you live on in the pages of *Miles*.

Table of Contents

Chapter 1 5

Chapter 2 23

Chapter 3 35

Chapter 4 63

Chapter 5 79

Chapter 6 95

Chapter 7 105

Chapter 8 115

Chapter 9 131

Chapter 10 143

Chapter 11 157

Chapter 12 167

Chapter 13 177

Chapter 14 189

Chapter 15 199

Chapter 16 215

Chapter 17 227

Chapter 18 237

Chapter 19 249

Chapter 20 263

Chapter 21 275

Chapter 22 287

About the Author 299

Chapter 1

I moved silently through the kitchen, avoiding the creaking floor-board. It was my first chance to explore since moving here last week, and if I could get out the door before a certain three-year-old woke up, I'd be in the clear. I love my little brother all to pieces, but some-times Tryon could be a little trying, if I had somewhere else to be, and he woke up before Mom.

As I filled a sandwich bag with a handful of baby carrots, my chocolate Lab pal, Chip, lightly wagged his baseball bat of a tail. I cringed at the thought of the drum-like effect it would have on the cabinet if he wagged any harder. Keep the enthusiasm down boy, we're almost out of here!

Grabbing the sack lunch I put together the night before, I passed the kitchen island. Slipping the bag into my backpack, I palmed my "Anika" emblazoned key ring, gave Chip's glossy forehead a quick rub, motioned for him to follow me out the backdoor, then closed it carefully behind us.

I stifled the urge to cheer as I locked the door. I zipped my keys inside my pack, and slipped my arms through the straps.

The scent of pine, changing leaves, damp earth, and a wood burn-ing fire permeated the air. The broadleaf trees scattered amongst the pine were tinted orange and gold. The few clouds in the sky glowed pink and orange as the sun rose and touched them with light.

I took a deep breath as we disappeared into the woods behind the cabin.

"You can shake now. No one will hear you," I said. Chip shook violently, and smiled his toothy grin. It felt indescribably good to breathe the clean mountain air and look forward to a day without worry and responsibility. Some of the stress I'd accumulated over the past year, slowly began to melt away.

When Dad lost his job, it was a complete shock. After working at the same company for over twenty years, we assumed he would stay put until he retired. Instead, Dad's entire team was laid off. Some say misery loves company, but it didn't make our misery less miserable.

In the city where we lived, there were no jobs available that matched his field of expertise, and the poor economy meant few op-portunities elsewhere, as well. Dad qualified for unemployment which was something, and I kept the part-time job I'd had since my junior year in high school. It still wasn't enough to handle the mortgage payment, and everything else we needed.

We would have said "at least we have our health" and been glad of it, if it were true. But it wasn't, adding to the emotional and financial strain. We cut back in every way possible, and put off my college plans. The money just wasn't there for it anymore. It was kind of an odd feeling to realize the friends I graduated with, started their first semester last month.

Dad's brother, my Uncle Mark, was convinced Dad should come work for him, at his software company. It meant moving to Glen Haven, an urban area with a high cost of living, and Dad wasn't sure working for his brother was such a good idea, either. But a year later and at the end of our rope, it sounded just pretty good.

In spite of that, the high cost of living meant we couldn't afford to live in Glen Haven until we were back on our feet, which wasn't going to happen unless Dad had a job, which he couldn't get unless we moved, which we couldn't afford to do unless… Uncle Mark thought of everything, and came up with a solution to that problem, too. Until we can afford to do otherwise, Dad is staying with Uncle Mark at his apartment in Glen Haven during the week, while the rest of our family lives in Uncle Mark's cabin, about an hour and a half away. It's close enough so Dad can spend the weekends with us, and close enough so we can drive into the city to see specialists, too. Glen Haven has a lot more doctors to choose from than where we used to live, which is encouraging. It's lousy that our family is separated part of the time, but it's loads better than the way it was. And it isn't forever.

The first week at the cabin was all about unpacking and running errands. But now everyone was settled in, Mom didn't need me today, and I was free to explore.

A frog croaked beside the stream that wound through the forest. The song birds were singing exuberantly, and a bee buzzed from one wild flower to the next.

I couldn't get over how beautiful the day was. Squirrels leaped fearlessly from tree to tree, doing crazy acrobatics, and the birds continued their singing. The shallow stream tumbled over stones as it made its way past us, making its own music. Nose to the ground, Chip made short excursions to examine shrubs and trees that he found particularly interesting. I walked along slowly, pausing now and then to appreciate the beauty that surrounded us, and to allow Chip to take as much time as he wanted to investigate. We didn't have anywhere we had to be, and this day was too exquisite to rush through.

The angry sound of my stomach reminded me it was long past breakfast. Whistling for Chip, I looked for a good place to sit and eat. Instead, I spied a small stone bridge. It was only a little further down the path. I decided I was more curious, than hungry.

The bridge was a work of art and clever engineering, each carefully crafted stone fitting snugly in place. I ran my hand along the railing, admiring the work that must have gone into building this.

I felt an indentation in the cool surface of the stone, and had a closer look. *M.D.B, June 30, 1869* was carved on one rail.

"Unbelievable," I said under my breath.

One-hundred and forty-five years old, and still providing safe passage across the stream. Beyond the bridge, a path led into the woods.

"This is way more interesting than lunch," I decided. "Come on, buddy. We have to investigate this!"

I stepped onto the stone bridge, and Chip followed.

"It's fortunate for you this is here," I commented to Chip, as we crossed over the stream. "Since no one's ever convinced you that Labs are water dogs, you'd probably tell me to take a hike by myself, if following meant getting your feet wet."

Remembering his reaction the last time I gave him a bath, I laughed.

Chip's only response was another smile. He was having a blast, exploring. Moving here certainly suited him just fine. I ruffled the fur on his back, and was thankful I still had him. I remembered with gratitude that when we lost our house, my parents didn't decide life would be easier if we no longer had a dog, either. Considering the neighborhood we relocated to at that time, Mom and Dad were probably glad to have Chip for the protection.

Life today, was certainly an improvement over life two weeks ago.

As we followed the path, the forest around us thickened. Intermixed with the pine were towering oak trees, their reddening leaves in vivid contrast to the surrounding forest. Their limbs arched overhead, blocking the sun. The occasional cry of a bird sifting through the leaves, and the pad of Chip's paws, were the only sounds.

The path was once cobbled, although many of the stones were now missing. The further we walked the more stones remained intact, until at last the path became whole.

It must lead to something worthy of the bridge and cobbled path, why else would someone take the time and effort to build either one?

I walked faster. I wanted to see what was at the end of this! Chip ran to keep up.

Leaving the shelter of the forest, we found ourselves standing at the edge of a garden. Late blooming roses and a wide variety of flowering plants and shrubs, grew unhindered. Vines crept over the ironwork tables, chairs, and statues, and a shower of morning glories draped the ornate fountain. What must have been a beautiful lawn at one time, was now overrun with dandelions and weeds.

But that, was not what held me rooted to the spot with my mouth hanging open.

In the center of the spacious garden stood a towering stone mansion. Turrets jutted from the sharply slanted roof, and tucked in its many gables, were windows of various shapes and sizes. Round towers pointed to the heavens with their cone shaped caps. The castle-like estate was four stories high, judging from the windows. On each side of the main structure stretched an additional wing, with towers spaced evenly along its walls. Filling the space between each tower, was a row of decorative stone which resembled saw tooth battlements.

I stared in astonishment. The size of the structure was stunning, in addition to everything else about it. There were hospitals that weren't *this* big.

"Wow, now *that* is worthy of the stone bridge and cobbled path!"

Chip stood beside me, more interested in the garden, than the humongous castle that I couldn't take my eyes off of.

I had no idea such a thing existed in this country, much less right here, practically next door to Uncle Mark's cabin! Does he know about this?

A freezing blast of wind destroyed the gentle breeze. It hit with such sudden force, I struggled to keep my balance. I looked up at the sky for the first time since crossing the bridge.

A black cloud moved toward us rapidly, blotting out the sun and plunging everything beneath it into darkness. The castle towers rose in sharp contrast to the rapidly darkening sky. Lightning flashed, briefly illuminating the green-tinged clouds from within, and thunder rumbled ominously.

"This isn't in the forecast!" I exclaimed a little indignantly, as if that declaration would bring back the blue sky, and send the interloping storm packing. Chip whined softly.

My mind raced, searching for shelter, and coming up with nothing. We'd never outrun this, and taking the path through the trees would be about as smart as traveling between two rows of lightning rods. The estate looked abandoned, but I wouldn't seek shelter there, even if it wasn't. Where I come from, entering the house of a stranger is risky, no matter how amazing the house looks on the outside.

A streak of lightning and deafening blast of thunder warned me I better quit thinking, and *do* something. Looking apprehensively at the castle, I blinked in surprise. Was… that a curtain falling back into place, in one of the upstairs windows?

I felt a chill that had nothing to do with the frigid wind.

Icy raindrops began to pelt the ground, and I turned to discover that non-water-dog Chip was already halfway to the castle, and a vestibule protected side entrance. The way the wind was whipping every which way, that vestibule wasn't going to give much protection from the rain, but it could prevent us from being badly injured if the storm brought hail with it. I hurried after him.

Running across the uneven and overgrown yard, I took a flying leap over a mass of tangled vines. I landed on the other side, and with a loud crack and the sound of splintering wood, the surface beneath me shifted. I fell forward, reaching out frantically in search of anything to grab hold of, as it completely gave way. My fingers came in contact with stone, and I latched on, my heart pounding as gravity exerted almost unbearable pressure on my shoulders and hands, nearly breaking my hold. The surface that gave way beneath me, struck the bottom of the pit with a sickening thud, and shattered.

Note to self, always look before you leap! I hope I live long enough to follow that very good advice, in the future.

I struggled to get a better grip, and with a stranglehold on the stone ledge, I fought to pull myself up, arms shaking with the effort. My legs swung helplessly in the open space that surrounded me. I gasped for breath, my hands cramping, as gravity's pull overcame my strength. My fingers slipped on the rain dampened stone, and I cried out as my hold slowly gave way.

The tears of desperation running down my cheeks turned to tears of relief, when I didn't fall after all. Instead of empty space beneath me, I found myself supported by a solid surface.

I had no idea how my flailing feet managed to miss that before! The pressure on my arms relieved, I took a few deep breaths. Tightening my grip on the ledge, I braced my feet against the surface in front of me that I'd somehow neglected to discover earlier, and managed to pull myself up. I got one elbow over the ledge, then the other, and with one last heave, I scrambled out of the hole and collapsed beside it.

Muscles burning like fire and shaking uncontrollably from the effort, I lay on the ground a moment, struggling to catch my breath and gather my scattered wits. Chip abandoned his run for shelter and now pressed against me, whining softly.

"It's okay, it's alright," I said as much to myself, as to Chip. I wiped the tears and blinding rain out of my eyes, and looked beside me at the hole in the earth where the ground gave way.

"This could be the entrance to a cellar..."

I pulled back the morning glory vines with arms that were almost too weak to do so, revealing a gaping doorway into the ground. The rain came faster, huge drops pounding the earth. We found the stairs at the same time, and hurried down.

I didn't like leaving the opening uncovered with the storm raging, but the door was lying in fragments at the foot of the stairs and there was nothing I could do about that. I was relieved to see the wood was rotten, though. It would not be a self-confidence booster to think I broke through a perfectly good door!

We reached the base of the stairs as the sky was torn with lightning, and rain drowned the earth.

We hurried further away from the open doorway, and what little light was left. The pitch-black darkness, chill air, and musty smell, reminded me of a cave. I slipped off my backpack and felt around for the flashlight I kept there *just in case*. Finding it, I panned the flashlight in a circle, the beam weakly illuminating my surroundings.

Assorted gardening tools were lined along one wall, and a few bags of potting soil, lawn, and rose fertilizers were stacked next to them. The bags were a recognizable brand. The refrigerator and upright freezer, were further proof that someone was here in recent years.

The thunder was so loud it was hard to hear anything else, and the wind howled through the open doorway, bringing rain with it. I moved to a dry corner and sat on the cold floor, rubbing my aching muscles. For the first time, I was thankful for what Mom kindly refers to as my "trim athletic build." If I was more abundantly blessed in the curve department, I never could've pulled myself back out of the cellar after falling through the doors.

I pointed the flashlight at the open doorway, and frowned a little. There beam of light revealed nothing but empty space between it and the floor.

I was confused. When my fingers slipped, what did I land on? It wasn't the stairs, they were set back from that end of the opening. My feet were definitely supported as I lost my grip on the ledge, though...

I shone the light at the stairs again. I wanted to figure this out. I didn't care when I was clutching that ledge for dear life, but now I did.

I spent several minutes puzzling and searching for a solution, then Chip moved into my line of sight, and sat down in front of me with a hopeful look.

"I'll bet you're hungry, aren't you?" I said loudly. I practically had to shout, to hear myself over the storm.

Chip tap danced in place, then sat waiting patiently to be served, as I took his collapsible bowl and a Ziploc bag of dry dog food from my backpack.

I set Chip's dinner in front of him, and opened my sack lunch. In spite of my near-death experience, I was hungry, too.

We ate, listening to the wailing wind and the pounding of the rain. I tossed my apple core to Chip and he finished it off, then sat and looked at me expectantly.

"No carrots right now bud, we'll save those for later. Who knows how long this storm will last."

Chip stared at me intensely.

"You want more water?"

No reaction.

"What, you want to go back out in *that*?" I exclaimed, looking toward the cellar stairs, where hail bounced and rolled across the floor like spilled marbles.

Chip huffed and stood.

I followed him with the beam of my flashlight as he crossed the cellar floor, and stopped at the foot of a second set of stairs. He looked back at me pointedly, then turned and climbed the steps toward the closed door at the top.

"Chip!" I hissed in alarm, scrambling to my feet. "Where do you think you're going!"

Chip reached the top of the stairs, pushed the door open, and disappeared.

I could not believe he did that! It was horrible behavior on his part, and not like him, at all. But like him or not, and like it or not, he was out of the cellar, and inside the estate. So, now what?

I stood there looking up at the open doorway and the darkness on the other side, as I wondered what to do.

There were so many good reasons not to go inside this castle. As bad as it is to go through the front door of a stranger's house by invitation, entering through their cellar without their knowledge is on a whole other level. We kind of broke and entered, and are already trespassing. I remembered seeing that curtain move, too.

But my dog is in there. I can't just let him go wandering around like that, who knows what he could get into. And I've got to admit, as crazy as Chip was acting, a part of me was crazy enough to *almost* be glad he was giving me an excuse to see the inside of the castle.

I felt a mixture of excitement and apprehension as I reached the steps, and began to climb. I remembered the old saying "curiosity killed the cat, but satisfaction brought her back." I sure hope the second part of that is true, I thought, as I reached the top of the stairs.

The open doorway revealed a broad, shelf-lined room with some sort of cabinet, kind of like a kitchen island, in the center. The room had to be a pantry. There was nothing on the shelves now, other than the indentation of cans and a few stains. And dust. I stifled a sneeze and hurried through the next doorway, anxious to collect my insubordinate dog.

Beyond the pantry loomed a large kitchen that retained its antique look, in spite of the updated appliances. There was no wood burning cook stove, ice box, and water pump, but the space retained its antique appearance, in spite of all the modern conveniences. The dust which lay undisturbed over every surface said it was abandoned, but sometime in the last few years, not century. I continued on, following the dog prints on the dusty hardwood floor.

12

That didn't make sense... Chip's prints crossed over a second set of paw prints. Another dog must have been here not long ago, but why? How did it get in, and where was it now? There was no evidence of human footprints, which did not disappoint me. It was spooky enough in here, already.

Chip's paw prints led through a butler's pantry to a large dining room. The light from the flashlight cast eerie shadows behind the mahogany furniture. Intricately carved figures and designs, were obscured by a thick layer of dust. Heavy embroidered wall hangings adorned the walls.

The light from my flashlight glinted off the glass doors of the china cabinet. In its reflective surface, I saw that my brown eyes were even larger than usual, my shoulder length brown hair was a mess, and my heart shaped face was pale. I looked almost as apprehensive as I felt.

Inside the cabinet was a gorgeous display of china. It would be beautiful in the light of day, minus the dust and cobwebs, but right now the sun was no match for the storm, or the heavy window coverings. The frequent lightning flashes didn't improve the eerie atmosphere.

I was glad I had a flashlight! I couldn't imagine stumbling around here in the dark. I was wishing I had my dog, too.

I continued through room after room and hall after hall, following the trail of paw prints. Every so often the second set of prints intersected with Chip's. I traveled deep into the left wing of the house, in pursuit. How far did he intend to go? This wasn't like him at all.

My heart pounded as the flashlight flickered and dimmed, then shone steady again. I needed to find Chip and get out of here before my batteries failed, but a sense of self-preservation kept me from calling out to him. I was overwhelmed with fear that someone else would answer, and if that happened, I would surely die of fright.

I spotted Chip as he passed through yet another doorway at the end of a dark hallway.

"There you are!" I shivered as I caught up with him, retrieving his leash from my pack, and clipping it to his collar. "What in the world were you thinking, taking off like that?"

As I turned to go back the way we came, a lightning flash revealed the walls of the room around us, and the paintings which covered them. We were standing in a portrait-filled gallery.

All thoughts of returning to the cellar in a timely manner were shoved aside as curiosity overcame me, and I stepped forward for a closer look.

The portraits were amazing. I'd never been so close to original works of art before. It was interesting to follow the changes in fashion over the years as I followed the paintings, but what fascinated me the most, were the people who once lived here. I walked slowly, taking the time to read each name and study each face.

Until the late 1800's the firstborn son in every generation was named Delevan. The last died in 1870.

I stood for a moment, studying the portrait of the last Delevan Bannerman. He was stocky, with thick black hair that wanted to curl. I couldn't decide what his eye color was, maybe gray. He had chiseled features and a firm chin, and looked serious and determined. His deep-set eyes had a look of kindness, in spite of his expression. He was only twenty-three at the time of his death. That explained why he was the last one, then. He died without leaving behind a son to carry on the tradition.

I felt appropriately saddened by that, then moved on to the next portrait, Delevan's younger brother.

Miles Delevan Bannerman. MDB. He must have built the bridge that led me here. I glanced at the year of his birth and death, which were engraved underneath his name, and was dismayed by what I saw.

Miles died the same year as his brother.

I stared back and forth from one portrait to the other. What happened? Were their deaths connected, or was the timing a horrible coincidence? A lot of people died due to illness before vaccinations became available. Was that the cause of this double tragedy? I studied his portrait, wishing I could make sense of it.

Miles didn't resemble Delevan at all. He was strong but lean, with short, dark blond hair that waved back from his forehead in what resembled a modern-day business man's cut. The laughter in his smile also filled his hazel eyes, and he looked as though he'd found the secret to happiness. The joyful light in his eyes promised if you were around him long enough, you'd find it too.

Miles' portrait stood out in extreme contrast to the others, whose subjects looked as though they could barely manage a smile, much less laughter. I did the math. Born in 1850, he was about my age. Only twenty years old, when he died. His eyes were filled with such life and optimism, it just didn't seem possible he could do anything other than live. It never felt right when someone died young, all their hopes and dreams and so much potential, just—gone from this earth. Sadness washed over me.

I stood in front of the portraits of the two brothers for a long time after that, wondering.

The Bannermans had other children as well, a younger daughter and son, who both survived them. How sad though, to lose two of their sons. Nothing would make up for their loss, and how horrible for the remaining children to lose their siblings. As I looked at the paintings soberly, I thought of my sister. Some of the worry I let go earlier in the day, returned.

I spent so much time on the earlier portraits, especially the two brothers, that I hurried to get through the rest of the paintings. I was anxious to see them all, but also wanted to return to the cellar so we could leave as soon as the storm allowed. I forgot my watch, but it felt like we'd been here for hours. The desire to explore was strong, but memories of the moving curtain continued to intrude, and left me feeling unsettled.

Judging by the paintings, there were two Bannerman descendants still living. Polly Bannerman, and grandson Miles. He looked an awful lot like his ancestor of the same name, though younger.

I spent a few more minutes comparing the two. The likeness was pretty close. More tragedy though, the second Miles' parents died five years ago. He didn't have the same joyful laughter in his eyes as the first, and that was probably why. Although, I'd never seen anyone with the light in their eyes that the first Miles had. It wasn't common.

Someone was here in the last five years, anyway, to have the year of the parent's deaths engraved and added to those two paintings. I wondered where Polly Bannerman and her grandson were now, and why the house stood empty and uncared for.

My flashlight flickered threateningly. It was time for us to go, if we didn't want to be left in the dark.

"Come on buddy, let's see what the weather's doing now," I said, pulling myself away from the paintings. Back through the darkened house we went, past the shrouded furniture. It was fortunate the the floors were so dusty, if I didn't have our footprints to follow, I'm not

15

sure we would find our way back out. Pulling aside a very dusty curtain at one of the windows, I breathed a sigh of relief. If the clouds held more rain, for the moment at least, they were holding it in.

Through the cellar, up the stairs, and we were standing in the garden once more.

I looked back at the open cellar ruefully. I hated leaving it that way, but didn't see an alternative.

A glance at the sky revealed dark clouds still lurking. It wouldn't be long before it was pouring rain again.

Chip and I took off running for the cabin. Maybe we could make it home before then.

Our feet flew across the garden, down the path, over the bridge, and through the forest. We kept up our break-neck pace, and made the trip from castle to cabin in a fraction of the time it took to go from cabin to castle.

We raced across the miniscule covered porch and through the door, as rain poured from the sky once more.

"Anika!" exclaimed Mom. She held a dish towel in one hand, and a wooden spoon in the other. A chocolate cake sat on the counter behind her. She brushed her short blond curls off her forehead with the back of her hand, and looked me over with her blue eyes. "I'm glad you're back. I was beginning to worry, with the weather like it is."

"Yeah, pretty crazy. The forecast was for clear skies. It came out of nowhere," I said, washing my hands at the sink. Ouch. The abrasions left on my hands after clinging to the ledge, didn't appreciate that.

"What on earth happened?" Mom asked, giving my muddy clothes a concerned glance. "You look like you got in a fight with something. You're not nearly as soaked as I expected, though."

"I slipped and fell, and Chip and I found some shelter. Are we having company tonight?" I asked, glancing at the cake and conveniently changing the subject, at the same time.

I rationalized that Mom would be happier not knowing about the fall that could have led to my death when the cellar door collapsed, and I'd be happier if I didn't have to explain where Chip and I spent the afternoon.

"Yes, Uncle Mark is driving up with your Dad. They'll be here in a couple of hours. Go get out of those filthy wet clothes and when you're done, come and help me with supper."

I hurried out of the kitchen and through the living room. Chip sank down in front of the warm fire with a deep sigh, and closed his eyes thankfully.

I quietly shut the door to the tiny room I shared with my sister, so as not to wake her, then took off my muddy, dirt stained clothes and changed into a t-shirt and jeans.

I looked at my reflection in the mirror which hung low on the wall. For most people that would be a problem, but not for me, since I'm only five foot two inches tall, anyway.

I quickly brushed my hair. The side swept bangs which were still in the process of growing out since my last haircut, fell across my large brown eyes as they always insisted on doing. That was the one feature I thought slightly remarkable. The eyes, not the unruly hair. That, could do with some taming. I mercilessly smoothed it all back, and corralled it with a clip. I put on my belted sweater, quietly set my brush back on the dresser top, and returned to the kitchen.

"How's Doreen?" I asked.

Mom sighed.

"Tired. Headachy, joints hurt… shortness of breath, but maybe that's from the higher altitude. About the same, I guess. I'm anxious for the appointment with the new doctor to get here. I'm really praying he'll know what she needs."

Me too. If another doctor said nothing was wrong… I wasn't sure which of us would wring his neck first. There would be a line.

"Here, fix a salad," Mom said, "then vacuum the living room."

"Sure, Mom," I replied, as I hunted through a cabinet for the large wooden salad bowl.

"How was your hike?" Mom asked.

"Really great," I said enthusiastically. "It's beautiful out there. The leaves are changing colors, and there's a stream. It was awesome. Chip loved it, he had the best time."

"Well good," said Mom. "I think this is working out really well for us all. Even though I do miss your Dad during the week."

"Yeah, me too, but it sure beats how it was," I said, as I chopped bell peppers and onions for the salad.

"No kidding," Mom said with feeling.

I finished the salad, and found the vacuum in the living room coat closet.

The cabin wasn't large, it was built to vacation in, not live in, like we were doing. It beat the horrible apartment we'd been in before moving here though, so no one minded the tight fit. It didn't take long to vacuum the small space either, who could complain about that!

I dusted the furniture for good measure. I was almost finished, when my three-year-old brother, Tryon, stumbled in. His blond baby curls framed his face and his big brown eyes, which lit when he saw me.

"Hi, Anika! Read to me, please?" he begged, holding out his favorite story book.

"Oh, Tryon!" groaned Mom from the kitchen doorway. She suddenly looked exhausted, and as if she might cry. "I thought you were taking a nap!"

"I woke up!" Tryon beamed, clearly proud of this accomplishment.

"Here, Try, if you'll be good for just a few minutes and let me help Mom, then I'll read you a story. But I've got to get done first. Okay?" I reasoned.

"OK!" Tryon smiled in consent.

Thank goodness the kid tended to wake up in a good mood.

I helped Tryon climb up on one of the breakfast bar stools with a coloring book and glass of milk, then finished helping Mom in the kitchen.

Tryon and I sat in the cozy living room where we'd hear Dad's car when he and Uncle Mark drove up. After reading Tryon's favorite story twice, the car pulled into the driveway.

"Hear that, Tryon? That's Dad's car! Go open the door for Dad and Uncle Mark," I said, as I tried and failed with an agonizing pain in both arms, to lift him out of our chair. Tears came to my eyes it hurt so badly. Tryon scrambled off the chair himself, and raced to the door and threw it open.

Mom hurried in to greet Uncle Mark, and thank him again for letting us use his cabin. Tryon held tightly to Dad's hand, and Mom gave Dad a hug. I managed to raise my arms enough to hug Dad, too. He looked good, like the weight of the past year was lifting. Doreen walked slowly into the room, and my heart sank a little. My nine-year-old sister was even more pale than she was the day before. Dad gave her a long hug, and some of the worry returned to his eyes.

"Why don't we all sit down and have supper?" Mom said. "It's ready, and on the table."

Dinner was excellent. Mom is a great cook, and the barbeque she made for dinner was exceptional. The rolls were, too. I was starving after being out all day. I could barely remember eating lunch.

After dinner, we sat in the living room to visit around the cheerfully crackling fire in the stone fireplace. Chip was still sprawled on the wood floor, dead to the world.

"There are times when I really appreciate paper plates," Mom said as she sat down.

"Me too," I agreed.

After a few minutes of peaceful silence, Tryon held his book out to our Uncle Mark.

"Read to me, please!"

We all tried, more or less successfully, to stifle a groan. Uncle Mark raised his eyebrows, looked back at Tryon, then raised his hand to his chin as though in deep thought.

"How about one story, and then to bed? If I remember right, it's about that time." Uncle Mark looked to Mom for approval, and she nodded.

After a reading of Tryon's favorite story, which we could all recite from memory, Mom put him to bed, then rejoined us in the living room.

"This is such a beautiful place. How do you stand not living here all the time?" asked Mom.

"Well, work, for one thing!" Uncle Mark laughed. "It's a little far for a daily commute. And I admit, I do enjoy living in the city."

"The buildings in Cedar Oaks are so cute," said Doreen, who was curled up on the couch next to Dad.

"Yes, many of them were built long ago. The city is determined to keep that old-time atmosphere, so there are strict building codes. Tourism is important to the survival of the town and that helps attract visitors."

"Do you know anything about this area's history?" asked Dad.

Uncle Mark thought briefly.

"I did hear an interesting story recently. It's about a wealthy family who built a castle on the mountain many years ago, not far from here... The House of Bannerman."

My eyes widened in surprise.

"The estate was built by the Bannerman family after emigrating here from England in the 1700's. It resembles an English castle, and is very impressive. You'll have to drive by and see it sometime while you're here.

"In 1870, two Bannerman sons, Delevan and Miles, lived there with their family. The brothers were best friends. Delevan was older, and more serious. He was a handsome fellow. But there was no question Miles was the handsomer of the two. There wasn't a girl around who didn't do everything she could to try and get his attention. But Delevan wasn't jealous, in spite of his brother's popularity. They worked well together, and as I said, were best friends... and so the story is all the more tragic."

Uncle Mark paused. For a really... long... time.

"What happened?" I finally urged, anxious to know.

"Like so many tragedies before and after, this one's about a girl. Her name was Sarah Williams, and she was extraordinarily beautiful."

"What did she look like?" whispered Doreen.

"Just like you," Uncle Mark said.

Doreen blushed shyly.

"She had beautiful curly blond hair and blue eyes, and was kind and sweet," he said, smiling towards Doreen. "No one remembers where she was from, or how she came to be here alone. Delevan's parents were concerned about their son's interest in this stranger. At the time, social order and caste were considered extremely important, and the Bannermans considered themselves akin to royalty. But that did not deter Delevan. He was in love.

"After Miss Sarah's introduction to the Bannerman family, Miles traveled west to handle some of the family's business affairs. They were extremely wealthy, including ownership of several gold mines. When Miles returned, his parents were away for the afternoon. He went straight to Delevan's room to discuss the business he transacted. What he found, was a letter from Delevan to the family, informing them that he and Sarah were on their way to elope. Miles was extremely upset. He rushed out of the house, taking his revolvers with him."

Uncle Mark paused for effect. Again.

What is with this man and his theatrics!

"And?" said Mom.

"Their little sister found the note and showed it to Mr. and Mrs. Bannerman when they returned a few hours later. She also told them Miles was back, and that he'd run after Delevan. They were upset by the news of the elopement, but it was nothing to how they would feel soon after."

Uncle Mark paused dramatically, once more.

Just tell the story already!

"What happened?" exclaimed Mom.

"Shortly after, Sarah rushed back to the house, hysterical. She finally managed to say that as she and Delevan followed the path in the woods toward town, Miles caught up with them."

This man and his pauses! He's killing me, here!

"Then what happened?" I asked impatiently.

"He said he was in love with Sarah. He was determined to have her, and he would fight for her, if he had to. He didn't take into account that Sarah loved his brother. He never met a girl who would refuse him, and expected her to be just as glad of his attention as the others. The brothers got into a heated argument. Miles drew his gun, and so did Delevan. Miles fired, and in self-defense, Delevan returned fire. The bullets met their mark, and both brothers were killed."

"Oh, that is just horrible!" choked Doreen.

"My goodness!" said Mom, utterly horrified.

"What a waste of life," Dad shook his head grimly.

My fists were pressed against my mouth. I could not believe the guy with the laughing eyes in the portrait would do such a horrible thing. He just *couldn't*. I felt sick.

"The Bannerman family was devastated. They were a proud family, and refused to accept Sarah's story. But she was the only witness, and the evidence supported her account."

"What... happened to Sarah?" asked Doreen.

"Crushed with grief, and blaming herself for coming between the two brothers, Sarah sailed for Europe as she and Delevan planned to do as a married couple. The ship was lost at sea, and she was never heard from again."

"Oh, how—how—horrible!" said Doreen, near tears. "That is just... awful!"

"So terribly sad," said Mom, with a frown.

"What a terrible waste of life! So unnecessary and preventable!" exclaimed Dad irritably.

I was silent, torn between horror and disbelief.

"The ghost of Miles Bannerman is said to wander the estate seeking forgiveness he will never find. He could have any girl he wanted, but instead he would only be satisfied with the one girl who loved his brother. He had such a bright future, and he threw it away, and destroyed the happiness of so many others in the process.

"Over the years many strange things have been seen and heard at the castle. I spoke with a fellow who did some work for the estate a few years ago, when the family still lived there, and before it was abandoned. He saw for himself a set of paw prints on the floor. That wouldn't be unusual, except... Miles' dog was the last to set foot on the estate. She disappeared the day he died, and was never seen again."

I felt a chill like an electric shock travel down my spine.

"Rumor has it, that the ghosts of Miles and his dog, may be searching for the family treasure which disappeared around the same time, hoping to use it to pay penance for the murder of his brother," Uncle Mark finished.

Apparently, the rest of the family was as speechless as I was.

Seeing that his story had fallen horribly flat, in an effort to redeem the situation Uncle Mark said feebly, "I'm sure there are lessons we can take from this..."

"Yeah," said Doreen thoughtfully. "Marry an only child."

Chapter 2

Monday morning before lunch, Mom asked me to run an errand for her.

"It doesn't matter what I do or what kind of list I make, I always forget something when I'm at the store," she said cheerfully.

I was glad to have a reason to go to town. It was the coolest place, there were so many little shops with such interesting windows to browse. We were still getting back on our feet with Dad having been out of work for so long, and I no longer had my job, but it didn't cost anything to look.

There were boutiques with unique purses and clothing, home décor items, and toys. Books, a bakery which smelled painfully delicious, and a chocolate shop which I would really like to become better acquainted with some day! There was even an old-fashioned drug store, with a soda fountain. All the shops and other buildings looked as though they were from another time.

Cabins dotted the surrounding mountains. Smoke curled from chimneys and I breathed in the scent of the juniper fed fires. The moisture from yesterday's storm gave quite a bite to the air, and I zipped my jacket with a shiver and shoved my hands in my pockets. I was very glad I didn't walk to town as I first intended.

"Good morning Anika, how are you today?" Susan, the owner of the grocery store, greeted me as I walked in.

"Great, and how are you?" I was struck once again by the friendliness of everyone I met here. It was a welcome change.

"Just wonderful," Susan replied. "And how's your family?"

"Doing pretty good," I said, not sure how much detail to go into.

"How about your sister?" asked Susan, a shadow of concern and sympathy crossing her face.

"About the same, I guess."

"Well… we're praying for your sister, and that you'll find the right doctor. Glen Haven's got some good ones."

"Thanks, Susan. That means a lot," I said.

A customer wheeled a loaded cart to the register, so I moved along with my shopping list.

Mission accomplished and back in the car once again, I looked at a map of the area on my iPhone.

My part-time job made it possible to keep our cell phones up and running while Dad was out of work. We needed to be able to communicate somehow, and I was glad I could help that way, and with the cost of feeding my big dog. I was so thankful to find I still had a signal after we moved here. Being in the mountains there were dead spots here and there, but for the most part, we had surprisingly good coverage.

I felt haunted by Uncle Mark's story, and spent most of the weekend dwelling on it. I couldn't get the castle and the story off my mind. If there was a road that went past the estate, I wanted to drive by and see it again. I felt drawn to it. I was pleased to see that the alternate route my iPhone displayed wouldn't take me that far out of the way. I'd easily be home in time for lunch.

Like all the roads in this mountain area, the way to the castle wound through the forest, trees growing thick on both sides. There were mostly pine, but now and then the gorgeous red of an oak and golden leaves of a birch tree made an appearance. I loved driving here. The roads were more twisty and narrow than I was used to, but the view was worth it, and who'd want to drive so fast they couldn't enjoy it, anyway.

I was startled out of my appreciation of the scenery around me, when I saw an elderly woman at the side of the road. She was hunched over, leaning heavily on a cane. She didn't seem aware of the approaching car, or much else.

I pulled over as far as I could, and parked. I knew better than to stop for a random stranger, but this was a tiny little elderly lady, in obvious distress. She could seriously die out here.

I switched off the vehicle and pocketed the key, and climbed out of the car. My hand was on the pepper spray in my pocket, as I looked around for signs of trouble. I didn't see any.

"Are you okay?" I asked, as I cautiously approached the woman. She looked up at me, tears in her eyes.

"No, my dear... I can't say that I am."

"Well... can I help you? I don't think you should be here on the side of the road, in the middle of nowhere," I said with concern.

"I don't believe anyone can help me," she said despairingly, as she swayed, losing her balance. I reached out and steadied her, alarmed to find that her skin felt like ice.

"You can't stay out here," I said decisively.

She didn't respond, and I didn't know what to do. That never stopped me before though, why should it this time!

I ripped off my jacket and put it around her, then guided her to the car.

"Here..." I said, opening the door and helping her inside. "We'll get this figured out."

As I hurried around to the driver's side, I hoped this wouldn't be considered kidnapping. Or elderly-lady-napping.

I cranked the heat full blast and turned around, heading back to the cabin. The castle would just have to wait.

I pulled into the driveway and leaped out of the car with a glance toward the cabin, then helped the little old woman climb out. As we slowly made our way up the walk, the front door flew open and Mom hurried out.

"What's going on?" Mom asked, putting her arm around the woman to support her from the other side. "What happened?"

"This lady seems to be in trouble, she was alone at the side of the road a couple of miles outside of town. She's freezing, and needs help. I didn't know what else to do, Mom."

"Okay," said Mom, getting a handle on the situation. "Let's get you inside," she said to the woman.

We seated her in the nearest recliner. Tears still ran down her cheeks, though she was no longer sobbing. Mom grabbed a blanket off the arm of the chair, and wrapped it around her. Doreen, curled up on the couch, watched with wide eyes.

25

"She's so cold. Get her a cup of tea, quick, Anika," Mom said, as she reached for another blanket. "There's hot water already on the stove."

I quickly prepared the tea, tempered it with cold water, and hurried back to the living room. Mom took the mug and wrapped the woman's hands around it. The warmth must have been a relief, some of the tightness left her face. After a couple of minutes, she slowly began to sip the tea.

I didn't realize how pale she was until faint color began to stain her cheeks. She took a deep, shuddering breath.

"I'm feeling a little better," she said weakly.

"You were freezing cold," I said. "No wonder you felt bad."

"Are you hungry? We were just about to have lunch," Mom told her.

The woman considered that, and nodded.

"That would be lovely, dear."

"Anika, could you..." Mom indicated the kitchen, then to the woman she said, "You just stay put. Anika will bring your lunch in here."

I snatched a bowl off the counter, and filled it with the potato soup waiting on the stove. My mind raced to remember where I'd seen the folding tray tables, and dragged one out of the front closet. I handed it to Mom, then the bowl of soup.

Tryon was in the kitchen, helping himself to one of the cheese sandwiches on the platter next to the stove. I sat him quickly at the table.

"Who's that?" he wanted to know, looking toward the recliner and the little woman sitting there.

"I don't know, but I'm sure she'll tell us when she feels like it."

"Okay," Tryon said, getting back to his sandwich. I squeezed his little shoulders and kissed the top of his curly blond head quickly, as I passed by on my way back to the living room portion of the room.

I was glad to see the woman continued to look better, as she ate and drank her tea. I fixed Doreen a bowl and brought her a tray, then

Mom. I was too interested in knowing what was going on with this little lady, to eat.

"Thank you," the little lady said, as she finished her soup. "I was terribly foolish to walk so far. I forget sometimes that I'm not as young as I used to be."

"We haven't exactly introduced ourselves yet," Mom said. "I'm Samantha Riley, and these are my daughters Anika and Doreen, and my son Tryon."

The little woman smiled.

"It is very nice to meet you all. My name is Polly Bannerman."

Polly Bannerman! My eyes widened in astonishment.

"I'm very glad to meet you, Mrs. Bannerman," said Mom.

"Polly is just fine, dear," she said. "That's what I prefer my friends to call me, and you've certainly shown friendship towards me today."

"It's nice to meet you," I managed to say. I was still in shock, realizing who it was that I picked up by the side of the road.

Doreen mumbled a greeting. She wasn't having a good day, and her eyes were heavy. Given another minute, she'd be asleep again. Tryon waved his sandwich in the air, his mouth stuffed full.

"I do greatly appreciate the kindness you've shown me. I should've known better than to go off walking like that. I was just so upset…" Polly paused, and a shadow crossed her face. She continued tremulously, "I didn't take time for breakfast this morning, and with the exercise I must have been a bit hypoglycemic. Thank you for stopping to help me."

"Of course," I said, wondering what upset her.

"Is there anything else we can do for you?" asked Mom, her eyebrows knit in concern. "You… said you were upset."

Polly looked thoughtful. She glanced away, then back at Mom and me. Chip padded into the room and sat beside her, and she patted him absentmindedly.

"Oh, I hate to burden you with my problems… everything is just so complicated. My grandson is missing, that's my primary concern. He spent the past three years boarding at an academy on the other side of the country. When he graduated last spring, he decided to spend the summer traveling, before starting college in the fall. He hasn't been heard from in four months."

"No one's heard from him?" I asked in surprise.

"No dear, no one has," said Polly, her eyes filled with worry.

"If he's been traveling… Is it possible he doesn't realize how it would worry you not to hear from him?" asked Mom.

"Yes, that could be the case. He never arrived at college however, and classes began last month. He was looking forward to attending, so his absence is greatly concerning. There are additional issues as well. When my son and his wife were killed in an accident five years ago," Polly used her napkin to blot her eyes, "I was appointed guardian of my grandson Miles, and of the Bannerman estate, to be held in trust. On Miles' twentieth birthday, he is to receive his inheritance. All rights and responsibilities as trustee and beneficiary of the Bannerman estate, will be transferred to him."

I refilled Polly's mug with more hot tea, as she talked.

"Thank you, dear," she said. "He may appear on time, ready to assume his place as trustee. But as he is currently unaccounted for, a distant cousin is seeking legal means to seize the estate, should Miles fail to return and take possession himself. I've no idea how this cousin, Alfred Sullivan, even found out that Miles is missing. But somehow, he knows. He intends to turn the House of Bannerman into a resort. I'm not against tourism, or honestly—even of the whole resort concept, maybe a museum, it that's what Miles wanted. Alfred however, if he succeeds in being named trustee, intends to market his resort by capitalizing on a family tragedy that occurred over a century ago, and I have a very big problem with that."

She looked grim and a little fierce, and Mom and I waited for her to continue.

"Perhaps you've heard the story of Miles and Delevan Bannerman?" She questioned, as Mom and I nodded. "Well, Alfred is responsible for that, I'm sure. The story that's been told over the years, has *never* been accepted by the family, however. Miles' and Dele-van's parents and siblings adamantly refused to believe it. They felt there was evidence to the contrary, but could never offer other explanation for what occurred. The Bannerman family as a whole, has never accepted the story told by the woman. It was her word over a lifetime of good character, and she a relative stranger. My grandson would never have been given the name Miles, had there been any doubt in our minds as to his ancestor's innocence. But what really happened that day, remains a mystery."

I was relieved to hear the family didn't accept the story Uncle Mark told us. I didn't believe it myself, and didn't want it to be true. I couldn't bear it if it was.

"Alfred's plan is to dramatize the woman's version of the tragedy even further than it already has been, and market the resort accordingly. It wouldn't be the first resort to gain notoriety from a dark past. Especially if he hints at ghostly activity…" Polly frowned, her voice fading.

"That's awful," I frowned.

"Yes, isn't it!" Polly replied with asperity. She was obviously feeling better. She also had more to say.

"And that isn't even the end of it! Alfred is attempting to paint me as incompetent in caring for the Bannerman estate! Mentally incompetent, if he can manage it," she rolled her eyes. "Those things would vastly improve his chances of taking over as trustee."

I thought of the neglected state of the House of Bannerman, and wondered reluctantly if maybe Alfred had a point.

"Okay, so how is he planning to prove this?" asked Mom.

"I was informed by my attorney this morning of Alfred's intentions, and that the House of Bannerman is in terrible disrepair, which could be used as evidence that I am not fit to see to the adequate care of the estate. For the past three years, while Miles was away at the academy and I traveled and visited friends, we employed a caretaker to see to the grounds and upkeep of the house. I've taken for granted

that it was in good hands. The Henderson's have always been trust-
worthy, I don't understand how this could happen. After the meeting
with my attorney, I was so upset that I just took off walking toward
the estate, and you know the rest."

"Can this Alfred legally get away with any of this?" I asked.

"There is a possibility, dear. As Miles is the last direct descendant
of the Bannerman family, and my age being what it is, Alfred may be
able to. He is prepared to take legal action if Miles is still unaccounted
for on his twentieth birthday."

"When was the last time you heard from the caretakers?" asked
Mom.

"Three years ago last May," said Polly. "Repair and maintenance
expenses, including salary, were reported to our accountant, who
managed payment. I did not routinely communicate with them myself."

"What are their names?" I asked, pulling my iPhone out of my
back pocket.

"Jim and Amelia Henderson," Polly said.

I did a quick internet search, and regretted to see that it located an
obituary for Jim Henderson. He died in June, shortly after Polly's last
visit to the estate. On a social networking site, I discovered that Amelia was living with a sister in Florida, now.

"Well then. I guess that explains that," Polly said. "I don't know
why Amelia didn't contact me or the accountant... or why no one
thought to mention there being an obituary in the paper... but now I
know why the estate isn't up to its usual standards."

Polly finished her tea, then set the mug down decisively. Her eyes
were filled with resolve.

"Regardless of everything else, I must find someone to see to setting the property to rights. The needs of the estate must be assessed,
and a service hired to tend the gardens. I'm sure the inside of the house
is a fright, not having been cleaned in three years... I'll need someone
to interview cleaning services and oversee the work. I'm not sure
where to start," she mused, lost in thought. "But first, I need to call

for a car so that I can see the property, and know what I'm dealing with."

Mom looked at me. I nodded, and she turned to Polly.

"Don't worry about calling for a car. Anika will be glad to take you."

Polly accepted another cup of tea, and rested a bit longer. She was alert and energetic, now. Amazing what encouragement, a warm blanket, hot tea, and some food can accomplish.

When she was ready, I helped her back into the car, and followed the road in the direction of the castle.

"Anika dear, I don't mean to pry. I couldn't help but notice, your little sister… is she quite all right?"

I sighed.

"No, she's not. It's very frustrating. She had the flu, which seemed to start everything off. She's never been the same since. She has a lot of strange symptoms that come and go. She's definitely sick, but the first doctor we saw couldn't find anything wrong, and instead of continuing to look he decided there *was* nothing wrong. My parents took Doreen to another doctor then, who ran a lot of tests but came to the same conclusion. Then Dad was laid-off work, and that made everything more complicated. No insurance, and so many expensive tests and expensive appointments, and they all say the same thing, that there's nothing wrong. Some have insinuated that Doree is making it up, which just infuriates us!"

"Well of course," said Polly indignantly. "No one could look as miserable as she does, without truly being ill."

That didn't exactly make me feel better.

"It must have been dreadful, your Father out of work. How are things now, dear?"

I told Polly about Dad's new job working for Uncle Mark, and our living arrangement. She wanted to know why "a bright young girl" like me wasn't in college, and I explained that I would be, as soon as I could afford it again.

"You know dear," she said. "When my son and daughter-in-law were killed in a car accident, my grandson and I started a scholarship in their memory. You really should think about applying. It's not too early to start thinking about next year."

I told Polly about the hike Chip and I took through the woods, and my abrupt meeting with the cellar. I told her we waited out the storm inside the house, and we both had a good laugh when she told me I should have turned the lights on. The electricity has never been disconnected. I didn't even think of trying!

We arrived at the castle and I pulled into the long driveway. There were no dark clouds lurking, today. It was beautiful and serene in the bright sunshine, as awe inspiring from this side as it was the other. The Henderson's were conscientious in caring for the estate while they were there, so the exterior was in good repair. The grounds had certainly seen better days, though. The three years of neglect had taken their toll. The sun brought out flaws I wasn't aware of last Friday, in the shadow of the encroaching storm.

"Oh my. I do see what everyone's talking about," Polly said grimly.

We walked slowly around the property so Polly could see the depth of the neglect. She was a very friendly little lady, and had all sorts of questions. She wanted to know all about Tryon. She said she just loves little boys, "so much easier dear, than when they're older" which sort of surprised me, but I guess we'll just have to wait a few more years to find out.

"When I followed Chip into the house last week, I saw something very odd."

"Oh? Did you, now?" Polly's expression was inscrutable, as she looked straight ahead at the path in front of us.

"There were two sets of paw prints. Chip's, and another dog's. It was very strange," I said.

"Hm." Polly sounded like I do, when I want to keep what I know to myself.

"I'm not certain, but before it started to rain and I fell through the cellar doors, I think I saw a curtain move."

"Oh my, just look at those two squirrels playing! I remember a time when I was filled with that much energy."

I didn't doubt it. She was pretty spry, even now.

The squirrels were cute, but I'm skilled enough at the art of redirecting, to know when someone else is doing it. Polly did not want to talk about this.

As we continued our walk around the perimeter of the forest which encircled the castle, Polly wanted to know all about my interests, what career I was considering, and so many other things. Eventually I had a question for her.

"The story of the two Bannerman brothers really haunts me. I saw the portraits when we were waiting out the storm, and I just can't believe the story is true. I'm sure their parents tried to learn what happened, but was there ever any evidence that might be useful in solving the mystery now? If there is, forensic science could prove what really happened that day."

"You know, I'm not sure," said Polly, with a gleam in her eye. "I would assume that Miles' and Delevan's father would have kept anything he collected. As you can see, the house is quite large. There are places that I have never been, even though I lived there for many years."

"Wow, that's something. It looks massive on the outside, but must be even bigger on the inside," I joked.

"Oh, it is. It would be quite something if Miles Bannerman could be absolved of the crime after all these years..." she said thoughtfully. "And wouldn't that just take the wind out of Alfred's sails!"

She was positively giddy at the thought.

Polly narrowed her eyes and gave me a searching look.

"You seem a very smart, responsible girl. How would you like a job?"

Chapter 3

"Now remember, dear. As we discussed before, I don't want you coming out here alone. You bring that dog with you," Polly said, waving her cane in Chip's direction. Her voice lowered to a conspiratorial whisper. "Yard men can be a rough lot, but he'll keep them in line."

I choked back an involuntary laugh at that unexpected comment, and ended up in a coughing fit. I wondered what her experience with 'yard men' had been, or if she was making a joke.

I was grateful that Polly liked Chip, and suggested he come to work with me. I wasn't sure I would've taken the job otherwise. I felt safe enough, but if Chip wasn't here, and I was alone in the silent house for very long... well, I was really glad to have Chip's reassuring company.

Chip and I walked Polly to her waiting taxi, which would return her to the hotel where she was staying.

"Room service, dear. A wonderful invention."

Polly and her attorney would interview PI's to search for her grandson Miles, and I would hire people to restore the grounds and clean the house, and repair anything in need of it. In addition, I would oversee the work, making the estate look so sharp, no one would be able to use it to question her ability to manage the trust.

I had Polly's blessing to search through the house for anything that could be used as proof of what actually happened to Miles and Delevan Bannerman. The chance to search for clues and maybe solve the family mystery felt right, like it's what I *should* be doing.

I stood and surveyed the outside of the house. The opportunity to work here and the ability to start saving for college again, taking that worry off Mom and Dad, meant a lot to me. I couldn't believe Polly was trusting me with such an important job. I couldn't help but think that the dire need to start the clean-up at once, and my immediate availability, had something to do with it. But I also think Polly is a very sweet, philanthropic lady who wanted to give me a chance, and help my family in the process.

I only hoped hiring a nineteen-year-old to manage the estate wouldn't backfire, and be considered evidence that Polly wasn't mentally competent!

Last night, I spent hours on the internet studying how to care for antiques, and clean rugs and drapes, and anything else that might be in the house. If I didn't know the right way to do things myself, I'd never be able to tell if the people I interviewed were up to the job, or not. This house was filled with antique treasures, not particleboard. I wasn't willing to trust the cleaning and handling of the contents to just anyone.

Armed with my newfound knowledge, I spent several more hours looking up cleaning services and landscape maintenance companies, and reading online reviews. The list was now narrowed down to a manageable size. This morning, I made appointments to interview four of the services on the short list. The interviews would start tomorrow.

I waved to the repairman installing the new cellar doors, then Chip and I turned and re-entered the double front doors of the house. We walked through the entry and on into the first living room, or parlor. I really needed to get online and figure out names for all of these rooms. Whatever it was called, this is where I'd start today. I wanted a clean room to conduct the interviews tomorrow.

I looked around me. Sunlight filtered through the curtains, dimly illuminating the room. Its fingers of light touched the mahogany end tables and curio cabinets, and caused the sheet enshrouded sofa and easy chairs to appear ghost-like. Beautiful paintings were scattered at intervals across the Victorian wallpaper, and a large fireplace stood in between two picture windows. Cobwebs covered everything like the softest blanket, and dust settled thickly on every surface.

I shivered, but not from the cold. The room was so quiet and still, as if it was sleeping.

Chip whined softly.

"It is too quiet, isn't it?" I agreed. "Let's get to work. Once we're started, it won't be so bad."

I crossed the room and drew open the curtains. The bright sunlight streamed in unhindered, warming and dissolving the ghostly effect of the room, and exposing the unchecked dust and spider webs mercilessly.

"Well, it looks like a real room now anyway," I said.

Chip sneezed loudly in response.

The heavy curtains were folded neatly, ready to be picked up by the professional cleaners. The rugs were rolled, awaiting the same destination. The hardwood floor gleamed, after a much needed cleaning. I surveyed the dust-free room, congratulating myself on a job well done.

I was a little disappointed not to find anything even remotely pertaining to the family tragedy while working in this room, and I looked thoroughly. I reminded myself that this wasn't the most likely place in the huge house for a clue to be kept. There were many other places to search, and I would search every one of them. If anything was here, I'd find it. I was driven. It might take me the rest of my life, considering the size of the house, but I'd get it done.

I turned to collect the cleaning supplies and put them somewhere other than on the floor of the clean room, when I heard a faint rustling.

The sound came from the entryway, which I could just make out through the large arched doorway to my right. The lighting was very dim there, compared to the parlor, where the sun poured freely through the clean curtainless windows. It took a minute for my eyes to adjust. I couldn't see anything.

I looked to Chip for assurance. I wasn't imagining it, he heard the sound, too.

As my eyes adjusted to the dim light, I began to make out the staircase. At the end of the gracefully curving banister, sat a statue. I was startled by it at first, until I realized that's what it had to be.

A golden retriever walked into the living room through the doorway on my left. Before I or even Chip could react, the "statue" turned toward the dog.

"Our visitor is back again," he said.

I jumped so hard my teeth rattled, and the bottle of glass cleaner I held in my hand, fell to the floor with a clatter. Chip and the retriever loped toward each other like long lost friends, no worries there.

Thanks a lot buddy, run off and leave me why don't you!

The statue, who now looked more like Polly's missing grandson, looked back at me again.

I tried to convince my heart to climb back into my chest where it belonged. It was a little late for calm cool and collected, but I was determined to gain back some semblance of control.

"Are you Miles?" I said.

Instead of answering, he lost his balance and fell off the banister, and onto the floor. There he stayed, staring at me as if, what, I have cobwebs in my hair? I look like I've been cleaning all day? I don't look like I belong here, my t-shirt and ripped jeans aren't exactly proper parlor attire?

I swept the hair that insisted on escaping my ponytail behind one ear, and resisted the urge to rub under my eyes to remove any smudged eyeliner. The boss' grandson was extremely good looking, and sharply dressed. In his white shirt with rolled up sleeves, dark vest, and pants, he looked great, even if he was sprawled on the floor. I, however, was a mess. It left me feeling off balance and self-conscious, like a scullery maid finding herself in the same room as the master of the house.

"Are you Miles?" I said again.

He was still sitting on the floor staring as if mesmerized, and it was getting to me.

"Your grandmother has been so worried!" I snapped at him, my patience gone.

"Are you… talking to me?" he asked slowly.

"Do you see anyone else in the room?" I raised an eyebrow and crossed my arms.

I could not believe this guy! I change my vote, he's not the cutest guy I've ever seen in my whole life, and not that smart either.

38

Glancing toward the retriever, he slowly rose to his feet.

"I'm sorry… I wasn't trying to be rude. You just *really* startled me." He stepped forward, studying me intently. "You're the first person to speak to me in over a hundred and forty years."

I was preparing a snappy comeback, when he stepped into the parlor, and out of the shadows. As the light from the windows touched him he faded, for lack of a better word. He wasn't all there, and I don't mean that in the mental sense.

"Whoa, I don't believe in ghosts," I stammered, taking a step back and running into a chair. My mind raced madly to find something else that would explain what I was seeing.

"I don't either, exactly…" he said, rubbing his forehead as if he, too, would prefer an alternate explanation.

This admonition on the part of semi-transparent guy surprised me so much, I found myself arguing the opposite.

"Well how do you explain—this?" I exclaimed, gesturing towards him.

"I can't really, it's… complicated," he said.

I sank into the chair behind me, not enjoying how it felt to have all the blood in my head rush out as fast as it possibly could. I dropped my head into my hands, to try and slow the rapid exodus. The retriever walked over and pushed on my arm, making room to rest her chin on my knee. Chip watched semi-transparent guy, and looked puzzled.

"So I see your dog is solid… real… alive… something…" I struggled for the right word.

"She sort of comes and goes."

What he said and the way he said it would make me laugh, if I weren't so freaked out.

"She made the choice to stay with me. Maybe that's why she can switch back and forth," he added.

My head swam. I was a little young to exhibit signs of schizophrenia, but maybe that was it. Maybe Polly didn't hire me, I wasn't even in a house, I'd been cleaning tree trunks all day. Maybe I was living out my own *A Beautiful Mind*! Not that I'm a math genius, or any-thing. Pretty terrible how that was the most reasonable of the two re-ally disturbing explanations for what I was seeing.

I would love to wake up now, but that required falling asleep as a prerequisite. I settled for closing my eyes, and taking a deep breath.

When I opened my eyes again, he was still there, a look of concern in his eyes. Trixie the retriever, still sat with her chin on my knee. I put my hand on the dog's head and felt her warm fur.

The dog was real. I wasn't imagining this.

"So what's your name, semi-transparent guy?" I asked, fairly cer-tain I already knew.

"My name is Miles... but I am *not* Polly's grandson," he said, slowly moving forward to sit in the nearest chair.

He's either afraid I bite, or that I'll run away. He needn't worry. Tryon's the one that bites, and I couldn't stand, much less run, if my life depended on it.

There was silence, and it was awkward, but I didn't know what to say. I needed a moment to process this whole situation, which was by far the most bizarre thing that ever happened... ever! Way beyond finding a castle in an abandoned garden in the woods. Or finding the castle's owner or whatever, wandering at the side of the road and then being paid to explore. How impossible this was. It just was! My brain short circuited.

Miles sighed. He looked sad.

"I take it you've heard about my family... about me."

I nodded. I started to glance away, when suddenly a sliver of my old not-stunned-out-of-my-wits-self returned.

"But I don't believe what I've heard. I don't believe you killed your brother," I said firmly, my gaze steady.

The sadness in Miles' eyes was replaced with surprise, relief, and curiosity.

"With the exception of family, everyone who ever heard the story accepted it without hesitation. But not you."

There was a question in there somewhere.

"Yeah, well… I'm not family, but I've never been accused of being like everyone else, either. Why start now?" I replied.

A smile flickered across his face.

"I'm glad you don't believe it, because the story isn't true. I didn't kill my brother, I wasn't in love with his fiancé, and Delevan and I didn't fight over her." Miles breathed a sigh of relief. "I can't tell you how amazing it feels to say that, and be heard."

The shock that I was talking to THE Miles of the portrait and horrible story, was starting to wear off. It dawned on me that the solution to the family mystery was sitting right in front of me.

"Would you mind telling me what really happened to you and your brother?"

"I'd appreciate the chance to, if you're offering to listen."

"Yeah, I'm offering. I know you didn't do it, but I'd really like to know who did. Was it Sarah Williams? Is that why she lied and blamed you?"

"No, she's not one of those responsible for our deaths," Miles answered. "She lied about me, but it wasn't to save herself. It was to save my family."

"Wow. You have got me so curious," I said. "So what really happened?"

"I'm sure most of the story you heard is a lie, as no one besides those who were there that day, ever knew the truth. Unless the story has changed, it and the truth have the same beginning, however…"

After four long weeks spent in the west finishing certain business transactions for his father, weary and travel-worn, Miles was more than ready for this journey to come to an end. He missed his family and everything else about home while he was away, and as he drew closer to his destination, his heart quickened with anticipation.

Giving his horse more reign, the wooded path was covered in no time, and soon the Bannerman stable loomed into sight. Miles rode into the fenced area surrounding the barn, and swung from the saddle nimbly. He gave orders to the stable boy to return the horse to the livery in town, and retrieve his trunk from the station. Then he turned and hurried down the short path that led to his home, swinging his satchel lightly at his side.

Stepping through the front door, he collided with his little sister, Cynthia.

"Miles!" she squealed, throwing her arms around him. "You're back!"

"I'm glad to see you too," Miles smiled, managing to give her a hug as he set his satchel on the entryway table. "Where are Mother and Father?"

"They spent the afternoon visiting the Henderson's," Cynthia answered. "James went with them. He'll be so happy that you've returned. They should be home very soon."

"Is Delevan here?" Miles asked.

"No, Delevan and Miss Williams went for a walk just a few minutes ago. But he left a note. He said not to read it, which I didn't," she said proudly. She took a folded paper out of the pocket of her pinafore, and held it out to Miles. "He said to give it to Mother and Father, but I think it's okay to give it to you."

She scrunched up her face for a moment, deciding whether or not that was really true. Her face cleared, and she handed him the note.

Miles unfolded the page. Inside was a paper with the name of an ocean liner, and voyage details. Puzzled, he set it aside and silently read the letter written by his brother.

Dear Father and Mother,

I have given thought to the concerns you expressed with regards to my association with Miss Williams. Please know that I have the utmost respect for you and your wisdom. I have made my decision however, and I will not be deterred from it.

To spare our family and Miss Williams further discussion on this subject, I have made the decision to elope with Sarah. We are on our way to be married and likely will have done so by the time you receive this letter.

We are traveling by stage and then steamboat to New York, where we shall sail to Europe for a brief trip. It is my hope that during this time, you will become fully reconciled to welcoming Sarah as my wife.

I shall write from the ship so that you know when to expect our return.

Your loving son,
Delevan

"How long since they departed?" Miles asked sharply, as he rose to his feet and snatched up his satchel. He rummaged inside, checking its contents.

"Wh-what's wrong?" stammered Cynthia, alarmed by the change in her brother's voice and demeanor.

"How long, Cynthia?" he asked insistently.

"It's been but ten or fifteen minutes," she managed to answer.

"How did they travel? By foot or carriage?" he asked, snatching up Delevan's note and pressing it into her hands.

"A walk, this is what Delevan said."

"By the main road, or the path through the forest?" he asked, throwing open the front door.

"The path, but Miles, please! Whatever makes you look so?"

"I must catch up with them before it is too late. Give Father Delevan's note the moment he returns." Seeing the anxiety in her eyes, his tone softened. "I'm sorry I've frightened you, Cynthia. I shall explain when I am able, but now I must go."

With that, he was out the door, and then he was gone.

Miles raced along the familiar path, anxiety for his brother and the cost to their family that Delevan's haste would incur, fueling his footsteps. He covered the ground quickly, and as he passed between two overgrown pines, he found himself in a clearing. On the opposite side, just vanishing down the trail, were Delevan and Sarah.

"Delevan!" Miles shouted. "Delevan, stop!"

Delevan turned in surprise.

"Miles!" He exclaimed, a smile lighting his face. He turned, and led Sarah back across the clearing and toward his younger brother.

Miles breathed a sigh of relief and remained where he was, intent on catching his breath.

"How good it is to see you again!" Delevan said, setting aside his and Sarah's satchels, so that he might give Miles a brotherly hug.

"And you," said Miles, returning his hug. "I feared you would be gone before I could reach you."

"Are our business affairs such, that they demand extraordinary haste on your part, and immediate attention on mine?" Delevan asked, his smile revealing his lack of concern that it was so.

"Our business endeavors are successful, but it is not of that which I feel I must speak."

"You've stirred my curiosity," said Delevan. "But see here, my joy at seeing you once again, has caused me to be forgetful. Miles, I believe you have met Miss Williams, have you not?"

"Only just," said Miles, acknowledging Sarah's smile with a nod, and thinking how very awkward this was for himself, if for no one else just yet.

"You're the first to know, Miles," Delevan said, holding Sarah's arm a little closer. They looked at one another and smiled. "Sarah has agreed to be my wife. We are on our way to be married. I'm so very glad you reached us when you did, or I fear it would have been a long while before we had the chance to see one another again."

The look that passed between Delevan and Sarah, caused Miles to hesitate. He could not doubt the affection they had for one another. He was confident in his ability to judge character, and if he must do so now, he would not question Sarah's.

Perhaps the information he possessed was wrong. Perhaps Sarah could explain. But if she could not, then Delevan must know of it at once. If Miles was silent and tragedy befell his brother as a result, never could he forgive himself, nor did he have the right to keep such concerns as he had to himself.

"Delevan, I take no joy in what I must reveal to you," Miles said, passing over Delevan's words, and turning to the undesirable task at hand. His eyes held no laughter. Such a rare occurrence this was, his brother was more concerned by that lack, than he was Miles' words.

"Miles, whatever can be wrong?" he asked, concern sharpening his voice.

Miles opened his satchel and removed a folded page. His eyes held the deepest sympathy as he handed it to Delevan, and then watched for a moment as his brother read, and understanding began to dawn.

Shock registered on Delevan's face, and Sarah paled.

"And so you discovered this during your travel," Delevan said evenly.

"It was necessary that I meet with the Sheriff a number of times as you will recall," Miles answered. "It was with dismay that I saw the paper you hold in your hand. I kept my concerns to myself, but brought the paper away with me."

Delevan sighed and nodded, then turned his gaze upon Sarah.

Miles turned aside. He made as if to sort through the remaining papers in his satchel, in order that Delevan and his fiancé might have a semblance of privacy.

"Have you an explanation?" Delevan asked evenly. "I should certainly like to hear of it, if you do. I cannot devise a way in which your photograph should be on a handbill, if you are not guilty in some way."

A tear rolled down Sarah's pale cheek, and her lips trembled. She looked up at Delevan pleadingly.

"I cannot explain in such a way that you will understand. It is impossible, I think."

"Do put forth the effort, in spite of it," he said.

Miles felt deeply for them both. Delevan's cold demeanor masked his grief, while Sarah's was plainly displayed.

She blotted the tears from her cheeks and took a moment to compose herself.

"I am not of your class as I encouraged you to assume, yet I am not so low as you now have reason to believe. My heritage is not so very different than your own."

"It is not that which concerns me," said Delevan, raising an eyebrow, as he held up the handbill.

Acknowledging his words with a nod, Sarah spoke quickly.

"Not everyone in my family has proven worthy of that heritage. My brother is a conman and outlaw. He grieved my parents until their deaths, at which time I came under his authority. He found me useful in the occupation he chose, but it is only under threat that I complied. It was only ever under threat that I allowed myself to be used in his schemes, and not without first learning the consequence of rebellion. If there was a means of escape, I did not discover it."

There was a brief flash of anger in Delevan's eyes at learning of her plight. Miles hurt for his brother, and for Sarah also. He saw no sign of deception in her. The situation she described, left her with little recourse.

"This then, is true," Delevan stated flatly, glancing at the handbill once again.

"What you see is the work of my brother, in both the crime, and in laying the blame at my feet. The paper you hold in your hand accuses me falsely. And yet, in all matters I cannot say that I am innocent."

Miles sighed quietly, as he averted his gaze once more. He focused unseeing eyes on the contents of his satchel. The papers, gun belt and revolvers, which he'd placed inside upon boarding the train for home, held little interest in light of the heartbreak playing out before him.

Sarah waited for Delevan to respond, but he did not. She wished for some sign that the affection and acceptance he had for her just moments ago, was not entirely destroyed. She sighed.

"I ran away from him and that life, the moment opportunity presented itself. I wished to leave it behind and to forget that miserable chapter. The woman you came to know and love is who I am, and who I would always have been, if my parents were not taken from me."

Delevan shook his head slowly.

"Why did you not tell me? To learn of this in such a way... it is a poor way to nurture trust."

"I wished to forget that life," she said, her eyes pleading to be understood. "I did not choose it, and ran from it, as soon as I had that chance. I do not wish to own it, and be overshadowed by it. Delevan, your parents despise me already, based on heritage and that I travel alone. Can you not imagine their position toward me if they were to know of this? I wanted desperately to start over, to forget my past, and to leave it behind."

Never did Miles feel so wrong about doing that which was right. This past which once imprisoned her would not now be threatening to do so again, if he kept his concerns to himself.

Delevan sighed deeply.

"In spite of it, you should not have kept this from me. You have placed me in a difficult position."

"Please forgive me," she said sincerely, seeing as she did not before. "I have thought only of myself in this. I did not give consideration to you. I was foolish to think that by the use of silence, I could leave this behind."

"We have a great deal to talk over," Delevan said. "I do not see my way clear to proceed as we intended. In spite of your words of reassurance and all other considerations aside, the accusation on this handbill is real and must be dealt with in some way, else the past shall forever threaten the future. Come, let us return to the estate. We shall do our talking there."

Sarah nodded in acceptance, but there was no hope in her eyes. To return to his home and have her past revealed when already she was considered unworthy, could only result in misery.

"Delevan... wait but a moment," said Miles quickly.

Delevan glanced at his brother, but before Miles could speak further, they caught a glimpse of movement on the other side of the clearing.

Miles remained motionless as he rapidly took account of their adversaries, for that is what they were. Three outlaws, revolvers at their sides and confidence in their eyes, and photos of all three on the handbill with Sarah's. He and Delevan were outnumbered, but they were not unarmed. He need move his hand only slightly, to grasp the nearest of the guns in the gun belt placed inside his satchel. He cocked it slowly, so as to make no sound.

"What is your business here?" asked Delevan, flecks of steel in his gray eyes.

"I've come to collect my sister," said one of the men, the leader by all appearances.

Sarah gripped her handbag tightly.

"Why did you follow me, Dan?" she asked, trying to still the tremor in her voice. "Why could you not let me go?"

"You're of far too much use to me," he said, his eyes cold. "Of course I followed you."

"This lady is my fiancé, and it is clear to me she wishes to have nothing to do with you," said Delevan firmly.

Sarah had no time to register relief at hearing his words.

Dan's gaze hardened.

"Until my sister comes of age, she is no one's fiancé." He glared at Delevan a moment, then addressed his words to Sarah. "You were a fool to leave, and a greater fool to become involved with this sort. I will not have it."

Before Delevan realized her intention, Sarah left his side and hurried toward her brother, and the other men.

"Sarah, no!" said Delevan, but she did not turn back.

Delevan's heart sank. The brothers watched with concern, the thought crossing their minds that she might be part of a con targeting Delevan. If she was, Miles would no longer feel so certain of his ability to judge character.

Crossing the clearing, she clutched her brother's arm.

"I'll go with you if that's what you want, but please, just leave them alone!" Sarah tugged on her brother's arm, trying to draw him closer to the woods, and further from Delevan and Miles.

"Sarah, no!" Delevan shouted.

Miles tightened his grip on the revolver in his hand and Delevan took several steps forward, as Sarah's brother flung her aside, and he and his men reached for their guns.

"No!" Sarah screamed.

What happened after was a blur. In a flash Miles' own revolver was out and he and Delevan fired. Two of the men fell to the ground. Miles pitched the second revolver to his brother as he re-cocked his own. As Miles took aim at Dan, one of the downed men fired again. Miles felt a searing pain in his right knee, and collapsed. As Delevan caught Miles' revolver, he used the second and last round in his derringer to still the shooter permanently. Dan shot at Delevan and missed, as Delevan cocked the borrowed revolver. Focusing through overwhelming pain, Miles steadied his arm and fired. Delevan's adversary clutched his arm with a scream of agony, and the gun fell from his hand. He staggered, then sat down heavily, nursing the wounded arm.

Sarah scrambled to her feet and flung Dan's gun out of reach.

"Tell me if he moves, Sarah," Delevan said, as he turned quickly to Miles.

"Miles! Are you alright?" he asked anxiously, kneeling to examine his brother's wound.

"I'll—be alright," Miles grimaced, wondering if that could possibly be true.

Keeping a wary eye on Dan, Sarah turned toward Delevan and started to speak, but her words were cut short as she gave a strangled cry, and pointed behind them.

Before Delevan could turn, the report of a gun rang out.

"Delevan!" Miles cried, as his brother fell.

Miles felt himself pulled deeper and deeper into the whirlpool of unconsciousness. By the time the second shot was fired, Miles was so far down, the bullet felt like nothing more than a tap on the shoulder.

Sarah screamed incoherently, wailing as she dropped to her knees beside Delevan.

The fourth man scowled in her direction, then turned to Dan.

"What's the plan?" he muttered, glancing toward Sarah as he wrapped a handkerchief tightly around Dan's wounded arm, and tied it. "Shall I…"

"No, Sam," said Dan. "She's going to get us out of this mess."

Sam added another kerchief to the make-shift bandage. "You're lucky it didn't hit bone. You're barely nicked. Should be alright."

Dan flexed his wounded arm, testing it. Wincing but satisfied he still had the use of it, he watched Sarah. His brows knit as he considered how best to approach her. He didn't have time for this.

"I'm sorry, Sarah. This didn't have to happen… but your friends opened fire. If Sam hadn't come along, we'd all be dead by now, not just Andy and Ron."

Sarah ignored his poor attempt at sympathy, and continued to sob over Delevan's body.

Dan's impatience grew. Time was wasting, and there was much they must accomplish before they ran out.

Dan grasped her impatiently by the shoulder with his uninjured arm, and jerked her to her feet.

"That's enough! Pull yourself together, unless you want to answer for your crimes," he said firmly, glancing at the handbill which lay where it fell when Delevan dropped it.

Sarah froze for the briefest of moments, then her eyes slowly focused on her brother. He took that as a sign of compliance.

"We can get out of this without the law hunting us down, and you're going to help," he said.

The grief in Sarah's eyes turned to hatred. She launched herself at Dan, taking him by surprise. He was almost knocked off his feet, as she barreled into his chest. As he struggled to maintain his balance, she clawed him hard across the face. Sam leaped forward and caught her by the arm and pulled her away, but not before she connected with Dan's injured arm. He howled in pain, the hatred in his eyes matching Sarah's. He moved a step back and further away from her reach.

They stood motionless, both breathing hard, as they glared.

"That's enough of that," he said through clenched teeth. "Try that again, and it'll be the last thing you do."

"And this should deter me?" she cried, her voice breaking.

Dan nodded to Sam. He drew his gun, then let Sarah go and stepped back, keeping her in his sights. She kept her eyes locked on Dan's.

"It better deter you, unless you want to suffer a worse death than your friends," Dan said ominously. He gave her a moment to consider this, before he spoke again. "We can get out of this without the law hunting us down, and you're going to help. Then we'll take a steamboat north up the Mississippi to Montana Territory, a comfortable distance from our reputation. But first, Sam and me have to dispose of Andy and Ron. When we're done, you're going back to the house and tell the Bannermans what happened."

Sarah looked at him in surprise. Dan watched her closely, and looked satisfied.

"So you *are* listening, then. Good. Now listen carefully, because this is what you're going to say…"

As Miles floated in and out of consciousness, he began to take in the lies Dan intended for Miles' family to hear. The thought of dying with a scandal of that sort dropped on his family and on his name, was unbearable. He struggled to remain conscious, fearing that if he did not he would never wake again, but to do so was impossible.

"How dare you think I will help you!" Sarah spat. "You've stolen my life and murdered two innocent men, one of them the man I love! I'll *die* before I ever help you again!"

Dan crumpled the handbill, stooped, and shoved it into Sarah's satchel. He then stood and shoved the bag into her arms roughly.

"I mean what I say. You will do exactly what I tell you, or die a worse death than your two friends."

Sam laughed mirthlessly.

Sarah paled, but her expression remained set. Dan watched her for a moment, then he smiled and turned to Sam.

"If Sarah won't do her part, we'll have to help ourselves, Sam. So… we need to buy some time, and delay the law getting involved. So tell me, Sam, who's going to discover the bodies and inform them?"

"The Bannermans," said Sam.

Alarm filled Sarah's eyes.

"That's right. We can't have that. So since Sarah won't help us, looks like we'll be paying a visit to the Bannermans. All of them. I understand your friends have a younger sister and baby brother."

Sarah's eyes widened in horror, then her gaze dropped to the ground and her shoulders sagged. What color remained in her face drained away.

Miles grew aware of faint voices, growing fainter. He was still in the clearing and he was still alive, but only just. Yet if Dan and the other man were leaving, it meant soon his father would come.

The long minutes dragged past, the only sound the whispering wind in the tall pines that surrounded the clearing.

It seemed he waited an eternity for each new beat of his heart. His strength waned and he lay struggling for breath, and yet his father did not come.

At what point it became too late for him he did not know, but he could no longer deny that it was. He grieved the loss of the future he would never have and resigned himself to his fate, relinquishing the hopes and dreams he held such a short time ago. All he now asked of what little life he had left, was that it would not leave him until his father came and heard the truth. Then he could rest, knowing he would not be blamed for coveting Delevan's fiancé, and murdering his brother. Then he could let go.

As night began to fall, the earth grew dark.

Still his father did not come, and he had nothing left with which to hold on. With his last breath, he pleaded…

"Please don't let me rest, please… don't set me free… until my innocence is proven."

Miles was silent, memories of the past obscuring the present. Trixie moved to him and pushed up on his arm, so it lay across her back.

My throat ached. I felt like I'd been there, a helpless observer, as I witnessed each tragic second of it. Chip rested his chin on my knee, looking up at me with his soulful eyes. I hugged him, burying my face in his thick fur. Judging by which, we were going to have a very hard winter this year.

Miles returned to the present and smiled slightly. He looked tired.

"So that is what happened… that's how I… died. And yet, here I am. Here, but not here." He shrugged.

I cleared my throat and pulled myself together.

"So you won't be able to rest in peace, until your innocence is proven?"

"Looks like it. When I prayed what I did, I hoped to live long enough to tell my Father the truth. But… instead, here I am."

"That—had to be disappointing," I said, not sure how to say what I was thinking.

Miles laughed, and shrugged again.

"Yeah, I guess you could say that."

"It had to be so hard, seeing your family grieve after what happened," I sympathized.

"I'm thankful I missed most of that. It would have been unbearable. A number of years passed before I returned like this," he indicated his semi-transparent form. "I gathered that the years I missed were very difficult for my family, my Father was obsessed with finding the truth. I was glad to see that he turned from that, and focused instead on my younger brother and sister, the children he had left."

"So like… when his quest ended, yours began?"

53

"That's the conclusion I've come to."

"So… why didn't you try communicating with your family, and tell them what happened? Write them a letter, something?" I wondered.

Miles shook his head firmly.

"No, seeing the effect on my family from the years my Father was searching for evidence that didn't exist, no. He would have become even more driven to find proof. I wouldn't do that to my family."

"Wow, you actually chose to be like this forever, instead?"

"Yes. If you have a family and love them like I did mine, you'll understand."

I thought about that.

"Yeah, I do," I said. I wasn't sure I had as much character as this guy did though, to stick with that resolve. How unbelievably hard it had to be for him, all these years. "You said proof didn't exist, but listening to what you've said, there would have been so much evidence left behind. Technology available today, would reveal the true story."

"Yeah, there was evidence. If only it was still there," Miles said. "It's been a while, though. Over a century."

"It's a wonder no one considered that you couldn't have shot Delevan in the back and killed him instantly, and then been shot by him twice, after he was already dead. What kind of Sheriff did you people have back then?"

Miles laughed.

"Not a very good one. I gathered that he would rather accept Sarah's word, than be left with two murders to solve."

"I'm not sure how we can use that information now, since we don't have the crime scene or a report of the investigation, or guns or bullets… I'm surprised by the way you described Sarah, that she never tried to tell your family what really happened."

Miles sighed.

"Yeah, that surprised me too. She was protecting the rest of our family at the time, but I don't understand why she didn't write and tell our parents the truth before boarding the ship to Europe."

"In the story my Uncle told, the ship never made it to Europe. It sank with Sarah aboard," I remembered.

"That's what I understood to have happened as well, from what I overheard my family say after I returned. If the boat didn't sink, I believe she would have contacted my family eventually, and told them the truth."

"Was her brother on the ship with her?" I asked.

Miles thought about that.

"My family certainly never mentioned him, as they never knew of him. He could have used Delevan's ticket, though. One thing I'm sure of, she didn't board that ship alone. There's no way he would let her go free."

"That Dan was horrible," I scowled. "I can't imagine having such an evil brother."

"Me either," Miles agreed. "It's tragic that Sarah died on her way to Europe and was never able to escape from that. I never blamed her for what happened in the clearing that day. If you could have seen and heard her, how she looked at Delevan, and then how she reacted to her own brother... My parents did blame her, though. They didn't give her much of a chance to begin with. And she *was* lying, they knew that, they just couldn't prove it. And then she was gone."

"Your brother would have been on that boat to Europe too, if things went the way he and Sarah planned," I said.

Miles' eyebrows rose in surprise and he processed that for a second.

"You're right. I never considered that before. I felt a lot of guilt for a lot of years, as if Delevan would still be alive if I didn't go after him. I eventually realized that wasn't true, I didn't bring Sarah's brother and his companions to the clearing. It's so strange though... to realize Delevan would've died, no matter what."

"His death wasn't your fault," I said, feeling the need to elaborate on that. "Getting that handbill to Delevan before he married Sarah was honest and right, regardless of the outcome. Otherwise, you're in a no-win situation where there is no right, because whether Delevan lived or died that day was out of your hands. Imagine if you didn't go after him, and he was confronted by all those guys with nothing but that little gun that had two shots, and wasn't very accurate, either. Wouldn't you feel just awful that you weren't there? Wouldn't you think that maybe, if you'd gone after him, you could've saved him?"

"Yes," Miles said quietly, as he rubbed his forehead. "That's exactly what I'd be thinking for the rest of my life."

"You'd be eaten up with guilt, and in that instance, you *would* be guilty of keeping that handbill to yourself, and letting your brother go off and marry some woman of questionable character. But you didn't. You did the right thing. Consider this too, is your sister responsible for your death, since giving you the letter caused you to be in the wrong place, at the wrong time?"

"Of course not!" Miles said with feeling.

I was on a roll. If this guy ever felt guilty again after I was done, well, it wouldn't be for lack of trying!

"Results don't determine if our actions are right or wrong. Wouldn't that be the ends justifying the means? It's the actions themselves that are either right or not, all on their own."

"You are very wise… Who are you, by the way?"

That made me laugh.

"I'm Anika Riley. Polly Bannerman hired me to manage the estate. Hire people to do the yard work, clean the house, see to any repairs."

Miles looked mildly surprised.

I wondered why. After all, he was going out to the wild, wild west on his own to manage the family gold mine, when he was my age.

"So why can you see me, I wonder? What's different about you?" Miles studied me curiously.

I shrugged, and paused before answering.

Yikes, I'm pulling an Uncle Mark!

"It might be because Polly gave me permission to search for clues to prove you're innocent."

That earned a set of raised eyebrows.

"Wait, you—you *asked* for permission? Specifically to—to try and prove me innocent? You came here—for that purpose?"

"Yes," I said.

He stared back at me, stunned.

"I believe I'll succeed," I said.

He shook his head to clear it.

"The first person I've been able to talk to in all these years, and somehow you keep leaving me speechless. I never would've believed that was possible!"

I laughed.

"Yeah, I sometimes have that effect on people."

"You're unexpected, that's for sure," he smiled.

"Uh—look who's talking!" I said, indicating his semi-transparent self.

We both laughed at that, then Miles continued.

"I love the idea of being proven innocent. I love that you want to do this. I'm completely blown away that you came here intending to do that, I think I'm in shock, actually. But after all this time, I wonder if it's even possible."

"Let's think about this for a minute. If there isn't any way to prove it, why are you here? That would just be cruel. 'Hey, really nice guy that didn't do anything wrong, live with false accusations against you for all eternity because you asked not to rest until proven innocent, and proof doesn't exist.' Really? I don't see it. The fact that you're here, makes me sure that proof *does* exist."

"I like the way you think," said Miles, a spark of hope reaching his eyes. "When you put it that way, it makes perfect sense."

"So, do you want to help me find that proof so you can get out of this semi-transparent mode?"

"Yes! Absolutely," said Miles.

"Plus, you don't want your family home turned into a resort marketed as the home of a murderous ghost, seeking and never finding forgiveness."

"What do you know that I don't?" asked Miles, a shadow of concern filling his eyes.

"Okay, so you're not all-knowing, then. Here's the thing. There's a distant cousin named Alfred, trying to wrestle control of the estate away from Polly. Polly's grandson Miles has been missing for the past four months, and if he doesn't show soon, then she's afraid Alfred may succeed. He's trying to declare her incompetent, partly because of the mess the house is in right now, which is really because the caretaker died, and Polly didn't know. So I'm here as I said before, to manage the cleaning and yard maintenance, to help prove her competence. But if Alfred wins, he plans to turn this place into a resort, and market it as I said."

"Okay...." Miles said slowly. "That makes a little bit more sense. But would you please repeat all of that, and this time use a few more words?"

I laughed.

"I can do that." I explained everything Polly said, in detail this time.

Miles listened and shook his head thoughtfully.

"After this long... I don't know how we're going to prove who was responsible and what the truth is... we've got to try though, I can't stand the thought of Alfred succeeding. I *really* do not want that to happen."

"Polly doesn't want that to happen either, that's why she hired me. I don't want that to happen, that's why I took the job."

Miles studied me.

"I can't begin to tell you how much I appreciate you believing in me. I can't get over it that you do. Other than family, that isn't what I'm used to."

I could tell he wondered why.

"When I was here last week during the storm, I had to hunt down my dog Chip, who wandered all over your castle. It's completely not like him to take off, but he did, so I followed him."

"Ah, yes. That's thanks to Trix. She's missed having another dog around. She wanted a playdate, and sort of lured him away. I didn't realize what she was doing until right before you found him, or I would have told her to stop sooner."

"Wow. I... did not know that. I saw the other dog prints, and I sure wondered. So I found him in the portrait gallery then, and while we waited for the storm to calm down enough to get home, I looked at the portraits."

"I know. I saw you," said Miles. "I wanted to know what you were up to."

"What?" I said. "I didn't see you!"

Miles smiled.

"You never turned around."

"It's a good thing I didn't, I would have died of fright! I was getting more stressed by the minute, until I found Chip and the gallery," I said with all honesty.

And note to self, look around more often! I wasn't aware I was so unobservant.

"I'm glad you didn't see me, then. Since you're the only person who *can* see me, it would be extremely ironic if that's what happened as a result."

I laughed.

"So you looked at the portraits," Miles prompted.

"Yes. I saw that you and your brother died the same year. I wondered why, and if it was related or not. I thought it was very sad."

"So you hadn't heard the story that I murdered my brother, before that?"

"No, my Uncle told the story that night after dinner. I was horrified at what he said, and... I couldn't reconcile that with what I saw in your portrait. I know you can't always judge by appearances, and I know it's a painting, but with that joyful light in your eyes, you just looked so decent and honest. I couldn't believe you would do that."

"I appreciate you giving me the benefit of the doubt," Miles said. "You wouldn't believe how everyone other than family turned on me after they heard Sarah's story. I'm talking about people that at one time I believed to be friends. People that knew I'd never hurt my brother, and would never want what I had no right to. After we were murdered, the Sheriff started spreading Sarah's story. People I'd known for years, analyzed everything I ever said and did, trying to find something dark and ulterior that wasn't there. I lived my life to bring honor to my family, and to have that happen… it was torture."

"That's terrible," I frowned.

"When you looked at my portrait so long, I thought it was because you'd heard the stories."

"I looked at your portrait because I thought it very sad that you died so young." And he was cute, really cute, although I'd never admit that had anything to do with it!

Miles thought about that.

"I'm glad Polly hired you. I'm being master of the understate-ment, when I say that. You believe in me, you can see and hear me, and you believe there's proof. After all these years… something has changed," Miles smiled. "Alright, Anika Riley… I'm in, all the way in. I don't know how you plan to accomplish this, but anything I can do to help, you've got it."

"Great! What we'll do, is work this mystery backwards. We al-ready know what happened, thanks to you. All we have to do now, is prove it. I've got plans, and together, we'll do this. It makes sense that when we do, it'll free you. If nothing else, it'll clear your name and you won't have that cloud hanging over you anymore."

"Either way would be a major improvement," Miles said.

I looked around.

"Where did the dogs go?"

We found them in the entryway. Trixie was trying to show Chip how to go through a wall. We both laughed, it was too funny! The puzzled look on Chip's face, and his reluctance to try and follow her.

"Sorry Trix, he knows that's not going to work. If you want to show him around, you'll have to use a doorway," Miles smiled.

"Speaking of doorways," I said, as I refastened my ponytail, in an effort to capture the hair that kept falling across my eyes. "It's time for us to head back for the day."

Miles and Trixie walked with us to the edge of the garden.

"We'll be back in the morning," I said reassuringly.

I would want reassurance if I was alone for as long as Miles was, and then the only person able to see me, was leaving.

Miles smiled.

"See you tomorrow, then."

Chip and I hurried down the path through the forest, and across the bridge that Miles built.

How crazy was that, I spent the afternoon talking to the guy that built this bridge a hundred and forty-five years ago.

Note to self, nothing is impossible. Today just proved it.

Chapter 4

I tossed and turned, wishing my brain would stop trying to assimilate all of the mind-blowing things that happened in the past few days. There were so many. Moving here, finding the castle, meeting Polly, meeting Miles... especially meeting Miles. He was such a nice guy, and didn't deserve what happened to him. I felt so much sympathy for him, not just because he was falsely accused and stuck in semitransparent mode, but also for the way his friends turned on him. It was nowhere near the same, but I lost so-called friends when our circumstances changed so drastically. Apparently, I was only popular because of my very cool car, and house, and clothes, and the ability to afford what everyone else could. Trouble is a good way to find out who your real friends are. It turned out I didn't have any outside of family, and neither did Miles. I could totally relate.

I had to find a way to clear his name, but what I really needed to do right now, was get some sleep. My mind was spinning out of control, and I couldn't make it stop.

I gave up trying to sleep, and tried reading a book instead, but still my thoughts raced madly. Several pages later, and I didn't remember a word I read.

It was hard to act normal when I got back to the cabin after work. I couldn't talk about what happened, and who I met. I would scare my Mom to death, she'd have me in a hospital searching for a brain tumor to explain my delusion. Come to think of it, I did have quite a headache. My brain felt ready to explode from everything I'd seen today.

I tossed my kindle aside, and clutched the sides of my head with both hands. It was no use.

I slid out of bed and snuck quietly out of the room, determined not to disturb Doreen. I plopped on the couch in the living room and reached for my laptop, which I forgot to put away earlier. I was sooo glad Tryon didn't mess with it, he had a tendency to get into electronic devices that didn't belong to him, and use them in unapproved ways.

I opened it and switched it on, then sat and stared blankly at the Google search engine screen for several long minutes.

Thoughts racing like mad, and I can't think of anything to search on? How additionally frustrating! Brain full, mind empty.

Fine. I'd focus on something completely different instead... I did a search on Doreen's symptoms. Not that we hadn't all done this before, but you never know... different day, different search engine, dig through enough results and just maybe the info we needed would be there.

The search results included multiple Lyme disease websites. She tested negative though, and the doctors she saw were certain she didn't have it.

I spent the next two hours searching for anything else that matched Doreen's symptoms, but which hadn't been tested for already. I didn't find anything new, but the change in focus slowed down my swirling thoughts.

I shut down the laptop, and went back to bed.

Bright and early the next morning, Chip and I hurried back through the woods to the Bannerman estate. I had interviews to conduct, and I was sort of anxious to see if Miles was still there.

As we walked out of the woods into the rose garden, Trixie ran up and play-bowed to Chip. He looked at me.

Oh, so it matters what I think now?

"Go ahead," I told him.

He accepted her invitation and they ran off through the garden, playing keep away with a stick.

"Hi," I heard Miles say. In the bright morning light he was a little harder to see, but he was there.

"Hi back," I said.

We walked toward the house. Sounds so normal, doesn't it. I wondered if the novelty of this whole situation would ever wear off.

"To tell you the truth, you surprise me in more ways than one," I said.

"How's that?" Miles wondered, as we continued up the steps.

"You seem pretty laid-back and—well—normal, for having been in isolation for so long."

Miles looked back at the dogs, who were still playing with abandon. He nodded his head towards the retriever.

"I don't know how I would have tolerated it, without Trix. It does get awfully lonely though. A little like watching families interact on TV. It's not even close to really being part of a family," he said with a note of sadness in his voice. "The past three years with no one else here, has been the worst. Without Trix for companionship, I don't know what I would have done."

I thought about how awful it would feel to have life going on around me, but without me.

"Well, at least now you can talk to me. And I believe we'll prove to the world you're innocent, and set you free."

"I look forward to that," Miles smiled.

I adjourned to the clean parlor to prepare for the interviews I scheduled for that morning. Miles didn't stay, he knew he would be a major distraction.

I watched a truck emblazoned with the Lawncare Extraordinaire logo, as it pulled into the long curving driveway and parked in front of the estate.

Right on time. That was a good sign.

The guy that got out of the truck was probably mid-twenties, with dark hair. He looked fit, it was easy to see he got a lot of exercise on the job. I moved toward the front door, as he began to walk up the stairs toward the vestibule.

I opened the door and stepped out.

"Hello," I greeted him. "I'm Miss Riley, the property manager."

"It's good to meet you, Miss Riley," he said, as we shook hands. "I'm Nate Harrison."

"If you'll follow me, I'll show you around the grounds," I said, leading the way. "So what is your position in the business, Nate?"

"I own the business, actually," Nate replied. "I'm the boss, and I create the plans, but I also work alongside my guys to make it happen."

"Impressive," I said. "I notice you have stellar ratings online, and I like the photos you've posted of the properties you regularly maintain."

"Thank you," said Nate. "Lawncare Extraordinaire's reputation is very important to me, and to each of the guys I've got working for me."

Nate was very professional, which was a point in Lawncare Extraordinaire's favor. I still wondered if Polly was joking about her 'yard man' statement, but she ought to be happy to know this guy was very unlikely to give me any trouble. He was pleasant to talk to and friendly, but in a respectful way.

We reached the rose garden. Nate examined one of the plants, his deep blue eyes narrowed in concentration.

"The roses are in good shape for being so neglected," he said, as he stood and looked around. "When was the last time the grounds had any care?"

I explained that the caretaker died three years ago, and the owner of the estate wasn't informed. He nodded as if considering that, and we continued on the royal tour of the grounds.

"When the rose bushes are trimmed, they're going to explode with new growth. You'll have roses before winter sets in."

"That's interesting. It isn't going to be too cold at night for that, soon?"

"Not at all. They'll withstand a lot of cold nights before they decide to hibernate, as long as it warms up during the day."

Nate and I continued touring the grounds. It took a while. With a house this big surrounded by a huge garden, it was quite a hike to go all the way around and see everything.

Nate mapped out his vision for the grounds on a Google earth printout of the estate. I was impressed with that, and with his ideas, which I could easily picture thanks to the page I was now holding in my hand. I liked his plans for planting in the spring, and his use of pansies and other cold hardy flowers to keep color in the garden during the winter months.

"I'm very pleased with your ideas," I said, as we completed our tour and returned to the front of the house. "When can you start?"

"I can have a crew out here first thing tomorrow," Nate smiled.

We set up a contract and pay schedule, and Nate went on his way to inform his crew that they had a very big job ahead of them.

I had a short break before the next interview, which I was grateful for. That walk around the grounds was a mini marathon. Nate and I walked at a much faster pace than I did on Monday when walking with Polly, and my muscles were feeling it.

While I waited for the next interviewee to arrive, I called and cancelled the appointment with the other landscape company that was scheduled for that afternoon.

I walked to the window and glanced from it, to my watch. The next interviewee was already thirty minutes late. Not a good sign!

After an additional thirty minutes of waiting, a car pulled into the driveway and screeched to a halt in front of the steps. A harried looking woman, somewhere in her fifties, got out and looked around with a glare, before heading for the stairs.

This could get interesting.

I walked out to the vestibule, and waited for her to make her way to the top of the stairs.

"Hello, I'm Miss Riley, the estate manager," I said with a smile, to the woman in front of me.

Her hair was black and cut in a short bob. She scowled and narrowed her eyes, which were so dark she looked dead inside. She looked me up and down critically. Ironically, her shirt and hat boasted the logo *Happy Cleaners*.

"And your name is?" I prompted her.

She was sure not making a good first impression!

She pushed past me on her way into the castle, making me once again thankful I wasn't more abundantly blessed with curves, and gave the entryway an appraising look.

"It's Lana," she said. "When's the last time this place was cleaned?"

She ran a finger along the entryway table, and frowned at the accumulation of dust.

"Three years," I said, starting to feel rather bristly, myself.

She shook her head and made a sound of disgust, as she moved into the parlor.

The interview went downhill from there. She had no clue how to properly care for antiques, any more than she did public relations.

"Alright then Lana, you've given me everything I need to make the right decision for the estate."

"And exactly what would that be?" she asked condescendingly.

"I've decided to go a different direction," like a positive one! "and will be hiring another service. Thanks so much for coming. Here, let me show you the door."

She stared, her lip twitching as if she could not believe what she just heard.

I smiled and motioned toward the front door.

She left, peeling out of the driveway. I hoped she didn't need the tread on her tires, because she left it behind.

I took a deep breath and shook off the encounter. She would not ruin my good mood, or make me doubt myself!

Note to self, never hire based on online reviews only. I wouldn't be surprised if she wrote them all herself, although I wondered how she managed to scrape up enough positivity to do even that.

I ate the sandwich I brought with me for lunch, and wondered where Miles was. He was serious about not distracting me, I saw no sign of him.

One o'clock came, and right on time, I was glad to see a Queen of Clean van pull into the driveway.

This was my last appointment of the day. I hoped it would go well, because if this appointment was as great as the last one, I'd be calling to arrange additional interviews!

"Hello there, I'm Molly, and you must be Miss Riley!" said the Queen of Clean lady. She was probably in her thirties, and the polar opposite of the not-happy woman.

"Yes, I'm Miss Riley. It's great to meet you, Molly," I said, as she reached the top of the stairs.

"What a wonderful place," she marveled, her short dark hair bouncing in excitement as she looked around. "And you're the estate manager. Well that's just wonderful, good for you!"

She patted my arm as I led her inside.

Molly knew not to use Windex on antiques, which was a big improvement over not-Happy Cleaners. She brought an e-cloth, which is what her business primarily uses, to demonstrate its miraculous cleaning powers.

"If you don't mind, I'll just demonstrate for you," said Molly.

"Sure, I'd love to see what it can do," I said. If it was as great as she said, I would get some for Mom.

"Now you just spray it with a little water," Molly used a small spray bottle she brought with her. "You don't want it really wet, just barely damp. The cloth has over a million and a half strands per square inch, and just wait until you see how well it picks up dust, and just keeps on picking it up!"

Molly enthusiastically ran the cloth along the entryway table, and I was amazed at the difference.

Molly zoomed through the whole entryway. She dusted the baseboards, walls, furniture, banisters, the whole bit. In my research, I found that many experts recommended cleaning antique wood furniture with a barely damp cloth, just as she was doing. It cleans off the dust without scratching, and doesn't leave behind a residue to attract more.

"Molly, I love your attitude and your e-cloth superpowers. When can you start?"

"Well, now Miss Riley, thank you! I do say there's not a day that can't be improved by a cheerful disposition."

"Very true," I agreed.

"I've got a large team that works in pairs to do regular cleaning jobs, but on Friday, we can all be here and start on the castle together," she said. "It's going to take a while to get the whole place spic and span, but we'll do it!"

"Awesome, Molly. Let's get a contract set up."

"You know this job is going to be good for Cedar Oak's economy. I'll have to hire more girls to add the estate as a regular client!"

I laughed.

"You can hire the entire town, and it will still take more than a week to get every room done," I said.

Molly laughed too.

"That's about right! But we'll get it done. Oh yes, we will."

As I closed the door behind Molly, I breathed a sigh of relief. I felt good about the two companies I chose to do the work. This was so exciting! I was impatient to see the house and grounds with their glory restored.

"Miles, are you around?" I asked, as I walked through the entry-way.

"Where else would I be," he responded beside me.

I was not expecting that, and jumped.

"Sorry," he smiled.

"Sure. Sure, you are," I said, giving him a narrow-eyed look. "That explains the smile, and the laughter in your eyes."

He laughed in response.

"I didn't startle you on purpose, how's that? I can't help that it was funny. Amusement is kind of involuntary."

"Fine. As a person who also possesses a sense of humor, I understand, and choose to forgive you," I replied, and he smiled. "So now, on to my news. I hired a landscaping company, so it's going to be very busy outside for the next week or so. I've got a house cleaning company lined up, too. They'll start the day after tomorrow. They have a large team coming, but still. This house is huge. It's going to take a while."

"That's great," Miles said. "I hope everything works out for Polly, otherwise I might have to haunt Alfred and dis-abuse him of his notion to capitalize on my murderous past. He could end up with more than he bargained for."

That made me laugh.

"Where are we going, by the way?" I asked, as I followed Miles up the staircase.

"I have something to show you," he said mysteriously.

Up two flights of stairs, down a hallway, through a doorway, and down another hallway, we came to a closed door. This house was a maze.

"This is where I've spent most of my time since Polly and her grandson moved out," Miles said, as he opened the door with a wave.

I stepped through the doorway to find an office, or library, I suppose it was called in the past. It still retained its antique aura in the way of furnishings. Floor to ceiling bookshelves filled the majority of each wall. An antique globe resided on a stand in one corner. Several comfortable chairs and cut-glass lamps were positioned around a gorgeous fireplace, surrounded by a carved mantle. An antique desk presided over it all. What I wasn't expecting to see, was the up to date office equipment.

"Wow, this is nice," I said, as I looked around.

"I think so," he agreed. "It's possibly my favorite room in the house."

"Great view, too," I noticed. "Were you looking out this window when Chip and I came here during the rainstorm?"

"Yes. I saw you right before you went in through the cellar."

In all my uncoordinated glory.

"Well at least I managed to get myself back out, and enter by the staircase," I replied. I could be proud of that, anyway.

Miles hesitated, either trying to find the right words, or deciding whether to speak at all.

Understanding began to dawn.

"You helped me. You caught me, when I lost my grip!"

"Don't feel bad about not being able to do it on your own, almost no one could," he assured me. "Movies make it look like all it takes is determination, but in fact, it takes stronger muscles than most people have."

"Well… thanks for the help," I said. "I really needed it."

"Any time," Miles smiled.

"I didn't see you in the basement though," I realized.

"I wasn't in the basement," Miles replied. "I didn't have to be."

Interesting. Like so many other things in the past few days.

He sat in front of the computer, and switched it on.

"I've kept myself from being bored out of my mind by learning as much as possible. You would not believe how things have changed over the years."

"Mom told me when she was in college, there was no such thing as the internet or cell phones," I said. "I can't imagine living without either one."

"Those were big changes," Miles agreed. "There have been more than I can count, in the past hundred and forty years. There have been lots of opportunities to learn new things. Books left lying around, especially school books when my younger brother James, his son, grandson, great-grandson, and great-great-grandson Miles, were growing up here."

"All of that must be why you seem so normal. You don't sound or act like you belong in the 1800's."

"I suppose," said Miles. "I spent very little time in the 1800's, when it comes down to it."

"Did you ever search the internet for information about Sarah, and what happened to her?" I asked.

"No," Miles frowned. "The thought never occurred to me. That was such a long time ago. Since her ship was lost anyway, what information could there be?"

"Passenger manifestos, for one thing," I said. "We could find out more about the ship she was on when she sailed to Europe. I know it sank, but still. You never know what you can unearth. One piece of information leads to another."

"Let's do that, then," Miles said. "That's why I wanted to show you this room, it will make a good Mission Control center."

"Try to remember everything you can about Sarah and the hand-bill. The other names on it might give us something to go on. As for the ship manifesto, she wouldn't have been sailing alone. Maybe you'll recognize other names that were on the wanted poster. Finding the actual handbill is a longshot, but remember where you were when you found it, and we can call around to museums in that area. Are there any photo albums still here from that time period? Something might spark a memory. And what about diaries, or files. If you didn't return, or whatever, for several years after the murders took place, then you don't know what evidence or information your Father might have compiled. If there is any, we need to find it. We might have the technology now, to interpret evidence your Father collected, that wasn't available then. We may not know a piece of information is critical until we have it, so let's search the house and search the net, for anything and everything."

"You've really thought this out," Miles said. He sounded im-pressed. "Your enthusiasm is starting to rub off and make me think we might actually be able to do this."

"Believe it, Mister!" I said. "We WILL do this."

I looked around the spotless office, comparing it for the first time to the dust laden state of the rest of the house. "How did it get so clean in here?" I asked.

"Dust is harmful to electronics," Miles said. "And I spend most of my time here, so I keep the dust to a minimum."

"How do you even do that, and since you can, why is the rest of the house still such a mess?" I wanted to know.

"The rest of the house is still such a mess because I don't want to fuel rumors that the house is haunted by an OCD scullery maid," Miles said. "And I clean the office this way…"

Miles motioned for me to follow, and we crossed into the next room. He waved the windows open, lifted the dust with another wave, and sent it right out the open window. I stared in astonishment.

"Quite a superpower you've got there. So what I want to know is, since you can do this…" I flicked my hand, "why did I just hire a cleaning service!"

Miles laughed at that.

We returned to the office.

"Tell me something about yourself now," he said. "I was so stunned yesterday when I found out you could see me, I didn't even ask. You know an awful lot about me, and I know next to nothing about you."

"Okay, that's fair. You know my name. You know I have a dog, your dog's new best friend," I pointed toward the window. We could see Chip and Trixie dashing around the fountain, playing keep-away with Chip's Frisbee.

"I'm nineteen years old, and graduated from high school last spring. I have a nine-year-old sister and three-year-old brother…" I told him all about our family, where we were from, and why we moved here. Miles had lots of questions, which I answered.

We talked about other subjects, too. We talked about Miles' family, and the family he observed over the years as he lived in the castle, unseen. Try as he did to stay under the radar, now and then people would still see strange things that made them wonder.

"I was amazed at how freaked out people could be when they mislaid items and I made sure they found them again. Half the time, instead of being glad the lost item was found, the person who lost it went on and on about how that's not where they left it. If they knew where they left it, they would have found it themselves, so I thought that was rather contradictory."

I laughed at that, as Miles continued.

"People began to suspect some sort of supernatural help was involved. I didn't want that, so I stopped. There were times though, when I had to intervene. Like when my younger brother James' little boy, who was less than two years old, fell from the top of the stairs. The little guy was supposed to be napping, but that was the day James and his wife discovered their son Jonathan learned to climb out of his crib. They were at the foot of the stairs and saw him fall, and then suddenly lifted back up and set down safely."

"Oh, wow," I said. "Then what happened?"

"After being hugely relieved their son was spared a fall that could have killed him, and after collecting him from the top of the stairs, my brother and the rest of the family talked about it over and over. They never came to any conclusions, how could they, but the general consensus was that Delevan or I saved him, or it was a miracle. There was no way for them to know for certain, because I didn't want them to. I couldn't see any good coming of it."

"I guess so… it would have made them sad to know you were trapped," I said.

"Yes, my sister and Mother were still living, and it would have grieved them. They suffered more than they ever deserved because of what happened to Delevan and I, and the lies that everyone around them believed as a result. I couldn't bear to add to that."

"What about your brother?"

"James was three when I died. He barely remembered me as his brother, so though it would have upset him to know, it wouldn't have affected him like it would my Mother and sister," Miles explained. "The servants who were aware of what happened were convinced I was responsible, but in every other way they were wrong. They began the stories that I was seeking forgiveness for Delevan's death. Anything unusual or mysterious that happened was attributed to me, and fueled the stories."

"That's such a shame they did that, I can understand how hard you'd try to keep your presence a secret," I said sympathetically.

"I did appreciate my family always standing by me," Miles said. "I appreciate you too, you really are the only person outside of the Bannerman family who has ever believed in my innocence."

"By the time I'm done here, everyone else will believe it too," I said firmly.

Miles smiled.

"I like your attitude."

I laughed.

"I'm pretty sure you're the only person who's ever said that!"

Miles laughed too.

"I can imagine. From what I can tell, you're not afraid to form your own opinions and stand by them. Most people don't appreciate a differing point of view that won't conform to their own."

"Yeah, most people would call that being stubborn," I said.

"Considering you want to clear my name, then I find that to be a very positive trait, no matter what label you put on it," said Miles, and I laughed.

We heard barking outside, and looked out the window. Chip and Trixie were running in circles. I had no idea what they were barking at, but they were having fun.

"I try to keep my presence a secret, but Trixie isn't so careful," Miles said. "She leaves evidence behind. If you've never had one, you have no idea how much hair a golden retriever generates. She doesn't have to be visible for long, to leave a mountain of hair behind. She's clogged the vacuum more than once, which really puzzles whoever's vacuuming at the time. She sometimes leaves paw prints, and has been known to take things that don't belong to her. She particularly likes sock,s and a few times I've caught her chewing on shoes. No one in the castle ever loses their keys, but if they don't hang on to their own shoes and socks, then there are no guarantees. I don't call her Trix for nothing."

I laughed at that.

If he was just a little more solid and talking about different subject matter, it would be easy to forget and think he was just a guy my age who was fun and easy to talk to.

The more we talked, the more Miles' eyes began to take on the sparkle I'd seen in his portrait. He could be very funny, and his sense of humor clicked with mine. When I made a joke, I didn't have to constantly explain what I meant. He got it the first time around. I loved that.

We talked too long, though. By the time I looked at my watch, it was past time for me to head back to the cabin.

"I'll see you tomorrow," I said, gathering my purse from the entryway table. "Maybe we can start searching. There's evidence, I am sure of it. We'll find it."

"I'm looking forward to it," Miles smiled. "See you tomorrow."

I turned as I reached the base of the vestibule stairs, and waved at Miles. He waved back, and with another quick "see you later," and a call for Chip, I hurried home.

He was such a nice guy. He deserved to be free from the false accusations, and freed from his semi-transparent state. I was confident that I had enough stubbornness to stick with it, and get the job done.

Sarah flew through the woods. Every few steps she threw a glance over her shoulder to reassure herself she wasn't being followed. Dan and Sam had their hands full disposing of their two dead companions, and in staging the clearing to look as though a duel took place between the two brothers. Dan knew he had her under his control, and it wasn't likely he'd feel the need to follow her as she composed herself and rehearsed her story, as she was supposed to be doing. But still she was wary, as her feet sped over the rough ground.

Where was it, the entrance was well hidden and difficult to find, and she'd only been here once before. But this—surely this was the place. She scrambled uphill, then looked down at the narrow fern covered rock ledge that protruded from a steep drop-off on the other side.

She carefully made her way to the ledge, and ran her hands along the wall of stone now in front of her. Parting the ferns that grew thickly, she knelt and entered the dark cavern. She fumbled for the candle lantern and matches, finding them where Delevan said they were. In the almost pitch-black darkness she stifled a sob, and glanced over her shoulder at the entrance. The first match broke, she was shaking so. The second match struck, and she lit the lantern and continued further into the cavern. She didn't have much time. If she wasn't back at the clearing and ready to go to the Bannermans before he and Sam were finished, they would surely carry out their threat and murder the rest of the family.

At the third narrow passage, she knelt and crawled down the sloping tunnel, pushing her satchel ahead of her. What a mess she was making of her dress, but how little things like that mattered anymore. Still, it was fortunate that the tunnel was not damp and covered in pools of water, as some of the cave was. She didn't want to be questioned as to where she had been.

She swiftly made her way to the hiding spot Delevan spoke of. Moving aside the stones covering the deep hollow in the rock behind it, she hurriedly forced her jewel case inside. She hesitated, then snatched the crushed handbill from her satchel. Smoothing it quickly, she placed it inside the case and returned it to the hiding spot. Replacing the stones, she rapidly retraced her steps and sped back to the clearing.

When she reached it, breathless and shaking, she was glad to see that Dan and Sam were still busy removing the signs left behind when their two partners were shot.

Brushing at the front of her dress to remove as much dust as she could, she knelt beside Delevan and Miles. She was almost overwhelmed with horror and grief. For just a moment she allowed herself to sob. She could afford no more than that.

Pulling herself together, she whispered, "I won't let you take the blame for this. I won't. I'll find a way to tell the truth and protect your family, too."

Chapter 5

"Hello, Mother dear," I said, as I walked in the kitchen the next morning, tempted by the smell of breakfast cooking.

"Hello, Daughter dear," she said, as she handed me a plate. "So what are you up to, today?"

"Yard clean-up starts today, so I'll be checking on the crew's progress. Queen of Clean won't be here until tomorrow, but I haven't seen the whole house myself yet anyway, so I'll explore today."

"Sounds like fun," Mom said.

"Yeah, I think it will be."

"I wish I could visit your castle, but with Doreen…"

"Yeah, I know Mom. Maybe someday I can give you the grand tour. It can wait, though."

"I talked to Susan yesterday," Mom changed the subject. "She has a daughter your age. You might like to meet her sometime, and see if you hit it off. I feel badly that you had to put off college, and move away from all your friends, too."

"Mom. Please do not feel bad. I'm fine. Work's going to keep me busy, so I'm not going to have a lot of time, but sure. I'll meet your friend's daughter sometime, maybe we'll become friends."

I put my plate in the dishwasher, grabbed my sack lunch out of the fridge, and Chip and I were out the door and up the path toward the castle.

"Anika!" Mom called after me. "You didn't eat breakfast! You just put a clean plate in the dishwasher!"

Oops, talk about mind being elsewhere.

Lawncare Extraordinaire trucks were parked up and down the long driveway when we arrived. Nate and several of his employees were hard at work cleaning out the flower beds and working on the weeds infesting the lawn. Large piles of rose cuttings, weeds, and dead plants were scattered about.

I waved to Nate.

"Looking good! You've accomplished so much already, I'm impressed."

"Thanks," Nate replied, waving back. "That's our goal, make our customers glad they trusted us with their business."

"Well you're succeeding," I said.

I was thrilled to see what a difference Nate and his crew already made, and it wasn't even eight o' clock! They were living up to their positive online reviews.

Trixie appeared, I sure hoped no one saw *that*, and she and Chip felt the need to examine the work that was done. One of the workmen gave both dogs a friendly pat, and tossed a stick for them. Instant friends. Well Polly, Chip's keeping an eye on them.

I went inside the house and set my purse on the entryway table, just as Miles appeared beside me.

"Hi," I said.

"Hi back," he smiled. "So what's on the agenda today?"

"We've got a free day, free of other people, since Queen of Clean won't be here until tomorrow. So now's the perfect time to explore. I'd like to get acquainted with the house, maybe pick a room to start, and search through drawers and trunks and that sort of thing, for clues."

"Let me start the grand tour then, but I warn you... it's going to take a while."

Boy, was he not kidding. I thought the marathon walk around the grounds was tiring.

"The house wasn't built all at the same time," Miles said. "The central portion of the estate is the original structure, as I'm sure you can tell. It's the most elaborate, what with the round towers and turrets and sharply pitched roofs. And so many windows, all shapes and sizes."

"I love that about it, there's so much character."

"As the family grew, the house was added on to in order to accommodate siblings and their families. That's the purpose of the two large wings on each side of the main house. The first-born son, named

Delevan until my brother's death, lived in the main house with his family and parents, and sometimes grandparents. If Delevan and Sarah married as they intended, they would have returned here to live in the main house eventually. I know it sounds odd now, but at any given time the Bannerman estate housed both immediate, meaning first-born, and several extended, meaning sibling, families."

"That does sound kind of odd," I agreed. "Kids taking care of elderly parents I can understand, but wasn't it difficult for a grown adult to try and have their own family and be an adult, while living in the same house as perfectly able-bodied parents?"

"That depends partly on who your parents are, I suppose," said Miles. "As you can see though, the house is large enough to get lost in. There's plenty of space for as much privacy as one could want. Still, I don't think I would have stayed here forever."

How ironic.

"Well the house certainly is massive," I said.

Room, after room, after room... it just went on. Sitting areas, bedrooms, a ballroom, storage rooms, it didn't seem as though it would end. And that was just the first floor!

I finally called for a lunch break. Maybe Miles didn't get tired or need to stop for food and water, but I did, especially since I so stupidly skipped breakfast. And it was way past lunchtime.

"How is your sister?" Miles asked, as I finished my sandwich.

"Hanging in there," I said. "Not good, though. It really worries me. She's so tired, her head hurts a lot of the time, and she's sensitive to light and sound. Maybe that's part of the headache, like a migraine. What's worrying us lately though, is that she's forgetting things. Like the times table, for example. She had that down hard and fast, now she struggles to remember it."

Miles looked worried.

"Maybe it's because she feels bad, she doesn't have the energy to remember."

"Maybe so," I said.

81

My iPhone began to ring. "Excuse me for a minute," I said to Miles, as I looked at it. I didn't recognize the number, but answered anyway. It might be Polly.

"Anika! How are you!" squealed the person that used to be my best friend in high school. I was really surprised she called.

"I'm doing fine," I said. Pressing mute, I told Miles, "it's someone I knew in high school. She talks a lot, I may be awhile."

"No problem, call me when you're ready," and he was gone.

I unmuted the call. Sheila hadn't missed me, she was talking a blue streak. Classes, parties, boys, parties, boys, classes, boys, boys, boys—she was getting on my nerves, she sounded so—shallow, actually. It's true she wasn't there for me when I needed a friend the most, but I didn't remember her being this bad when things were good and we hung out. Then again, I'd been pretty distracted my last year of high school with Dad being out of work, and my sister so sick. Maybe I just didn't remember.

"So, what are you up to?" she finally asked.

"Working, and saving for college. Dad got a new job, which is great. For now we're living in my Uncle Mark's cabin, and Dad drives up on weekends."

"Well cool, I better run. Talk later, Anika."

I felt sort of put out with her. She didn't even ask about Doreen, and I didn't have a chance to tell her. I looked at my iPhone. She talked for fifteen minutes straight!

I walked to the entryway and up to Mission Control. Miles was there, studying the computer monitor.

"Well! I hope I wasn't that shallow in high school," I said. I also told him about the conversation, which still had me miffed.

"Whether you were then or not, you aren't now," he said. "Difficulty creates the opportunity to rise to the challenge and grow stronger. Your family has been through a tough time, and that's built character in you."

Wow, I was flattered. I hoped I deserved that.

"Look," he said, turning the monitor to face me. Miles spent the time Sheila was on the phone, searching.

I looked at the screen.

"I've thought it sounded like Lyme too, but Doreen's previous doctors tested her. The ELISA test came back negative, so that was ruled out."

How thoughtful of him to want to help, though.

"The ELISA test is known for being inaccurate. Check out this statistic," Miles said, pointing to the screen. "I've spent a lot of time reading articles and researching different topics to pass the time. I'm not saying that makes me an expert, and the subject is controversial. There are many, including the CDC, who don't believe chronic Lyme exists. It could be worth checking out, though."

I looked closer at the site Miles had on the screen. I was surprised by what I saw. I wrote down the web address.

"I'll give this to Mom when I get home," I said. "This is definitely not a site I've ever looked at before. I doubt Mom has either. Thank you, for doing this. Sheila didn't even ask about Doreen."

"Any time," he smiled. "I hope it helps. I remember when my sister was nine. I can imagine what it's like for you to see her suffer, and feel helpless."

"Yeah, it's pretty awful."

"Earlier today I also searched for museums like you suggested," Miles said, clicking on a bookmark. "I found this one. I would have called, but you know…"

"Not one of your superpowers, huh?" I said. "Alright then, let me give it a shot."

I called the museum, but unfortunately, they were unable to help us. A call to the Sheriff's office led to my sanity being questioned, I'm sure. The person who answered the phone just couldn't wrap their mind around why I'd want a wanted poster, also known as a handbill, from the late 1800's. And I didn't even tell them my real reason! So that was a dead end, no help there. Maybe if I knew the right person, or was an investigative reporter, but random citizen Anika Riley wasn't getting anywhere.

"Don't be too disappointed," said Miles reassuringly. "This is the most that's been done toward proving my innocence in a very, very long time. Consider it one down, a whole bunch more to go."

"Right, we've got lots of other possibilities to look into," I agreed.

We continued the tour of the house, which I was beginning to realize would take more than a day to complete.

"This is a major workout," I said, as we climbed the stairs to the second floor. "No wonder Polly said it was bigger on the inside, than on the outside."

Miles laughed.

"It does seem that way. Maybe because of all the hallways and the maze-like arrangement of the rooms. It would be easy to get lost."

"Thank goodness I've got such an excellent guide," I said.

Miles smiled, and I smiled back.

Before I saw even half the house, it was time for me to head home for the day.

"Maybe we should just start searching tomorrow," I considered. "If we wait until I've seen the whole estate, who knows when we'll finally get started."

"That's a good idea," agreed Miles. "I vote for that."

Miles led me back to the entryway, which was fortunate. I might have been lost in the house forever otherwise! We said good night, and Chip and I began our walk back to the cabin.

Following the cobbled path between the towering oaks was like being in a cathedral. A dimly lit cathedral, the days were getting shorter, and the leaves didn't let in much light even in the daytime.

Chip and I arrived at the cabin. I opened the back door into the kitchen and took a deep breath.

"What is that awesome smell? I'm starving now!"

Mom laughed.

"Well no wonder, running off without breakfast this morning. As for what we're having for dinner, it's a new recipe I'm trying out," she said, as she lifted a pan out of the oven.

"Oh, wow, that is the best looking pizza I've ever seen," I said, as I washed my hands at the sink and began setting the table.

"Thanks, I'm hoping it will also be the best tasting," said Mom, as she cut the pizza into large squares.

"How's Doree today?" I asked.

"About the same," Mom said, concern washing over her face.

If only someday that question could be answered with "she's doing better," how happy we'd all be.

"And how about Try, what's he up to?" I asked, right before my exuberant little brother nearly plowed me over.

"Hi," he said, looking up at me as he held onto my knees.

"Hello to you," I said, ruffling his short, curly blond hair.

"I'll get this guy settled at the table, can you wake your sister and see if she feels like eating?" Mom asked.

"Sure, Mom."

I found Doreen asleep in the bedroom we shared.

"Hey Doree," I said softly, brushing back her curls. "Feel like coming to dinner?"

She blinked, then looked up and blinked a few more times. I felt bad waking her, but she really did need more than just sleep. She needed to eat, too.

"Yeah," she said.

I helped her up, and we made our way to the table.

After dinner, which was indeed the best pizza I've ever eaten, I got out my laptop. I entered the web address Miles gave me. It brought up the homepage for the International Lyme and Associated Diseases Society.

"Hey Mom, have you read this before?"

"Hmmm…" Mom peered over my shoulder. "Yes… well, no…. not this one."

I handed her my laptop. Mom read for a while.

"Can you print this off for me?" she asked. "I want to take this to the next doctor appointment. And do a search and see if you can find any Lyme literate doctors in the area, and print that for me too."

"Will do," I said. I looked over at Doreen, asleep on the couch. The living room light was turned down low, so it wouldn't hurt her eyes.

"I look forward to Tryon's naps and bedtime more than I should," Mom said with a sigh. "Doreen doesn't complain, but she's so sensitive to sound now. Tryon does his best to be quiet, but he is three, after all."

"Yeah, I doubt there's another three-year-old boy out there that does as good a job at keeping the noise level down," I said.

Mom didn't reply, and I thought about that for a minute.

"Mom, do you need me here? Did I do the wrong thing by taking the job Polly offered me?"

I wanted to help Miles, I would find a way to help him no matter what, but I suddenly felt guilty about being gone all day.

"Oh, honey, no. Your Dad and I don't expect you to live with us and help out with the other kids until they're grown, themselves. You weren't home all the time before we moved here because of school and your previous job, so there really isn't that much difference. This is the best chance you'll ever have to rebuild your college fund. You did the right thing in taking it. I wouldn't be a very good Mom to my already nineteen-year-old daughter, if I expected you to put your life on hold any more than you already have."

I was relieved.

"Okay, Mom. Good. I was feeling pretty guilty."

"Well, stop that!" Mom said, patting my knee. "I'm proud of you, and happy for you. There's nothing to feel guilty about."

"Thanks, Mom. And I can still help sometimes, even though I'm working during the day. I can take time off to babysit during doctor appointments, you know."

"Thank you, Anika, that's the best way you can help."

Mom got up to replenish her mug of hot tea, and I went to the desk in Mom's room to print the pages she asked for.

There was a cool fall breeze softly blowing, as Chip and I walked to the castle. It wouldn't be long before the changing leaves were changed. In spite of the chill, I enjoyed the walk. I loved the mountain air, full of the scents of autumn in the woods. Chip romped ahead, no doubt anxious to play with his friend Trixie. Every few yards he turned to look at me, encouraging me to pick up the pace.

I'd have to run full-out to be fast enough to suit him! I kept my own pace, and my frustrated yet loyal chocolate Chip stopped long enough for me to catch up, before leaping ahead again. From cabin to castle, that's how he traveled. There was no risk he'd use up all his energy. He may not be a water dog, but in every other way he's all Lab.

"Hello, Nate," I waved, as Chip and I entered the castle grounds, and he took off to find Trixie.

"Good morning, Miss Riley," Nate said, smiling.

"Your team is awesome," I said, admiring what they'd accomplished already.

The piles of rose cuttings and weeds and overgrown vines from yesterday were gone, and more piles were rapidly taking their places, as the cleared area in the garden grew larger.

"I'm very pleased with your progress," I said.

"I'm glad to hear it," said Nate. "I'm also glad we ran into each other, as I have a question for you. Would you prefer to have the entire grounds of the estate cleared before planting the beds, or plant as we go?"

I looked around and thought about that.

"I'd like the entire grounds to be completely cleared first. When all of the old growth is trimmed back or removed, then I'd like the beds planted as we discussed."

"Very good, Miss Riley. That's what we'll do."

"At the rate your guys are working, how long do you expect it will take to have the grounds cleared?"

Nate looked around and considered that.

"As long as we don't get stalled by the weather, I'd say two weeks."

"That sounds great! Thanks, Nate," I said, as I turned and headed toward the stairs to the castle.

I unlocked the heavy door with the ancient key, and Chip and I went inside.

"Hi," I said, as Miles appeared beside me.

"Hi back," he smiled.

"Hello!" said Molly, from inside the arched doorway to the parlor.

Miles held in a laugh and stepped back, as I turned to Molly.

Note to self, before speaking to a friend that no one else can see, make sure no one else is around!

"How are you doing today?" I asked her, recovering quickly.

"Just fine, Miss Riley. I got here a little early today, I hope it's alright I let myself in…"

"Of course, Molly, that's why I gave you a key," I said.

"My team will be arriving in about ten minutes, and we're all looking forward to getting started. Is there a particular place you'd like us to begin?"

"Yes, actually there is," I said. "Start at the top of the main house, and work your way down. Then move to the west wing, then the east."

"That's just what we'll do then," said Molly.

There was a knock at the door.

"That'll likely be my girls," she said.

I turned and opened the door, and sure enough it was Molly's girls, all fifteen of them, and all looked much happier than the not-Happy Cleaners woman.

"Hello ladies," I said as they trooped in, looking around in awe. "I'll leave you to your work, and head off to mine. If you need me, Molly, I'll be in the east wing."

I glanced at Miles, and he led the way. Which was fortunate, the house was such a maze I might have ended up somewhere else!

"That was a close one," said Miles.

I nodded, and looked behind me. There was no one there. They probably wouldn't even get to the east wing and west wing halls today.

"I think we're in the clear," I whispered.

Miles smiled.

"You're going to have to be careful, people will start thinking you have an imaginary friend."

I laughed, then clapped my hand over my mouth and looked behind me. Still all clear.

Miles laughed at that.

"Yeah, people will start thinking I'm crazy if they hear me having one-sided conversations."

We walked on, winding down maze-like hallways and through large rooms.

"This house is just crazy big," I commented. "Polly said there are places she's never been."

"Hmm. I think I've been through the whole house. But then again, I've had over a hundred and forty years in which to do that," said Miles.

I laughed.

"I don't have that long, we're going to have to search like mad to find the proof we want if we have to go into every room to do it!"

Miles smiled.

"The wings aren't likely to hold much, I wouldn't bother with the majority of the bedrooms and parlors, at all. There are storage rooms that might possibly be worth searching, though. Since this is the least likely place for you to be discovered chatting away with your imaginary friend, it's the best place for us to start."

Miles stopped in front of a door, and opened it.

"This is the storage room furthest east in the east wing," he said.

"That is just amazing to me, to think of having multiple storage rooms in one house," I said.

"If you think that's something, wait until you see the two ball-rooms," said Miles.

"Two?" I stared at him. I was stunned. "Are you serious?"

"Yes, two," Miles smiled.

I turned and walked through the door into the storage room, and Miles followed and closed it behind us.

"Lock it too, please, just in case," I said. I heard the key turn as I looked around.

Chests of drawers, a massive wardrobe, and several cedar chests and trunks filled the room. There were no wall hangings, and no wall-paper. The wood floor was bare, although several rugs were rolled and stacked against one wall. There was also a bed, which I found surprising.

"So this is where you put the overflow guests, huh?" I commented.

Miles laughed at the thought.

"I suppose if we ever invited the entire state, once this area became a state, and everyone came, we might've needed it. But no, at some point in time someone wanted different furniture, so this was stored with the other pieces," he said, and he pointed out the matching furniture in the room.

"It is just crazy," I said, turning in circles as I surveyed the contents of the room. "If a person in your family wanted to go shopping for furniture, then hey, let's go check out the storage rooms. Whatever we want, it's probably already in there."

Miles opened a drawer and sorted through the contents as I opened the door to the wardrobe and looked inside.

"You do know this isn't how other people live, right?" I questioned.

"Of course. Other people didn't live this way when I was still the all-me solid guy I used to be, either. Life here has always been different than what I would agree is normal," Miles said. As we continued to search, he added, "The castle does have a television, so between that and the internet, I haven't been entirely isolated from the rest of the world in spite of not being able to interact with it."

"You watch TV?" I don't know why that surprised me.

"Sure," said Miles. "Sometimes. Enough to have an idea of how society has changed over the years. I saw that with the Bannermans that lived here, as well."

"Huh. No wonder you seem like just another guy born around the same time I was," I said, then gave that some thought. "Aside from the fact that you're a lot more fun to talk to."

"Thanks," said Miles. "I like talking to you too."

"Yeah, it's not like I've got a lot of competition," I pointed out.

"I'd enjoy talking to you even if there was. I like your sense of humor. You're different than other people that have come and gone over the years."

"Well, let me just say, if you were some other semi-transparent guy, I wouldn't have come back! I'd probably still be running."

Miles laughed at that thought, and so did I.

I continued sorting through the wardrobe. A very elaborate hat was in my way, so I plopped it on my head rather than find a new place for it. I turned to carry out a pile of books and papers I found on a shelf. Glancing up, I saw Miles give me a very funny look.

"What?" I asked.

Oh—the hat.

"What do you think?" I spun around, nearly dislodging it from my head and almost dropping the books and papers in the process.

"Hmmm…." said Miles.

It was obvious he was trying not to laugh.

I caught the spilling papers and lay them on the dresser top, then spun again and looked in the mirror set in the door of the wardrobe.

I looked hideous, if I do say so myself. Who would wear this thing... on purpose?

"What, this isn't a good look for me?" I asked, my hand on my hip, pretending to be offended.

"That's not a good look for anyone," Miles smiled. "You should have seen my Aunt when she wore it. Between that and the dress that matched, she looked like some sort of deranged rooster."

91

I laughed and put the hat back where it came from.

As I continued to rummage in the wardrobe and Miles dug through the drawers of a large dresser, I was impressed—in one way or another—with the various articles of clothing I unearthed.

"There have been some strange fashion trends over the past couple of centuries," I commented.

"Yes, yes there have," agreed Miles. "And that particular Aunt tried as many of them as possible. Delevan and I wondered how our Uncle could stand it, and why he never said anything."

"It's called self-preservation, baby," I laughed. "Your rooster-Aunt would have about pecked your Uncle to death, if he had."

Miles laughed too.

"You're probably right."

"Did you have a large family?" I asked. I saw the portraits the day Chip and I were hiding out from the rain, but I paid more attention to Miles' than any of the others.

"When I was very young. By the time I was ten, I believe it was just my immediate family and grandparents living here at the estate."

"You don't know for sure?" I asked.

"Have you seen the size of this house?" Miles asked.

"Point taken. And how creepy, by the way, to think of people living in the same house and not even knowing it!"

"Now that you mention it, yeah. Stuck here alone at night, it's enough to make me glad I'm semi-transparent guy."

"Even though it's daytime, I'm glad I'm with you, and that you've got semi-transparent guy superpowers," I said. I finished placing the contents of the wardrobe back inside. "Well, I think we've exhausted the opportunities in this room."

I looked around, hands on my hips, and blew a loose strand of hair out of my eyes. Maybe I should give up and just cut some bangs, it would be easier to see.

"So, on to the next one?" suggested Miles.

"Lead the way," I agreed. "I feel sure that somewhere in this massive house we'll find something… but I sure do wonder where! It really is a needle in a haystack we're searching for."

"That it is," agreed Miles.

"But we'll find it!" I said, pointing at him.

"I know you will," Miles smiled. "I have faith in you."

"Good," I said, and smiled back.

We searched until it was past time for me to collect Chip and go home for the evening. Miles and Trixie walked us out. With a quick "see you tomorrow," we headed home.

I never stayed late at my last job, I thought, as we crossed the bridge and I marveled over the colors of the sunset staining the sky and clouds vivid shades of pink and purple. But then again, I never before worked with someone I got along with so well. Miles was fun to be around and it made all the difference.

The job wasn't half bad either. It was exciting to see the estate come to life as Nate and Molly did their work. And who wouldn't enjoy searching for clues in a castle!

Chapter 6

"Hello Miss Riley," said Nate the next morning, as Chip and I emerged from the forest path and stepped into the garden.

"Hello, Nate," I waved, as we headed toward the castle.

Here came Trixie, walls and locked doors didn't slow *her* down any. She ran up to us, and she and Chip began to play.

"Is this dog yours also?" asked Nate, indicating Trixie.

"No, she's... the estate dog," I said, not exactly sure what else to say about the subject.

Nate accepted that.

Well, he ought to, I'm the boss, after all!

"I've thought about getting a dog. These two are sure friendly," he said, as they stopped in the midst of running past, to receive affection from him.

"They are. Both are excellent breeds. Although... I hear that golden retrievers are notorious for leaving hair on everything," I remembered. I looked toward the castle. "See you later, Nate. Keep up the good work."

"Wait, Miss Riley..." said Nate, and I turned back to look at him. "A couple of my guys found something you might not be aware of."

"Oh? And what's that?" I asked, anxious to see Miles.

"There's a path over there," Nate said, as he pointed to one side of the estate grounds. "It leads to a family cemetery."

"Really?" I was surprised.

But come to think of it, of course the Bannermans would have one. They added two wings to their already huge house in order to accommodate every member of the family that ever lived, of course they'd have a cemetery on the grounds to accommodate every member of the family that ever died.

"Yes. It's overrun just as the garden was. Do you want my guys to take care of that, as well?"

"Yes I do, Nate. Thank you for bringing this to my attention. I'd like you to care for that just as you are the rest of the estate."

"Very good, Miss Riley. I'll get some guys right on it."

"Thank you, Nate."

I continued on my way to the castle, and hurried up the stairs and through the front door.

Miles was waiting for me in the entryway. I listened carefully and looked to Miles for confirmation.

"They're upstairs," he smiled.

"Okay then," I acknowledged. "Hi."

"Hi back," Miles smiled.

"Ready to search?"

"You bet," he said.

"Alright then. Lead the way, sir," I said.

We investigated yet another storage area. I wondered how many this huge estate had, after all! We didn't find anything useful to our endeavor, but Miles had all sorts of stories about growing up in the castle, and the various family members that lived there over the years. The time passed quickly as we talked.

"Wait, you're kidding—right?" I said, holding up my hand.

This was one story I was finding hard to believe.

"No, I'm completely serious. We were out prowling around the forest, and Delevan thought bringing home that baby skunk was a great idea."

"Oh my goodness. How old were you?"

"I was eight, and Delevan was eleven."

"What on earth happened next?"

"Well… Delevan thought the parlor was the perfect place for his new pet."

"Oh, no!"

"Oh, yes. It was as tame as a cat, and maybe it would have been fine if something hadn't startled it… but something did."

Miles began to laugh, remembering.

I started to laugh too.

"I have never seen anyone as angry as my Mother was that day. And I've seen a lot of people over the years!"

I had to stop searching for the time being and sit down so I could laugh, as I imagined Mom's reaction if I brought a skunk into the house!

"It's funny now, because it happened so long ago, but believe me, I was not laughing then!"

"I can't believe he did that!" I gasped out.

"He only did it once," he smiled, and I laughed some more.

"Were you in trouble, too?" I asked.

"I was charged as an accomplice, so my sentence was lighter," he said, and smiled, as I attempted to overcome the amusement I felt over the whole crazy scenario. It didn't seem quite appropriate to laugh hysterically over him getting punished as a kid.

Miles laughed to himself though, as he thought about it.

"Honestly, I'm a little surprised Delevan and I made it past the ages of eleven and eight, considering."

Appropriate or not, that was my undoing. I gave up and laughed so hard, I fell over.

There was a knock at the storage room door.

I clapped my hands over my mouth and froze, staring wide-eyed at Miles. Whoever was out there must have heard all that. Or… my part of it, anyway.

Miles quickly held his hand to his ear

"Phone," he said.

I gave him a thumbs-up, and pulled my iPhone out of my pocket as I unlocked and opened the storage room door.

"Oh, hi Molly. Hang on just a minute," I greeted her. Into the phone, I said, "Gotta go, I'll call you back."

I put my iPhone back in my pocket, and looked at Molly expectantly.

"I hate to interrupt Miss Riley, but I wondered if you'd like to see our progress before we leave for the day," she said.

"Sure, that'd be great. Lead the way."

I followed, and as I left the room I turned and mouthed the words "I'll be back" at Miles, and he nodded.

I walked with Molly into the main part of the house, and she showed me around the freshly cleaned hallways and rooms.

"Thanks Molly, your girls are doing a fantastic job!"

"You're very welcome, Miss Riley," said Molly. "We do appreciate the business. I declare, you're the only client we need, you've got so much for us to do!"

"I don't doubt it," I laughed along with her. "So you'll be working on the second and third floors of the main house the rest of the day, correct?"

"Yes, that's right. We'll be here until four o' clock."

"Sounds great. Thanks, Molly!"

I hurried back to the east wing of the house, to the storage room Miles and I were searching before Molly came calling.

"They're all set," I said, after shutting the door and locking it with the ancient skeleton key, for good measure. "There shouldn't be any more interruptions."

"No problem," said Miles, as he placed items back in a trunk. "So far I haven't found anything helpful in achieving our goal."

"Well thanks for the phone idea, I was too stunned to think what to do! The ideas I had weren't very good."

"Like what?"

"Oh, climbing out the window for example."

Miles laughed.

"Yeah, that would convince the cleaning crew there's something not quite right about you. Especially since these windows don't open."

I laughed at that, as we resumed our search.

In a trunk filled with books and papers, I found something.

I sat on the floor staring at the documents I held in my hands. I was reluctant to tell Miles what I found. As uncomfortable as it made me feel, I wondered what it would do to him. Finally I looked up.

"Miles… I found something."

"What?" he asked, as he sat beside me.

I held the papers out to him.

Miles read in silence for a minute, before replying.

"Wow. Kind of strange, seeing your own death certificate. I mean… it's not telling me anything I didn't already know, but still."

I sympathized in silence, then looked at Miles in shock.

"This proves you didn't fire the first shot, anyway," I said. "So that's something! But not enough? You're still here."

Miles rubbed his chin as he thought.

"That alone makes it look as though Delevan shot me twice, then I shot him in the back after he turned away. It changes the story, but it doesn't tell the truth. Now my brother's guilty of shooting me first, and I'm guilty of shooting him in the back, for what... revenge? And this doesn't absolve me of the claim that I wanted to take Sarah from my brother," said Miles, a slight frown on his face. "I would really like to prove otherwise, if I have a choice."

I looked at the papers in my hand and frowned, lost in thought.

"We really need a letter or diary telling what happened," I said.

"I'm afraid the only one who could provide that would be the only other decent person in the clearing that day," replied Miles.

"Sarah," I said.

"Sarah," Miles nodded, rubbing his forehead as if his head hurt.

I reached out to put my hand on Miles' shoulder, but then stopped, remembering that my effort would be futile.

"We'll find proof, okay? Don't give up. I can understand why you would after all these years, but you aren't alone now. I'll search until I find it, no matter how long it takes. I promise you that."

"Thanks," Miles said with a shadow of a smile. "I won't give up."

"Why *do* you have more than one ballroom?" I finally remembered to ask, thus changing the subject.

Miles thought about that.

"Your guess is as good as mine."

"Hm, well then let me think," I said, shaking out the linens I found folded in a drawer. "It helps to have an extra ballroom, when... you forgot to clean up after the last party. Now it's your turn to come up with one."

"Okay, I'll have to think about this," Miles said.

I jumped in.

"It helps to have an extra ballroom, when you have friends that don't get along and you know if they're in the same room they'll fight, but if you don't invite them, they'll hate you."

Miles laughed.

"Hey, I thought it was my turn!"

"You're too slow, Mister!" I said. "It helps to have an extra ballroom, when you want to waltz in one room and rock out in the other."

Miles laughed again, and I kept going.

"It helps to have an extra ballroom, when..."

"When you have a party, and want to have dancing in one and rollerblading in the other," said Miles triumphantly.

I laughed.

"That's a good one. I can see actually doing that."

"Do you rollerblade?" asked Miles.

"I have," I said. "I wouldn't say I'm good at it, though. I've got some scars to prove it."

I pulled back my sleeve to reveal a faint scar just below my elbow.

"That must have hurt," said Miles sympathetically.

Not nearly as bad as the scar on my hip that wasn't up for discussion.

"Yeah, it kind of did."

I pulled more heavily embroidered linens out of a drawer, and searched them for hidden papers or diaries or anything else that might be helpful.

"How about you, how did you get that?" I indicated his jawline, where I'd seen a very faint scar.

"Funny you should ask," Miles said, holding up what I recognized as items used many years ago in shaving. "I've no idea why these things would be stored, but I got this in a shaving mishap."

"Oh, no! That had to hurt."

"It did. Guys these days have no idea how good they have it compared to how shaving was done back then."

Miles placed the straight razor back in its case, and returned it to the trunk he was searching.

"No kidding," I said. "Why didn't you guys rebel, and all have beards instead?"

Miles made a face.

"It was considered the mark of a gentleman not to have a beard, that's why. My ancestors would have turned over in their graves at the very idea! Not to mention what my Mother would have said about it."

It struck me as funny that it was such a big deal, and I couldn't help laughing.

"Hey, if you grew up when I did, you'd be just as horrified at the thought as my Mother," Miles said.

"So on a scale of one to ten, which would you say is worse. To set a skunk loose in the parlor, or grow a beard?"

Miles laughed, then had to give that some thought, which made me laugh. Why was growing a beard such a big deal? I wasn't going to understand this.

"I'd say... it's too close to call. But, it's easier to shave with a straight razor, than to rid a parlor of the scent of skunk."

I laughed again.

"The smell resurrected every time it rained, the humidity in the air I guess," he said. "For years afterward, Delevan had a tendency to make himself scarce at the sight of thunderclouds."

I laughed so hard my ribs hurt.

"Stop making me laugh, or I'm going to be sick!"

"One thing I can say for sure, I'd rather face a straight razor than my Mother, after setting a skunk loose in her parlor."

"Hush!" I laughed, and threw a pillow at him.

He caught it and smiled, then took pity on me and kept to himself the rest of the things he could've said. Just looking at him almost set me off again. He smiled, then looked away.

I re-folded the linens and put them back in their drawer, while Miles sorted through yet another trunk.

I looked around as I thought of all the rooms and places where something could be hidden, and for just a moment, I felt over-whelmed.

Then firming my resolve, I pulled myself back together and re-membered what I *knew* on a gut-level to be true.

Miles wouldn't be here if it was impossible to free him. Evidence *does* exist. I glanced at him as he loaded items back into the trunk he searched. If anyone ever deserved to be proven innocent, it's Miles.

It may take me the rest of my life, but I'll find that proof. When I do, I won't laugh nearly as much on the job, anymore... but he'll be free.

Sarah quietly closed and bolted the door to the stateroom. She knew the reason Dan chose to travel as cabin passengers aboard the steamboat making its way up the Mississippi River to Montana Territory, had everything to do with access to the cabin saloon, and nothing to do with kindness towards her. It didn't make her appreciate any less the chance to be alone, that having a stateroom afforded. The past few weeks had been unbearably hard.

She placed her hatbox on the floor, then sat on the solitary berth and leaned heavily against the wall. For just a moment, she closed her eyes and let her weary muscles sag. But no, until she did all she could to make right the terrible wrong that was committed, she would not rest.

Opening her satchel, she retrieved her fountain pen and writing paper. Using the small dresser as a writing surface, Sarah wrote feverishly. She filled the page with the truth of what happened in the clearing, the truth of why Miles followed after them, her deep regret and sorrow for the Bannerman family's loss, and her own. She begged forgiveness for her lies, and pleaded for understanding, as her only thought was to protect them from further harm.

Sarah sealed the letter in an envelope and addressed it.

She sat still and thought. She couldn't trust the letter to the steamboat. She couldn't run the risk of Dan finding the letter, and the Bannermans must not receive the letter until Dan was far away from here. It wasn't Dan's safety for which she was concerned, it was theirs. The thought of little Cynthia and James at the mercy of her soulless brother, sickened her.

Sarah knelt on the floor beside her hatbox. Opening it, she swiftly emptied the contents onto the bed. Running her fingers probingly along the stiff fabric lining the bottom, she worked carefully to dislodge it. Finally the lining lifted, revealing a thin compartment underneath. Inside were two even thinner tin cases, which together, filled the space completely. Prying the cases out, she emptied their contents on to the dresser. She placed the envelope inside one, then tightly closed the lids to both cases and returned them to their place in the hatbox's hidden compartment. Sarah deftly wedged the stiff lining back in place, then packed her belongings inside once more. She shut the lid with a snap of finality, and turned the key in the lock.

Sarah relaxed slightly, then turned to face the money which now lay on the dresser in front of her. She looked at the handbag, but thought better of it. Finally, with an exasperated sigh she picked up the bills, folded them tightly in a handkerchief, and fastened them inside the bodice of her dress.

Sarah took up her pen again, and began a second letter. It was brief, and she thought with satisfaction that if Dan read it, he wouldn't understand. She addressed the envelope, then placed it in her handbag. This she would send from the steamboat.

Satisfied with her efforts for the time being, Sarah lay down and closed weary eyes, seeking a few moments of rest. All too soon it would be necessary to join the others for dinner, and it would be all she could do not to push her brother overboard.

The thought made her laugh for the first time in what felt like an eternity.

Chapter 7

The air was cool and moist as Chip and I walked back to the cabin that evening. It was raining, somewhere nearby. Clouds moved across the darkening sky, passing over the half moon. The lights from the cabin glowed ahead, and we hurried the rest of the way home.

"Hi Mom," I said as we walked in the door.

"Hi, honey," said Mom, as she stirred the broccoli cheese soup on the stove. The scent of homemade rolls permeated the room, making my mouth water.

Mom looked tired, though. Worried.

"How is everything?" I asked, worry clouding my own face. "Did—Doreen have a bad day today?"

"They're all bad days," Mom said, running a hand through her blond curls. She sounded really depressed. She sighed, then tried to smile, but it didn't reach her eyes. "I'm sorry I'm not in a more cheerful mood. Today was fine. I think everything we've all been through in the last couple of years is just catching up with me."

I gave Mom a hug. I wished I could do more, though. Fix everything, that's what I wanted to do.

"I'm sorry, Mom," I said.

Mom hugged me back for a minute, then returned to stirring the soup.

"Mom… take a break. Dinner looks done, so go eat. Then relax and do something fun, for a change. Talk to Dad on the phone, or read a book or something, then go to bed early. Don't worry about anything else. I'll clean up, and get the kids to bed."

Mom blinked back tears.

"Just do it, Mom. You're always so strong for us… and we need you, you can't go have a nervous breakdown on us! But you might, if you don't give yourself a break now and then."

Mom looked at me, then nodded.

"Okay. Thank you."

Mom gave me a hug, and I fixed a tray for her. I walked with Mom down the hall to her room. I handed her the tray, told her not to come out until morning, and shut the door behind her.

I looked in the room I shared with Doreen, but she wasn't there. She must be on the couch.

That's where I found her, pale and listless. Tryon sat on the floor coloring.

Maybe crayons wouldn't be too difficult to scrape off the wood floor... Good thing Mom went to bed early.

"Okay funny boy, let's get you a coloring book next time you want to color," I said, as I put away crayons.

"But that's for Uncle Mark," said Tryon.

"Well, tell you what. Color a picture in a book. A coloring book!" I quickly added, "And then give that to him."

"Okay," Tryon sighed.

"Dinner's ready," I said as I stood, the box of crayons safely in my hand.

Doreen stirred.

"What do you think, Doree, can you make it to the table, or would you like to eat right here?"

"Here," Doreen whispered.

"Okay then, that's what we'll do."

I got the kids fed, read them some books and got them to bed, cleaned up the kitchen, then scrubbed crayon off the floor. It could have been worse. Tryon could have tried decorating the walls or the carpet!

The next morning when I walked into the kitchen, I was relieved to see that Mom was feeling better.

She looked up from the pan of eggs she was stirring.

"Thank you for giving me a break last night. I'm feeling much better this morning."

"You're welcome," I said, taking toast out of the toaster and re-loading it with more bread. "You know, when you need a break, tell me. I'm not always the most observant person in the world, so don't wait on me to figure it out."

"Thank you, Anika, I will do that."

Good, because if Mom burns out, then the rest of us are going to crash and burn! I can handle things for a day, but I'd make a lousy replacement.

"I feel a lot more optimistic," said Mom. "The chronic Lyme information you gave me the other day fits Doreen so well. This new doctor will have the answers we've been looking for, I'm just sure of it."

"I think so too, Mom," I said, as I buttered toast and she turned the bacon in the pan.

"How did you ever find out about it?" asked Mom.

"A friend looked it up for me," I said.

"That's nice, how on earth did your friend know about it?"

"He's really smart, and knows a lot, and Doreen's symptoms made him remember reading about it," I said.

"Who is this friend?" Mom wanted to know.

Ack! I need to get my brain in gear, before I start talking in the morning. Of course she's going to want to know who my friend is, especially since my friend is a guy!

"Um, well... is that a MOUSE?!" I screamed, jumping backwards.

I could answer that question. No. It was not.

"What, where?" Mom jumped too, she *really* does not like mice.

I reached around the stove and threw open the back door, then kicked violently in that direction. Fortunately the kitchen is small. A mouse *could* have been next to the stove and *could have* run out without Mom seeing.

"Whew, close call!" I said with the utmost sincerity.

Mom breathed a sigh of relief.

"A mouse is the last thing we need in here! This is enough to make me want a cat. If your Dad wasn't so allergic, I'd get one right now."

"Yeah, that's a shame, I always wanted a cat," I said.

Oh please, let's not talk about my friend anymore! Please, forget I have a friend that's a guy!

"I know honey, I love cats too."

"So what do you think about those hairless cats, Mom?"

"Oh those are just the creepiest looking things!" Mom shuddered, and the conversation was all about bald cats from that point forward.

Crisis averted. But I have got to do a better job keeping my mouth shut from now on! How many mice can I see before Mom either insists on moving, or having my vision checked?

I have never eaten breakfast so fast in my life, I was anxious to get out the door. The more time that passed between Mom and that slip of the tongue I made, the better the chance she'd forget about it.

I put my plate in the dishwasher and shot out the backdoor. It was sprinkling outside, but I wasn't going back for an umbrella. Chip had to run to keep up with me this time.

We burst through the door of the castle, completely out of breath. I'm not sure why I didn't stop running somewhere along the way. It wasn't like Mom was going to leave Doreen and Tryon, to chase me down.

Chip greeted Trixie, and they took off down a hall. Going where, who knows.

"Hi," I gasped at Miles, seeing him in the entryway.

"Hi back," he said, a look of concern in his eyes. "Is… something after you?"

I shook my head.

"Okay, well, that's good," he said. He looked puzzled. "You were trying to avoid the rain?"

I shook my head, my hands still on my knees as I made up for the oxygen I lacked.

"You're training for a marathon, then?"

I shook my head again.

"Alright, fine…" Miles thought. "You've qualified, and are preparing for the next Olympics."

I gave him a thumbs up. Miles shook his head and laughed.

"Lead—the way," I said, still breathing hard. "You pick."

"Okay then, follow me," Miles said, then paused. "If you can make it up the stairs, that is."

I stood and walked past him, making a slapping motion at his arm on the way by.

"Ow!" Miles said, an injured look on his face as he held his arm.

I was shocked, and felt terrible!

"I'm so sorry! I am sooo sorry, Miles! I didn't know you'd even feel that!"

"I didn't," Miles smiled.

I stared at him for a second, then gave him a narrow-eyed look and pointed at him.

"You… have no idea how lucky you are."

I gave his semi-transparent shoulder a slap that would have really stung, if he could actually feel it.

"Actually, I think I do," he smiled.

I rolled my eyes, but laughed too, as we continued up the stairs.

We were searching one of the second floor bedrooms today, in the main part of the house. A huge room, but then again, I'd seen very few that weren't. Faint thunder sounded through the closed windows and rain softly pelted the glass. It was a peaceful rain, not like the wild storm that blew Chip and I in through the cellar.

The four-poster bed in the room was absolutely huge, I did not know they made them that big all those years ago. I thought furniture was smaller then! It was mahogany with the most beautiful grain. The two chests of drawers were the same design. There was a cute little vanity, a very fancy wardrobe with claw feet, and a sitting area arranged around a large fireplace.

The window hangings and bed covering were in shades of antique white and gold, and a luxurious rug covered the floor.

Miles and I dug through a cedar chest filled with quilts. Some he recognized, which reminded him of the people who made them. He told me stories about the Bannermans who lived there over the years, and answered my many questions.

Miles recognized a crazy quilt sewn by his little sister, Cynthia. It was made of all different sorts of fancy dark materials. I recognized some of the oddly shaped pieces as silk and velvet. It was heavily embroidered.

"That's amazing, your sister made that," I said, admiring her work. "It does live up to its name, though. It looks pretty crazy."

"Yes, it does. It was used as a couch throw in the parlor, at one point in time."

"That had to be so bizarre, seeing your sister grow up while you stayed the same," I commented.

"It was. Although," and Miles sort of laughed, "there were benefits to that."

"Like what?" I wondered.

"Like when a guy came courting her that didn't have the most honorable intentions."

"Oh my goodness, dare I ask how you knew this?"

"I heard him talking to another guy during an afternoon party, here at the castle. You might be surprised at how easy it is to overhear people when you're standing right next to them," Miles said, and I laughed at that.

"Okay, so you heard something he never would have wanted her big brother to know, and what did her big brother do then?" I asked.

"I made sure he didn't get anywhere near her. He hit several invisible walls, was forced down paths he wasn't intending to take, ended up in the fountain at one point, made such a fool of himself—

or rather, I did—that my sister wanted nothing to do with him. After all that, he was so freaked out he ran and never came back," Miles said, as I fell over laughing.

"Oh my goodness, that is too funny!" I said. "Every girl should have a protective big brother with semi-transparent guy superpowers!"

"It was pretty funny in retrospect," said Miles. "At the time it took more self-control than I knew I had, not to fling him right off the mountain, and onto another continent."

Trixie suddenly appeared. She shoved her nose under Miles' elbow and lifted up hard to get his attention.

"What's up?" he asked.

A look passed between them.

"Someone's here," he said abruptly.

"That's interesting how you two can communicate with a look," I said. I was impressed.

"It's living together all this time, and someone isn't just here, they're *right here,*" he said in a rush.

Who on earth? Molly and her girls weren't scheduled for today.

I scrambled to my feet and hurried to the open bedroom doorway, where I discovered Polly just a few short feet away, petting Chip.

OH MY. I do hope she didn't hear that.

"Hi, Polly!" I said. "What brings you out in the rain?"

"Oh, Anika dear, there you are! Thanks to your dog, I found you. I wanted to see how you're getting along, and I am seeing a big difference already. I'm very pleased."

"Thanks," I said. "It's important to me, to prove the faith you have in me is justified."

"You've certainly done that," she said, patting my arm and looking through the doorway behind me.

"We—I've been searching for evidence to solve the mystery," I said. "I was just going through this cedar chest."

"Oh, my dear…" Polly walked slowly into the room. "This was my room, you know, ours I should say, when I married into the Bannerman family."

"Oh, wow, I had no idea," I said. "I guess there's nothing here to find, then."

I gave Miles a puzzled look. He seemed like he wanted to say something, but didn't, and I couldn't interpret his look. I didn't spend the last hundred and forty or so years living with him, like Trixie.

"I wouldn't say that..." Polly's voice drifted off as she looked around the room, picking up an old-fashioned brush from the vanity and turning it in her hand absentmindedly. She set the brush down, and turned around.

"I wouldn't say that, dear. Very little in this house has not been here for a hundred years or more. My son and grandson made some changes, but for the most part it has stayed the same, just rearranged to suit the occupants. After all, when you have furniture like this..." Polly ran her hand across the mahogany footboard of the bed. "Why replace it with something else. They just don't make things like they used to."

"Totally agree with you, Polly," I said.

She sat at the vanity, and looked around again.

"So many memories," she sighed. A slight cloud crossed her face, then it was gone. "You know this wasn't only my and my husband's room. This is the master bedroom. Of course you might very well look around and wonder what sets it apart, all of the rooms are spectacular. But this... this, for some reason, is the master bedroom, and this is where the heads of the house slept."

Polly paused in thought for a moment.

"You know dear, the Miles Bannerman whose name you are working to clear... this was his parents' room, as well."

Miles gave me a 'there, THAT'S what I was trying to say' look.

Polly suddenly narrowed her eyes and gave me a piercing look.

"Did I hear you speaking to someone, as I was walking down the hall, dear?"

"Uh... I sometimes talk to myself when I'm thinking... maybe I was doing that?"

Polly considered the possibility.

She appeared to accept the explanation, and rose from the chair. As I walked with her back to the front of the house, she stopped to remove something from one of the tapestries lining the hall. She held it up and looked at it.

"Curious... very curious," she said under her breath, as she dropped it and continued walking.

I looked back to see what it was. Several strands of Trixie's hair, of course.

Polly moved on to a completely different subject, which was fine by me.

"We used to have wonderful parties here, Anika dear," she said, as we passed through a large ballroom. "The women wore such beautiful gowns. And the food! And the orchestra, and the dancing..."

Polly had a faraway look in her eyes.

I looked around, imagining. The wooden dancefloor filled with dancers, the orchestra in the corner, the chandeliers lit, family and friends enjoying food and good fellowship. For just a moment, I thought I saw a glimpse of the past and the whirl of ball gowns.

I walked Polly out, then returned to the bedroom as Miles finished searching the cedar chest.

"Good job, Trixie," I gave her head a good rub. "If you hadn't warned us, Polly might have thought I was crazy, talking to myself like that."

Miles laughed, then became serious.

"I don't think we'll find anything here," he said, looking around the room. "It doesn't appear to hold any of my parents' things. Too much time has passed."

"Yeah, but it doesn't look like anyone ever got rid of anything," I said. "Your parents' things were moved, but they're surely here. We'll search until we find what we're looking for."

"Sounds good," Miles said. He moved to look out the window. "The rain has stopped, and the workmen have gone for the day. How about we take a break, and play ball with the dogs for a while?"

"Yes, let's do that," I said. My back was tired of searching trunks and cedar chests.

The garden was breathtakingly beautiful after the rain. The colors were more vivid than they were at any other time, and the raindrops hung from the rose petals like diamonds. The stone walls of the castle were damp with rain, and reflected glittering shades of pink and purple that weren't visible when dry. A rainbow spanned the sky above the castle. It was a fairy tale world. I wouldn't be surprised if a unicorn stepped out of the forest. But then look who I was with! Why should anything surprise me, ever again.

The dogs had a blast chasing after the balls we threw. I couldn't help imagining how strange it would look to anyone passing by, balls rising in the air by themselves, and sailing across the garden! As out of the way as the castle was, no one would just wander by, though. Well, except me!

We played until time for me and Chip to go home, and then said goodbye until tomorrow.

The scent of the forest after the rain was intoxicating. The air felt so fresh and cool. As we walked home under the towering oaks, rain drops from the afternoon shower filtered through, lightly dotting the path's cobbled stones.

We crossed the bridge, marveling in another gorgeous rainbow over the cabin.

"Hi Mom," I said, as we walked inside, and I stopped to clean my shoes on the rough mat.

"Hi honey," said Mom. "How was your day?"

"It was good. Polly came by, and was pleased to see what's been accomplished so far. I really love what I'm doing. I could see doing this sort of thing forever, and not getting tired of it."

Of course it wouldn't be as interesting if I wasn't searching the castle with Miles to find evidence. Still, I did enjoy it. Seeing the castle come back to life as rooms were cleaned, repairs made, and the grounds restored... I did enjoy that a lot.

"Good, I'm glad," said Mom, as she patted me on the back on her way to the stove where dinner was cooking. "I knew you had it in you, and that's wonderful for Polly that she has such a conscientious estate manager."

Relieved that Mom wasn't inquiring further about *my friend*, I walked into the living room where Doreen lay on the couch. The TV was on, but without sound. She looked barely awake.

I knelt beside her.

"How are you doing?" I asked her, gently moving one of her beautiful gold curls away from her equally beautiful blue eyes.

"Same..." she said lethargically.

"Need anything?"

She gave me a weak smile, I could see a little bit of her old self in it.

"A diagnosis would be nice. Maybe a cure."

I gently kissed her forehead.

"That's what we're all praying for... maybe the next doctor will be the one."

Doreen nodded, and closed her eyes. I walked softly out of the room.

Tryon just about ran over me in the hall.

"Anika!" he shouted, quietly, for Doreen's sake. "You're home!"

"Yes I am, funny boy," I said, trying to pick him up.

I grabbed my back and groaned dramatically, making a face.

"I need—some—ibuprofen—"

Tryon giggled, and ran back down the hall for his favorite book. I knew what I'd be doing until dinner was ready!

Chapter 8

"If I'm back by one o' clock, will that give you enough time to get to Doreen's appointment?" I asked Mom, as I put the breakfast dishes in the dishwasher.

Mom thought for a minute, calculating in her head.

"Yes, that ought to work."

"Okay, great. I'll be here at one o' clock then," I said with a wave, and headed out the door. I whistled for Chip, and he came running.

The weather looked ominous. I hoped there wouldn't be another violent storm like the one that led us inside the castle. If there was, I supposed Mom could pick me and Chip up, then drop us and Tryon off at the cabin before heading to the appointment. It wouldn't be very nice weather for driving to the city, though.

As Chip and I entered the garden, I saw Nate and his guys hard at work. The grounds were now free of weeds and overgrown plants and vines, and they were preparing the flower beds for the cold-hardy flowers that were soon to be planted there.

"Very nice," I said to Nate, as Chip and I walked by. "I love the progress you're making. It's looking great."

"Thank you," Nate said, looking around at the grounds. "It won't be much longer before the work is done, and we'll switch to maintenance mode."

"Awesome," I said, as I continued on to the house.

As I walked up the steps, the Queen of Clean ladies arrived, and I ushered them in. After they were well on their way deep into the west wing, I followed Miles to the east wing.

"Hi," I said, when I figured it was safe to talk.

"Hi back," he smiled.

"Today's my sister's appointment with the new doctor, so I need to be home by one, so I can babysit my brother," I said.

"How's she doing?" asked Miles.

"Not better, that's for sure. After Mom visited the website you recommended, she made an appointment with a doctor on the Lyme literate physician list. That's who she's seeing today."

"Good, I hope this one figures out what's going on," said Miles.

"Me too," I said. "It's a desperate feeling to know something is badly wrong, but the medical community at large won't believe it, because they can't figure out what it is."

Miles shook his head.

"That's faulty logic to say it doesn't fit what I'm familiar with, therefore it must not exist."

Miles stopped and opened the door to yet another storage room.

"I seriously cannot get over the amount of storage space in your house," I said, as Miles closed and locked the door behind us.

"I can't either. I never went through any of them, before you came along. I had no idea how ridiculous it was."

I tackled the contents of yet another wardrobe, and Miles sorted through a trunk.

"Is that rain?" I asked.

Miles listened.

"Sounds like it."

"Ug, I hope it doesn't storm the way it did the first day I came here."

"More than likely it won't. This is probably the last rain we'll see this year. The next time, it will be snow," Miles said.

I found what might have been a diary, it was filled with spidery writing.

"Can you read this?" I held it out to Miles.

"Hm. Not without an extreme amount of difficulty," he said, turning to the inside cover. "Fortunate for both of us, this was written in 1805, so we don't have to interpret it one painful word at a time."

Miles handed the book back to me, and I looked through it just to be sure there wasn't a note or some other bit of pertinent information inside of it.

Nope, just a diary I was thankful not to have to try and read.

116

"It sure is full of history though," I said, using my fingers to comb back the hair that wanted very much to shield my left eye.

"That it is," said Miles.

"Imagine what a great museum curator you'd make," I commented. "You'd know all about everything!"

Miles laughed.

"You overestimate me. I was here for a great deal of our country's history, before this part of the country even became a state. However, we didn't have the flow of information that's available now, so there's a lot I never knew until long after the fact."

"Well you are still the smartest guy I know," I said stubbornly. "Anything you didn't already know, I know you'd learn it faster than anyone else could."

"I may need a few hundred more years of learning, to live up to that opinion of yours," Miles smiled. "But thank you, for the compliment."

We sorted in silence for several minutes, listening to the sound of the rain gently tapping against the window panes. It didn't sound like anything my umbrella wouldn't be able to handle.

"The rain makes me think of another time I intervened for my sister," Miles said, as he lay aside a bundle of needlework.

"Really? Another guy?" I asked, wondering if Miles was the only gentleman in the late eighteen-hundreds.

"No, thank goodness she met and fell in love with a guy that was good enough for her. And that's saying a lot. He was a minister, actually. Quite poor by Bannerman standards. Cynthia was very happy though, and together they did a lot of good during the time they had on this earth."

I finished searching the wardrobe and sat back to listen, as Miles talked.

"Cynthia dreamed of being married in the garden amongst the roses she loved. It was thick with roses, even then. Preparations were made, and all was in readiness for the wedding she dreamed of. Mother and Father spared no expense of course, as you can imagine.

The Bannermans as a whole, had more sons than daughters, and my family was no exception. So when there was a daughter, her wedding was made much of. Cynthia's wedding was the event of not only the season, or even the year or decade, but if you were to ask any one of the guests who attended, it was the event of the century. Far more importantly, it was significant for my family, as they focused entirely on celebrating a new beginning rather than on remembering previous losses. Family from all over the country traveled to attend, and for a time, the house was full again."

"Really?" I said in awe.

"No," he smiled. "Of course not, can you imagine? No, but there was enough family to fill half of the east wing."

"Oh my goodness, you completely had me!" I laughed.

"Yeah, I could tell by the size of your eyes," he smiled.

"Well I didn't know how that was possible, but you said it, so… still, even filling half a wing of the castle equals a crazy amount of people."

"Yes, it does. So the day arrived, and all was in readiness. However, just before noon, the sky filled with clouds."

"Oh no!" I said, imagining Cynthia's disappointment, and his whole family's, really. And after they chose to focus on celebrating instead of grieving, too! It just seemed so unfair! "Well… it helps to have an extra ballroom when your humongous family shows up for a wedding, and it gets rained out."

There was laughter in his eyes, but he held in the rest.

"This is a somewhat serious story, and here you are trying to make me laugh…"

I laughed, then pretended to zip my lips. He smiled, and continued.

"It seemed inevitable that rain would force the wedding inside. It came closer and closer, and at last it reached the grounds. But then it stopped."

"It stopped raining? Oops, sorry, faulty zipper," I said, zipping my lips again. Miles smiled and shook his head, then kept going with his story.

"No, it didn't stop raining. But the rain stopped. It stopped right at the edge of the grounds, and then went all the way around. While outside of the Bannerman estate, right up to the encircling trees, the rain came down... from one side of the estate grounds to the other, there was none."

"You did that?" I was awestruck.

"Yes. It required a great deal of concentration, but yes. There isn't anything I wouldn't do for my sister, although there were so many things I couldn't do, after I returned like this.

"When I was alive, she once told me the reason she talked to me so much is because it was easy. I never looked disinterested or found amusement in the serious things she had to say. I understood her even when others didn't, and I always gave good advice."

Miles paused, lost in memories.

Outside, the rain fell softly against the window panes, and the grandfather clock in the hall announced the half hour.

I watched him silently. His eyes were sad, and my own eyes now stung with suppressed tears.

"There was so much I couldn't do anymore. See her grow up, for one thing... when I returned like this, she wasn't the little girl I last saw when I hurried after Delevan that day. She was four years older, and so grown up. She was still my little sister, though. She still needed someone to understand her, to care what she had to say and take her seriously, and give her advice. She didn't always have that, and I couldn't fill that gap for her, no matter how badly I wanted to. I could talk to her, and I did, but she couldn't hear me, and so she couldn't respond. I loved my little sister, and it grieved me that I couldn't be the big brother I used to be. I was so glad, and relieved, when she married Matthew. He loved her unconditionally, and gave her the listening ear and understanding she needed. He gave her advice too at times, which sometimes she appreciated, and other times not so much." Miles smiled softly, remembering. "In spite of all that I couldn't do, throughout her life I watched out for her and was there for her in every way that I could be. Giving her the wedding she wanted and seeing her so happy, and seeing Mother, Father, and James enjoying family without a shadow of grief in their eyes… controlling the rain tested the limits of my abilities, but giving that to them… I felt truly happy."

"Okay, you are just going to make me cry," I said very honestly, tears pooling in my eyes. "That is so sweet, but so *incredibly* sad at the same time. The thought of you being so totally alone, while the family you loved continued their lives right beside you… and the way you watched out for your sister all her life… You have got to be the nicest guy that ever lived, and it's just *wrong* what happened to you. You've just succeeded in breaking my heart. That's movie material, you'd win an Oscar, and every girl in the country would be completely in love with you."

Miles laughed. He thought I was joking.

"You laugh, but I'm serious," I said, trying unsuccessfully to hold back a few sobs as I wiped away the tears that insisted on spilling out onto my cheeks.

"I didn't mean to make you cry," Miles said in dismay. "I had no idea—you were laughing just a second ago! What happened? I can't believe I made you cry!"

I couldn't help laughing, he was so disturbed by the effect his incredibly emotional story had on me. I wiped the remaining tears off my face with my sleeve.

"Well then, Miles Bannerman, I'd say in spite of being very smart about a lot of things, even after all these years, you don't know very much about women!"

Miles laughed too, then.

"Considering how I thought you'd say something like 'wow Miles, that's so cool how you used your superpowers to save your sister's wedding!' and instead you burst into tears, I don't think there's any hope I ever will!"

"Oh well, then you're just like every other man in the world," I said, rolling my eyes and dismissing any hope of change with a wave of my hand.

Miles smiled and shook his head, he knew I was kidding.

We sorted and searched through the rest of the storage area and determined there was nothing useful to our cause, but before we had a chance to move on to the next room, the alarm on my iPhone sounded. I pulled it out of my pocket and silenced it, then began gathering my things.

"I better go, it's almost time for Mom and Doreen to leave for her doctor appointment."

"I'll walk you out," said Miles.

He unlocked the door and we stepped into the hall.

"It *was* a really great story, and really cool how you did that," I said, as we walked.

He raised an eyebrow and gave me a dubious look.

"Are you sure we should be having this conversation?" he asked. "I'd rather not send you home in tears, and clearly I don't know what's safe to say and what isn't."

I laughed, and then he smiled, but I'm afraid he may be hesitant to share any more cool stories with me for a while!

All was quiet at the front of the house, but I wasn't taking any chances. I waved, and whispered, "See you tomorrow," and Chip and I walked home. I didn't even need an umbrella after all, because it stopped raining.

Or did it? I looked up and all around. Yeah, it really stopped. It's a good thing, because if Miles shielded the path home, I would reach the cabin in tears!

We arrived at the cabin without tears, and went inside.

"Thank you so much Anika, for coming home early!" said Mom, as she put on her jacket and helped Doreen into a warm coat. "It's so much easier on Tryon, and on me too, if I can concentrate on what the doctor has to say."

"It's not a problem, Mom, I totally understand."

We saw Mom and Doreen off, and then Tryon and I read, and played, and read and played... I baked cookies, which he ate, and unfortunately that only seemed to replenish his already un-depleted energy.

We went outside and walked for a while, which finally wore Tryon out. Which meant I had to carry him back to the cabin, which wore me out!

As we neared the cabin, I saw Mom's car was back in the driveway. I hurried inside, I really wanted to know how the appointment went.

I heard Mom on the phone when I walked through the door and into the kitchen. I could tell she was talking to Dad about the doctor visit, so I plopped Tryon down, grabbed a bottle of water, and listened in.

"I'm hopeful. He listened, really listened, and took Doreen's symptoms seriously. He asked a lot of questions, and then referred us to a specialist. He thinks Doreen's symptoms really are chronic Lyme disease, which is hard to get a diagnosis for. It depends on the doctor, there's a lot of disagreement regarding it. I've been reading about it ever since the appointment, and it sure does fit Doreen..."

Wow. I hope this doctor's right. He took it seriously, which was more than the others did. I was so thankful Miles learned as much as he did, and cared enough to look it up for us.

I walked through the kitchen to the living room, where Doreen lay on the couch with the TV turned down low.

"How are you, kiddo?" I asked Doreen, as I sat on a chair beside her.

She gave me a wan smile.

"Okay."

"So I hear maybe you've got a decent doctor now," I said.

"Yeah. Maybe."

I walked back to the kitchen as Mom finished her call to Dad.

"So?" I asked.

Mom smiled, and there was hope in her eyes.

"I think we're on the right track. The doctor referred Doreen to a specialist, someone who's Lyme literate, he said. He sent us to the lab for blood work, but not the same test as before, it's often negative, he told us."

"Yeah, that's what the website said. So why in the world do they even use it?"

Mom's eyebrows knit as she frowned in thought.

"I have no idea, honey. I really don't. It makes me sick to think of all the time and money that test may have cost us, the suffering Doreen's gone through..." Mom stopped and closed her eyes. She took a deep breath, then released it. "But. If we're on the right track now, I'll take it. It will be a while before we have the Western Blot test results, but we have an appointment set up with the specialist because the doctor is so sure this is what it is."

Oh, how wonderful if that's true. Not that Doreen has something so awful, but if she does... finally she can get treatment and start getting better!

The Bannerman estate showed vast improvement since the landscape maintenance crew began work just over a month ago. I waved at two of the crew who were already hard at work this morning. The roses were trimmed, weeds removed, paths swept. It wouldn't be long before really cold weather arrived I thought, as I looked around at the bare oak trees and piles of colored leaves, and wrapped my coat tighter around me. I was glad I wore my tall suede boots today.

"Good thing you've got that coat Chip, you're going to need it," I said. Winter in the mountains would be very different from what we experienced in the past.

I stopped to smell the roses. It's what you're supposed to do, after all. Soon it would be too cold for them. The trimming they had the month before resulted in an explosion of new growth, including rose buds. There were roses of every color, and they filled the garden with beauty. The dew on the velvety crimson roses looked like tiny, multi-faceted diamonds. I would be sad to see them hibernate during the winter, but they would be beautiful again in the spring. The whole garden would, now that it was being cared for again.

The inside of the house sparkled as well. With so many rooms, it would still be a while before each one was thoroughly cleaned, but no one in their right mind would think the House of Bannerman was uncared for, if they saw it now. No one would believe it needed a different trustee to manage it.

We hadn't found the proof we were seeking, but we did mark a number of rooms off our list. Searching through storage room after storage room could have gotten tedious, but Miles was funny and fun to talk to, and a good friend, and was around during so much history. There was so much to talk about, and it made the time go by quickly. I was pretty sure we could talk forever, and not get bored or run out of things to say.

It would be easier to search wherever we wanted, now that the cleaning crew had a maintenance cleaning schedule. They wouldn't be at the castle every day, and not so much stealth would be required on our part.

I walked through the front door of the estate and set my purse on the entryway table.

"Hi," I said, when Miles appeared.

"Hi back," he smiled.

"Just so you know, Polly will be here soon, she's coming to check on the estate's progress."

"Looks like she's already here, there's a taxi pulling up," Miles said, and nodded toward the window at a yellow cab.

"Oh, good. I'm anxious to see her, she said she has news. I'm hoping it's about her grandson."

"I'll get out of your way then. I wouldn't want you to forget and talk to me, she might think you're crazy."

"Thanks for having my back," I laughed, and he smiled and winked.

"Any time," he said, then vanished upstairs.

Man, is he ever cute.

I did NOT just say that!

Slapping myself mentally, I turned to welcome Polly.

We toured a good deal of the house, and Polly was pleased with the care the cleaning service took with the irreplaceable furnishings. As we toured the grounds, she pointed out the guest house.

"This is where the Henderson's lived when they cared for the estate."

It was a cute little place, and it did work well as a caretaker's cottage. It was cozy, consisting of a bedroom, bath, and a combined kitchen, living, and dining area. I couldn't imagine needing it as a guest house though, as big as the castle was.

As I locked the door after us, Polly looked up at the little house thoughtfully.

"It's hard to find conscientious people these days. I never would have imagined Amelia would just pack up and move after Jim's death, without a word. But now I have you, dear," she said, turning with a smile as she patted my arm. "And very thankful for it, too."

As we continued to walk, Polly asked about Doreen and Tryon and the rest of the family. I appreciated her interest. She really cared, she wasn't asking out of politeness.

After Polly was satisfied she'd seen all she wanted to, she told me her news.

"I've an appointment to meet with my private investigator today. He has news about my grandson!" Polly beamed.

"Oh Polly, that's wonderful! Did he give you any hint what it is?" I didn't know how she kept this news to herself for so long.

"No," she said, sounding slightly miffed now. "He's making me wait. He suggested I bring a friend, I'm under the impression he thinks I'm too excitable. Perhaps he believes I'll forget what's been said. I'd like you to come with me, dear."

"I'll be glad to, Polly."

I called for a taxi and we arrived at the coffee shop where she was meeting the PI. We chose a table and waited for him to arrive.

The coffee shop was just as cute on the inside, as it was on the outside. Little round tables which would seat up to four people, were scattered about. I noticed they were well made, there was no wobbling. That alone made it upscale compared to what I'd been used to in the past. There was an amazing assortment of coffee and tea drinks to choose from. Several people sat with laptops in front of them, taking advantage of the free Wi-Fi available.

"I love what you've done with the Bannerman estate dear," she said, as the waiter delivered her hot spiced tea, and my latte. "It looks wonderful, it can't possibly go against me now."

"And if the PI has good news, it won't matter anyway!" I said, "Your grandson will be back, and everything will be on track again."

Polly beamed.

A tall lanky fellow with a graying military haircut approached the table and introduced himself as Jackson, Polly's hired PI, then took a seat and got to the point.

"I followed bank and credit card charges since the last time you spoke with your grandson, Mrs. Bannerman. The last charge was about six months ago. There's been nothing since then."

Polly was silent, but the look on her face said she knew that wasn't a good thing.

"It's taken time to track down his friends, but I confirmed that the last time he was seen was when he made the final bank charge."

He pulled an Uncle Mark, and paused.

"Mrs. Bannerman, I received confirmation this morning. I believe your grandson is here..." he placed a piece of paper on the table with the name of a hospital located half way across the country. "It appears he was hiking alone, and fell from a cliff overlooking the trail. He was found unconscious. Your grandson is alive, but he's been in a coma since he was found. He had no identification, and is listed as a John Doe at the hospital."

Polly's eyes were filled with tears and she looked ready to collapse. I jumped out of my seat and put my arms around her to keep her from falling out of her chair.

There was sympathy on the PI's face as he showed her a photo of a patient in a hospital bed. In spite of all the medical gadgets he was hooked up to, we both knew the PI had found Polly's grandson.

Everything was a blur after that. I called Polly's attorney to apprise him, called the hospital to tell them Polly was on her way, and called friends in her address book to let them know she needed their support. They arrived right away, and I was relieved to see they were true friends, and intent on going through this crisis with her. One of the ladies made arrangements to fly with Polly to the hospital, and said she would keep me informed of Polly's grandson's progress and let me know how Polly was holding up.

I eventually left Polly in their able care and started walking in the direction of home, too dazed to think of calling Mom for a ride.

My head began to clear after the first mile, and as I reached for my iPhone, a truck pulled up beside me. It was Nate.

"Hi, Miss Riley," he said with a look of concern. "Are you having car trouble?"

"Hi, Nate. No, I didn't have a breakdown. I'm just... out for the fresh air," I said, thinking how cold that fresh air was and that my coat seemed to be providing less protection by the minute.

"Well... I'm headed back to the estate, I just got through picking up some supplies. Would you like a ride?"

I thought about that. I knew enough about Nate to know it was safe to accept.

"Sure, Nate, thank you," I said, as I climbed in the Lawncare Extraordinaire truck.

Hopefully Polly will never find out I hitched a ride with a yard man.

"Not a problem," said Nate, as he pulled back onto the road.

"It's very impressive that you have your own business, and such a successful one," I said. "How did you happen to get started?"

I did not feel like talking, my mind was swirling with the news about Polly's grandson. If Nate talked enough, I wouldn't have to.

Nate did talk, so there was no uncomfortable silence. I did my best to listen and make appropriate comments. I don't think he could tell what a tangled mess my thoughts were in as I absorbed what the PI said about Polly's grandson.

After we reached the estate, I couldn't remember a single thing Nate said, and felt terrible about that, but my focus was too fragmented. Today was not an ordinary day.

"I can give you a ride home later if you need one," said Nate.

"That's nice of you to offer, but I'll just walk. It's what I do every day."

"It wouldn't be any trouble," he said.

"Thanks Nate, I appreciate that. I live so close, it's not a big deal. It takes less time to walk than to drive, actually, and I enjoy the exercise."

I thanked Nate for the ride and walked slowly toward the steps to the door of the castle. This news would be hard on Miles... after all, Polly's grandson was also Miles' great-great nephew.

I took a deep breath and opened the door, then walked into the entryway, giving Chip and Trixie each a distracted head-rub.

"What's wrong?" Miles asked, his eyebrows knitting in concern.

"Miles... I'm so sorry. Polly's grandson has been found, but he's hurt. He's in a coma, and has been for the past six months."

I watched in sympathy as various emotions washed over his face. He sighed.

"That's terrible," he said. "What happened to him, how did he end up in a coma?"

I told Miles everything the PI told Polly.

"Well... Polly will see that he has the best of care," said Miles. "That could make a big difference."

"Yeah, it sure could," I said optimistically. "It can't hurt to have his grandmother there to talk to him, too. Sometimes people in a coma can hear what's going on around them, I've heard."

"That's what I've heard also. Maybe with Polly's presence and better care, he'll recover," said Miles.

We stood mulling over everything.

"I wonder why he was out hiking, and alone?" wondered Miles.

"Was that out of character?" I asked.

"Well... I guess he could have changed a lot in three years... but when he lived here, yeah. He had a lot of friends, and hiking wasn't a pastime he cared anything about. He was into video games and skateboarding."

"The whole thing's just so sad..." I said. "We should do something to get our minds off this. We aren't helping him by worrying and feeling depressed."

"You're right," agreed Miles.

"Lead me to the next storage area," I said. "We can't help him, but I'm determined to help you. The faster we work our way through this house, the faster we'll accomplish that."

"I want to accomplish that too," said Miles. "But to be honest, it's okay if we don't find it right away. I enjoy being around you, it's making up for the hundred and forty years of being alone."

"That is very sweet of you to say," I replied, truly flattered that he felt hanging out with me could make up for that much loneliness. "I've had more fun getting to know you and talking to you every day than in the whole rest of my life combined, so maybe I understand what you mean."

I smiled at Miles and he smiled back.

"Alright then, follow me," Miles said. "On to the next storage room."

"Which we'll search, but slowly," I said, as we both laughed.

It was a real shame we couldn't stay friends forever. I wondered if I'd ever find anyone else who clicked with me like Miles did. It was very unlikely.

I'll be sad when we find proof and I lose the best friend I ever had.

Chapter 9

After the horrible news about Second-Miles, which I called Polly's grandson to keep my head straight, I called Polly or her friend daily for updates. There was no change in his condition, but Polly arranged a move to a top hospital with a state of the art neurosciences department. They dealt with brain injury day in and day out. If anyone could help Second-Miles, they could.

Miles and I sat on the floor of one of the downstairs bedrooms. Late autumn sunlight filtered in through the tall narrow windows, casting fingers of light about the room. The ancient flowered wallpaper was all in soft shades of pink, antique white, and green. The wood floor was covered in a soft rug, oriental by the looks of it. What else would be in the Bannerman castle? The cherry furniture pieces were each carved with matching accents. The canopy portion of the bed was covered in a thin antique white fabric to match the whole cloth quilt. It was a beautiful room, like every room I'd seen so far.

We sat on the rug looking at old photos. Miles had relatives who lived through some pretty crazy times in our country's history. He was semi-transparent guy during those times, but he was still present for it.

"This is amazing, these World War II letters and photos and documents. So that's what a telegram looks like!" I said, as we paged through albums and folders filled with objects from that period in time. "So you had family in the war, then."

"Yes. Several. They were all proud to go and serve our country. Some returned, and some didn't," he said thoughtfully.

"So then you had family overseas?"

"Right. Like I mentioned before, our family used to be a lot larger than it is today. The young men lost in the war are only one part of why that is, though."

"What are some of the other reasons, then?" I asked.

"People started having fewer children, at least my family did. Some didn't have children at all... some by choice and some not, like my sister."

"Cynthia never had children? I had no idea," I said in surprise.

"Yeah... she and her husband would have been good parents, too. The church where Cynthia's husband was a minister also helped fund an orphanage in the same town. They worked with the children there, and made a huge impact on their lives. She and Matthew brought good to others through, and in spite of, the sadness they felt at not having children themselves."

"Did they ever adopt any of the children, and make them their own?"

"Seeing how much good they accomplished in the lives of the children at the orphanage, they made the decision to pour everything they had into all the children, instead of focusing on a few. They labored over the decision, but felt it was the right one for themselves and the children there."

"Wow. I don't even know how to say what I'm thinking, your sister was just—really something," I said.

"Yeah, she was," Miles smiled softly, lost for a moment in a memory. "She really was."

"You know... I wouldn't expect her to be anything other than amazing and selfless," I said.

"What do you mean?"

"Considering the kind of guy her big brother is, I wouldn't expect anything less from your little sister. You haven't let what happened to you cause you to be bitter. Talk about a disappointment in life! Yours was so cruelly and needlessly cut short, when all you were trying to do was help your brother. You had every excuse to be very bitter. But you aren't. You watched out for your family over the years, helping others, knowing you'd never get the credit. I don't even have to ask, to know, that you never retaliated against those so-called friends that believed Sarah's story and turned on you. Even when you were alone for the past three years, you kept your sense of humor and were ready to help my sister by finding the information that allowed us to find a knowledgeable doctor. Your sister was an amazing woman, and you're an amazing guy."

"I guess all of that's true, but I never thought of it as being amazing. Me, not Cynthia, I mean," said Miles.

"That's because you're humble, another admirable thing about you. Just take my word for it, you're awesome," I said.

Miles laughed.

"Well, thanks then, if that's what you think."

I rolled my eyes.

"I don't think, I know." I held up my finger and pointed at him before he could respond. "And don't tell me 'I don't think you know, either!'"

Miles laughed again.

"Fine then, all I'll say is thank you."

I smiled and brought us back to our earlier topic.

"So what else caused your family to grow smaller?"

"Sibling families stopped living here. That began during my lifetime. They branched out and made homes elsewhere, and over the years, lost touch with the family here. We did lose several during both world wars, and eventually it was down to Polly's husband and son, and when they were gone, Polly's grandson. And... Alfred Sullivan, I suppose. Although his tie to the family is very distant, indeed. Before Polly's grandson was injured, he had very little chance of gaining access to the estate as trustee. Now though, it's anybody's guess. I really hope Polly's grandson pulls through."

"Me too," I said. "No one who thinks you're guilty, or wants to capitalize on that lie, has any business being here."

"My sentiments exactly," said Miles.

"Polly told me she isn't against tourism or using the castle as a museum or hotel or something, if that's what her grandson wants to do, just not the way Alfred is planning," I said, as I continued to flip through papers and albums and several patches and medals, which I didn't recognize, that not being one of my fields of expertise.

Miles was thoughtful for a minute.

"This place is huge. You're seeing that for yourself. Think of how we've only scratched the surface, and we've been searching for weeks now. There is a lot of family history, and United States history here. It wouldn't be a bad thing to share it. The museum idea is kind of growing on me."

"Well you'd be a great curator," I said.

"I don't know how I'd be able to work the curator part," he laughed.

"Too bad, because you'd be a good one," I said.

"Perhaps a resort or hotel could be in one wing of the house, and a museum in the other, with separate entrances and exits. Then the original part of the house would continue to be a private residence for the Bannermans still living here."

"Maybe Polly's grandson will do that. I can't imagine rattling around in this huge place. I mean it's amazing, and I love it, but I think it would feel sort of lonely with only a few people living here," I said.

"Yes, it can be," Miles said seriously. "I appreciate how much time you're spending trying to clear me. I sure hope you succeed before Polly's grandson gets the idea to implement that spur of the moment plan we just came up with. Being all alone in the house is one thing, but being surrounded by strangers... not a pleasant thought."

"Well, we'll do our best. And I believe we'll succeed."

"You make me believe it, too. Thank you for all the work you're putting into this. These last couple of months getting to know you, and having you to talk to, have been great. Even if we don't succeed, you've done a lot for me."

"We will succeed," I said. "And I like hanging out with you too, Miles Bannerman. You're a pretty cool guy."

"You're just pretty cool yourself, Anika Riley," he smiled.

The weather turned cold, and snowflakes gently floated down from the clouds that covered the sky. The ground was probably too warm for them to stick, but maybe not. I'd need to get someone lined up to shovel the drive and walks before long. I was glad to have on a thick sweater in addition to my heavy coat, and warm boots. I was beginning to wish I'd worn gloves and a scarf, too! The walk from the cabin to the castle wasn't terribly far, but far enough to get pretty chilled in cold weather.

As I walked up the steps to the front door, a man stepped out of the vestibule. He was in his mid-fifty's, he had an unpleasantly superior demeanor, and was well-dressed in what was probably a very expensive suit. Miles stood in front of the door, arms crossed, watching him.

I motioned for Chip to stay, and stopped where I was.

"Do you need help with something?" I asked.

"To whom am I speaking?" he asked with a superior smirk.

Me, can't you tell? I felt like responding. I didn't like the condescending look in this guy's eyes. The look on Miles' face told me to be cautious.

"I'm Miss Riley, the property manager. And who are you?"

The snooty jerk looked me up and down with an increasingly condescending sneer. I was being judged for the clothes I was wearing, for being a girl, for not being as superior as he imagined himself to be, there was probably a long list. Miles still stood in front of the door, and missed the look the guy gave me.

I motioned for Chip to heel, and walked up the rest of the stairs. This guy was not going to keep me from my job. Plus, it was really cold outside.

"The name's Alfred Sullivan," he said.

Ah. So *this* is Alfred Sullivan, distant cousin and wannabe trustee for the estate. Not to stereotype, but that's about what I expected him to look like. No wonder Miles was on guard.

"And what brings you here today, Mr. Sullivan, besides your car?" I asked, crossing my arms.

Alfred switched to an ingratiating smile so fast, it was disconcerting. He gestured toward the vastly improved landscaping.

135

"I'm impressed," he said. "And I'm not easily impressed."

I found that hard to believe, he seemed pretty impressed with himself.

"Polly is fortunate to have found such an expert manager," he said with a broad smile.

I didn't realize a person could have teeth that large. He'd rival the Dentastix dog.

He looked me over again unpleasantly. I was glad Chip and Miles were there.

"It's a pity about poor Miles' condition…" he said, looking at his shiny manicured nails.

I couldn't imagine Dad or Miles with a manicure. And I didn't believe Alfred thought it a pity that Second-Miles was in a coma.

"How fortunate, that the house isn't in more disrepair than it is," he said, as he ran his hand down the doorframe, inspecting it. "I'll need to see the entire property, of course. I shall be assuming responsibility as trustee of the estate soon."

"You're assuming an awful lot," I retorted. "Without Mrs. Bannerman's permission, you are not putting one foot inside this house. And in case you haven't noticed, the heir to the estate is in a coma. He's not dead."

Reaching into his jacket, he pulled out a folded sheet of paper.

"This document gives me full access to this property."

I reached out to take the paper, and as Alfred, aka Mr. Creepy, tried to pull it out of my reach, a flick of Miles' hand sent the paper straight into mine.

Mr. Creepy was confused by that. It was all I could do not to laugh out loud.

I stepped back, unfolded the paper, and had a look at it. I know legalese can be a foreign language, but this looked to me as though it was intentionally written to confuse. I looked Mr. Creepy in the eye and sized him up.

"You may tour this property when you bring the Sheriff with you to prove the legality of this document," I said, giving it a thump for good measure.

Mr. Creepy looked sinister, and reached for the paper. Chip stood and growled at his sudden movement toward me, and I whipped the paper out of his reach and held it behind my back. With a wave of Miles' hand, Mr. Creepy slid several feet backwards, increasing the distance between us and startling Mr. Creepy considerably. I glanced at Miles quickly out of the corner of my eye, and he winked. Mr. Creepy better watch it, or he'd find himself in the fountain, next.

"I'm sure Mrs. Bannerman's attorney will want to see this," I said, composing myself.

Mr. Creepy straightened, shaking off the confusion over his sudden move to the other side of the vestibule. Any semblance of congeniality now vanished. A look of evil washed over his face so quickly, it frightened me. Chip's hackles rose, and he growled menacingly.

Mr. Creepy walked toward me.

"I have worked too long, and too hard, to let a little thing like you get in my way. Give me that paper and unlock this door, you—"

With a wave of Miles' hand, Mr. Creepy was suddenly at the bottom of the stairs.

There was a mix of anger and satisfaction in Miles' eyes. I must admit it was very satisfying to see Mr. Creepy sail all the way to the bottom like that. Chip was so impressed the growl stuck in his throat.

"Get inside," Miles said firmly.

"Yes sir," I said under my breath, as I unlocked the door, and Chip and I hurried inside and bolted it. I ran to the parlor window to see what would happen next.

Mr. Creepy slowly got up, and wiped himself off. He took a step forward as if he intended to climb back up the stairs, then thought better of it. Glaring at the house, he walked down the driveway toward what must be his vehicle.

Miles appeared beside me, and whistled for Trixie. A look passed between them, and she vanished.

I turned from the window.

"Well! So that's Alfred Sullivan," I said, shaken by the experience. "Lovely individual."

I eyed the paper I still held in my hand.

Miles moved to face the window, watching to ensure that Alfred really left. He turned suddenly, and smiled.

"Yeah, the guy's a real jerk. He visited a few times over the years. I can't say I ever cared for him."

The discrepancy between the smile on Miles' face and the subject matter confused me, until Trixie walked back in the room.

She had a triumphant gleam in her eye, and the bedraggled seat of a very expensive pair of pants grasped between her teeth.

Trixie and Chip began a spirited game of tug with the pants.

Miles and I both laughed. Maybe Alfred would think twice before coming around again!

"Thank you, Miles," I said sincerely. "I would have been scared to death if you weren't there with your superpowers."

Miles looked at me softly, and suddenly I knew what it meant to go weak in the knees.

"Any time," he said.

I pulled myself together.

"I need to get this to Polly's lawyer," I said, waving the document in the air. "I better get home and borrow Mom's car."

"You aren't walking home by yourself," Miles replied.

He and Trixie walked us the whole way home so I could borrow the car and get Alfred's "document" to Polly's lawyer right away.

I gave myself a talking to on the drive there.

My life is now, his was in the past. The fact that he's painfully cute, the way he looks at me makes me feel like I'm melting, he's fun to talk to, he is the nicest guy ever, he just rescued me from a creep and insisted on walking me home, doesn't change that. I have got to get a grip. We are friends, and I can't think of him in any other way, I just can't.

Having firmly slapped some sense into myself, I arrived at the office of Polly's attorney.

Polly must be a very important client, because when I identified myself I was ushered right in.

Polly's attorney was a trim, middle-aged fellow. He looked sharp, as in mentally sharp, I was glad to see. I explained why I was there. After examining the document, he tossed it in a folder.

"Absolutely fake. A person can print anything these days with the kind of software that's available. Thank you for bringing this by, it's going to come back and bite Mr. Sullivan on the posterior."

Oh, sir. If you only knew, that's already been done once today. I pushed aside the image of Trixie with Mr. Creepy's pants so I could keep a straight face, thanked him, and left.

I drove back to the estate. The day was still young, it wasn't even lunch time yet. It was getting colder though, so I was glad to have Mom's okay to keep the car and drive it back in the evening.

I drove up the long curving driveway and parked near the front stairs.

Trixie appeared as I hurried up the steps. The temperature was dropping fast.

"I'm sorry Trixie, Chip didn't come with me this time. I'll bring him tomorrow though," I said, stopping to pet her before going inside.

"Hi, again," I said to Miles, as I closed the door against the cold.

"Hi back, again," he smiled.

"Polly's lawyer now has the paper you so kindly commandeered from Mr. Creepy," I said.

"That's a good name for him," said Miles. "It fits."

"Yeah, a lot of people end up with nicknames. Of course they seldom ever hear them. Mainly I use them when I'm thinking," I said.

"I see," Miles said, pondering that, as I took off my coat and lay it on the entryway table. "Do I have a nickname?"

"Yes, as a matter of fact you do," I replied.

He waited for me to tell him what it was.

"My friend. That's your nickname. You're my friend. When I think of you, that's what I think."

"I like that. I thought it would be semi-transparent guy."

"No... that's just something about you. It isn't who you are," I said.

The look in Miles' eyes gave me that weak-kneed feeling again.

This was one superpower of his I would never be pointing out to him!

I looked away and pretended to be very busy making sure both my gloves were in the pockets of my coat while I ordered my knees to cut it out, and tried to compose myself. I really needed to get a grip! If he didn't stop looking at me that way, it was going to make it very hard to stick to my resolve and only see him as a friend. Just a friend. That's all.

Rather than search yet another storage room, which neither of us felt like doing, we went to Mission Control. A fire burned brightly in the fireplace, casting a friendly flickering glow about the room. Snowflakes gently made their way past the panes in the windows, and we spent the rest of the day talking. I told Miles what the lawyer said, including the part about the document coming back to bite Mr. Creepy. We both had a very good laugh over that. Trixie did too.

The afternoon flew by. When it grew dark outside, I thought clouds must be covering the sun. But no, the sun was dropping behind the mountains.

Miles and I said our goodbyes, and I drove back to the cabin.

Mom was setting the table for dinner when I walked in the door, rubbing my arms and hands to try and increase circulation, as I stomped snow off my feet.

"It is really cold out there," I said. "Tomorrow I'll have to dress warmer, I think."

"So tell me what happened today," Mom said, turning back to the kitchen. "You needed to drive into Cedar Oaks to see Polly's lawyer. What was that all about?"

"Sorry I was in such a hurry earlier, Mom. I appreciate you letting me wait to explain. Polly's grandson's distant cousin, Alfred Sullivan, do you remember her talking about him?"

"Right, he wants to take over as trustee?"

"That's the one. He was at the estate when I got there this morning. He wanted me to let him in the house to look around, he claimed he would be assuming responsibility as the trustee soon, and claimed a paper he had with him gave him the right to go anywhere he wanted on the property," I said.

Mom looked concerned, so I hurried to finish my story.

"So I looked at the paper, and didn't believe it was a real legal document, so I wanted to give it to Polly's lawyer, and he confirmed it isn't legitimate."

"And... what did this Alfred Sullivan do?" Mom wanted to know.

Hm. What did he do? I might have to see another mouse, depending on how this conversation goes.

"Well, he left."

"He just left?"

Well... he got thrown down the stairs and the seat chewed out of his pants, but why be wordy about it.

"He left."

"Huh," Mom said, considering that.

"Dinner smells great, Mom," I said, turning on the oven light so I could see what was cooking. "It looks awesome, too!"

Mom would not be re-directed, but she wasn't overly concerned, either.

"Well, I'm glad you have Chip with you at the castle," she said.

"Yeah, and there are so many people working there off and on. I'm never alone," I said truthfully enough.

"Oh, well that's good," Mom said, the faint crease in her forehead smoothing.

"So is dinner almost ready, shall I round up the others?" I asked.

"Sure, I think Doreen will eat in the living room on the couch, but you can get Tryon's hands washed, and bring him in."

"Will do, Mom."

Crisis averted. I hated not being fully honest with Mom, but the truth would cause her unbearable stress. I felt caught between a rock and a hard-place, and the rock of not-telling-Mom-everything was a lot softer and gentler on everyone than the hard-place of telling Mom everything and completely freaking her out and being institutionalized because I have an imaginary friend.

I'm sticking with the rock, and going to avoid the hard-place for everyone's sake.

Chapter 10

We woke to a white world. Snow blanketed everything between earth and sky, and there was frost on the windows of the cabin. Mom had a fire roaring in the fireplace, and I stood there warming my hands a moment.

"It's really howling out there!" Mom said. "Do you want to take the car today?"

I thought about that.

"Hm, well... I think Chip and I will be okay. I mean I know he will, have you seen his fur? It's crazy thick! I'll bundle up, and honestly I'd rather walk through the woods than try and drive on an icy mountain road."

"Smart thinking," said Mom. "But you sure will need to bundle up, that wind is going to cut like a knife."

I ate a quick breakfast, then grabbed my cold weather gear.

"I'm so glad you broke down and bought a good coat," Mom said. "We didn't exactly come from a place that prepared us for this kind of weather."

"I really hated spending the money though," I said ruefully. "I want to save it all for college."

"I know, honey," said Mom sympathetically. "I hate that things happened as they did, and we weren't able to send you like we'd always planned to."

"Don't feel bad, Mom," I said. It sure wasn't her fault, or Dad's. "Polly is one generous lady. I'll go to college, and hey, maybe I'll appreciate it more because I had to work for it."

"I appreciate your attitude," Mom said. "A lot of kids would pitch a fit rather than pitch in and be willing to give up as much as you have."

I considered that as I fastened my coat.

"Well... difficulty creates the opportunity to rise to the challenge and grow stronger," I said.

I did *not* say that my smart friend Miles told me that, although he did.

"I'd rather be better, than bitter," I added, as I pulled on my boots.

Mom blinked back some tears.

"Mom, do not cry! For pity's sake, will it make you feel better if I try real hard to work up some bitterness?"

Mom laughed, and dabbed at her eyes.

"No, I'm just—proud of you, that's all."

"Well," I said, ready for a change of subject, "I'm glad I got the snow boots, can you imagine trying to wade through snow in cross trainers or my suede boots?"

"No kidding," said Mom. "Call me when you get there, okay? I'll feel better if you do."

"Sure Mom," I said, giving her a hug as I headed out the door with Chip.

He ran out into the snow and dove into a drift. He stood back up and shook, sending snowflakes flying.

"Silly guy, you like the cold better than the heat, huh?" I laughed. "Well, me too."

Everything around us was varying shades of white, even the sky. It was too bad the wind was blowing, Tryon would be disappointed when he woke up and discovered he couldn't come out and play in the snow.

After we crossed the bridge, the path through the forest provided a welcome respite from the biting wind and stinging snow crystals. Once we reached the garden, it was at us full force again. Even Chip was ready to play inside for the day by the time we reached the front doors of the castle.

"Hi," I said, breathless from our trip through the winter world, as I closed the door behind us and began unwinding my scarf and removing layers.

"Hi back," smiled Miles. "I didn't think you'd come today, it's so bad out."

"Hey, I'm like the post office. Rain, sleet, snow, whatever... it's not going to stop me. Although it may slow me down. We really had to push against the wind to get here."

"It's not what you're used to, I suppose," said Miles.

"Not a bit," I agreed. "I'm used to blowing sand, not blowing snow."

"That doesn't sound pleasant."

"Oh, it isn't. You can lose a few layers of skin just by standing outside in the month of March," I said.

Miles laughed.

"I'm not joking," I said. "It's ridiculous!"

"Have you heard anything new about Polly's grandson?" Miles asked.

"Oh, no, but—I need to call Mom. She'll worry if I don't," I said, ripping my iPhone out of my pocket.

After reassuring Mom that Chip and I arrived safely, I turned back to Miles.

"So where to, today?" I asked. "Molly and her crew aren't coming, which is smart. I need to hire a service to plow the driveway so they can get to the house, but there's no point in that when the snow is still coming down so thick."

"I suppose we might as well continue on the same hall we've been searching through," said Miles, leading the way.

"Back to Polly's grandson though," I said. "There hasn't been any change so far. Polly hopes the change in hospitals will make a difference."

"I hope so too," said Miles.

"Wait." I stopped abruptly, and looked at him. "Your parents' room was on the second floor. Let's check out the storage area that's closest to their room."

"Alright. Let's do it."

We turned, and Miles led the way.

We reached the storage room, and began going through wardrobes and drawers and trunks. It seemed as though every room held a cedar chest or trunk of some kind.

"So what was your favorite period in history?" I asked.

Miles thought.

"I'd say now. The technology available today is amazing compared to when I was, well, solid. It's amazing compared to even last year."

"I guess having a computer now, and the internet, helps you stay connected with the outside world," I said, laying aside a bundle of baby clothes that filled the cedar chest I was searching.

"It does. I've read every book in Mission Control—"

"You're kidding! Every book?" I exclaimed.

"You might be surprised what can be accomplished in a hundred and forty years when you don't need sleep, or have anything else to do."

"Wow. I guess. That's still pretty impressive, considering how many books are in that room."

"Having a computer has allowed me to keep up with current events. Not that it matters I suppose, but it is nice to know what's going on outside these walls. Even if I'm not really a part of it, I feel better connected and less isolated."

"I don't even know how you did it, staying so laid-back and sane all these years. Even with Trixie here, it just seems like torture," I said.

Miles shrugged.

"I guess when there's no choice, you just—deal with whatever it is you have no choice over."

That sounded sort of like what I said to Mom earlier. Miles had it way worse than I ever did, though.

Miles continued.

"It's made a huge difference though, that you can see and talk to me. And didn't run screaming when you realized I was semi-transparent."

I laughed.

"Are you kidding? I hardly stayed conscious, I can't even imagine how I would have run."

"So that was it. You sure did look terrified. Well, you looked like you saw a ghost."

We both laughed over that, for some reason it struck us both as very funny.

"Yeah, but," I said, "it turned out you were actually my good-friend-to-be, semi-transparent guy, who has amazingly cool super-powers. I would have missed out on a really good friendship, if I'd run off. I'm glad I didn't."

"Me too," smiled Miles.

I stood and stretched my back, surveying the room as I did so. I moved to have a closer look at a group of assorted pieces of furniture that filled a corner of the room.

"Hey, it's an old roll top desk," I said, squeezing between a wardrobe and chest of drawers to get closer to it.

"Here, let me," said Miles, moving the furniture so that I had plenty of room.

"You really are very handy, you know," I smiled, and Miles smiled back.

I raised the front of the large desk to reveal pigeonholes. Lots of pigeonholes. They were each stuffed full of papers. I sighed. This was going to take a while.

Miles whistled under his breath.

"This is going to take a while."

I couldn't help but laugh.

"What?"

"Nothing, I was just thinking the same thing," I said. "And I'm going to look on the bright side, this is better than breaking my back over more trunks."

"Then I'll search through the trunks, while you do that," said Miles considerately.

I removed the papers from one of the pigeonholes and began to go through them one at a time. We sorted in silence, as I focused on scanning each paper for relevant information.

"I'm finished with the trunks," said Miles. "Let me help."

He began looking through the drawers of the desk. They were full to the brim as well.

"So what on earth happened, someone decided to stuff every miscellaneous paper in the entire castle into this desk?" I asked, struggling to pull one particularly large mass of pages out of the pigeonhole in which they were stuck.

"That's what it looks like," said Miles, as he leafed through the contents of his drawer.

"Oh! Miles-Miles-Miles!" I breathed. "I found something!"

"What?" Miles asked, trying to see what was in my hand as I bounced up and down. I held a stack of folded papers, tied with a ribbon, out to him.

Miles took it in his hands. Written on the top page of the stack was "Evidence, Miles and Delevan".

Miles' hands shook in his eagerness to unbind the papers. I could hardly stand still myself, maybe we'd finally found something we could use! I restrained myself from snatching back the bundle and helping him loosen the ribbon that bound it.

Miles and I sat on the floor at the same time, and he began to unfold the papers and read them.

"It's a diagram of the clearing," said Miles.

"Your Dad did a good job of mapping that out, from what you told me," I said.

The diagram indicated signs of blood stains and earth that appeared to have been disturbed in places other than where Miles and Delevan were found.

"They were in a hurry," Miles remembered. "They knew they had to be out of there in case my Father returned home and went looking for Delevan."

"Your Dad should have been a CSI agent," I said. I was impressed.

On another paper, he noted how many people he judged to be in the clearing, based on what he found. He was right about how many were there, but he didn't list the fourth man, which was understandable.

Miles didn't say anything, he was searching each page with intense concentration.

"This says he found Delevan's blood-stained handkerchief here," I pointed at another page, "a distance away from both of you."

Miles struggled to remember.

"He was trying to bandage my knee, to stop the bleeding. I forgot about that. We were ambushed before he managed to."

We continued to sort. While some of the papers had relevant information, others didn't. I felt for his poor Dad, trying so hard to unravel the mystery of what really happened that day and never receiving anything but a deaf ear from the Cedar Oaks Sheriff. From what Miles said, I imagined the residents of Cedar Oaks were less than supportive as well.

"Look!" I said, holding out a news article that was folded inside a page.

Miles and I both read it at the same time. It was about two unidentified men who were found shot to death.

"That has to be them," he said.

The page in which it was folded held copious notes detailing his Dad's search to identify the men. He noted that the bullets used against them could have come from Miles' revolvers and Delevan's derringer. He also noted that he would point this out once he had enough evidence to exonerate Miles, otherwise he was sure the information would be used against him. I was sure it would have been, too.

"You're still here," I said, looking at Miles. "So I guess this and the death certificates aren't enough, although it seems like they ought to be."

"To be totally honest with you, what I have no peace about is the accusation of being in love with my brother's fiancé, and trying to take her from him," said Miles. "I'm sure it sounds strange, but that's worse to me than being accused of murdering him."

I nodded.

"You're an honorable guy. That doesn't surprise me, Miles," I said.

I gathered up the papers.

"Okay then. I think this and the death certificates ought to be plenty to prove half of the story is false. The death certificates prove you couldn't have been shot by your brother after he was already dead, and this indicates there were other people there that day too. We'll keep hunting until we find proof that the other half was also a lie," I said.

"That sounds good," said Miles, a shadow of a smile crossing his face.

"Hey," I said. Forgetting he was semi-transparent, I tried to shoulder bump him and nearly fell over in the process, which at least made us both laugh. "We'll find that proof. It exists, it's out there, and every day we're getting closer."

"I believe you, I'm not giving up," Miles said, giving me a genuine smile.

"Good," I said, as I bundled and retied his Dad's notes. "Let's go put this in the safe with the death certificates."

I was sure we would find proof. Just as sure as I was that he deserved to be free, and that I was really going to miss him after he was gone.

Chip and I returned to the cabin after a long day of searching at the castle. We hadn't found anything else, but at least Miles and I had fun talking and looking at more of his old family memorabilia.

We hurried inside, and I slammed the backdoor against the howling wind and snow.

There was howling inside too, it sounded like a crazy kids' party was going on. Tryon was running around the cabin screaming, Mom was jumping up and down laughing and crying, and Doreen was smiling broadly.

"What's going on?" I asked.

"Doree's got limes!" yelled Tryon.

Mom half rolled her eyes, which sparkled with excitement.

"The doctor called, the test results came in. Doreen tested positive. Dad picked up her prescriptions in Glen Haven on his way here for the weekend, so any minute now, we can get started with the treatment protocol the doctor outlined!"

"Oh my goodness! I can hardly believe it!" I exclaimed.

If we never came here, and I never met Miles… I'd never know for sure, but there was a good chance we never would have found out what was wrong.

"I'm sure we'd look crazy to anyone who could look in and see the way we're acting right now," said Mom, smiling ear to ear as she hugged a laughing Tryon, and swung him around.

"Yeah, well, we're not glad Doree's sick, we're glad that now, finally, she can get better!" I said.

"No kidding," said Mom, setting Tryon down, then sitting herself down at the table, breathless. "Watching her suffer and get worse while the doctors told us nothing was wrong, and didn't believe us, and didn't believe Doreen…"

"I know, Mom," I agreed. "To finally have a diagnosis for a treatable illness, it's better than Christmas."

Dad arrived, and the celebration continued, as Doreen took her first dose of the medications that would ultimately bring her back to health. We had a very merry celebratory family dinner, then the rest of the family settled in for a movie.

I put my cold weather gear back on, reassured my perplexed mother that there was something I absolutely must do at the castle, and was out the door like a shot.

I flew down the path and back through the icy woods. I was so excited that Doreen had a diagnosis, and couldn't wait to tell Miles the news and thank him.

"Miles!" I yelled, skidding into the entryway in my snow covered boots, as the door slammed behind me.

"What's going on?" Miles appeared beside me, his eyes filled with concern.

"It's my sister!" I beamed. "You were right! We've got a diagnosis, and now she can begin treatment! You were right!"

"I'm so glad," Miles said, his smile making his hazel eyes light up even more than usual.

I spun around in a circle, I was so glad, glad, glad.

"I would give you the biggest hug if I could," I grinned.

Miles blushed and glanced away.

"I mean, I'm just so thankful… we would have kept the other doctor appointment, and it's almost certain he would have done more expensive tests and claimed there was nothing wrong," I said, feeling a tiny bit awkward now.

Miles looked back at me, and smiled again.

"I'm very glad. I really am. It isn't often that I can help anyone."

I stopped and looked at him incredulously.

"Are you serious? You are constantly finding ways to help people without them suspecting. How about one of Nate's guys, I think his name is Ben. If you didn't intervene, he would have been injured when the ladder he was standing on to trim the large hedge of roses near the fountain, started to fall. And when Susie was cleaning the chandelier, with a flick of your hand, you kept her from taking a dangerous tumble off of that ladder. I don't know what the deal is with the people I hire and ladders, but if it wasn't for you, there would be some serious on the job injuries. I've seen you do lots of other little things for the people that come and go here at the estate. You think I haven't noticed?"

Miles shrugged. I rolled my eyes.

"It may be no big deal to you, but it is to the people you help. I can only guess how much good you've done over the last hundred and forty years, because you're too modest to admit to it. Do you realize I owe you my life? You saved me when the cellar door collapsed. I couldn't hold on. My fingers were slipping, and if you hadn't caught me, or whatever you did, I would've smashed against the floor the way the pieces of the door did. I don't even want to imagine how badly I would've been hurt if you didn't save me."

"I don't either," Miles said, with that soft look in his eyes.

Now it was my turn to blush and look away.

"Well you've helped, big time," I said, getting back to the original subject. "You saved my life, and you just may have saved my sister's life, too. If you could see how sick she's been... but now she can start getting better!"

The very thought made me spin around the entryway some more, I was too happy to behave like an adult.

Miles laughed, and Trixie caught the enthusiasm and started pirouetting, too.

Finally I calmed down enough to be serious again.

"I should go, I just wanted to let you know right away. And... thank you, Miles. Thank you. For everything."

"Any time," Miles said softly, with that look in his eyes again.

I didn't blush this time, but I did melt inside. Which is saying a lot, considering how cold I was after my trip through the freezing night air.

I recovered as best I could, but it wasn't easy. Miles insisted on walking me home.

"It's dark, and you didn't bring Chip," he said. "You can't expect me to let you walk off in the dark by yourself. What kind of friend would I be, if I did that?"

So he walked me home, and I was glad it was dark, because it meant there was a chance he couldn't see the struggle my brain and my heart were in.

We said good night. I went inside the cabin and locked myself in the bathroom, the only place I could be alone, and ordered myself to get a grip and quit crushing on my semi-transparent friend! This was happening way too frequently, and it had to stop. Myself wasn't very cooperative, but in the end, I regained control.

~***~

Cynthia stood on the sun-dappled bridge, gently tracing her brother's initials as fresh tears brimmed, then tumbled down her cheeks and into the stream below.

The rose scented breeze ruffled her hair and cooled her forehead, as a wisp of a cloud passed overhead. She glanced up at the late afternoon sky, and sighed.

Cynthia swallowed hard, blotted her eyes, and left the bridge behind. She walked slowly down the path through the trees, and back to the garden.

Her striped kitten crouched near the fountain, watching a beetle lumber across the paved path. With a leap, he batted it with a white tipped paw, then leaped away again, as though terrified the bug might bat back. The kitten saw her and came running, rubbing its furry sides against her legs as it purred. She picked him up and buried her face in his soft kitten fur.

Cynthia sighed, and wondered again where Trixie, Miles' dog, was. She hadn't been seen since the day he and Delevan were killed.

The kitten wriggled out of her arms so he could continue examining the beetle, and Cynthia turned toward the house. As she neared the entrance, she heard her Father's voice drift through the open front door.

"That girl is a worthless little fool, what Delevan saw in her I'll never know. She's lying, there isn't a word of truth in her."

Someone else spoke, but too softly for Cynthia to understand who it was or what they said. Father, however, was easy to hear.

"The ammunition used for one thing, the firearms involved, the time frame. I'd like you to explain to me how Delevan managed to shoot his brother twice, after he was already dead! I'm positive from the markings on the ground there were more than three people there. Someone went to a lot of work to try and make the clearing support Miss Williams's story. Miles' dog went missing that day, and has never been found. You have a responsibility to find the truth, why you're content to accept the word of that woman is unfathomable..."

Cynthia hurried by. Father must be meeting with the Sheriff again. It made her feel even worse than she already did, to hear Father try and convince the Sheriff to look deeper into the cause of her brothers' deaths. It would do no good... she shared Father's opinion that the Sheriff wanted Sarah's story to be true. Otherwise there was a murderer still at large, and everyone would look to the Sheriff to determine who that person was, and to see that justice was served. The Sheriff didn't want neighbors to begin doubting one another, he'd rather they believe Miles and Delevan killed each other. It infuriated Father, and sickened Cynthia and Mother.

As she silently passed through the entry on her way to the stairs, familiar handwriting caught her eye. On top of the stack of mail which lay on the entryway table awaiting her Father's attention, was an envelope addressed in Sarah's handwriting.

Cynthia looked toward the parlor where her Father was still arguing for justice. She paused a moment, then slipped the envelope off the table and into her pocket.

Cynthia hurried up one staircase and then another. She was out of breath and shaking by the time she reached the top. She opened the attic door and slipped inside, then dropped onto the cushions she'd piled in a corner to create her secret hiding spot. She'd spent hours here, playing with her doll and reading... and in the past few weeks, grieving.

Cynthia took the letter out of her pocket and looked at it in the light of the round window beside her. She remembered how kind Miss Williams was to her. Nothing made sense... Why was she lying? Maybe this letter would answer that question.

Father and Mother would be upset if they knew Cynthia took Father's mail. But the letter itself would upset him, unless it contained a confession.

Hands still shaking, she carefully opened the envelope, took out the letter, and unfolded it.

A puzzled frown crossed Cynthia's face.

The letter was very strange. Cynthia wondered if Sarah's mind was not right.

She sighed. It was well that her Father was spared reading it.

Cynthia folded the letter and hid it where she was sure it would never be found.

Chapter 11

I woke up when the breath was knocked out of me by my little brother, who saw fit to pounce on me.

"Ug, Tryon...you are getting way too big for this!" I groaned, rubbing my ribcage.

Tryon laughed, and ran out the door.

By the time I was dressed and ready for the day, Tryon was making himself at home on top of the kitchen counter.

"Well, Mr. Tryon!" I said, removing the bag of cookies from his little hands. "Why don't we try, try again, and find you something better for breakfast."

I lifted him off the counter and brushed the crumbs from his face.

"Nothing better than cookies for breakfast," Tryon tried to reason with me, then did an about-face. "Fix me breakfast?"

"Sure, Try," I said, as he grabbed me around the knees and squeezed, then took off for the living room where I heard the sound of cartoons in the background. It was kind of unusual for Mom not to be awake by now.

I pulled out the instant oatmeal, bacon and eggs, and cooked a quick breakfast.

"Come and get it, hungry boy!" I called towards the living room.

Tryon skidded in on his pajama covered feet and crashed into the table, knocking over a chair and sending his cup to the floor with a splash. Really Polly, little boys are easier? I shudder to think!

"Chip, get it," I said, pointing to the milk spill.

Should I clean it up? Probably. But Chip was an awesome mop for things like this when I was in a hurry. And I was.

I got Tryon going on his breakfast and poured a bowl of food for Chip, then hurried down the hall for my coat.

I bumped into Mom as she came out of her room.

"Oh, sorry Mom!" I said, regaining my balance.

"What are you doing up so early?" Mom asked, a puzzled look creasing her forehead.

"Uh...well, I need to get to work. What are you doing up so late?"

"Anika, it's Saturday."

Oh, wow. I was so busy lately, we'd been searching through the rooms of the estate, and the days of the week were starting to meld together.

"Well silly me!" I said. "I forgot. I've got a lot to do though, so I better get going."

"Okay," said Mom, the crease deepening. "But remember, your Dad is here. And you're gone so much during the week, and you've been getting home late... you went back yesterday, after dinner."

Well of course, I had to tell Miles what the doctor said! He's the one who pointed us in the right direction, after all. Of course Mom didn't know that.

"You need to stop and take a break sometimes. Even God rested on the seventh day."

What's with the frown?

"I will Mom, I won't stay all day. But especially now, with all she's going through, I don't want to let Polly down."

I also don't want to let Miles down, I thought, as I hurried over the snow-covered ground. I couldn't imagine how he stood being isolated for so long, and until such time as I proved his innocence and got him out of this limbo-ness, I was going to make sure he didn't spend any more days alone.

And it isn't like I was ignoring my family... I cooked the kid breakfast this morning! Still, Mom was right. Dad was home, and we didn't get to see him much these days. I needed to take advantage of the opportunity.

I reached the end of my very cold walk and hurried up the stairs and into the entryway, blowing on my hands. The warm air of the castle felt good. I looked around, thinking what a fortune it must take to heat the place. The Bannermans certainly weren't church mice. No wonder Alfred was trying to weasel his way in.

Second-Miles' condition hadn't improved. His birthday wasn't until spring, but the fact that he'd been in a coma for months had everyone worried. Except Alfred, who hoped he would never wake up. It's despicable what greed does to people. I saw Alfred positively skipping down the sidewalk the last time I drove into town. I'd no doubt he was just counting on Second-Miles not pulling through.

"Hi," I said, as Miles walked down the stairs.

"Hi back," he smiled.

"What, no superpowers today?" I asked, indicating the stairs.

He looked down, and laughed.

"I've spent so much time with you lately, I'm getting used to doing things the old-fashioned way."

"Speaking of which," I sighed. "I can't stay long. My Dad's here for the weekend, and I need to participate in family time."

I'm ashamed to admit, I kind of rolled my eyes and used air quotes.

Miles looked serious.

"Go home, Anika. Spend time with your family. I'd give anything to have that opportunity again… don't waste yours."

I hesitated.

"I hate to think of you here all by yourself, with no one to talk to, though… and I was hoping to search more of the second floor today."

Miles shook his head.

"It isn't your responsibility to keep me company. I love the time I get to spend with you. But I'll stop being here when you are, if I think you're sacrificing family or friends to do it. If there are clues, they'll still be here Monday."

"What, I'm not allowed to come back until then?" I exclaimed, more than a little bit irritated.

"If you do, you won't find me here. Now go, spend time with your family. I'll see you Monday."

He ushered me back out the door.

Well! I'd think he'd been talking to Mom, if that was possible.

I hung out with Dad that afternoon. He was splitting logs for firewood. I stacked, and we talked, between the blows of the axe.

"So how is it, working for Uncle Mark?" I asked, picking up a piece of wood.

"Good. Real good. I enjoy the work, and benefits are better… I'm starting to think we're going to be better off than if I never lost my job."

"That's great, Dad. I'm glad you're happy."

"Mom and I are going to start looking for a place to live soon. Cost of living is higher, but so is the pay."

I processed that while Dad split some more logs. He placed another on the chopping block, then took a moment to rest and continue the conversation.

"It would be good for Mom and Doreen to not have to travel so far to see her new doctor. It might be good for you too, Mom says you've been spending all your time working, and haven't made any friends."

"I've just been busy, Dad. I love what I'm doing. And it turns out I'm good at it. I might want to major in hotel management, when I start college. I think I'd enjoy managing a lodge or upscale bed and breakfast. I'm saving a lot because of my job, and Polly suggested I apply for a scholarship her family set up."

"Okay, honey. I'm glad to hear that. Just be sure and take time for yourself. We all need friends, it isn't healthy to be alone."

I was mulling over Mom's and Dad's words of concern as I picked up a few forgotten groceries at the store the next afternoon.

Maybe I *should* make more of an effort with people. It was just so time consuming to try and make friends, and I already had a good friend in Miles. I sighed in frustration.

"Hi, are you Anika?" asked a girl about my age.

Tall, gorgeous curly red hair, blue eyes. Somehow managed to be stick thin and have curves all at the same time, no less. She had that top model thing going on.

"That's right," I replied. "Have we met?"

I could answer that. No. We have not.

"I'm Susan's daughter. Our moms are friends. I'm Jenny," she smiled.

"Hi Jenny, nice to meet you."

"So how do you like it here? It must be a big change from where you lived before," she said.

Jenny was really, genuinely nice. I could see it in her eyes and hear it in her voice, now that my insecurities backed down a bit. There wasn't anything snobbish or superior about her.

Note to self, do not judge a book by its cover! Even if that cover leaves you feeling short and insignificant, by comparison. My brown hair and eyes would be no match if there was a contest going on. And I'd bet a dollar if she stepped on a rotten cellar door, it wouldn't collapse on her.

I brought my thoughts back to the conversation, and Jenny's question.

"I really like it here. Everyone is so nice. It's very different from where we're from."

"That's great. Have you made any new friends here, yet?" she asked.

"Not really, I'm busy working most of the time," I said.

"Some of us are meeting at the coffee shop later today, why don't you join us. We always have a lot of fun, sometimes we play Jenga or dominoes or Scrabble… it will give you a chance to get to know some people, if you want."

"Okay…" I said hesitantly. Fine, Mom and Dad. This is for you.

And so, at seven o' clock that evening I was at the *Bean There, Bun That*. Kind of a dorky name, but the lattes were good.

The store front, like all those on Main Street this time of year, was decorated with Christmas lights. Inside there were more decorations, and Christmas music quietly played over the sound system. It wasn't as upscale as the coffee shop where Polly and I met her PI. It was a better fit for college age students, though. There were booths along the walls as well as tables scattered about the room. There was free Wi-Fi here as well, and a few people sat glued to their laptops. Most were in a group with Jenny, though.

"Anika!" Jenny said. "I'm so glad you made it!"

"Hi Jenny," I smiled, as I walked over to her group.

She gave me a hug.

"Hey everyone, this is Anika. She moved here last fall."

Everyone yelled out some form of greeting, and I was surprised to recognize one of the guys in her group.

"Nate, I didn't expect to see you here."

"I'm here most Sunday nights," he replied.

"I had no idea you knew each other," said Jenny.

"Nate is responsible for how wonderfully the gardens at the estate look now," I said. "Well...they're covered in snow, actually. He's responsible for how wonderfully they'll look in the spring."

And we *don't* know each other. He works for me, and I hope being in the same social group doesn't change the good working relationship we have. That concerned me.

Jenny led the way to the two empty chairs next to Nate, and I reluctantly followed.

"How is restoration coming along on the castle, Miss Riley?" he asked, as I settled in my chair.

"Might as well call me Anika," I replied. "Everyone else will."

"Alright then," said Nate. "So, how is restoration coming along on the castle, Anika?"

"Not a lot can be done to the outside right now, but the three years of neglect didn't affect the exterior much. Although, the guest house does need work. The roof leaks, and that's a mess. Restoration on the inside of the estate itself, is going awesome. I think our cleaning crew is beginning to wonder if the house goes on forever though, they still haven't gotten to every room yet. What they have freed from years of dust, is amazing."

"That's right," Jenny said. "I heard about that, Mom was telling me about your job. That's really cool."

"It is. I love it. I can't imagine a job I'd enjoy more," I said.

"I've never been so anxious for spring to arrive," said Nate. "I'm looking forward to getting back out to the estate again and watch the grounds come to life. It's going to be amazing."

A couple more people arrived and joined in, and the topic quickly switched to games.

I like Jenny a lot, we got along well. I could see being friends if we had enough time to get to know each other. Nate is a nice guy too. I am not a fan of board games though, so that part was rather torturous. I can't say for sure, but I'm not exaggerating much, when I say I just might prefer being alone with my dog for a hundred and forty years.

I did my best to be engaged in what was going on around me, in spite of it. The majority of the guys in her group, with the exception of Nate, were awfully immature. They really got on my nerves. But then again, I was used to Miles. I've come to the conclusion they just don't make 'em like they used to. I would so much rather be hanging out with him, instead.

I said goodbye around eight-thirty, and left. I wanted to get an early start in the morning.

I drove home carefully. Mom's car is not suited to mountain driving in the winter and I had no opportunity to learn proper driving technique in the past, considering we lived in a desert before coming here. The snowplows did a good job of keeping the snow cleared and the roads de-iced though, so it wasn't too bad. Still, it was a relief to get home.

I parked the car and waded through the snow to the cabin.

"It is so cold out there!" I said, as I closed the door behind me and stomped the snow off my feet.

"So how was it?" Mom asked, obviously thrilled I went out.

"It was okay," I said neutrally.

"Well did you have a good time? Did you make any new friends?"

I made a face.

"Well, I do like Susan's daughter. She's nice."

"That's great!" said Mom. "So do they get together every Sunday night?"

"Uh, well, maybe. I'd have to ask I guess."

"That would be so wonderful if you could have something like this to look forward to every week," said Mom brightly.

Who looks forward to torture?

"Why's this so important to you?" I questioned.

"Well," Mom was a little taken aback. "You've given up a lot in your life, and I know how social you've always been. You had a crowd of friends around you all the time, and now you're so isolated."

"I am not isolated!" I protested.

I had to bite my tongue to keep from mentioning my unmentionable friend who I talk to almost every day. But no longer on weekends, apparently, I thought with some annoyance.

"Well I just want you to have a chance to make some friends, you need that. Interacting with the people you hire to care for the Bannerman estate isn't the same thing."

I almost laughed out loud at that. Nate, a person I hired to care for the estate, is part of this group she's so gung-ho about. So technically, that ought to make the group invalid.

I didn't think she'd accept that logic as a reason to avoid game night from now on, though. Instead, she'd borderline insult me and suggest I become a lawyer since I'm so good at twisting truth and arguing technicalities. We've had this conversation before.

"Okay Mom," I said. I was not going to win this one, I couldn't put all my cards on the table. "I'm fine though, so please. Do not worry, and please do not pressure me. Friends either happen or they don't, you can't force it, or you end up with the wrong friends."

"Alright, fine," said Mom, holding up her hands. "I just want what's best for you."

"I know you do, Mom," I said, giving her a hug. "I'm going to bed, I'm really tired. I'll see you in the morning."

I got ready for bed as quietly as possible so I wouldn't wake Doreen, and slid under the cold sheets. Brrr! Maybe I ought to switch to warm pajamas, instead of a tank top and yoga pants as my sleep-wear of choice.

I lay there thinking about game night at the coffee shop. Honestly, if I clicked with the people there like I do with Miles, I think I would've enjoyed it. But I didn't really know them, and I don't really like games, and Jenny was the only one I sort of clicked with, and that still wasn't on the same level as Miles.

In spite of spending quality time with Dad, I was glad the weekend was over. I missed hanging out with Miles. My last thought as I fell asleep was how much I looked forward to seeing him in the morning.

Chapter 12

Monday morning on the way to the castle, I made my usual phone call to Polly.

"Hi Polly," I said.

"Oh hello, Anika dear."

"How are you doing?"

"Hanging in there," said Polly. "No change, I'm sad to say. We're not giving up hope though."

"Of course not," I said.

"How is the estate, dear?"

"Great! Right now, it's covered in snow. The grounds are in great shape for spring though, and the inside of the house sparkles."

"And how about the mystery, dear? How is that going?"

"It's going. I haven't found anything conclusive yet, but we... I'm making progress."

"Well, wonderful dear. Oh... visiting hours have begun, I'll let you go for now."

"Talk to you tomorrow," I said.

I really felt for Polly. How disappointing, that after months of being in a coma, there was no improvement. I could only imagine how hard that was for her.

I ran up the steps of the castle, looking forward to the warmth I would find inside.

"We're searching the house again today!" I said, as I walked in the door, and Trixie tore past me and ran outside to hang with Chip in the snow-covered garden. The wind wasn't howling, and the sun was shining, making the day much more pleasant than it was on Friday.

"Okay, where do you want to start?" Miles asked.

"There you are, you usually meet me at the door. I was wondering where you were! I thought maybe you got your days confused, and were still boycotting me."

"No, I'm not boycotting you today," he smiled. "So, where to start?"

"Do you have an attic? We've searched the storage areas on the first floor. Instead of moving to more rooms on the second, let's start over from the top this time."

"Follow me," Miles said.

Three staircases later and approaching the fourth, I gave him a sideways glance.

"Miles and miles to go before we sleep, huh?"

"Very clever," said Miles, "Never heard *that* one before."

He was obviously teasing. Still, I slapped at his shoulder unsuccessfully.

"Nice try!" Miles smiled. "Being semi-transparent may be a good thing after all, seeing as you're so violently inclined."

That earned him another attempted whack before we reached the end of the fourth set of stairs, and started up another. At the top was the door to the attic. It swung open with a wave of Miles' hand, and we stepped inside.

"What an awesome place," I said. "This is an Antique Roadshow dream come true!"

It was truly a treasure trove of history. Dust motes sparkled in the rays of soft light that shone through the small windows that dotted the walls of the room. A Singer treadle machine stood against one wall, a dress maker's dummy wearing an unfinished dress, beside it. Multiple steamer trunks were scattered about the room, intermixed with furniture, lamps, paintings, rolled up rugs, vases and small statues, a harp... It was overwhelming, there was such a conglomeration of items.

And dust.

Of course Miles took care of that part, straightaway.

"Show off," I said.

He just grinned, then looked around.

"I haven't been up here in a very, very long time. I forgot what it was like."

We walked around looking at the contents. It was hard to know where to begin.

"What a gorgeous old wardrobe," I said, admiring the detailed carving on the huge piece of furniture in the center of the attic. "The mirror is perfect, it doesn't warp the reflection at all. Only the edges have lost a little bit of their silvering."

I continued to study the design carved in the beautiful grain of the wood.

"That was my parent's, I think," said Miles reflectively. "It was a long time ago, but I seem to remember that being theirs."

"Then let's start here," I said, opening the single door on the front left side of the wardrobe.

I searched through the items that filled the interior while Miles searched the drawers.

"I found something," Miles said suddenly.

I leaned back and looked. It was a set of old pistols like I remembered seeing in western movies.

"These were mine," he said softly. His eyes had a far-away look. "And this, was Delevan's. The one he had with him that day."

Miles lifted a small gun with an odd looking barrel from the open drawer in front of him.

"Here," he said, after making sure the guns weren't loaded. "Take these for me, please…"

I reached out and took Miles' gun belt and Delevan's odd little gun, and Miles returned to his search of the drawer.

"Nothing there…" he said, searching another.

A thorough search of the entire wardrobe revealed nothing more. No bullet casings, no letters, no documents, no written information of any kind. No one would guess those were the guns Miles and Delevan had in the clearing that day, just by looking at them.

"I don't suppose that helps the cause much," said Miles.

"At the moment, perhaps not. That could change though, we might find something else that will make them useful."

"I used to be a pretty good shot," Miles said, taking back the gun belt and spinning one of the revolvers on his finger. "Of course I never did that, I've only ever seen it done in movies."

"How about Delevan? Did you target practice together?" I asked.

"We did. There was always a competition between us over who was the better shot. We had business dealings in the west you know, and it paid to be prepared. I never did run into trouble, but if I didn't have these, I would have."

"So who was the better marksman, you or Delevan?"

A smile flickered across Miles' face.

"I was. But Delevan was stiff competition."

He thought some more, as he turned the pistol in his hands.

"Three against two... not including the guy that ambushed us. Delevan only had this derringer, and it's got such a short barrel it isn't very accurate. Dan and his men weren't very good shots. It would have been over a lot faster, if they were."

"I've wondered... why did you only shoot to disarm Dan that day?"

"I believe in defending oneself, but given the chance, I'd prefer to disarm rather than shoot to kill. I didn't have that chance when Dan's men first fired at us, and neither did Delevan. With Dan, I did. I was shaking with pain and had to take time to steady my arm to shoot straight, anyway. Might as well take Dan's gun out of the equation, rather than kill him."

It was so unfair what happened to Miles. It was just wrong on so many levels.

Miles sighed, and put the guns back in the drawer.

"I don't know about you, but I'm ready to think about something else!"

I said the first thing that popped into my mind.

"Any idea where the photo albums would be?"

"They could be in this trunk by the wall, it was my Mother's," Miles said.

"Bingo, look at all of these..." inside were several albums from the various generations of Bannermans. I found them fascinating, but they didn't contain anything helpful to the cause.

I sat looking at a page covered with pictures of Miles and his family.

"Well, weren't you cute when you were little," I said. He really was adorable. I felt sad though, looking at that little boy, and knowing what happened to him later.

"I hope you know that all boys under the age of six dressed that way at the time," said Miles.

I laughed.

"Yes, I do know that. I can't imagine why they made boys wear dresses, but I know they did. I wasn't making fun, you really were cute."

In every photo of Miles, he was smiling, like he did in the portrait. I turned several pages and found one that must have been taken when he was nineteen or twenty, he looked just like he does now. Well, other than the semi-transparent-ness.

"How old were you in this photo, nineteen or twenty?" I asked, holding up the book and pointing at the photo in question.

"I was nineteen," Miles said. "I didn't quite make it to twenty."

"I'm sorry, I didn't know," I said. Going by the years 1850-1870 on his portrait, I assumed he was twenty-years-old when he died.

"It's fine, don't worry about it," he said.

I looked back at the photos of Miles, always smiling. In so many early photos I'd seen, people looked so serious, but not Miles.

"Why is that?" I mused.

"Why is what?"

"Why did other people look so serious in photographs back then?" Miles sat on the floor beside me.

"If you didn't hold very still for several very long minutes, the picture wouldn't come out right. It would be blurry. It's easier to have a straight face than to hold a smile, so that's what most people did."

"You've never stopped smiling, have you," I said. "In spite of everything, you've kept your sense of humor."

"So have you. You don't make a big deal of it, but I know it's hard seeing your little sister so sick, your Dad being out of work for so long, and losing so much. It's been a big disappointment having to sacrifice college, but you've kept your sense of humor, too. You're pretty amazing, Anika."

I felt myself blush.

"Yeah, well, nothing I've gone through compares to what happened to you," I said. I looked back at Miles' picture. "Can I keep this?"

Miles looked at me, and I felt myself start to blush again. Cut that out, self!

"It's just… when we get the proof we need, you'll go, you won't be stuck here anymore. I'd like to have a picture to look at, and remember my old friend."

"Sure, you can have it," Miles smiled. "And I won't be your *old* friend until I'm at least two-hundred."

I slipped the photo out of the album, and set it carefully aside.

"Looks like someone made themselves a little nook here," I said, pointing out a pile of old pillows in a corner next to a round window looking out on the back gardens.

Miles' eyes softened as he walked over to look at the spot.

"My sister," he said. "This must have been her hiding place. She told me she had one, but never where it was."

He picked up a delicate paper doll and held it in his hand. I stayed silent, hesitant to intrude on his memories.

Suddenly his forehead creased. He looked intently at the paper doll, then held it out.

"Do you see what I see?"

I bit back the desire to sing a Christmas carol in response. After all, 'tis the season.

"I think so, those are words. Your sister must have recycled a piece of paper to make her doll," I said, wondering why it mattered.

"Anika… look again," he said intensely.

I looked closer, and on the foot of the doll was written the name *Sarah.*

"A letter?" I said, as understanding beginning to dawn.

"A letter!" Miles said back, searching for more dolls and paper scraps.

Feverishly, we lay all the bits of paper we could find on a patch of empty floor, and pieced them together.

Thank goodness Cynthia didn't keep a trash can up here, and no one ever cleaned out her corner! I guess in a house this big, it wouldn't be hard to have places that were seldom visited. That's what Polly said, there were still places she'd never been.

All the pieces assembled, we hurriedly read Sarah's letter.

Dear Mr. and Mrs. Bannerman,

I hope this letter finds you well. I was reminded recently of a poem Delevan once wrote, and am moved to share it with you. I hope you will understand.

> Down the path and through the hole,
> Does the little rabbit go.
> Count to three, and through again,
> Wonder where the carrots been?
> Find the little pile of stones,
> Lift it out and take it home.

I know Delevan would like to think of his sister reciting this in one of their favorite play places. I pray that you will understand.

I will write again soon.

With the greatest of sincerity,

Miss Sarah Williams

We each read it over a few times. Miles looked very puzzled.

"Your brother wasn't very good at poetry, was he," I finally said. After pausing to consider it some more, I added, "I wonder why she never wrote again... or if she did, what happened to the letter."

Miles continued to focus on the words, as if fighting to understand or remember.

Finally he shook his head.

"I don't know, whatever Sarah was trying to tell my parents... it's a riddle. Delevan never wrote that."

We stared at the words some more.

"Do you remember any of the places that you liked to play as a kid?" I asked.

Miles shook his head and shrugged.

"That was so long ago... I'll have to think about it. I just... don't remember."

~***~

With each passing day, Sarah struggled to think of a way to escape so that Dan would never find her. She looked across the ladies' cabin toward the saloon, and disgust washed over her face.

Gambling as always, stupidly drunk, laughing as though he hadn't a care in the world. As though the blood of so many wasn't on his hands, including that of the man she loved.

She turned away. The pain was too great, the desire to fly across the space that separated her from her brother and tear him to pieces, almost too much to bear.

It was fortunate she took the chance while she had it, and hid the heirloom jewels Delevan presented to her as a wedding gift. She knew better than to count on an opportunity to return them, if she waited. Before forcing Sarah to go to the Bannermans and tell them that Miles and Delevan died fighting over her, Dan searched her belongings. It wasn't the first time. It was a small miracle he was too distracted to do so before she had a chance to hide what didn't belong to him. She hoped the Bannermans would read between the lines of the carefully worded letter she mailed at the steamboat's last stop. She hoped they would understand where to find the jewels. She couldn't be direct in her letter. If the message was intercepted, it mustn't give away the hiding place or its contents to anyone else.

She didn't know how, or when, or where, but she would find her freedom, or else die in the attempt. As for now, she couldn't bear to sit here another second. She stood and proceeded to the promenade deck, and fresh air.

She stood, looking out at the muddy water, thinking her sad desperate thoughts. Going to the authorities would backfire, that wasn't even a consideration. Dan somehow pinned the stagecoach murders on her, the handbill revealed that. She'd sought and experienced the consequences of seeking help before. Dan could be so convincing… she knew if it came down to her word against his, he would charm the sense out of anyone within hearing, and she would be the one to suffer. It was no different now, than it had ever been.

She looked up into the sky with a silent plea for help, as a tear escaped and rolled down her cheek. She couldn't go back and change what happened… but what she wouldn't give to be able to start over. To forget.

Sarah turned and walked back to her stateroom. Closing the door and locking it behind her, she threw herself onto her berth. Eventually she was lulled to sleep, the closest thing to escape she would find here.

Chapter 13

"Hi," I said, as Chip and I walked through the door on yet another snow filled day.

"Hi back," smiled Miles.

Chip and Trixie ran upstairs, probably headed for Mission Control, their favorite place to hang out, as well as ours.

"Happy New Year, too," I said.

"And the same to you," said Miles.

"So, did you do anything interesting on New Year's Eve?" I asked, unwinding my scarf and slipping off my snow boots.

"Actually I did," he said.

I stopped what I was doing and looked at him.

Miles smiled.

"I spent the day searching with you, remember?"

I laughed.

"Okay, so that's what you meant. I really had no idea what you were going to say."

"How about you?" asked Miles.

"Well, as I said I would, I went straight home and hung out with my family at the cabin. I did do something fun, though."

"And what was that?" asked Miles.

"I hung out with you all day," I smiled, as I lay my coat across the entryway table.

Miles smiled back.

"For just one day," I said, getting down to business, "how about taking a break from the attic, and searching somewhere else."

"What do you have in mind?" asked Miles.

"We searched your parents' room and didn't find anything. What about yours and Delevan's rooms? Is there any chance your Father would store evidence there, that he collected?"

A shadow crossed Miles' face so quickly, I wondered if I imagined it.

"We can look," he said.

"But you don't want to?" I asked. "Is this too painful?"

"It's fine. And you're right, we need to search those rooms just in case."

"I could search on my own," I said.

"No, let's do it together," Miles said. "Follow me."

I followed Miles up several sets of stairs until we reached the fourth floor.

"So which room are we going to?" I asked.

"Mine," said Miles.

"You really got a workout every day, living all the way up here," I said.

"I did, but wait until you see the view. It was worth it."

Miles opened a door and I stepped into a large room. Miles waved and the drapes opened, letting in the winter sun. I walked to the center window and looked out.

"Wow... that *is* some view."

All around were snowcapped mountains. We were up above the treetops, and the view of the mountains seemed endless. Looking down, I saw the snow-covered garden, the oak tree lined path through the forest, and a plume of smoke that must be from Uncle Mark's cabin.

"Climbing the stairs is definitely worth the view," I said, turning from the window to look around the room. "Let's start with the trunk."

I opened it and began sorting through the contents. I stopped suddenly, and looked at Miles.

"This is yours," I said, holding a worn and much used bible with his name written inside.

Miles nodded.

I looked at the bible in my hand, then back at Miles.

"Did... anyone else use this room after you?" I asked.

"No," said Miles. "Although my parents gave up the search to find out what happened that day in the clearing, they kept my room and Delevan's exactly as they were the day we left them. No one has touched them since. There are plenty of rooms to choose from, I suppose no one felt there was a need to use ours. What you're looking through right now, is the trunk that I used on my last trip. It was delivered after I was, well, gone."

"My goodness, Miles," I said in dismay. "No wonder this is difficult for you. You never come here, do you."

"No," he said. "It just... no, I never come here."

"Well come on," I said, slamming the trunk shut. "We're leaving. The longer I'm in here, the less I believe we'll find anything useful, anyway."

Miles hesitated.

"Come on!" I urged him. "It's not like I can drag you out of here."

A smile flickered across Miles' face at that thought, and he followed me out of the room.

"If there is *ever* a place where you don't want to go, or search, then tell me," I ordered. "No trying to be Mr. Tough guy. You are tough, but come on, you don't deserve to be tortured. So don't let me, in my ignorance, do that to you."

"Okay," Miles agreed. "No more torture. I'm all for that."

I led the way to Mission Control.

"Let's hang out in here," I said. "It's New Year's Day anyway, it's a holiday. What were we thinking, intending to work!"

Miles looked much more like himself again. He coped so well, it was easy to think his semi-transparent state didn't bother him, he just took it in stride. But the truth was, he lost so much. He lost everything. Seeing his old room brought all of that back.

"How about checkers, ever play?" I asked, seeing the checkerboard on a low table near the fireplace. I sat in one of the chairs beside it.

"Are you suggesting that we play?" he looked surprised and a little confused.

"Yes, let's do. If you know how, and want to."

"Okay... I thought you hated games, though."

"I do, I abhor them," I said.

179

Miles laughed, and looked even more confused.

"What is this then, an attempt at penance? What can you possibly have done that's so terrible?"

"I'm not trying to pay penance for anything," I laughed. "I thought with you, checkers might be fun. Don't you think so?"

"Yes… maybe. But at the first sign of misery, we stop," he said, and I laughed again.

"Okay, agreed," I smiled.

"Alright, then. I'll set them up. I'm not convinced you aren't trying to pay penance for something, though…"

There was laughter in his eyes.

"I'm not. I can't imagine why you think that," I said, as if I hadn't spent several hours regaling him with tales of game-night misery.

"I wonder," he smiled too, then turned his attention to the checkers and checkerboard.

"That is just too convenient, that superpower you have," I said, as the checkers neatly marched to the appropriate places on the board. "You'll have to teach me how to play though, I only vaguely remember."

"Alright then," said Miles. "I'll start, and tell you the rules as we go."

I would feel tortured if I were playing this game with anyone else, but with Miles it was different. I had fun, and it was a huge relief to see him smiling and laughing again.

We played several games, and then moved on to dominoes. I asked if he knew how to play poker, since he travelled in the wild, wild west, and he laughed and said absolutely not.

The time came to wake my sleeping dog, who was none too anxious to leave the warm fireside, and head back home.

Miles and Trixie walked with us to the entryway as they did every day that we came to the castle, and I began the task of bundling up to brave the cold, dark, winter outdoors.

We said goodbye, and Chip and I walked back to the cabin through the frigid evening air.

"Brrr, it is really cold!" I said to Mom, as Chip and I hurried through the door. "Do you have a fire going?"

"Well of course," said Mom. "We've got to burn all that wood your Dad chopped, after all. We'd hate for him to feel unappreciated, wouldn't we."

I shed my layers as quickly as possible, and knelt in front of the roaring fire. It was amazing how cold it got at night once the sun went down.

"Here," Mom said, handing me a mug of tea.

"Thanks, Mom," I said, wrapping my hands around it, and taking a sip. "Why is it that once you start to get warm, then the shaking starts?"

"I don't know honey, but that does happen, doesn't it. "

I'd have to ask Miles. I'll bet he would know.

"So how are the kids?" I asked. "It's awfully quiet."

"Well, Tryon is sound asleep. We may be up late if he gets woke up, but I'm hoping he'll sleep through the night. He missed taking a nap today. I took him outside and let him play in the snow for a while, and he wore himself out."

"How about Doree?" I asked, drinking more tea and appreciating the warmth.

"She's asleep too. I'm looking forward to the day when the treatment she's on starts to make her feel better. It's a process. One that finally we're embarking on."

It was nice getting to chat with Mom for a minute. We ate dinner together and then went to bed, knowing if we did that, then Tryon was less likely to wake up wide awake and stay up the rest of the night!

As I lay in bed wrapped in blankets and still shivering a little from the cold walk, I thought about Miles and the search we started on. I never imagined that his and Delevan's rooms would be untouched after all these years.

We absolutely had to find that evidence and free him. If Alfred managed to get himself appointed trustee, I could just imagine the sick tour he'd arrange for the resort he had planned. If Miles interfered and let his presence be known, then he'd have no peace whatsoever. Alfred would probably get the castle on an episode of Ghost Trackers, and the lies about Miles would be broadcast for the whole country, or anyone who watched that show anyway, to hear.

It made me angry just thinking about it. Miles was quite possibly the nicest guy that ever lived, and what happened to him was just worse than wrong. Thinking of the further insult and injury Alfred would inflict if he had the chance, made me furious. I'd make sure he didn't get that chance.

Fresh snow powdered the ground as Chip and I made our way to the castle. We saw footprints made by different animals and birds, and it was interesting trying to figure out which creature made them.

The limbs of the deciduous trees looked as though they were covered in white velvet. Two doves sat together on a limb. It was picture worthy, so I took one with my iPhone.

It was pretty cold though, and I was thankful to reach the castle.

"Hi," I said, as I walked in the door. Trixie was outside, and Chip stayed there with her.

"Hi back," Miles smiled, but seemed a little distracted.

"What's up?"

Something clearly was.

"Alfred was here last night," said Miles.

"What happened?" I asked, as I began taking off my snow boots and other winter outerwear.

"He was sneaking around outside the castle. I don't know what he intended to do, but I sent him packing."

"How did you do that?"

Miles couldn't help smiling.

"His car drove down the mountain without him, and he followed after it as fast as he could."

I laughed. I could just see it.

"That's too funny," I said. "Serves him right, he's no business being here."

"No, he hasn't," agreed Miles. "Unfortunately if Trixie or I don't see or hear something, we're not aware of it. We'll both be paying attention though, in case he returns."

"If he does, I have a feeling he'll decide the murderous ghost he wants to market along with the resort, isn't a fan of his, and neither is his dog!"

Miles laughed.

"No kidding, Trixie and I could have all sorts of fun with that."

"It sure is strange though, isn't it," I mused. "Polly doesn't know how Alfred found out her grandson was missing. But he did, and has been hanging around town. He's been here twice that we know of, since her grandson was found."

"Are you thinking Alfred had something to do with his accident?" asked Miles with concern.

I thought about that.

"Maybe I do. The timing is just awfully peculiar."

"Well... I'm not sure he'll show up again after the strange things that happened the last two times he was here, but if he does, I'll follow him around and see if I can get any information."

"I'm probably experiencing a case of over-active imagination," I admitted.

"Still... if he does come back, I won't send him hurtling down the mountain road until I figure out what he's up to."

"Okay, good. And try and stay under the radar, because if he does get control of the castle, I don't want him knowing you're here. He would find ways to make your existence miserable, and I wouldn't be able to do anything about it."

"Alright. I'll cause trouble in as subtle a way as possible," Miles said.

"Good," I said. "So... on to the attic?"

"On to the attic," Miles agreed.

After the long walk upstairs, Miles and I continued where we left off after our last search. The attic was huge, and jam-packed with such a vast assortment of furniture and other items. A museum would have a field day if they got ahold of even a small portion of its contents.

"Are you quite sure your ancestors built this house to hold people, or was it for storing furniture and other things?" I asked, looking around for a moment at all of the places still left to search. "It looks like no one ever got rid of anything, they just put it in storage rooms and the attic."

"It's excessive, isn't it," agreed Miles. "I hope Polly's grandson pulls through, and maybe he'll do something better than leave all of this in storage. You could suggest that, as estate manager. I doubt he has any idea what's in the castle, I didn't realize myself, until I started searching with you."

I sneezed.

"Bless you," said Miles.

"Thanks," I said. Something was starting to get to me, allergies maybe.

"So has Sarah's poem triggered any memories yet?" I asked.

"Not yet. I'll keep trying to figure out what she meant. I hope it wasn't something only Cynthia and Delevan knew."

Me too. How awful if that's the case!

We searched some more, and I sneezed several more times.

"Do I need to dust again?" asked Miles.

"I don't think so, maybe I'm allergic to something. But it's so cool how you can do that. Mom would love you, if she could see you that is, and got to know you, and you came over and cleaned once a week."

Miles laughed at that.

"Interesting, I'd need to clean in order for your Mom to like me."

I rolled my eyes. "She'd *love* you if she just knew you, although she'd need to see you to do that. I just meant, what woman wouldn't love to never have to dust again."

"How is Polly's grandson, by the way?" asked Miles.

"The same," I said. "No better, no worse."

I pointed to the rafters, where an old bicycle with a huge front wheel hung.

"That's some bicycle. Did you ever ride one?"

"No, that was after my time," said Miles. "They weren't very safe though, the Bannerman who owned it was thrown headfirst over the handlebars when he ran into a rut in the road."

"Yikes, was he hurt?" I asked.

"He lived, but yeah, he was badly injured. That's when the bike came to live in the attic."

"How did he go over the handlebars?" I wondered.

"Well, look at how it's made. If it ran into anything on the road, it would tip forward easily. With the handlebars in the way of the rider's legs, he's got nowhere to go then, but headfirst over the front of the bicycle. Later on, bikes were made so the rider's legs went over the handlebars. That way, if they were thrown off they had a chance of landing on their feet instead of their head."

We continued searching and talking, and I continued sneezing.

When it was time to leave I bundled up again, preparing to brave the outdoors.

"I keep thinking we'll find something else in the attic, since we found the guns and the note there."

"Me too," said Miles. "Searching with you is fun though, even when we don't find anything."

"I agree. I look forward to it every day. Well, other than week-ends, when you boycott me," I said, rolling my eyes.

Miles found my annoyance amusing, but didn't comment.

We said goodbye, and I called Chip and headed for home.

I hate being sick.

I bundled my coat tighter around me and pulled my cap down over my ears. My scarf protected my face, lungs and throat from the freezing air, to some extent. It was better than nothing, anyway.

I stomped my boots as free of snow as possible outside the door of the castle, then Chip and I went inside.

I basked in the warm air, and Chip loped over to see Trixie, who lay on the floor chewing... something. I hope whatever she has isn't important. I just don't feel like wrestling her for it to find out.

"Hi," I said to Miles as I unbundled.

"Hi back," he said, then looked at me with concern. "Are you okay?"

"Just a cold... hey, we just discovered a new superpower you have. I can't make you sick."

"Maybe not, but you can make yourself a whole lot worse by walking all the way here in the freezing cold. What did you do, sneak out before your Mom saw you?"

"You know me so well," I said. I was impressed.

"I also know you ought to be home in bed."

"Yeah, maybe, but I'd like to see you try and take a sick day with a very energetic three-year-old brother in the house. Somehow the parents have instilled in him that he's not to disturb Doreen, but I think he takes all her share of his crazy boy energy, and heaps it on me. I doubt I'd get any rest."

Miles still looked concerned. "Well, you don't need to be searching through any rooms, anyway. Take it easy here, if you can't at home."

"Okay," I said. I really wasn't feeling very well. "I want to search more in the attic, though."

"We'll do it later. I'll search when you're not here, if it makes you feel better. Come on, follow me."

Miles led me to a room that was much more up to date than the rest of the house. What I'd seen so far, anyway. It had fat sofas and recliners, and a very large TV.

I dropped onto the couch and Miles used his superpowers to pass me a throw to wrap up in, then brought me a Sprite. Good thing I stocked the fridge in the cellar for the yard men Polly was so concerned about. My good deed was coming back to bless me now.

"Want to watch a movie?" Miles asked.

"Sure," I said.

"What would you like to see?" he asked. "We can get almost anything using the Roku."

"Nothing I have to concentrate very hard on," I said. "How about *Tangled*?"

"Okay," Miles smiled.

It probably wasn't his kind of movie, being neither a kid nor a girl, but I appreciated him humoring me.

Miles started the movie and we watched it together. We laughed in the same places, and at the end when Flynn Rider sacrificed himself for Rapunzel, I'm pretty sure he was as choked up as I was. It never fails, no matter how many times I see it, it gets to me.

I watched Miles as the credits passed by and realized I was going to have to make a huge sacrifice. When we found the evidence we were looking for, I'd need to give up our friendship and let him go. That was going to be an almost unbearable loss. Just how much I'd be losing when he was gone, hit me hard in a way it hadn't before. Being the one left behind... now I knew on a whole different level what Rapunzel felt like. But she was a Disney Princess, she got Flynn back in the end.

Lucky her.

"Good movie," Miles said.

"You choose the next one," I replied, glad that my cold was a good cover for the sudden case of watery eyes I suffered from.

"Okay, let me think..." he thought. "Have you seen the *Mummy* movies?"

"The really ancient movie with a mummy in it, or the new ones with Brendan Fraser?"

"The new ones. The first is my favorite," Miles said.

"Let's watch it, then."

"Okay, I'll find it... how are you feeling, by the way? Can I get you anything?" Miles asked.

"I'm okay. It feels good just to lay here, and not have a three-year-old try and crush me. Or get me to read. Or play."

"If you do need anything, let me know and I'll get it for you," said Miles.

If only it was so easy.

Miles' movie was really good. I enjoyed it. I couldn't help wishing I could find a Book of the Dead for Miles.

"Think what you're saying, though," he said. "I wouldn't want someone to die so I could be solid again, and I find the thought of living in someone else's body extremely disturbing."

I said that out loud? I must be feverish. I need to stop thinking, who knows what random and private thought I might make public next.

We watched movies all day. *Night at the Museum, Journey to the Center of the Earth...* the new one. We started out watching the old one, but had enough when they started to sing. Who thought *that* would be a good idea!

It was the best day I'd had in a long time, in spite of how sick I was. I enjoyed the movies, but it was Miles' company that made the day for me. It's amazingly fun to be able to just joke around with someone who understands my sense of humor and can hold his own.

The day came to an end, and Miles convinced me to call Mom for a ride home.

It was Friday, so when we reached the cabin I crawled in bed and that's where I spent the rest of the weekend.

Chapter 14

After finding Sarah's paper doll letter and Miles and Delevan's guns, I felt sure the attic would hold more clues. So far though, we'd found all sorts of fascinating things and I'd learned a lot about history, but no evidence from the crimes that were committed. We'd been searching the attic for over a month, it was unbelievable how much was packed in there.

As I prepared to walk out the cabin door into the cold January day, Mom stopped me.

"Wait, before you go... you've been gone so much, we haven't had a chance to *really* chat lately," she said.

Uh-oh. Didn't I have this talk with Mom *and* Dad just a few weeks ago?

"What's going on, Mom?" I tried to sound casual.

Mom's forehead puckered.

"I know you're taking your job very seriously, and believe me, your Dad and I are so proud of your work ethic and the job you're doing. Dad was so impressed when you took him for a tour, and he saw what you've been up to."

So where's the great big *BUT* fit in?

"But... you have been gone so much lately. I'm still concerned that you aren't taking time to hang out with people your own age, at least part of the time. You've been invited to go out every weekend, but you rarely take advantage of those opportunities. You're either at work, or here at the cabin. This isn't like you at all. You've given up so much, having to move here, and I—we—want to make sure you're okay. You went to the castle on Friday, in spite of being so sick you needed me to pick you up later. I'm just concerned about you," she finished. Mom looked so worried, I felt bad for her.

"I'm fine, Mom. Really. And I'm saving for college, that's important to me."

"That all sounds wonderful, but it's not good to spend all your time alone, there are opportunities to make friends here if you'll take them," she said.

Poor Mom, I wish she wasn't worried about me. I didn't need that, and she didn't need that, but I didn't know what to say.

"Well, I'm kind of friends with that red-haired girl, what's-her-name... Susan's daughter, she's really nice..." well that didn't help my case any.

I gave Mom a bear hug, told her I was great and not to worry so much, I still had friends I talked to on the phone (I *did* talk to Sheila once) and how did she know I didn't spend all my time at the castle talking to them? Okay, I didn't, but how did she know I didn't?

Mom hugged me back and smiled, although not a hundred watt.

"Okay," she said. "Just... remember, Anika, you need more than a dog for companionship. Make sure you invest in more than that."

"Okay, Mom," I said, as I went out the back door to join Chip, who wondered what was taking me so long.

As we trudged through the snow to the castle I thought about what Mom said. She had no idea I spent all day talking to Miles. He was so easy to be around. It was a lot easier hanging out with him than spending time trying to make friends with other people who might or might not be friendship material, anyway.

Suddenly I got what Mom was trying to say. And she had no idea how right she was, either. I was working hard to free Miles. In essence, I was working hard to get him out of my life, and when he was gone... I'd be alone with my dog.

"No offense," I said to Chip. He wagged his tail at me.

I suddenly felt depressed. I had to move past it though and keep going, no matter how bad I felt just thinking of not being able to hang out with Miles anymore. He shouldn't be stuck here alone. I couldn't stay with him forever... it wasn't my house, for one thing!

The right thing to do was to keep searching for proof. That was the only way to keep him from being alone with *his* dog again in the future. He'd already spent over a hundred and forty years that way.

I stepped out of the woods and into the garden, and waved at the fellow making repairs to the roof of the guest house. Chip bounded over and rolled on his back next to another workman, and got a belly rub from him. I laughed inside, wondering what Polly would think about that. Chip was really keeping them in line.

I ran up the steps of the castle and through the door.

"Hi," I said.

"Hi back," said Miles. "Any news on Polly's grandson?"

"Nope, nothing new. There's been no change in Second-Miles' condition."

"Second-Miles?" he looked puzzled.

"I have to keep you two apart in my head, so you're Miles and he's Second-Miles."

"Got it. If I ever hear you burst through the door and yell 'Second-Miles!' I'll know not to answer."

I tried to hit him with my purse.

"I'd be black and blue hanging around you, if I didn't have my superpowers," he smiled.

I rolled my eyes dramatically.

"Have you remembered anything that would explain what Sarah was trying to say?" I asked.

"I do remember playing in the woods when Delevan and I were really young," Miles said. "I don't think Cynthia knew about that... but there was a cave on the property. Even before I became semi-transparent guy, I hadn't been there in years. It's the only place I can think of, though."

"Well, she does say *through the hole,* maybe she means a cave entrance," I mused, as I looked at the letter again. "Do you remember where this cave is?"

"Maybe. We can look and see," he said.

"Let me grab a flashlight, and we'll be on our way."

The dogs followed us as we walked through the garden and found the path Miles thought was the right one. It led uphill at first, then dropped sharply. We looked down and saw a narrow rock ledge surrounded by frost covered ferns.

"There," Miles said, pointing to the snow and fern covered ledge. The dogs were rooting around tracking something on the ground, so we left them to play and turned back to the path.

We, or more like I, scrambled down to the small ledge in front of the cave opening.

"I'll go first," said Miles.

"After you, little rabbit," I said under my breath, as I pulled out my flashlight and stooped to crawl in behind him.

Stepping into the cave was like entering a whole different world. The sound of dripping water echoed, and pools of water lay at intervals on the cave floor. It smelled… like a cave, and the air was cool and moist.

"We used to keep candles here, and matches," Miles said, as he pointed just inside the mouth of the cave.

"Looks like something ate your candles," I pointed out.

I used the flashlight to explore our immediate surroundings.

"See those?" Miles pointed. "They're called soda straws."

"That's a good name for them, very descriptive," I said, looking at the formation that indeed looked like a bunch of soda straws stuck to the roof of the cave.

"And there are some fried eggs," he pointed out.

"Oh, how strange! That's exactly what they look like."

"There are some pretty delicate formations in here, so be very careful and don't touch anything if you can help it. It takes a long time for these to form, and we don't want to damage them."

He was so smart. I don't think I'd be able to learn all the things he knows, even if I had three-hundred years to do nothing but study.

"So what's the difference between a stalactite and a stalagmite?" I asked.

"Think of it this way," Miles replied. "A stalactite holds tight to the roof of the cave. A stalagmite rises up, mightily."

"Cool, I just may be able to remember that then," I said. "What makes caves smell like this?"

"Do you really want to know? Because once I tell you, there's no taking it back," he said.

He seemed amused by something. He had me really wondering what on earth he was talking about.

"What on earth are you talking about?" I asked.

"Part of what makes up the cave smell, is bat guano," Miles said.

"And what is that?" I asked, feeling no more enlightened than before.

"Well, that would be bat droppings," he enlightened me. I looked disgusted, and he tried unsuccessfully to hold back a grin.

"So there are bats in here?" I asked, looking overhead a bit nervously.

"Yes, but they aren't going to bother you, and let's don't bother them, they're hibernating this time of year. If they're disturbed too much or too often, they won't have enough energy to survive until there are insects for them to feed on again. And believe me, the time will come soon when you'll be thankful to have the little mosquito catchers out hunting."

"Well! You are a walking encyclopedia," I said.

Miles just grinned at me again, and we moved on to the point of our spelunking endeavor.

"Okay, so how does the poem go...

> *Down the path and through the hole,*
> *Does the little rabbit go.*
> *Count to three, and through again,*
> *Wonder where the carrots been?*
> *Find the little pile of stones,*
> *Lift it out and take it home."*

Miles looked around and pointed to the third opening from the entrance. We knelt and crawled down the sloping tunnel.

Standing, I searched the cavern we were in with the flashlight. It was a lot bigger than the one we were in before. There wasn't time to explore though, we needed to continue with our riddle note.

"There," Miles said.

I could make out a stone filled crevice in the wall to the left of the tunnel we passed through.

Moving forward slowly, we looked at each other for a long moment.

My heart suddenly felt like lead.

"Well, this is it," I said, trying to sound upbeat. It didn't work.

We stood and stared at the crevice for several minutes, then looked back at each other.

"If this works, I'm... going to really miss you," Miles said softly.

I wiped my eyes with my sleeve.

"I don't feel like I'm ready for this, and I'll miss you too... but you shouldn't have to stay here forever. If you do, then someday you'll be alone again..."

Miles looked down and nodded, and we began to dig out the rocks in the crevice. Underneath was a decorated case. It looked extremely old, of course. With another long look at each other, I opened it.

A heavy bag slipped out and slithered across my knees. I opened the drawstring.

"There's a bunch of jewelry in here," I said, holding the bag out to Miles. "Carrots, as in diamond karats."

Miles' eyebrows knit as he studied the jewels.

"I recognize some of this. My Mother used to wear these. They were passed down in the family, so Delevan must have given them to Sarah when he proposed."

"And she hid them here... to save them from her evil brother Dan? And then sent the coded note in case it was intercepted."

A wrinkled paper lay in the case, and I picked it up.

"It's the handbill. There's Dan," I pointed. "Grrr!"

"My sympathies exactly..." said Miles.

We sat a moment looking at the bag of jewelry and the handbill. There was nothing else here. Nothing to indicate what really happened that day.

"We have the handbill," I said. "That might shed some doubt, at least…"

Miles made a face.

"It would just support a different lie, like the death certificates would. Sarah said she didn't murder those people, and I believe her."

"You have a lot of respect for Sarah," I said.

"My brother loved her. And she lied to protect my family from her brother, not to hurt them. Or me."

I folded the paper and put it back in the case with the jewels.

"So you had no idea these were missing?" I asked.

"No, I didn't. All of this would have belonged to Delevan's wife someday, so my Mother's jewelry wasn't something I thought anything about when I was alive. It may have been discussed after I died, but by the time I returned, the topic was laid to rest and never mentioned within my hearing. But I guess this is the family treasure mentioned in the story your Uncle told you."

"I guess so," I said. "So what now?"

"The jewelry belongs to Second-Miles, or will, once he comes into his inheritance," Miles said. "Let's bring it back to the house and put it someplace safe so you can give it to Polly to give to him, whenever they come back home."

All the way back through the cave and back to the castle, I couldn't help being relieved that Miles was still here.

I ought to be prepared for him to go, considering accomplishing that was the goal since the day we met. And yet we'd become such great friends, the thought of losing him grew more horrible with each passing day.

I was completely at war with myself. The selfish side wanted to quit searching. The unselfish side, the one that cared more about Miles than about myself, wanted to keep searching and track down the proof I knew on a gut level was out there waiting for me to find it.

The unselfish side was going to win, but not today. Today, both sides were relieved to have a little more time.

We climbed the front steps and went straight to Mission Control.

"What do you say we take another break from searching for the rest of the day?" suggested Miles.

My sentiments exactly!

"Sounds like a great idea," I replied.

Miles opened the safe which was hidden behind a moving book-case, and I put the bag with the jewels and the handbill inside. Miles closed the safe and moved the bookcase back in place.

"You know..." Miles said. "That was a lot harder than I expected it to be."

"Moving the shelf?" I asked.

Miles laughed.

"No, not moving the shelf! I meant, when I thought we were about to succeed. When I thought we found proof."

"Yeah, I know what you mean," I said. "I feel very guilty that I'm glad you're still here."

"Me too," said Miles.

"It's just... you're the best friend I've ever had. You are so easy to talk to, and funny, and I can't imagine what I'm going to do when you're gone," I said. "But, I don't want you stuck here for my sake. We do have to keep searching. And yet, I'm glad today wasn't the day we found proof."

Miles nodded.

"I feel the same way... if I could talk to you forever, I'd be per-fectly content. But I worry about you, that I'm your only friend right now."

Miles flinched when I took a whack at him, which made us both laugh, since of course I can't actually touch him.

"I know you're sick of your Mom telling you that you ought to go make some friends. But she's right, and I can't stand the thought of you being alone in the future. I'm selfish enough though, to be glad I'm still here, and that we can be friends for a little while longer."

I sighed.

"I can tell you right now, there isn't another person out there that's going to fit me as a friend as well as you do. But fine, I will make an effort to make some solid friends."

"It sounds like Jenny would make a good one," said Miles.

"She probably would. I'll try to invest some time in that."

"Okay, good," said Miles. "Then I won't worry about you."

"Okay, good, because there's nothing that bugs me more than someone worrying about me!" I said. "You just watch it Mister, or I'll stay up all night looking for proof!"

Miles laughed at that, and I laughed with him.

We spent the rest of the day talking and played a few games of checkers. It was growing on me. Although I can't imagine wanting to play it with anyone else.

The time came for Chip and I to head home, and Miles and Trixie walked with us. Someday we'd each lose our best friend, but at least today was not that day.

Chapter 15

Mom's talk made me think, but the experience in the cave convinced me. She and Miles were both right. I needed to add some new relationships to my life, otherwise I was going to curl up and die, assuming Miles "moved on" once we cleared him. I might curl up and die anyway, but I needed to at least try to build some friendships to fall back on.

So when I ran into Jenny in town as I was running an errand for Mom, I accepted when she invited me for another game night. It wasn't really my thing, but it was something.

At seven-thirty on Sunday night, I arrived at the *Bean There, Bun That* and searched for a place to park. The spaces in front were taken, so I pulled into the parking lot behind the coffee shop and found an empty spot. I parked the car and walked through the narrow alley between two buildings to reach the front of the shop. Opening the door and stepping inside, I basked in the warmth and the scent of fresh roasted coffee.

"Hi Jenny," I said, speaking loudly to be heard above the music that blared, as I made my way through the crowded establishment.

Hi, Anika! I'm so glad you made it!"

"There are a *lot* of people here tonight," I said, looking around. I was thinking it was awfully loud, too.

"Yeah, there are, and some of our regulars aren't even here. Like Nate, you know him, but then several others, too."

We both looked around.

"Are you getting anything?" I asked. "I thought I'd get a latte."

"That sounds good. I'll wait with you in line."

We talked and got to know each other a little better. Miles and Mom were both right, Jenny would make a good friend. Too bad Mom and Miles couldn't know each other. They'd get along great, even if Miles didn't do all the dusting. They agreed so much about what would be good for me.

As we waited for our orders, several people I remembered from the last time I showed up for game night, came in and stood talking with us. A guy I didn't recognize walked over and pulled Jenny aside. He said something, I wasn't sure what, and she seemed hesitant. I wondered what was going on. Finally she turned, and introduced him to me.

"Anika, this is Bill."

"Hey there," said Bill, lifting his chin as he said it.

Not a bad looking guy, but definitely not my type. I've never thought the muscle-bound look was a good one. It wasn't a low attractiveness rating on my personal scale that gave me a bad feeling about him, though. Part of it was Jenny's hesitation and demeanor when she introduced us. The rest of it was the way he looked at me, and a strong gut feeling.

"Hi, Bill," I said, glad my order was called right then. I turned away to retrieve my drink, then walked over to the straw, sugar, creamer, napkin station, for napkins I didn't need.

Jenny got her drink and we sat in a booth with a couple of other people she knew. Jenny did her best to include me, but it's hard when you're in a group that knows each other well, and has common experiences and memories. It's impossible to keep up with the conversation half the time, it's as if they're talking in code. It was ridiculously loud, too, which didn't help any.

"I hate to do this," Jenny said after a while. "I have to get going. I promised Mom I'd help her tonight."

We said goodbye. Before long, the other two friends also had to leave, which really was not a disappointment to me. I'm sure they're nice, maybe I'll get to know them eventually. But if we were friends, they'd be the sort of friends that take work. Not effortless, like Miles. Not like Jenny, either.

I was about to leave too, when Bill, the guy Jenny introduced me to, slid into the booth across from me.

"So you're Anika," he said.

"Since the day I was born," I replied.

He looked confused.

"Well hey," he recovered, "some of us are about to head to Joe's. I'll give you a ride."

Joe's is a bar outside of Cedar Oaks. No way would building codes allow it in city limits, it would ruin the atmosphere. I didn't like his assumption that I was going with him, or the look in his eyes. It made me feel like prey.

"I don't know how old you are Bill, but I'm not twenty-one."

When I'm twenty-one I won't be hitting up bars, either. A good friend of mine was killed driving under the influence, and even if I'd been so inclined before, which I wasn't, that would have cured me of wanting anything to do with alcohol.

"What difference does it make?" he asked.

My hand was on the table, holding my latte. He moved his hand and ran a finger along the back of mine. I jerked away, bristling.

"The difference between legal and illegal," I retorted.

"Aww, you're kidding!" Bill the jerk laughed. "You can't be serious. So don't tell me, you've never been to a bar before. No, wait. You've never even had a drink!"

I gave him the raised-eyebrow look.

"Aww, that's just wrong! You've gotta come. It's about time you got out and lived a little," he laughed some more.

Miles laughs, and I know everything is right with the world. Bill the jerk laughs, and I know everything isn't.

While those thoughts ran through my head, Bill the jerk leaned back and propped his foot on the seat beside me, invading my personal space, and blocking me from leaving the booth. I did not like that. At all.

"No thanks. My kind of living and yours don't combine."

I turned sideways and got one foot out from under the table and onto the seat, then stood and jumped over Bill the jerk's leg and out of the booth. Being short pays off at last! I couldn't do that if I had longer legs.

I walked to a table and sat. I barely remembered meeting these people, but there wasn't a place for Bill the jerk to sit. I felt shaken after that encounter. My gut instinct was screaming Red Alert.

When my heart rate slowed, I left the coffee shop for home. I watched until Bill the jerk was busy talking to someone else, so he wouldn't see me leave.

I hurried through the narrow space between the two buildings. Mom's car was in sight, when my arm was grabbed from behind. I was nearly jerked off my feet as I spun around, struggling for traction on the icy pavement. Bill the jerk had hold of my arm.

Adrenalin made my heart pound so hard, I could barely breathe.

"Let go Bill, I'm leaving," I managed to say as I tried to wrench my arm free.

He smiled, and I felt sick. My efforts to free myself amused him. He squeezed my arm so tight I thought it would break.

"So am I," Bill the jerk said, "And you're coming with me."

"No! I'm not going with you." I struggled to keep my balance and gain traction and get my hand in my pocket without falling.

"You might as well reconsider," Bill the jerk said in a tone that meant I had no choice, as he sneered at my efforts to free myself.

"FIRE!" I screamed at the top of my lungs.

That startled Bill the jerk, and for a brief second his grip on my arm slackened. I tore free, but he managed to grab hold of my forearm, nearly crushing it.

"No one's gonna hear you with that music blaring, and we're all alone out here," he smirked, looking around. "Nice try, though."

He started to walk, dragging me along with him through the parking lot. It was all I could do to stay on my feet on the slippery surface as I struggled to keep as far away from wherever he wanted to take me as I could. If he would just slip and get off balance or better yet, fall down, I might have a chance. But his weight was giving him an advantage in more ways than one.

"Let go!" My hand lost all circulation, he was squeezing my arm so tight.

"If you haven't noticed, I'm a whole lot bigger than you are. Fighting's only gonna make this harder on you," he said.

I slipped and went down on one knee.

Bill the jerk stopped, and I stuffed my hand in my pocket. He looked down at me as he took out a set of keys and pressed the unlock button. The van in front of us chirped.

My breath came in shallow gasps as panic threatened to overwhelm me. I fumbled with the contents of my pocket, my fingers numb with cold, as he pulled me to my feet and reached for the latch.

In a tone that insinuated something entirely different than his original invitation to go to a bar with friends, he said, "You need a lesson on how to have fun, and you're about to get one."

My blood turned to ice as he pulled the door open.

Shaking, I managed to flip the nozzle on the can of pepper spray in my pocket to the "on" position and gripped it tightly in my hand. You don't go out walking a dog without pepper spray, especially in the woods. You never know what kind of wild animal you may run into. Same for coffee shops, apparently.

As he shoved me towards the open door, I leveled the pepper spray at his face and let him have it.

He let me go and jumped backwards. It probably wasn't the first time he was on the receiving end of one of these. His reaction kept the pepper spray from hitting him full in the eyes, but it did get on his face and all over his chest.

"Geeez, what's the matter with you?! I was only having a little fun," he choked out indignantly, starting to cough as the fumes began to envelop him.

I kept the pepper spray trained on him, and backed toward Mom's car. Bill the jerk coughed some more, angrily swiping at his face with his hands.

"I was just joking around! You don't have to take everything so serious," Bill the jerk exclaimed angrily, as if I was too stupid to know the difference between fun and assault.

Sure, it's all my fault, a big misunderstanding.

"Do not *ever* touch me again!" I glared.

I reached Mom's car and got in. I locked the doors and somehow managed to get the key in the ignition in spite of how badly I was shaking, and drove away.

I shook so bad I had to pull into the grocery store parking lot and wait for the adrenaline to work its way through my system. Then I started to cry. I've never been so scared in my life. What almost happened made me physically ill. I fought to keep from losing the latte I had earlier. I wasn't unlocking the door for anything. If I threw up, I'd just have to clean the car later.

I wanted more than anything to go straight to Miles and tell him what happened. But then he'd be upset, and use his superpowers to annihilate the guy. The annihilation part I was okay with, but I couldn't stand for Miles to be worried about me, and he would be. I thought about telling Mom, but the last thing our family needed was for Mom to be strung up on murder charges.

It would only hurt the people I loved if I told them, I decided. There were no witnesses, and I couldn't prove what he tried to do. If I went to the Sheriff, it would be my word against his.

I leaned back and tried to take deep breaths and calm my pounding heart. I looked at my watch and groaned. I needed to figure out a plan. If Mom saw me now, she'd know something horrible happened. I was in no shape to come up with a clever re-direction.

One thing was certain, I couldn't go home yet. Mom would still be up, and insist on knowing how my evening went. I'd have to wait, it was my best chance of getting past her.

I huddled in the car, pulling my coat tighter around me in the extreme cold and tried to get a handle on the tears that were still running down my cheeks.

I waited until ten-thirty. Frozen nearly solid, I drove back to the cabin and parked the car, exiting as quietly as I possibly could. Mom's bedroom light was on… if she just had her door shut, I'd be okay.

Without a sound I snuck into my and Doreen's room, and quickly changed into my tank top and yoga pants. I breathed a sigh of relief as I slid under the covers of my bed, wondering if I'd ever be warm again, and pretended to be asleep.

Mom would never know.

No one would.

Talking about it would only upset people.

Talking about it only upset people.

Mom bumped into me as I walked out of my and Doreen's room the next morning. She grabbed me by the arm.

"WHAT HAPPENED?!"

I looked down and saw that my bicep and forearm were badly bruised, in varying shades of black and purple. Yeesh.

I gently extricated my arm, drew a blank on ways to redirect or distract her, and told her what happened.

Mom was upset. Very upset. She was upset it happened, and upset at me for not telling her.

Then I got upset. I said the only reason I went to the stupid thing, was because of all the pressure to get out and "make friends". I air quoted and eye rolled. The only reason I didn't tell her, is because I wanted to avoid *this*. Then I started to cry.

Then Mom started to cry. Then Tryon started to cry, and Doreen, who really didn't need any excitement.

This is why I didn't tell her!

I angrily wiped my eyes with the back of my hand, and set to work reassuring Doreen that everything was okay.

Mom fed Tryon breakfast and got him settled down, while I got dressed and snuck out of the house. I was so done for the day.

I trudged to the castle in a bad mood. I even forgot to bring Chip. Poor guy, he hates it when people argue. He was probably hiding under my bed.

I tried to snap out of it.

Fortunately the piano tuner arrived as I walked up to the door, so seeing Miles was delayed. If he saw me he'd know I was upset, and I didn't want to explain why.

I tried to put on a happier face than the not-Happy Cleaners woman, and ushered the man inside.

It took over three hours. Piano tuning done right isn't a speedy process. He played several trilling notes in rapid succession, then made an adjustment, played again, not a song, but it sounded cool.

I stayed in the piano room, and by the time he finished, I was calm again. I scheduled additional appointments for him to tune the other pianos in the house (yes, there were several), and he saw himself out. I heard the front door close behind him.

"Are you okay?" asked Miles, as he appeared beside me.

"Yeah, fine," I said, and hoped I sounded genuine. "So, ever play the piano?"

"Some," said Miles. "I did spend a lot of time alone the past three years. I had to do something to keep busy. How about you?"

"I know how to play fake music," I said.

Miles pulled an Uncle Mark, and paused.

"What is that? Surely it's not how it sounds."

I laughed. I was feeling better. That's what happened when I was with Miles.

"No, it's not pretend music like my brother would play. It's sheet music that has the letter of the chord written above the melody. So if you can read the treble clef and memorize the chords, then you can play fake music. It's a lot easier to learn than traditional, or classical, or whatever it is, where you have to follow a different staff for each hand. My mind just does not work that way. But since you know how to play not-fake music, why don't you play something for me?"

"Alright," Miles smiled.

He sat down at the piano and began to play. It was absolutely beautiful. I didn't recognize what he was playing, but that was no fake music. I sat and listened, feeling more relaxed and at peace.

Until I heard Mom.

"Anika," she called, following the music.

I should have locked the door behind the piano tuner.

"My Mom," I said to Miles, and hurried to the doorway.

"Up here, Mom," I said.

"Anika, I had no idea you play so beautifully!" Mom said.

"So what are you doing here, where are Doreen and Tryon?" I redirected.

"Dad and Uncle Mark are here."

"Oh, MOM!" I wailed.

Miles looked very confused.

"Honey, calm down," Mom said. "You couldn't expect me not to tell your Dad what happened."

I groaned and covered my face with my hands.

"What happened to your arm?" Miles exclaimed.

I groaned again, and pulled my sleeve back down so it covered the bruises.

"I called Susan, honey. I'm sure you would have talked to Jenny at some point, but I called her and told her what happened last night. She's with Doreen and Tryon right now."

"And Dad and Uncle Mark?" I wanted to know.

"After hearing his first name and your description, Jenny knew exactly who the guy was. Dad and Uncle Mark are probably dealing with him right now."

I groaned, for so many reasons! Now everyone knew, and—Miles looked worried, sick, and angry.

"He hurt my arm when he grabbed me, but I had pepper spray so *nothing* else happened, I got away. I'm okay," I said for Miles' sake.

"I know, you told me," Mom said. "But honey, you need to stop trying to protect me and your Dad and everyone else from worrying about you. If something worse happened, I'm afraid you would try to hide that, too. Stop trying to be so self-reliant, let us know what's going on with you, so we can help. I'm sorry I was so upset when I saw your arm this morning. I shouldn't have yelled at you, I took my feelings of powerlessness out on you, and that's not what you needed."

Mom's eyes teared up, and she hugged me. To Miles' credit, he didn't say a word, though he ran his hands through his hair and paced. He looked like he wanted to join the Dad and Uncle Mark posse.

I hugged Mom back.

"Your entire arm is bruised," she said quietly. "I don't see how that could happen if you escaped right away. Is there anything you haven't told me?"

"Are you going to yell at me if there is?" I asked, still feeling raw after getting yelled at earlier.

Mom was silent, her grip on me tightening, as Miles collapsed on the piano bench with his head in his hands.

"No," Mom said, managing to remain calm.

"The parking lot was slippery. I fought to get away, but he wouldn't let go and kept me so off balance, I couldn't get my hand in my pocket. I've never been so scared in my life," I cried. "No one was around, I screamed 'fire' like you said to do if I ever needed help, but there was no one to hear me. I managed to get out the pepper spray as he was shoving me into the back of his van, and sprayed him, and then I got away."

Mom squeezed me tight and rocked back and forth.

"You *have* to tell the sheriff, Anika," said Miles, looking very worried.

I nodded at him.

"You know we can't let this go, right?" said Mom. "He injured you, and tried to do worse."

"I know," I sighed, resigning myself. "I didn't know he bruised my arm last night. I didn't think I had any way to prove any of it."

"Well, you do, so..." said Mom.

"What if he gets away with it, though?" I asked. I was concerned about that. "It's my word against his."

"He better hope the law deals with him, instead of..." Miles said quietly, as he ran his hands through his hair again and took a deep breath.

"We'll be right there with you, honey. We'll get this figured out, one step at a time," said Mom.

"Okay," I nodded.

If I didn't talk to the Sheriff and then found out another girl was hurt later... I couldn't live with that.

Finally Mom let go.

"So this is where you work, huh?"

"Yeah," I wiped my eyes for the umpteenth time that day. "Pretty cool, huh."

"Pretty cool," agreed Mom. "Well, I'm here and Susan's watching the kids… have time to show me around?"

"Sure, Mom."

I walked Mom around the main house, and she exclaimed over it. She never had a chance to see it before, and was astonished. Descriptions just don't do it justice.

"Hello?" I heard from the entryway.

Dad and Uncle Mark.

"In here," I said.

Dad hugged me hard and looked at my arm. He looked grim.

Uncle Mark gave a low whistle.

"He's lucky you didn't see that *before* you got hold of him, John."

"You've got that right," Dad agreed shortly, as he hugged me again.

"He's lucky you didn't hear everything that happened, either," said Mom, her eyes shooting fire.

Dad and Uncle Mark looked at me, both concerned, and ready to go back out and finish whatever they started.

I explained what happened. Everything that happened.

Dad and Uncle Mark both looked furious, but held it in. Dad hugged me again.

"Honey, I am so sorry you were put through that. But don't you worry, that guy will never bother you again."

"What did you do?" I asked, really wondering.

Uncle Mark drew a finger across his throat.

I couldn't tell if Miles was shocked, or impressed.

"Uncle Mark!" I said. "Be serious. What did you do?"

"We played good cop, bad cop," Dad said.

He and Uncle Mark looked at each other.

"Okay, more like bad cop, psycho cop."

Wow, they were having so much fun with this. But it made me feel good that my family had my back.

"We confronted him and put the fear of John and Mark into him. He knows what'll happen if he ever comes near you again," said Dad.

"This is a small town, kiddo," said Uncle Mark. "There probably isn't anyone I don't know, so we talked to his mom after that. We let her know what a gentleman her son is. She's a good woman, and wasn't happy with him. At all. What we left behind, I have a feeling she finished off. My good friend the Sheriff, who happens to be his Uncle, was on his way over to put the fear of the law into him for good measure, as we left."

"Now that we know the extent of what happened, I want him charged. We can get him on assault at least," said Dad firmly. "The Sheriff needs to see for himself what this guy did, and take Anika's statement."

"I'll take care of it," said Uncle Mark, as he took out his phone and stepped away to make the call.

Dad turned back to me.

"I will see to it that you never have to worry about this guy again. Whatever it takes."

"I like your family," Miles said with satisfaction.

I ran up the steps and through the door the next morning, as Chip and Trixie tore off to play in the garden as usual.

Miles greeted me as I set my purse on the entryway table.

"How are you?" he asked gently.

"Okay," I said unconvincingly.

We weren't able to talk the day before. After my family joined us, they insisted I go home with them, since I forgot and left my chocolate guard dog at the cabin. Then the Sheriff came over and had a look at the damage Bill inflicted, and took my statement. By the time he left, he looked so angry I almost pitied Bill the jerk. Almost.

"How's your arm?" Miles asked with concern.

I lay down my coat, then held up my bruised arm and looked at it.

"It doesn't hurt as much as it did."

"Good... I wish I'd been there, Anika. That jerk never would have touched you. I would have..." he ran a hand through his hair, trying to decide which of so many options he would have chosen to use.

"Thrown him in the fountain?" I offered, trying to lighten the mood.

"No," Miles said very seriously. "He'd be lucky if all that happened to him was a trip to another planet."

I hated how stressed this was making him, it was so rare for Miles not to smile.

"How about a star, instead?"

If that was laughter in his eyes, it was quickly extinguished.

"Anika, I am so, so sorry I put additional pressure on you to make friends. I had no idea this is what would happen."

I sort of laughed, but not because anything was even remotely funny.

"This is not your fault Miles, at all, so please don't feel responsible. I am not friends with this guy. I don't even know him. Jenny invited me to game night at the coffee shop again, and I went. She introduced me to this guy because he asked her to. She had no idea what would happen as a result. I knew he was bad news just from the gut feeling I got, and I did everything I could to avoid him. He followed me out to the parking lot, and this..." I held up my arm, "is what happened. But I had pepper spray, so that's all that happened."

Miles breathed a sigh of relief.

"I was afraid you... well, I was afraid you were on a date with this guy."

I did laugh at that, because *that* was funny.

"Wow, you don't think I've got very good taste, do you! And even less sense."

"No, I just—of course you've got sense. I'm relieved to know you weren't with this guy by choice, though. And that you were able to defend yourself since I wasn't there to do it, or your Dad and your Uncle Mark."

A smile flickered across Miles' face at the thought of those two, but then he went serious on me again.

"It's reassuring to see that you've got a good family, one that will defend you. Promise me you won't try to keep things to yourself anymore. That you won't try to protect people who love you from being upset by what isn't your fault."

I looked down at the floor and shrugged my shoulder.

"I do feel guilty when telling them something makes them upset," I said.

"Someone very smart once told me our actions are either right or wrong all on their own. The response or result is not what determines that."

I rolled my eyes. I just love it when my words come back to haunt me.

"Trust the people who love you to be big enough to handle the feelings they have when you tell them you need help or have a problem. You aren't sparing any of us grief by keeping things like this to yourself. If your Mom hadn't found out, the Sheriff wouldn't have gotten involved... you'd be in more danger than you were last night, once that guy realized no one else knew what happened. Do not try to handle big problems on your own ever again, please, Anika."

"Alright, fine, if it will make you happy... I'll be more open about problems, and let my family help."

"You promise?" asked Miles.

I rolled my eyes again.

"Yes, I promise."

Miles sighed in relief.

"Good," he said very seriously. "Because otherwise, I will refuse to be set free, and will follow you the rest of your life, protecting you. You don't know how tempted I am to do that anyway, right now."

Would that be so terrible?

For him it would, I reminded myself. For him it would. He would end up alone again someday.

"Forget searching," Miles suddenly said, in a more cheerful tone of voice. "Let's do something completely different."

"Like what?"

He had me curious now.

"Follow me."

We walked to the family room where we watched movies the day I was sick, closing several double doors in the halls between us and where the cleaning crew was at work today.

Miles flipped on the TV and tossed me a Wii remote.

I laughed.

"You're kidding, you play video games?"

"I have since Polly and her grandson moved out," he grinned. "I couldn't spend every second learning things I never thought I'd be able to use. I had to unwind somehow."

"I'm glad you spent all that time studying though," I said seriously. "It's making all the difference in my sister's life."

"I'm glad too," Miles said.

"Amazing, the different gaming systems you have in here," I said.

"Second-Miles loved his video games, that's for sure," said Miles. "Some hit way too close to home for me, but he has others that are just fun."

I could imagine how the violence in some games would bring back memories of losing his brother and being mortally wounded himself.

Miles sorted through the games, looking for one we could play together.

"Ever play the Xbox?" I asked, looking at it and thinking it was the more advanced system in the room.

"Kinect can't track me, so no."

I laughed.

"Wow. It is so hard to remember you aren't solid," I said, shaking my head.

"Since we've been hanging out, it's sometimes hard for me to remember, too. You make me feel like me again, the all-me guy I used to be."

I could tell by his wistful expression that I wasn't the only one who wished he could be that guy again.

Reluctantly accepting what we had no ability to change, no matter how badly we wanted to change it, we both got back to the business of choosing a game.

We played some competitive games, and then some fun games. Not that competition isn't fun, but Miles is way better than me! I could count on one hand the number of times I played before at a friend's house, so he was by far the more experienced player. Wii Go Vacation wasn't all about competition, and was a lot of fun. We travelled all over the resort, and now and then played a mini game. Which he won.

I didn't know how long it would take for thoughts of my encounter with Bill the jerk to stop haunting me. I was able to defend myself and get out of that situation, and Dad and Uncle Mark totally backed me up. But the memories were still there, how scared I'd been, and thoughts of what would have happened if that pepper spray wasn't there in my pocket when I needed it, tormented me.

Hanging out with my friend Miles, a truly nice guy, helped erase those memories so that they weren't as strong and not as haunting.

By the time the day was over and it was time for me to find Chip and head back to the cabin, I felt a lot more like myself again.

Chapter 16

I was in a hurry to load the groceries I bought and get back to the castle. Sometimes I liked to have something to snack on while I was there, particularly since I often forgot to bring lunch with me. The last bag safely inside the car, I closed the passenger side door and headed back to the store to return the cart.

Jenny was on her way into the store as I approached with the basket.

"Anika!" Jenny hugged me, and almost started crying. "I am so, so sorry about what happened."

She looked down at my arm, and I pulled my coat sleeve back so she too, like the rest of my world, could examine my black and blue arm.

Jenny clapped her hands over her mouth, her eyes wide.

I've got to admit, it does look absolutely awful. I was still thankful none of my bones were broken.

"Jenny, it's okay. I don't blame you."

"I'm just so sorry. I had no idea he would do something like that. I mean I never liked him myself, but I didn't realize…"

"I know. If I were in your shoes I'd feel bad, but being in my shoes, I can tell you this wasn't your fault. So let yourself off the hook," I said.

"Well… at least some other girls have come forward, since you did," said Jenny.

"Yeah, it isn't my word against his," I agreed grimly. "He's got so much stacked against him, I heard today he's pleading guilty in order to accept a plea bargain."

"That's good," said Jenny in relief. "You and the other girls won't have to go through a trial."

"Yeah. I can't say I'm sorry about that, anyway," I said.

"Well—we may start meeting somewhere else, since this happened. It's shaken everyone up, parking behind the building never was a safe thing to do. We may move game night to the Rec center at my church. Maybe you'll want to join us there sometime."

I decided to level with Jenny.

"Here's the thing…" I said. "I *really* do not enjoy board games. I never have liked them, and it has nothing to do with what happened…"

Jenny laughed. And laughed.

Okay, so… maybe most people don't feel the way I do, but it's funny… how?

"Anika—" she finally gasped. "I absolutely despise playing games, too!"

"What? Why in the world do you do it, then?" I asked.

"Because all my other friends do!"

"Well now Jenny, if all your other friends jumped off a building, would you jump too?" I asked.

Then we both started to laugh. We agreed we should get together sometime and do something other than play games, like watch a chick flick, and try every kind of chocolate in the chocolate shop in town. We exchanged numbers and made plans to find a good day and time to do that.

We said goodbye and Jenny went inside to visit her Mom, who owns the small but well stocked store where I enjoy shopping. I put my cart in the row by the door with the others, and headed back to the car.

As I passed the corner of the building, I heard a cat. I looked around, but didn't see one.

I listened, and there it was again, loud and echoing. There was a narrow gap between the grocery store and the shop next to it, which led to the alley where the yowling originated.

I held my pepper spray at the ready and walked cautiously between the buildings toward the back of the grocery store. Not because I don't like cats, I do, and I was concerned by the sound this one made that it was in trouble. But there are certain people I don't trust, and a girl's got to be careful not to fall into a trap.

Reaching the back of the store, I slowly looked around the corner. I didn't see a cat, although I did hear one. What I did see though, was far more interesting.

Alfred Sullivan.

What is Mr. Creepy and his expensive suit doing in the alley?

He held a phone to his ear.

"I'm sure. No one survives a brain injury like that. What do you think, I'd botch it like you've done before? He may be in a coma, but he'll never wake up."

I had my iPhone in my hand now, recording. Maybe not admissible as evidence, I don't know, but I sure wasn't going to inform him first.

The cat wailed again.

"Have you seen the cliff? I sent you a photo. That's why I chose that particular spot. He'll never wake up again. I don't know why you're so worried about it. His stupid grandmother will have to pull the plug eventually. Or her plug will get pulled, that's an option too."

I could not believe what I was hearing. I mean... I wondered if he was responsible for Second-Miles' accident, but to hear him talking like this, and about Polly too. It was so callous!

"I'm done talking about this. I've no idea why you think this conversation can't wait a few more minutes. If you want to argue, do it then."

Mr. Creepy finished his call and looked around, making me thankful the gap between buildings was narrow. He probably wouldn't even fit. The alley was kind of a mess too, littered with boxes and cans, and a big dumpster helped to block me from view.

Mr. Creepy headed down the alley toward the street and his car, which I now realized was parked there.

Why not just call from the car? Oh. When he got in the passenger side and it sped off, I understood. Someone picked him up. Too bad the license plate wasn't visible from my vantage point.

I stopped the recording and took off for Mom's car, when I heard the cat again. I needed to figure out what to do with the recording, but the cat sounded like it was in trouble and probably stuck inside something. Either that, or it had a megaphone.

"Kitty?" I called softly, as I stepped into the alley.

Pitiful cries and frantic yowls echoed loudly right beside me. The cat was definitely stuck somewhere, and if I had any doubt where, the scrambling and thrashing coming from inside the metal box of stench beside me would have cleared that right up. No wonder the poor thing was frantic!

I wasn't exactly thrilled myself, but in the grand scheme of things there was an easy fix for this problem. Dumpsters have doors. I made a face as I gingerly reached out to grab the handle on this one, reminding myself that Mom keeps sani-wipes in the car.

Grasping the handle tightly, I proceeded to pull and strain until I was out of breath, and then pull and strain again, but it would not slide. It was completely stuck and wouldn't give an inch no matter how hard I tried. It might as well be welded shut, as impossible as it was to get it to budge. I gave it a roundhouse kick for good measure, hoping that would jolt something loose, but no, all it did was make the cat howl louder.

It was either concede defeat, or spend the rest of my life standing in the alley fighting with that door and listening to the cat wail.

The only way out for that cat was through the opening in the top, so I looked around and considered my options. There weren't many. There were cardboard boxes though, and that gave me an idea. I dragged several of them over to the dumpster, then stacked wooden pallets beside it. There weren't enough. The alley did contain other assorted items, and that included some galvanized trash cans lined up against the back wall of the store. I borrowed several.

I made a pile out of the pallets and other items, then turned a galvanized trash can upside down on top of the pile so I could stand on it and look inside the dumpster.

Inside was a filthy orange striped cat, and it really wanted out. It was too small to jump out by itself, although it certainly tried. I had no clue how it ever managed to get inside in the first place. Or why it would. Did it have no sense of smell?

"Hang on, I'll get you out of there," I said, in what I hoped was an encouraging voice, as I gagged on the odor emanating from the box of refuse.

I carefully dropped cardboard boxes inside, hoping they would stack so the cat could climb out, but I wasn't up high enough to see or aim well, and was determined not to get close enough to actually touch the dumpster.

The cat didn't appreciate the boxes invading its personal space, especially the one that landed on it. The cat retaliated by using language I'd probably find offensive if I understood it, and I was thankful I didn't. Then, to prove how helpful it wanted to be in assisting in its own rescue, it tore around in circles, sabotaging my engineering efforts, and the boxes toppled instead of creating the tower I was hoping for.

I got off my trash can about ready to give the cat as big a piece of my mind, as it was giving me. I looked around in frustration and wished that Miles had a cell phone, or email, or something! But he didn't, and the only other people I knew here and whose numbers I had, were Mom and Jenny.

Well Mom was certainly out, and when Jenny and I talked about getting together it was to watch a movie, not fish cats out of dumpsters. They were no better equipped to deal with this than I was, anyway.

So I thought some more while the cat yowled, bounced off the sides of the dumpster, and hurled epithets.

If I had a hammer I could pound on the handle of the door and maybe then it would slide. I took off on a hunt for one, when it dawned on me. I can't leave the cat. If the garbage truck comes before I get back, the cat has no chance. What a horrible death, crushed under piles of garbage! I couldn't possibly leave and risk that happening. I'd never be able to live with myself if it did.

I dialed Jenny's number. She could surely bring me a hammer, or maybe she knew a cat lady that would go in after the cat, if that didn't work.

Jenny didn't answer.

I looked at my iPhone and thought. Then I asked Siri, "how do you get a cat out of the dumpster," and she gave me web links that told me how to rent a dumpster, how to coexist with raccoons... as if that helps!

I sighed, and groaned, and kicked a box rather viciously.

Then I took off my coat and lay it on a semi-clean box. It was bulky, and I didn't want it touching the outside of the trash receptacle, which was almost as filthy as the inside. Shivering, I stacked more alley-finds to make my pile taller.

Now I had a good view of the inside of the dumpster, and better aim. The cat looked up at me with big orange eyes. I looked back.

"I'm trying to help you, alright?" I said.

The cat wasn't sure if it wanted to plead for help, say thank you, or chew me out or what, the thing had a multiple personality disorder. Or maybe the stench was getting to the cat, it was sure getting to me. I gave up trying to befriend or reassure.

I balanced carefully on my pile of pallets. Breathing a shallow sigh of relief and nearly gagging anyway, I congratulated myself on constructing such a stable edifice out of such sub-standard materials. Feeling quite proud of myself, I reached over, box in hand, as my sub-standard materials decided to overthrow my stable edifice, hurling me over the side of the dumpster and landing me flat on my back.

Oh I have never been so grossed out in my life. I fought to keep my lunch from joining all the rest of the decaying matter in the box of stench that surrounded me. My only consolation was that I wasn't paralyzed, stuck here until the trash pick-up came and put me out of my misery. The semi-clean boxes I tried to free the cat with, broke my fall. I *was* however, covered in... I didn't even want to know what, as piles of garbage toppled all over me as I made my unceremonious landing. Why don't people bag their trash!

As I struggled to stand, the cat proceeded to dig in, run right up my back, and leap to freedom.

"You're welcome!" I yelled after it.

Ungrateful feline!

I took stock of my situation. The getting out part of it, anyway. I was trying hard to block out the rest. I was able to jump and grab hold of the edge of the dumpster. The molded—not moldy, although there was that too—metal sides of the dumpster and the track of the non-sliding doors served as slippery footholds. After several disgusting failures, I managed to get out.

Note to self, before attempting any maneuver that could necessitate pulling oneself out of a hole, make sure Miles is around to help!

I worked my way back to the front of the store, really hoping no one would see me, or smell me, on my way to the car.

Mom would not appreciate eau de parfum of dumpster all over her car, and this is no job for sani-wipe. Mom wouldn't much appreciate me coming home like this either, but… she also wouldn't appreciate it if I never came home at all. I ruefully spread my coat out on the seat to protect the vehicle.

I had to do something about what I learned before I did anything else, though. I had no idea what to do with this recording, but Miles would know.

I raced back to the castle and tore into the driveway, parked, and jumped out.

"Where's the fire?" asked Miles, instantly beside me. "And what in the *world* happened to you?"

"Big—major—fire. Come on."

Looking very confused, Miles followed me into the castle.

"Miles, what do I do with a video recording of a person admitting to murder?"

"What?" he exclaimed. There was silence for a moment, as I waited and he stared. "Anika… where have you been, and what have you done?"

"I tried to save a cat stuck in a dumpster, okay, and I fell in, and you just be glad," I said, pointing a soiled finger at him, "that one of your superpowers is not being able to smell!"

"Good grief, you are a mess," Miles said, continuing to look askance at me.

Apparently I had something in my hair. Oh, eggshells. Well isn't that nice.

"So what are you more shocked at, someone confessing to murder, or my trip into the dumpster?"

Miles hesitated.

"I'm not sure. I'll have to think about that and get back to you. In the meantime, tell me what you know about a murder."

"Here, I'll show you... after I wash my hands," I said, not wanting to touch my iPhone until I did.

"Molly is not going to be happy with you when she gets here Thursday," said Miles, as I walked away, leaving bits of refuse in my wake.

Scrubbing my hands repeatedly at the nearest sink, I looked around and wished I could take a shower. I was standing in a castle filled with bathrooms, but nothing other than garments from the 1800's to replace what I really would love to not be wearing any more. I returned to the entryway and took out my iPhone.

"Watch this," I said, holding it so Miles could see.

For the most part, what Mr. Creepy said came through clearly, and the image was sharp. I had to be really cautious, I couldn't just hold my iPhone out around the corner where he'd see it, but I was impressed with what I managed.

Miles ran both hands through his hair.

"We have to get that to the authorities," he said. "I would really like to keep you out of it, though."

"What do you mean?" I asked.

"This isn't enough to put him away, and I don't want him coming after you if he finds out about it," Miles said, looking worried.

"I don't want that either," I said, also looking worried.

"Call Polly's PI," Miles said. "Get it to him. He'll know what to do with it, and you can remain anonymous. He won't reveal you as the source."

"Okay," I said, my hands shaking as I called Polly for the number.

"Hi Polly," I said when she answered.

"Oh, hello Anika dear," said Polly. She sounded worn down.

"I'm so sorry to bother you, but do you happen to have the number for the PI you used to find your grandson?"

"Why, yes, I'm sure I do. Is everything all right dear?"

Wow, how to answer that.

I looked at Miles. He had no suggestions to make.

"Um…"

"Does this have something to do with the mystery, dear?" asked Polly.

Well, *a* mystery…

"Sort of."

"All right then dear, just as long as you're all right. Here's the number…"

I wrote it down quickly. We talked a few more seconds, just enough time to enquire about Second-Miles. There'd been no change since we talked earlier in the morning.

I immediately dialed the PI.

"Hi, this is Anika Riley, I work for Polly Bannerman."

"Yes, I remember."

"I overheard a conversation in which a person admitted to a murder. Or attempted-murder, of Polly's grandson. I managed to record most of it with my iPhone. I don't know what to do with it. I don't want to end up the next victim," I said, as Miles ran his hands through his hair again and paced the entryway. "I also don't want him getting away with it."

"Get it to me, and I'll handle it," he said, and Miles and I both breathed a sigh of relief. "Miles Bannerman's accident has been suspicious from the start. I've kept up with the case since locating him.

Send the video to the same number you just called, and I'll get it to the detective handling the investigation."

"Oh, so there's an investigation! I had no idea."

"Yes ma'am, there is."

We ended the call and I sent the video right away, then turned to Miles.

"I wonder if Alfred is already a suspect?"

"If he wasn't before, he will be now," said Miles. "I wonder who he was talking to? I hope the detectives investigating will figure it out."

I looked in the entryway mirror. Oh, lovely. I picked more egg-shells out of my hair.

"Just a quick run to the grocery store, huh?" said Miles.

"Yeah. I'll never be able to say that again, without remembering how I got way more than I bargained for on this trip."

I held out my iPhone and looked down at my extremely disgusting attire.

"I'm horrified you took the risk of being discovered when you recorded that, but glad the detective for the investigation now has it to use however they can," Miles said.

"So you can't decide if you're pleased or upset with me, huh?"

"Yeah, pretty much!"

I laughed, he just looked so conflicted, and maybe the stress of the situation was getting to me.

Miles rolled his eyes at me. Apparently I've taught him a few things too, over the course of our friendship. Then he smiled and shook his head.

"You are something else, Anika Riley," he said. "And consider this, if you ever find a cat in a dumpster in the future. You have an iPhone. Call the humane society, and they'll take care of it."

"Ug, now you tell me!" I said.

I drove home, leaving my coat and shoes and as many layers as I decently could, outside the cabin door.

"What in the world—" Mom said, when I walked in.

I held up my hand, palm out, as I made my way to a very long shower, and said, "Do yourself a favor and don't ask, Mom. You do NOT want to know!"

Sarah awoke with a start as she was flung headlong from her berth and hit the floor and opposite wall of the tiny stateroom with a sickening thud. It was dark, the only light the pale glow of the moon dimly filtering in through the closed curtains of her stateroom window. The steamboat no longer moved through the water, but listed hard, instead.

Heart pounding, Sarah struggled to her knees. She heard frantic cries and the pounding of feet on the other side of the door. Using the doorknob to pull herself up, she opened the door and stumbled out of her room, and into pandemonium.

Sarah was swept with the rushing tide of people out of the ladies' cabin, and onto the promenade. So many voices screaming in the dark, bodies pushing, and the sharply tilted deck.

"We hit a snag!" someone shouted over the heads of the panicked passengers. "Everyone, in an orderly fashion, get to the upper decks!"

In as disorderly a fashion as seemed possible, the deck passengers below, scrambled and struggled to gain higher ground. Sarah clung to the wall behind her, struggling to remain on her feet. She was jostled and shoved first one way then the other, as terrified passengers fought for a place on the upper deck. The ship tilted sharply and she lost her balance and fell. She felt a flash of pain as her head smashed against she knew not what, and she remembered no more.

Chapter 17

"Hopefully we won't be too long," Mom said, then hugged Tryon and gave him a kiss goodbye. "You be good for your sister."

I was home with my brother once more, freeing Mom to take Doreen to her latest doctor appointment. I kept the little guy busy, and he was busy. Very busy. How does Mom do this all day, every day?

I had an idea. Whether it was bright or not, remained to be seen. Taking Mr. Busy by the hand, I left Mom a note in case she got home before we did, whistled for Chip, and headed for the castle.

Through the woods, over the bridge, and up the path we went. Tryon had a blast, he wasn't used to getting out like this.

Mom has to stay in with Doreen all day, and that means Mr. Busy has to stay in, too. I don't know how Mom does it... how does Tryon?

Mr. Busy might not be so busy if he had the opportunity to get out and play every day, like he was doing right now. From now on, I'd make sure he had that chance.

Tryon paused to examine everything on the way to the front doors of the castle. Trixie bounded up and greeted him with a friendly lick.

"Two doggies!" he said, as Chip and Trixie chased each other across the garden.

"Yep, two doggies," I said, hoping he'd forget all about that by the time we got home. It would make my life easier if he did.

Miles looked surprised when we walked in the castle.

I mouthed "Hi" to him.

"Hi back," he said in a normal tone. There was no need for him to be stealthy about it.

"I thought it would be fun to come visit the castle, and maybe we can find something entertaining to do here while Doree's at her doctor appointment. What do you think?" I asked, looking at Tryon, and then glancing at Miles.

"I think I see where you're going with this," said Miles. "Come on."

We followed Miles to the family room/game room, and Tryon was thrilled with the Wii games. He had his own way of doing things, after all, he's only three. He liked the bright colors and the figures moving, and being able to move his own Mii.

I stood back to let him play, and so I could talk to Miles.

"Doreen's appointment is today," I said. "I forgot to tell you, and I didn't want you to worry when I didn't show up like I usually do. And honestly, Tryon was wearing me out! I ran out of things to keep him busy."

"I'm glad you brought him. It's nice to see more of your family, and better to use this..." he indicated the room, "than have a bored brother on your last nerve."

"Yeah, he kind of was. But I realized on the way here what his life is like. It's good, I don't mean that, but the poor kid is stuck in the house all day. I'm going to spend more time with him from now on, and give him a chance to get out of the cabin and play."

"That's great, Anika," Miles smiled. He looked really glad.

We watched Tryon play his own version of tennis. He did better than I did. He wasn't following rules, and his way of doing things worked.

"Your brother is the same age my brother James was, the last time I saw him. When I was solid, I mean."

"Kind of odd how my brother and sister are both so close in age to your younger brother and sister."

Miles sighed. Seeing how much he missed his family made me appreciate mine even more.

"I'd share with you if I could," I said.

Miles smiled softly.

"I know you would. You've done so much though, believe me. Being my friend these past months, you've done more for me than you'll ever know."

"Yeah, well, right back atcha," I said.

I alternated between playing games with Tryon, and letting him play solo games so I could talk to Miles. The time went by faster than if we stayed at home.

I looked at my watch.

"Okay Try, time to go, Mom and Doreen might be home by now."

"Thank you," I whispered to Miles.

"Any time," he smiled.

As we walked through the house toward the entryway, Tryon turned suddenly.

"Anika, who's that guy?"

Miles and I stared at each other, we were both stunned.

"Um... what guy, Try?" I asked, trying to sound nonchalant. Good thing the kid is as young as he is, my sudden pallor and the need to hang onto the doorframe next to me in order to stay upright, would have been a dead giveaway of my panic, otherwise.

Tryon turned, and pointed.

"Him."

Miles and I both looked. Tryon was pointing to a painting on the wall.

Miles thought the whole thing very funny, but I slid down the wall and had to take several deep breaths and wait for my heart to slow down before continuing down the hall.

"Not funny!" I hissed under my breath toward Miles, once I'd collected myself, and Tryon, and we began our journey to the front door once again.

Miles laughed so hard, he could only wave goodbye. He didn't even react when I took a whack at him on the way out the door. He really is fortunate to have his semi-transparent superpowers!

But then again, if he didn't, it would be perfectly okay for Tryon to see him, instead of a Red Alert event.

Sigh.

It was Saturday, "boycott Anika day" at Miles' place. I understood his point though, and appreciated the opportunity to spend time with my family. When you see someone who's lost what you have, and how much they miss that, it tends to make you appreciate what you have, more than you did before.

I sat on the couch in the cabin reading a book to Doreen and Tryon. It was a new one, his favorite having mysteriously disappeared. I wondered which desperate family member hid it away somewhere. I must say, I enjoy reading a new story more than I do reciting one from memory.

Mom and Dad walked into the room together, Dad's arm across Mom's shoulders, and her arm around his waist. He was home for the weekend as usual, and apparently they had news. Their eyes were so bright with excitement, I considered suggesting they invest in sunglasses before their children were permanently blinded.

"Come on kids, gather 'round!" they said.

Even though we're already sitting right here. Clearly they're over-the-top thrilled about something.

"Dad and I have been looking for a house to rent closer to where he works," said Mom.

"Eventually we plan to buy again, but we aren't going to wait until then to have our family back together," said Dad.

"We found a place," Mom beamed. "It's convenient for Dad to get to and from work, and is so much closer to Doreen's doctors. We won't have to make the long drive there and back."

Doreen looked relieved to hear that. Doctor visits took three hours longer than they otherwise would, living at the cabin. That would be hard on anyone, but especially when you feel terrible to begin with.

"The house has a yard, and a play set," Dad said, looking at Tryon.

"Yay!" Tryon tore around the room until Dad caught him and swung him up in the air, squealing with laughter. Dad laughed too, and Mom.

They were all so happy... I was happy for them. This was good. For them.

I love my family... but moving wasn't the right thing for me to do. Miles had something to do with that, I wouldn't even consider leaving until he was free. I didn't want to live with Mom and Dad forever, either. I had a good job, and I wanted to go to college... I was impatient for Monday to arrive, so I could see about making an alternate plan.

I skipped breakfast Monday morning and left the cabin before anyone else was out of bed. I was anxious to get my immediate-future plans in place.

The weather was beginning to warm up, although this early in the morning it was still quite cold. The ground remained covered in snow, but there'd been no new flurries over the past two weeks. Maybe spring was preparing to arrive.

I called Polly on my way to the castle. The birds were singing a blue streak, I hoped I'd be able to hear her!

"Hi Polly, how are you holding up?" I asked.

"Oh Anika dear, I'm holding... it's so hard, though. The doctors don't sound good, Miles hasn't had any improvement the whole time he's been here."

"I'm sorry, Polly..."

"So what's going on with you, dear? How are things at the estate? How is the mystery solving coming along?"

"Good, actually. We're... I'm getting closer. I wanted to ask though, if it would be possible to have the same arrangement you had with the previous caretaker."

"Not if it includes running off without a word," Polly laughed. It was good to hear, the poor woman didn't have much to laugh about lately.

"No, of course not," I laughed too. "But I would like to move into the guest house, if that's okay."

"Why certainly dear, but is everything all right?"

"Yes, everything's great. My parents found a house near Dad's work, and are planning to move right away. I don't want to leave the best job I could ever have, though. I love working for you, and I'll be able to start college before long, at this rate."

And I'm not leaving Miles alone in semi-transparent limbo, even if it means camping on the lawn.

"Well then dear, you just move right in. You've got the key. And dear... use one of the vehicles if you need to. If you look around, eventually you'll find the garage. It's on the ground floor."

Funny Polly.

I thanked her, and ended the call.

Chip ran to meet Trixie, who was waiting in the garden for us. They ran circles around the fountain and flower beds. It didn't take much for them to be happy. Just each other. I sighed. I could relate. It was going to be hard on Chip too, when Miles and Trixie were gone.

Miles was also waiting in the garden.

"Hi," I said.

"Hi back," Miles smiled.

"Guess what," I said.

"What?"

"My family is moving to Glen Haven. They found a house to rent. They'll be closer to Doreen's doctors, and Dad's work. They're really happy about it."

"You're not going with them?" asked Miles.

"Nope. I'm staying here," I pointed at the guest house. "There's no reason for me to give up my job. It'll pay for college, which is really important to me. And seriously, Miles, do you think I'd for even one second consider leaving you here in this semi-transparent limbo? I care way too much about you to do that. I'm staying put, as long as I have to. You're not going to be stuck here alone, ever again."

Miles smiled softly.

"Thank you. But if we don't find that evidence, then don't you dare stay here and sacrifice your life over it."

"It wouldn't be a sacrifice," I scowled at him. "But it won't come to that. I've been sure all along, and even more so as time passes. There's proof, and I'll find it. It's a gut feeling, and mine have never been wrong."

"Okay, then," Miles smiled. "I'm very glad you're staying."

"Me too," I smiled back. "Come on, I want to get the key and check out my new house!"

"Okay," said Miles, laughing, no doubt, at my enthusiasm.

Hey, this is the first time I've lived on my own! Or the first time I will, I still need to tell the parents and move in.

We walked to the castle, and I retrieved the key to the guest house from amongst all the other keys pertaining to the estate.

I skipped back to the guest house and unlocked the door. I remembered going through the guest house with Polly, and I'd been there to check on it and hire a repair man to fix the leak in the roof. But I'd never been in it when it was my new place to live, and I was more than a little excited.

"I love this," I said, looking around.

Like everything else at the estate these days, it was neat as a pin and in perfect condition. The cottage was freshly painted and outfitted with new carpet, bedding, and curtains per Polly's instructions. It might as well be new, it certainly looked it. All I needed to do was move over my clothes and laptop. Maybe stock the kitchen, that would be wise, since I'd be in charge of fixing my own meals from now on. If I intended to continue eating anyway, which I did!

"What do you think, Chip?" I asked, as he and Trixie investigated.

They wandered through the small cottage, using their noses to gather who knows what kind of information, then took off outside again.

"Nice place," said Miles.

"Great neighbors, too," I grinned at him.

"The best," Miles smiled back.

I rummaged in the kitchen cabinets, looking to see what I'd need to put on the shopping list for the next time I went into town. Food was about the only thing, it was very fully furnished.

"Cool, the TV is even hooked up," I said.

"Well of course. Did you think you were somewhere ordinary? Nothing is ever shut off here, which is fortunate for me, I would have been in poor shape the past three years if I didn't have electricity, internet and satellite. I would have had to resort to reading the entire library again."

I laughed.

"I'm going straight home to talk to Mom and Dad. He took the week off since they're moving, so he's still here. I'll be back later, I'm sure Dad will help move my things. Then I'll run to the store, and then I'll be back to stay. Movie at my place tonight!"

Miles laughed.

"Okay, see you when you get back. But Anika… just get groceries at the store this time, okay? No more diving for cats and recording murder confessions."

I rolled my eyes at him, and he laughed again.

I left Chip playing with Trixie, and ran through the wooded path and over the bridge and back to the cabin.

I walked in the kitchen where Mom and Dad sat at the table eating breakfast.

"Mom… Dad, I need to talk to you about something."

"Anika, I thought you were still in bed!" said Mom, surprised to see me come in through the backdoor.

"No, I had something I needed to do, and I need to talk to you about it now."

Mom set down her coffee and Dad set aside the newspaper, and they waited expectantly for me to continue.

"I'm so excited for you all, finding a house, and being closer to Dad's work, and Doreen being closer to doctors… that's what's best for all of you. It isn't what's best for me, though. I don't want to leave my job. I would make minimum wage if I were in the city. I'd never be able to save enough to go to more than a junior college, and I do want more. I'm saving everything I earn. If I stay, I'll reach my goal before I'm twenty-five, not forty."

Mom and Dad gave each other a long telepathic look.

I really hoped I wouldn't have to pull rank. I was four months away from my twentieth birthday, definitely of legal age to make this decision. But I would prefer to have their approval.

"The previous caretakers for the estate lived in the guest house. I talked to Polly, and she said we can have the same arrangement she had with them. She told me to use one of the Bannerman vehicles whenever I need to drive somewhere."

Another long, telepathic look.

"We'll miss you, honey," Dad said, "but we knew this day was coming. We had you longer than we thought we would... if life went the way we expected, you would have started college and moved out last fall. Your Mom and I aren't surprised you want to do this. I talked to Mark last week, and he said if you want to stay, you're welcome to continue living at the cabin. I'm proud of you, of your work ethic, and the excellent job you've done restoring the estate. I know how badly you want to go to college, and that you're working to accomplish that. I couldn't possibly fault you for it, or expect you to give up on that and come with us."

"Thanks, Dad," I said, relieved at how well they were taking this.

"I know you need to do this, and I'm proud of you too," said Mom, as she gave me a hug and got a little emotional. "We're going to miss you so much, though. You better call and check in a lot, and if you need anything, or run into any difficulties, you promise to tell us immediately. Don't try to handle big problems alone."

"I promise, Mom."

She had no idea I already made that promise.

"Alright, then... as long as we hear from you often, I'll try not to worry too much," said Mom, brushing her hand across her misty eyes.

Dad smiled and rubbed Mom's shoulder.

"Take care of yourself and call like your Mom said, and I'll make sure she doesn't worry too much."

"Thanks, Dad," I laughed. "That's great of Uncle Mark to say I can stay here, but I'll be right on the estate grounds if I stay at the guest house. So I want to do that. Since you're going to be moving to the city tomorrow, I'd like to move my things to the guest house today. Can you help me, Dad?"

"Of course, honey. I'd like to see where you'll be living."

"Me too," said Mom. "We'll take turns, that way one of us will be here with the kids."

Dad helped me carry over my things. There wasn't that much, which is great when it comes to moving.

Then Mom drove with me to Cedar Oaks and we grocery shopped together. It was great to have a chance to spend time with Mom, just her and me. I was going to miss her and the rest of my family, but staying was the right thing for me to do. I had a sense of peace about it that I didn't have when I imagined going with them.

That night Miles and I had movie night at my place. It was so much fun. I hoped we would get to do that again many times before finding the evidence that I felt was looming closer by the day. I was glad of all the memories we were making. At some point, they'd be all I had left, and they'd need to last me the rest of my lonely life. I'd have friends in the future, but I had no illusions that I'd ever find another friend that fit me like Miles did.

Mom and Dad moved to the city with Doreen and Tryon the next day. It didn't take long to pack up, they didn't have much more to move than I did.

Tryon and Doreen turned to look back one last time before the car disappeared around a bend in the road. I waved, and then they were gone. I stood watching and listening until the sound of their vehicle faded into the distance and the whisper of the wind in the pines was the only sound.

It felt strange seeing them drive away to their new life in the city, while I stayed behind. I was no longer under the shelter of Mom and Dad's wings. Their home and mine were no longer the same, and never would be again. It was a milestone moment.

I turned, and signaling for Chip to follow, I walked back through the path in the woods to the guest house. My new home.

Chapter 18

If the house held more clues, they were well hidden. We hadn't found them yet, in spite of our many searches.

Miles and I were camped in the office taking a break from searching the estate. For a change of pace, we were searching the internet.

The only sounds in the room were the hum of the computer, the dogs chewing their Nyla bones, and the crackling of the cheerfully glowing fire in the library fireplace. Being neighbors was very cool, and so was having no curfew.

"I can't believe how many cars are in the garage," I said, as I pored over the search results displayed on the monitor.

"Really? You expected less? I think you're forgetting where you are," smiled Miles.

"I suppose so. Any family that has two ballrooms should be expected to have at least five vehicles per family member. That's actually quite conservative, considering everything else we've seen while searching."

"Isn't that the truth," said Miles.

"It'll take a while before all of the vehicles are serviced and returned," I commented, as I continued to search. "I'm glad to have one of them back and ready to use, anyway. That's all I need."

I wasn't turning up any relevant information in my searches for Sarah Williams, so I tried a different tactic.

"Aha!" I said triumphantly. "I've got something."

Miles lounged in the chair next to the desk, but now he sat up. "What did you get?"

"I found her on this genealogy site one of my Aunts uses," I said as I continued to scan the monitor. "She's tried to get my Mom interested, and I heard her say this is the best site out there. It's kind of her hobby. She's found out all sorts of family history here. As people find information and add photos and documents, families start linking together. If anyone related to Sarah is a real genealogy hound like my Aunt, then we'll be able to find something."

I read in silence for several minutes, clicking various links, searching for any useful information.

"There's a lot more here than I thought there would be..." I said slowly, as I continued to scan the page. "Everyone should have a completely different name, with no repeats. It would make searching a lot more successful."

"If you don't want repeats, then you have to accept that names will be long, and keep getting longer. It could take all day to introduce two people, and forget remembering each other's names. It's hard enough remembering your own."

I laughed.

"Fine, destroy my brilliant plan why don't you..."

My voice trailed off as I sat up straight and my eyes widened with excitement.

"Oh my goodness Miles, I found her! This is her, and she never boarded that ship to Europe! She wasn't on the ship!"

I spun around and Miles and I stared at each other.

"Anika, please tell me you're not joking!"

"No, look, she's listed on the manifesto, but not on the list of passengers who boarded. She didn't go down with that ship when it sank!"

I wasn't the only one on the edge of my seat now, we were both glued to the screen.

"Everyone assumed she stuck with that plan," said Miles, processing this shocking revelation, as I scrolled and searched for more. "She didn't tell the truth about how Delevan and I died, so why I thought she told the truth about her future destination, I've no idea."

"Yeah, in hindsight, I can see how that awful Dan would want to throw off anyone who might come looking for them. If they found Sarah, they'd find him too."

"Maybe there's a diary out there somewhere then, since she never sent the letter she promised," said Miles

"That means searching outside the estate," I replied.

"The estate seems small compared to the entire world," Miles commented.

"Oh my goodness, don't say that!" I glanced at him and saw he was teasing. "I had no idea when I accepted this position that it would require so much travel."

Miles laughed.

"You may get away with doing all your traveling from the desk chair," he pointed to the screen. "We haven't reached the end of the internet trail just yet."

I clicked on the link he pointed out.

"She's listed as a passenger on the steamboat Capricious," I said. "They were traveling North on the Mississippi."

"Why don't you do a search on the steamboat," he suggested, so I opened a new window and did. "If we find out its route, then we'll narrow down the list of cities where they may have disembarked."

"Yikes… the bottom of the Mississippi," I said, my heart dropping. "It hit a snag, and sank."

We were both silent, digesting this.

Miles thought, then shook his head slightly.

"No… we assumed she went down with the ship on her way to Europe, let's not assume she went down with the steamboat, too."

"Okay, you're right. Pressing on, then."

Switching back to the genealogy site, I continued to go through information and discovered an old newspaper article.

"Does it say whether or not there were any survivors?" asked Miles.

I had control of the mouse, and therefore controlled how quickly the article scrolled across the screen.

"You read faster than I do," I commented.

"I've had more practice," he replied.

"That's right, you have! A *lot* more. Hang on, I'll try and find it…"

Miles spotted the list before I did, and pointed.

"Not all of the passengers died, in fact, most didn't…"

"Oh my goodness, Miles!" I said, pointing violently at what I read on the screen. I skipped a bunch and got ahead of him, apparently. "Sarah's brother was killed in the accident! And that horrible Sam, who ambushed you and Delevan. Good riddance to them, but look! Sarah survived!"

We continued to read.

"Wow, she got married in 1871," I pointed out. That was fast. I snuck a sideways look at Miles, but couldn't read his expression. "And had a LOT of kids. Well, she did marry a doctor."

"What in the world does that have to do with it?" wondered Miles.

"If doctors made as much then as some of them do now, they could afford all those kids," I replied.

"Well... I'm glad she survived. I don't understand though, her brother was dead. She was no longer under his control. Why didn't she contact my parents, and tell them the truth?"

"I don't know, it doesn't make sense," I said.

Miles sat back in his chair again, but unbridled curiosity forced me to keep going through her large list of descendants.

"A lot of her kids, and theirs, and so on, are listed on this site..."

My voice trailed off as information and photographs became familiar. Why was this linked to my Aunt's site? I checked and double-checked.

"Anika, what's wrong?" Miles asked, concern filling his eyes. He probably noticed the color drain out of my face.

"I... can't believe this. This can't be right... this *can't* be right!" I said frantically.

"What?" asked Miles, as he moved to look over my shoulder.

I pointed mutely at the monitor and a photo of... me.

Miles was silent as he stared at the screen. His silence worried me.

"How is this even possible?" I exclaimed, desperate for him to say something. I wanted to know what he was feeling.

"Major, major... coincidence?" Miles said slowly.

I turned to look at him as I began to panic, my words stumbling over one another.

"I didn't know, I promise you I didn't, I never even heard of her before Uncle Mark told us that story! I thought she died on the way to Europe just like you did, please believe me!"

"It's okay," Miles said, shaking his head as if to clear it. "It's okay, Anika. We're okay."

I stared unblinking at the screen.

"I just... feel so weird about this."

How could he not feel different? I felt different. I felt bad.

"It's going to take a while to process," said Miles. "But maybe... maybe this has something to do with why you can see me, when no one else can."

"Like I'm finishing something, and righting a wrong my Great-great-great Grandmother Sarah Williams Lawrence, didn't."

Miles nodded, and we were silent a moment, staring at the information in front of us.

"You know the horrible thing..." he said with a grin, "is that you're also related to Sarah's brother."

I glared at Miles, and grabbing a book off the desk, I took a swing at him. I didn't care for having that family skeleton pointed out. There's the slim possibility I never would've figured it out on my own!

But, it was a huge relief to know he could make a joke out of it, rather than feel differently towards me.

Miles laughed at my unsuccessful attempt to pummel him. But then he was serious.

"You're not responsible for a past you had no part in. So... don't feel differently about yourself. Okay?"

I felt another rush of relief at hearing him say those words. I glanced up at him and nodded.

"Okay. I won't."

"Good."

He sat back down, then turned so he could study me.

"You don't look anything like her," he said.

241

"Yeah, I hear she was a ravishing beauty," I replied, half rolling my eyes and thinking Mom and Doreen did bear a strong resemblance. I was sort of resenting that great-great-great grandmother Sarah didn't pass on a little something to me, too.

"So are you," Miles said, then looked away.

I think he blushed. I know I did.

"Oh really. Look at my hair... no curl to it at all, and a common shade of brown at that. Brown eyes, too, not amazing like yours," I said, as I remembered his hazel eyes. I wasn't looking at him, I'd blush again.

"There's nothing common about you, Anika," Miles said firmly. "You are incredibly beautiful. Stop selling yourself short."

I was embarrassed, but at the same time, I longed for what I was hearing. I'd never been complimented like this, and I *did* feel short changed when I looked at my Mom, and her spitting image, Doreen. I wanted to hear more.

"Yeah, but look at her gorgeous blond curls. I know it's a black and white photo, but still. And those blue eyes. I can't compete with that."

"You think there's only one kind of beauty. That isn't true, there are many kinds. Hers is like... a Queen Elizabeth rose. You've seen them in the garden, the pink ones. Pretty, but the buds have few petals. They bloom and reveal nothing more than what's seen at first glance.

"You're completely different, Anika. One glance from you reveals there's so much more to you than meets the eye. You're mysterious and alluring, like a deep crimson rose filled with layer upon layer of velvet petals. You're absolutely beautiful, and each layer is even more so. It's hard not to get lost, looking into those eyes of yours... if there was a competition, you'd win," Miles said, and looked away.

I was stunned into silence for several seconds.

"Where do you get this stuff?" I finally managed to ask, too embarrassed now to continue this line of conversation. "What movies have you been watching lately, and please don't tell me you're hooked on Lifetime, Television for Women!"

The spell was broken, and Miles laughed.

Oh, how I was going to miss that laugh.

"No, I do not frequent that channel. I don't know where all of that came from, I kind of surprised myself. But that's what I see, when I see you."

The spell was back, and the way Miles looked at me made me wish for the millionth time he wasn't semi-transparent.

"What are the crimson roses in the garden called?" I asked softly.

Miles looked away.

"They're... Taboo. The crimson roses are called Taboo."

I sighed. How ironic.

We sat thinking our separate thoughts, then returned to the subject of Sarah and the information on the genealogy site.

The snow was melting fast, spring was anxious to arrive. I waded through the mix of snow and mud on the way to the castle. It was a good thing I was only walking from the guest house! Even with as little unpaved ground as there was to cover, these boots were going to need a major scraping and scrubbing if I ever hoped to get them clean again.

And Chip!

"Oh my word, you are a mess!" I said, my hands on my hips, surveying his feet. He looked like he was wearing mud boots.

When we reached the garden, I searched for a garden hose to wash off Chip's horribly messy feet.

"What are you up to?" wondered Miles, as he appeared beside me.

"This dog! Do you see his feet? The boy's a mess! Molly from Queen of Clean would be justified in having a fit if I let him in the house like this. Not to mention Polly!"

"You don't need to give the poor guy a cold bath over it, let me handle it," said Miles, using his superpowers on Chip's feet and my boots.

"You are just too handy, Mister!" I said, admiring my extremely clean footwear.

"Oh, and hi," I said.

"Hi back," said Miles with a smile.

Once inside the castle, I plopped my purse on the entryway table and took out my iPhone like I did every morning first thing, to check on Polly and Second-Miles.

"Still no improvement," said Polly's friend Enid. "Polly's holding up, but it's hard. We both wanted to believe moving him to this hospital with specialists in the top of their field would bring him out of the coma. But... after all this time, there's been no change."

"I'm so sorry to hear that," I said. Poor Polly. It was too horrible.

Enid lowered her voice.

"The doctors don't sound positive at all, Anika. He's been in a coma for almost eleven months. They're talking about bad EEG results, and some sort of test they feel should be done. I'm worried he's too far gone, and there might not be anything left to come back."

"Do you mean as in brain-dead?"

"Yes... I don't understand all their medical chatter, but it sounds as though that is what they believe. Polly doesn't want to let go, but she's starting to realize she has to."

I hung up with Enid, feeling stunned. Poor Polly...

I turned to tell Miles the details of the conversation.

"How awful," Miles said.

We were both silent, lost in thought.

"That would be terrible, to be stuck like that... I guess I was lucky, I went fast." He paused. "Wait a minute, no I did not! It took a long time, and really hurt. Maybe Polly's grandson is the lucky one, if he's already gone and no longer suffering."

"Yeah... but poor Polly. I can only imagine how badly she's suffering right now."

"It's unbelievable how many used to be in the Bannerman family. You look around and see all the rooms... they used to have occupants.

And then somehow it's all reduced to one boy, and then he's gone as well."

"Wow," I said. "I am seriously depressed now."

"Me too," Miles admitted.

I looked at him, and realized.

"You're losing all of your family, too."

"Yes," he nodded.

"I'm sorry," I said, and reached out to pat his arm, then patted the air near his arm, instead.

It really is hard to remember he's semi-transparent, he's more real than a lot of solid people are.

Miles laughed softly, and I did too.

"I'm glad I can be comic relief for you, anyway," I said.

"You're always able to make me laugh," said Miles, with one of those intense melting looks. "But there's nothing comical about you."

Why does he have to be semi-transparent? I'd kick and scream and throw a fit about it, if it would do any good. I may do that anyway.

"We're slacking off on our search horribly, I know, there've been a lot of days we haven't done a thing. But I'd rather eat chocolate ice cream and watch a movie, preferably a comedy, than do anything else right now."

"Let's do that," said Miles. "My place, or yours?"

"Yours," I said. "You've got a bigger TV."

Miles laughed.

"Fine, then."

We watched several of our favorite comedies, and I ate ice cream. I really pitied Miles that he couldn't enjoy it too. Fortunately he's a guy, missing out on chocolate didn't seem to torture him, as it would me.

We stayed up late with our movies, but eventually I was tired, and Miles walked me back to the guest house.

And then I tossed and turned, having another sleepless night, as thoughts swirled in my head. Why is it that as soon as I lie down, I'm no longer tired!

Why didn't you leave a note with the jewelry, Sarah, I mused. And why, since you survived the accident, did you never send the letter you promised? I can't understand that, it isn't like you.

Why, why, why…. and what to do next. More searching I suppose, we had the names of the men on the handbill with Sarah, maybe something would turn up there. I could call Aunt Louise, she was the family history expert… and Sarah is family. Wow. I just cannot get used to that.

I was so relieved to know that Sarah survived though, and apparently had a good life. It was hard to understand how she could marry someone else so soon after Delevan's murder, though. Come to think of it, I wouldn't be here if she didn't survive and get married and have kids! Newsflash, if Sarah and Delevan made it on the ship to Europe, Dad would be the only person in our family. The rest of us would never have been born.

Those thoughts are too deep for one o' clock in the morning, or any other time! Resolving to call Aunt Louise bright and early, I rolled over and drifted off to sleep.

~***~

"Sarah?" A voice from far away slowly drifted towards her.

Sarah wanted the voice to drift away, it threatened the peaceful sea in which she floated.

But the voice persisted. She tried to ignore it, but it only drifted closer and closer, until...

"Sarah!" said a white garbed woman.

Sarah blinked, confused and dazed. Her whole body hurt as if she'd been thrown from a horse and then run over.

"There you are, it's about time you woke up. You've had enough of a sleep..." the woman in white turned away. "Doctor! Our patient is awake."

A thin young man with spectacles and kind eyes approached. He smiled gently at Sarah, and felt her pulse.

"I'm Dr. Lawrence, your physician. How do you feel?"

"I do not know… I hurt everywhere," she said.

The doctor smiled sympathetically.

"I'm sure you do. That was quite a fall you had. Do you remember what happened?"

Sarah struggled to think back.

"I... no," she said.

"That's all right, it may come back to you at some point. Do you remember your name?"

Sarah thought again, and was relieved to find the answer.

"It's Sarah Williams. Miss Sarah Williams."

"Very good, Miss Williams. You were injured aboard the Capricious last week, when she hit a snag on her journey up the river. The ship went down, but not before most of the passengers and crew were rescued."

Sarah tried to remember, but couldn't. She didn't remember being on a boat at all. She didn't remember… much.

The doctor gave her a moment to speak if she wished to do so, then continued.

"Aside from the blow to the head that resulted in your prolonged unconsciousness, you were not much injured. I think that now you are awake, you shall make a rapid recovery."

The doctor gave directions to the nurse and another smile to Sarah, then moved on to the next patient.

The nurse poured a glass of water for Sarah.

"You know Dr. Lawrence is the reason you're here. He kept you from going overboard when you were injured, and brought you to this hospital. He saved your life in more ways than one, though you'd likely never hear it from him, he's that modest."

"I'm in a hospital… how will I pay for this?" Sarah was suddenly distressed.

"Don't you worry, now. I suppose you forgot that as well. You've plenty enough for anything you'll need for some time to come. You did a smart thing pinning your money inside your dress the way you did. It would have been lost with everything else, otherwise."

Sarah sipped the water the kindly nurse held out to her, and lay her head back on the pillow. There was so much she didn't remember. For reasons she didn't understand, she was glad. She felt at peace, she felt... free.

Dr. Lawrence looked back at Sarah wistfully as he turned to walk away. He would like to become better acquainted with the beautiful, sad eyed girl he remembered from the brief time he was aboard the steamboat. Maybe now he'd have the chance.

Chapter 19

Aunt Louise was our best chance at finding more information about great-great-great-grandmother Sarah. Chip and I reached the estate with Second-Miles' condition, and a call to Aunt Louise, on my mind.

Miles and Trixie met us at the door, and Miles took care of our mud-caked feet.

I took off my coat and hung it on the coat rack we found in the attic. There was no maid or butler to carry off one's wraps, as there were in times past, so it was a useful addition to the entryway.

"How's Polly and Second-Miles?" asked Miles.

"The same. Polly's not ready to let go yet, but the doctors are encouraging her in that direction. There's one test left which will determine whether he's brain-dead or not, and she's getting closer to letting them do it."

"What test is this?" Miles asked, as we walked slowly up the stairs towards Mission Control.

"Remove the respirator. If he doesn't breath on his own, they'll know for sure. I'm convinced Polly knows if that respirator is removed, it will be all over. She just isn't ready yet. She hasn't said all of her goodbyes, I guess."

"Understandable. She was put in a tough position, trying to raise a teenage boy at her age. Polly is a kind-hearted lady, but she wasn't equipped for it, which is why she and Second-Miles decided attending the academy would be better for him than staying here. In many ways, it probably was. I'm sure she has regrets though, and wishes she stayed in touch and kept better tabs on him. It's Alfred's fault he's in that hospital bed, but I wouldn't be surprised if she blames herself, too."

"The whole thing is just so sad," I agreed.

We reached the door of Mission Control, and I changed the subject.

"I should have thought of this before, but better late than never. I'm going to call my Aunt Louise and see if she can give me any new information about Sarah."

"And hi, by the way," I said.

"Hi back," he smiled.

Adjourning to the office, I pulled out my iPhone. Putting it on speaker, I dialed, hoping Aunt Louise would answer.

"Well hello, Anika!" she greeted me after a couple of rings. "I've got your picture and your name right next to your number in my phone, so I knew it was you right away!"

We exchanged a few additional pleasantries, then I got down to business.

"Aunt Louise, I've heard you telling Mom about your interest in our family's genealogy. Well I was kind of interested in some of that myself. I'm managing an old estate for a friend," I glanced at Miles, "and learned that my great-great-great-grandmother was at one time engaged to one of the gentlemen who lived here in the late 1800's."

"Oh what an exciting find!" bubbled Aunt Louise. "That's what I love about tracing family history, you never know who is out there that you may be related to, or who may have been an ancestor."

I could hear Aunt Louise as she bustled through the house, then began rifling through papers.

"What was your grandmother's name, Anika?" Aunt Louise asked.

"Her name was Sarah Williams, and she married a Dr. Philip Lawrence in 1871."

There was the sound of rustling papers and a dropped phone. After an unpleasant clattering noise, Aunt Louise was back on the line.

"Let's see, let's see..." she said. "I remember finding this information. Yes, a particularly fascinating bit of history. She sailed on the steamboat Capricious, which sank in 1870. She was injured during the panic among the passengers when it hit a snag, and rescued by the man who treated her at the hospital, and then became her husband. She suffered permanent memory loss from the injury she sustained."

Miles and I made eye contact. Now we knew why Sarah never tried to contact the Bannermans again. In the truest sense, she forgot.

I was blown away by the Fort Knox level of info Aunt Louise had amassed, and she wasn't finished yet.

"You know Anika, you and your family should really visit the High Ridge Museum. You know the Capricious was salvaged in the early 1990's. The items salvaged have been restored, and are traveling on loan from museum to museum right now. The High Ridge exhibit opens the end of next week. I wish I lived nearby, I'd go with you. Here… I'm sending you the link right now. You really should go, you might see some of your great-great-great grandmother Sarah's things. It all went down with the ship, you know."

Somehow I managed to thank Aunt Louise. I was stunned almost speechless by all that she'd been able to tell me about Sarah. Stuttering out my everlasting appreciation and gratitude to my absolutely amazing Aunt, I ended the call and turned to Miles.

"Did you hear that?" I asked.

"Yeah, it was on speaker phone," he teased, as I lightly pretended to slap his arm.

I turned and woke up the computer, checking my email and clicking on the link Aunt Louise sent.

There it was. High Ridge Museum, Steamboat Capricious exhibit, opening in just a very few short days.

"Sarah didn't have amnesia until the boat sank," I said.

"Exactly what I was thinking," said Miles.

Maybe, just maybe, Sarah left something behind for us to find.

The next day, I got the clock man started on the cleaning and oiling all of the many wind-up clocks in the house. Grandfather, wall, mantle, there were so many. I didn't have him take them all at once, it would take all day just to collect them.

The clocks had to be taken to the shop where they would be dismantled, and each piece cleaned in an ultrasonic cleaner. Then the clocks would be re-built, then oiled, then tested to ensure they kept the right time, bushings replaced if necessary, then returned. It was quite a process.

Miles didn't think his superpowers were a good fit for the clock cleaning business. Some of them were over-oiled in the past. Dust then stuck to the oil, and it was just a mess. They needed the care of a professional, so that's who I hired. Sam from *Tick Tock Clock* thanked me for my business, and drove away. Probably thinking he could afford to retire in style, once he finished cleaning all the clocks in the house!

I ran up the stairs and met Miles in the hallway outside Mission Control. He was playing with the dogs, rolling a ball along the floor for them to chase. They had to sit patiently waiting for their turn, so it was good mental exercise for them. It was also loud. Now I knew why every few minutes, it sounded like a herd of elephants running back and forth upstairs.

"Not being very subtle and low key, are you!" I said, and Miles grinned.

"Hey, if the clock man came this far upstairs, all he'd see would be two crazy dogs having fun with a ball."

"With all that racket, he was afraid to come upstairs," I laughed, thinking of how the poor man cringed and looked overhead, every time a dog thundered by.

"What's on the agenda today?" asked Miles.

"Well, I'm thinking, why wait in suspense for the Museum exhibit to open. Let's just call, and see if they can tell us if any of Sarah's things have been identified, and are included in the exhibit," I said.

Miles considered that.

"If her items aren't marked and identified in some way, we'll have a hard time figuring out whether something belonged to her or not."

"Fingers crossed then," I said, as I dialed.

After several agonizing minutes on hold listening to the world's least easy listening music, I had the museum curator on the phone.

"Hi, this is Anika Riley. I'm thrilled to see that the Steamboat Ca-pricious display is opening soon at the museum. You see, my great-

great-great grandmother Sarah Williams was a passenger on the Capricious when it hit the snag on its journey up the Mississippi and sank. I'm looking forward to seeing the exhibit when it opens, and wondered if you could tell me whether or not any of my grandmother's things will be on display."

I waited, as the curator mulled that over.

"You do realize, according to the laws of salvage..."

"Of course, I completely understand! I'm not laying claim to any of the salvaged items, but I would love to be able to see a piece of my family history, if any of Sarah Williams' belongings will be on display."

The curator mulled that over some more, then shuffled some papers and had a muffled conversation off the phone. Finally, he returned.

"Yes and no, Miss Riley. It looks like there is a hatbox and satchel belonging to a Sarah Williams, which was salvaged and restored. Those, however, are not part of the museum collection."

I was puzzled.

"Do you know where they are, then?"

"The salvage company is auctioning off some of the items salvaged from the Capricious, and those are among them. I can give you the number of the salvage company, if you would like."

"Thank you, yes."

I wrote down the number and immediately called.

Miles and I both crossed our fingers as we waited for someone to answer.

"Western Salvage," said a deep voice. "Rich speaking."

"Hi Rich, my name is Anika Riley. I just spoke with the curator at the High Ridge Museum, where artifacts from the Capricious will be on display soon. I was told you also have items that will be up for auction, and I'm interested in hearing more about that."

I could hear the sound of papers shuffling.

"Looks like that auction is in two weeks, in Allendale."

"Rich, let me ask you this. Is it possible to buy a piece outright, rather than wait for the auction? My great-great-great grandmother was onboard the Capricious when she hit that snag, and sank. There is sentimental value involved in a satchel and hatbox Sarah Williams had with her on the boat. They were lost with the ship. It would mean a great deal to our family to have an opportunity to secure these pieces of our family heritage."

There was silence for a moment.

"Waaaaall… I reckon. I'm the boss, so I can do pretty much whatever I like. Bring documentation to prove your claim, and we can work something out."

Rich scheduled to have Sarah Williams' items unloaded and removed from storage. It would take a week and a half to accomplish this. We made an appointment to meet after that time.

Miles and I looked at each other soberly. I knew this was it. I think we both did. So many mixed feelings.

The cheerful, joking atmosphere in the room was decidedly dampened.

"I won't have to leave again until my appointment with Rich at Western Salvage," I said, remembering with dread that we only had a week and a half until then.

"We'll make the most of the time we have," said Miles.

"We will," I said, knowing that time had a limit that was fast approaching.

I made the trip to and from the grocery store in record time. I didn't use much discernment in my shopping though, it was difficult to stay focused.

I arrived back at the guest house and Miles helped me unload the vehicle.

"Quite an odd assortment you have here," he commented.

I looked to see what he was talking about.

"Yeah... well, chocolate may be my only comfort a week and a half from now. I think my subconscious mind took over when I went down that particular aisle."

Miles smiled softly, but his eyes were sad.

"I'm not looking forward to this either... but we never know how much time we'll have. It would be a shame to waste the time we do have, grieving a loss that hasn't happened yet."

I nodded, my eyes brimming with tears. "I know, you're right."

"Let's use the time we have to make good memories," he said softly.

"You're right," I said again. "We'll do that."

I blotted my eyes with my sleeve, and managed a smile.

I cancelled the castle's regularly scheduled cleaning appointments for the next week and a half. I felt very protective of the time Miles and I had left, and didn't want to spend any of it on anyone or anything else.

We spent every possible minute together and used every second for all it was worth, to try and make up for all of the years we wouldn't have. Thoughts of a lonely future did intrude, especially when I was alone in the guest house at night, resenting the need for sleep that wouldn't come. When Miles and I were together though, we pushed those thoughts of the future aside.

We talked about everything under the sun, watched our favorite movies together, played video games, and Miles played the piano while I recorded it with my iPhone. We crammed a lifetime's worth of memories into that week and a half. But in spite of trying to hold on to every moment and make it last, our reprieve ended, and it was time to visit Western Salvage.

I was thankful Polly gave me permission to use one of the family vehicles. I could get used to driving around in this sporty SUV. Did it ever handle the curves! It accelerated quickly too, there was a lot of power behind it. Living here year-round as the Bannermans used to do, I'm sure they appreciated having a four wheel drive vehicle capable of handling the snow and ice. It was so much better than Mom's car, which was more equipped for the city where they now lived.

Most of the snow was melted, and there were unmistakable signs that spring was coming. I wouldn't be surprised if this was the last of the snow until next winter. Soon it would be time for Nate and his crew to tend the estate grounds once again.

I pulled into the parking lot of Western Salvage and walked across the pitted and pothole laden parking lot to the double front doors. The windows were guarded by security bars, as were the glass doors, and Security Maxx Inc. stickers were heavily applied, warning anyone who got the not-so-bright idea to try and break in.

I walked through the doors and across the cracked vinyl flooring to the front desk.

"Hi, I'm Anika Riley," I said to the receptionist. "I'm here to see Rich."

The receptionist picked up a phone and punched some numbers. I wondered how she could hear through her abundant, tightly permed blond hair. I looked around at the peeling paint on the wall, and the stained ceiling tiles. I was surprised by how run down it was.

"Hi Rich, Anika is here," she said.

Within seconds, the whir of what must be a state of the art lock sounded, and the heavy metal door behind her desk opened. Rich stepped through, and motioned for me to follow. They may not care much about how the building looks, but their security could rival a bank.

Rich was a tall, gray-haired man with a large handlebar mustache, and deep smile lines. He used them all, when he saw the information I printed from the genealogy site.

"You've done your homework, Miss Riley. I'm real glad to see that. Now while I don't deny the salvage business pays the rent, I got into the salvage business for this very thing. To connect people with pieces of their heritage. Follow me."

Rich swiped an electronic key card on another vault like door, and I followed him into a warehouse. We walked past row after row of crates stacked from floor to ceiling, each labeled with a combination of letters and numbers. I followed Rich through a maze of these crates until we reached another door. A large window in the wall beside it, revealed a climate controlled room filled with storage units. On display inside the glass units was a huge assortment of salvaged items. Tray after tray of buttons, leather boots and silk dresses, satchels and trunks, china and cookware. There were bottles of wine and perfume, and jars of pickles, and jam.

Rich swiped his key card again and opened the door, ushering me inside, then led the way once more. He paused in front of one of the cases and unlocked it.

"This is it, the satchel and hatbox belonging to Sarah Williams."

"That's amazing. How did you figure out these belonged to my great-great-great grandmother? Is her name on the items?"

"They were found in her stateroom, and that's how we know they belonged to her," Rich said.

I stared at this piece of my history, this connection to Sarah. The trunk was Miles' ticket out of his semi-transparent state. I'd never been so sure of anything. Except how much I was going to miss him.

"How much?" I asked.

Rich was reasonable, but reasonable wasn't cheap. I cringed to think of the huge hole I just made in my college fund. It sickened me more to imagine waiting for the auction instead, and possibly losing my only chance to acquire these pieces. The thought was intolerable.

I paid the man, then he packed and loaded Sarah's things in the back of the SUV for me. Service with a smile.

On the way home I didn't feel like smiling, though. I felt more depressed than enthusiastic. My heart was so heavy I was surprised the car would move at all. This was going to be hard. Very hard.

I pulled into the Bannerman garage, which was huge. And of course, it was on the ground floor. Did Polly really think I'd look for it upstairs?

I rested my forehead against the steering wheel, dreading what was to come.

Miles waited for me to open the vehicle door and climb out, then carried the hatbox and satchel as we walked through the door and into the house.

We sat together on the floor of the parlor and stared silently at the two pieces.

My heart filled with dread, I pulled the satchel forward and began to examine it. I didn't expect to find anything there, but it put off the inevitable. I was sure, on a gut level, that we'd find a letter somewhere in that hatbox.

"Sometimes... I wish we wouldn't find it," said Miles, rubbing his forehead.

"Yeah... me too. But when I think of you stuck in semi-transparent mode year after year after year, then I want to find it. I don't want you stuck here forever. That's no life. The thought... it's unbearable. I care too much about you to be that selfish."

Miles sighed.

"I don't want you to give up living, either, feeling like you need to stay here the rest of your life to keep me company. I care too much about you, to allow that."

My eyes burned with suppressed tears. Miles was silent for a moment, but he had more to say.

"When I'm gone... I don't want you to stay alone. But be really careful of the friends you do make, and for pity's sake, promise me you won't go out at night by yourself anymore!" He sighed again. "At least I know you've got a good family that loves you, and will take care of you..."

"Cut it out, you're making me cry," I said, using my sleeve to wipe the excess moisture from my eyes. It felt good that he cared, but it hurt, too.

I set the satchel aside.

"Nothing there," I said. I pulled the hatbox closer and opened the hinged lid. "Guess we should see if there's anything here."

We looked inside the trunk and removed the tray. I turned it over in my hands, looking for anything resembling a secret hiding place. Placing the tray on the floor, I looked inside. The trunk was empty. The inside was lined with a heavy fabric. I felt of the sides, and inside the trunk lid.

"A letter could be hidden easily enough underneath the lining…" I said.

"It would be a shame to damage the trunk though, unless we're sure. This did belong to your great-great-great grandmother, after all."

I felt the bottom of the trunk. It was also lined, with a rolled fabric trim that ran all the way around the inside edge of the bottom of the trunk. I felt along the edges, but it fit snug.

I sat and thought for a minute.

"Hang on," I said. "I need a measuring tape."

"I'll get it," said Miles, using his superpowers to place one in my hands.

I measured the height of the trunk on the outside, then on the inside. The measurements didn't add up. Which made sense, the bottom of the trunk would make the inside measurement shorter. But not that much shorter.

"It's here," I said firmly. "It's here. There's a secret compartment here."

I tried to pry the bottom panel loose, then let Miles take over. Even for him it was difficult, the panel was really stuck.

At last the false bottom of the trunk was out, and we were looking at two tin boxes that fit tightly together underneath it. Miles lifted them out and set them on the floor.

"This is it. I know this is it," I said. I felt sick.

I picked up both boxes. One felt empty, but I heard something rattle in the other.

I put both boxes down and covered my face with my hands.

I felt the faintest whisper of air on my shoulder as Miles rested his hand there.

"Ug, this is unbearably hard," I said. "So much harder than in the cave."

"I know… it is. Anika, just… take good care of yourself. Have a good life. Do good things, and…"

"If you tell me to be good, I may wallop you one last time," I said.

Miles wouldn't be joked out of his speech, though.

"You're the best friend I've ever had. You mean everything to me, and… I don't know how I'll ever be able to rest in peace… I'm going to miss you so much."

"You're my best friend too," I managed to say. "And I'm going to miss you."

Once he was gone, there would be no resting in peace for me ever again.

I picked up the metal box and carefully worked the lid to remove it.

"Strange it didn't rust," I said.

"Tin doesn't rust," said Miles.

If only it was made of some other metal… then it would be out of our hands. We wouldn't have this choice to make. I'd gladly live my whole life the way we were now… if it didn't mean Miles would be alone again someday.

The lid popped off, and inside was an envelope addressed to the Bannerman family.

I picked up the letter, my hands shaking. I slit open the envelope carefully and pulled out a folded sheet of paper. For a moment, I hoped wildly that the ink had faded to nothing.

It hadn't. The ink was dark against the paper.

I looked at Miles.

"Just... go ahead and say it."

"What?"

"You know what. Please, don't go without telling me. I'll feel worse, if I never hear you say it."

"It won't make this harder for you… to move on?"

"No," I said, swallowing back tears.

Miles paused.

"I love you, Anika. With all my heart," he said softly. I memorized the look in his eyes as he said it.

"I love you too, Miles. I love you too. So much," my voice cracked.

"I don't want to say goodbye," he said.

"Then we won't," I said, a tear falling on the page I held in my hand.

"I do love you, Anika, more than anything, but don't let that stop you from living. Please."

I nodded, my throat aching so that I couldn't speak.

"You won't hurt me by living the best life you can… you won't help me by spending the rest of your life grieving," he said, almost pleadingly. "I'm not sure I did the right thing telling you I love you, even though I do. So much."

"Okay," I managed to say, wanting to erase the worried look in his eyes. "I'll try. I really will. Because I love you."

"Okay," Miles nodded.

"This whole thing just—I hate it. I don't want you to have to go," I said, wanting another option.

"I'd stay if I could, Anika—in a heartbeat, I would," Miles said. We both had tears in our eyes.

"I love you," I said one last time.

"I love you too. Always," said Miles.

A long look later, I blotted my eyes on my sleeve and lifted the page.

Miles and I silently read it together. He began to fade, and then he was gone.

I huddled on the floor crying silent tears of agony until long after the sun went down and the moon cast its ghostly light through the long narrow window and across the polished wood floor and the letter in my hand. Cold and feeling more alone than I ever thought possible, I stood and left the room.

Chapter 20

Cynthia crept past the parlor on the way out of doors, when she heard her Mother speak softly. She stopped a moment to listen.

"They were my sons too, and not a moment goes by that my heart does not feel torn to shreds. I wish we knew what happened as badly as you do. I wish we knew why Sarah lied as she did, and what the truth is."

Cynthia heard her mother stifle a sob, and her own throat swelled with grief.

"But Del... you are destroying yourself. Your anger, though justified, is hurting you, and hurting us. Hurting the two children we have left."

Cynthia looked down at her hands. Mother was right. She never knew how badly one could suffer until her brothers were killed.

And then, so many lies were told about them... and Father became angry, so angry, all of the time. James was young when Miles and Delevan were taken from them. He didn't remember Father as he used to be, before tragedy changed him so.

Cynthia heard Father's voice, low and rough.

"If I let go, I'm letting my son down."

Cynthia heard her Father sob for the first time.

"I can't bear that. Someone murdered our sons, Ellie! I just want the murderer brought to justice, I want my son's name cleared. He never... Miles never did such a thing, he loved his brother, he never looked at Sarah the way that she claims!" he choked out. "A more honorable young man never lived, and to have his good name tainted with such lies..."

"I know Del, I know," Mother sobbed too. "But Del, do we allow the murderer to destroy our family? He has already taken our sons. We mustn't let him take us all!"

"But what of Miles? He would be sickened to realize what people say about him now, even those who once claimed to be his friends. I want the truth to be known. The Sheriff was nothing but a hindrance, and it was my great pleasure to see him out of office," Father said with grim satisfaction.

"Miles would be even more sickened if he knew your quest for the truth is destroying you, and the rest of us. Miles loved James and Cynthia, and he would be grieved beyond measure if he knew the agony they are now in. Let go of this hunt for truth, Del. It isn't there to be found. If Sarah didn't vanish the very night she told us this story, we'd have hope of finding it. Without her, we have nothing to go on. Absolutely nothing."

"And her ship went down, all hands lost…" Father said.

Cynthia heard the rustle of Mother's dress as she went to Father.

"I don't know why Sarah lied. We both know that she did. But can we doubt the grief in her eyes and voice were true? I cannot fathom an acceptable excuse to say the things she did about our blameless son… but her grief was real. Her reason, whatever it may be… I cannot believe she felt she had a choice."

Father took a deep breath, then exhaled.

"All right, Ellie. I know what you're saying is true. I know what Miles would want for us… and Delevan, as well. I don't know how… but I'll try to forgive Sarah, and move forward."

The pinched look on Cynthia's face relaxed a bit. For Father to speak so, it meant a change. She hurried to find James, to tell him what she overheard. They would never have their brothers again, but they would have their Father back.

As she climbed the stairs, she felt a soft whisper of air brush her cheek. She looked around, but couldn't tell from where it came. Puzzled, she continued on, wondering why it was that it comforted her so.

~***~

I lay in bed staring at Miles' photo. It hurt unbearably that I'd never again see those laughing eyes and hear his voice. Why were we in such a hurry. Why didn't we wait to read that letter? Wait until I was ninety or a hundred… then we could've read it.

I lay there, throat aching, chest so tight I couldn't breathe, tears pouring silently down my face, holding his photo and wishing with all my heart I could follow him. Or that he could return to me.

In the early hours of the morning, something scratched at the door. Chip woke up and went to investigate, as I dragged myself off the bed. Chip whined, and outside there was an answering whine, so I opened the door.

Trixie stood on the other side, her head low and her tail drooping. She whimpered and looked at me pleadingly, her brown eyes filled with sorrow.

"You poor thing! You couldn't go with him this time?" I hugged her tight, and was overtaken by uncontrollable sobs. Tears ran down my face and onto her golden fur. My heart was broken for both of us. Of course I felt sorry for me, but poor Trixie! How could she possibly understand where her beloved friend had gone. She chose to follow him before, but now she was left behind.

I broke my rule of "no dog on the bed," and invited Chip and Trixie to join me as I lay back down. I needed the companionship and the comfort.

I tried to fall asleep, hoping for an escape from the pain, but sleep refused to come. I didn't bother getting up in the morning. There was no one to get up for... nothing for me to do. I could have spent the whole day talking to Miles, if only...

How is it possible to feel dead inside and hurt this much, at the same time.

I couldn't bear to talk to anyone, so I skipped my usual first thing in the morning phone call to Polly. But then I realized I couldn't quit caring about other people, just because I was hurting. Polly would want to know that I found the proof and solved the mystery. I forgot all about her part in this, and that one of the reasons she hired me was so I would accomplish this very thing. I had to let her know we... I succeeded, and maybe it would brighten her day. She hadn't had much to smile about herself, lately.

"Hi Polly, it's Anika. How are you?"

"I'm doing alright, dear. I've been better, but I'm sure we all have. And how are you, dear? You don't sound well."

"I'm... feeling sick." Heart sick.

"Do take it easy dear, don't overdo."

"I'm staying in bed today... How is your grandson?"

"The same," Polly stifled a sob. "I took the morning shift, and Enid is there now, taking the afternoon. Our old bones just can't handle sitting in waiting room chairs all day long, so we've started taking turns."

Poor Polly.

"I'm glad Enid is with you," I said. "I have news to tell you, if you feel up to it."

"Is it good, or bad?"

"I think you'll like it," I said, as I thought of all the things Polly didn't know. "It's a long story... a lot has happened since you've been gone."

I told Polly why Sarah lied, and about Sarah's first letter, and that Cynthia cut it into paper dolls. She was fascinated to hear of the riddle that pointed the way to the jewels hidden in the cave, and that Sarah never boarded that ship to Europe, she survived and was my great-great-great grandmother. She was stunned to learn that Sarah was injured and lost her memory of that day in the clearing, and that's why she never contacted the Bannermans. She exclaimed in astonishment when I told her about the hatbox that hid the letter naming the men responsible for Miles and Delevan's murders, which was salvaged from the Capricious, and how I tracked it down.

When I finished, Polly was ecstatic.

"I knew it, I knew you would do it! You are such a smart young lady, Anika. I hired you that day as we walked the estate grounds, because you believed in Miles' innocence. And now to learn that you are Sarah's great-great-great granddaughter as well. Perhaps that is what I could see in you, that you were meant to solve this mystery and finish what she couldn't. I'm so proud of you. I couldn't be more proud! Even the Bannerman family heirloom jewels! Thank you, my dear!"

"You're welcome, Polly. I'm glad I was able to do it."

I was glad to hear her so happy.

"I want you to call someone for me, Anika. Here, let me give you the number..."

I wrote it down.

"This is a reporter friend of mine, Phil Walker. I'll let him know you'll be calling. He's covered items of news concerning our family for many years, and I want you to tell him everything you've found. We'll clear the family name and show the world proof that Miles Bannerman is innocent."

"Okay Polly, I'll call today."

"Won't this just get Alfred's goat!" she said.

But what really cooked Alfred's goose, was when Polly's grandson awoke from the coma.

I first heard about it on the news late that night as I lay in bed, feeling numb and aching with pain, impossible as that seemed.

"Alfred Sullivan, charged with attempted murder of billionaire heir, Miles Bannerman, on News Channel seven, at ten."

Whoa, what? I talked to Polly just this afternoon. A lot must have happened since then. I stayed close to the TV, not wanting to miss this.

I was shocked at what I learned.

Polly's grandson was out of the coma. Not only was he awake, he was naming the person who attempted murder when they pushed him off the cliff.

Alfred Sullivan now had a lot bigger things to worry about than giving Polly fits by threatening to seize the position of trustee for the estate. And the heir was in stable condition and making a rapid recovery, so all was well in that regard.

I called Polly immediately, I was pretty sure she wouldn't be asleep after all this!

"Oh it is just the most marvelous thing, dear!" Polly beamed over the phone. "The doctors are calling it a miracle. Miles is awake, and doing well. The doctors aren't ready to release him, they said it would be dangerous to leave the hospital just yet. There have been some complications, but he's recovering."

"Wow Polly, I am so happy to hear that! I'm so glad Alfred didn't get away with it, too. I imagine he's pretty busy being charged with attempted murder now."

"Oh, yes, Anika dear! Miles has been interviewed by the detective, and Alfred has been arrested. Once we knew Alfred was guilty, a search warrant was issued. The detectives found Miles' driver's license and other identification hidden in Alfred's home. He needn't try and escape punishment with some hotshot defense attorney, either. The D.A. has the Bannerman fortune behind them, there will be no skimping when it comes to building their case. Money is no object."

I never heard a real person say that before.

Polly's PI called me the next day.

"Hello, Miss Riley. I thought you might like to know what your recording accomplished."

"What did it accomplish?" I wondered.

"I turned it over to the detective handling the case. It convinced him he was pursuing the right suspect. As a result, his time wasn't wasted on other possible leads, and evidence was discovered which otherwise might not have been. The detective wanted to thank you, so as you remain anonymous, I'm passing that on for him."

"With Polly's grandson awake and naming him as the attempted murderer, did it really matter after all?" I wondered.

"Every piece of evidence is crucial, Miss Riley. It matters," he said with certainty.

"Wow... I'm so glad that cat got stuck in the dumpster, then."

The PI's response was a moment of silence.

"I'm not sure I heard that right, what did you say?"

I explained what happened, which the formerly stoic PI found extremely amusing. If I weren't sick at heart, I probably would too. I managed to laugh along pretty convincingly, I think. Enough that I didn't seem as though I had no sense of humor. Although, I wondered if perhaps I lost mine when Miles left. Nothing was funny or fun anymore.

Mom and Dad and the kids were thrilled with life in the city. Who knew urban would suit them just as well as suburban did. Dad loves his job, and he and Uncle Mark work well together. Think how they handled Bill the jerk! They're quite a team. Doreen was on a treatment regimen to eradicate the chronic Lyme she was diagnosed with. It would take time for her to start feeling better, but we knew it *would* happen, and eventually she would be past this. Knowing it would end made it easier for her, and for us. It made it bearable, if only just.

They were all stunned when I told them what I'd been up to. Mom said now she understood why I spent so much time at the castle, and was so driven. I was careful not to talk much about my efforts to solve the Bannerman mystery over the past year, for fear of mentioning conversations or interactions that I had with Miles. If they'd gotten any impression I was friends with a semi-transparent guy, or thought *I* thought I was, they would have totally freaked out. They would consider the whole thing unhealthy, no matter how you sliced it. They didn't know Miles… and it made me sad to know they never would.

Mom and Dad were floored to realize our family's link to Sarah, the woman in Uncle Mark's story. They were fascinated by the whole thing, and I had to tell them over and over about every step it took to find each clue. It was difficult to do without mentioning Miles as in "he was right there with me," but it was good practice for the television interview I did later. Doreen was thrilled to know that Uncle Mark was right, Sarah did look just like her.

Bill the jerk was serving time, and the parking lots of Cedar Oaks would be safer as a result for the next few years. I was glad in retrospect, that Mom saw my arm that morning, and I was forced to deal with what happened instead of getting away with hiding it. It really was dumb to try and handle everything on my own. Some things are too big for one person.

I wanted to avoid everyone and be alone forever, and I knew the longer I stayed isolated the more strongly I'd feel that way. Miles didn't want me to be alone, and I needed to try to survive the agony of losing him. I called Jenny.

"Hi Jenny, it's Anika."

"Hi, Anika! How are you?"

I couldn't help it, my voice broke and I almost lost it.

"Um—I lost someone really important to me. My best friend," I said, choking back a sob. "Can you come over? It hurts too much to talk about it, but I need someone to hang out with."

"Oh, Anika! I am so sorry. I'll be right over."

Jenny was as good as her word, and she brought pizza and chocolate with her. Lots of chocolate. Jenny set it all on the kitchen counter, then hugged me. I felt some of the horrible pain drain away just enough to allow me to hold it together.

The dogs came out to greet her, then went back to their places on my bed. So much for my rule.

I managed a weak smile. "Thanks for coming over, Jenny, I just need to not be alone for a while."

"Anika…" Jenny put her hand on my arm, trying to comfort. "I'm glad you called me. Do that, any time you need anything."

I nodded. Miles was right, friends are important if you can make a good one. He was right about Jenny, too. She was a good friend.

"Here, let's dig into this pizza," said Jenny. I appreciated her taking charge, I was in no condition to.

Jenny located the plates. She put a slice on one and handed it to me.

"You need to eat, Anika. I can't believe how much weight you've lost since the last time I saw you. You are way too thin. Your friend wouldn't want you making yourself sick."

I had to blot my eyes repeatedly. I nodded. She was right.

"I know something that might cheer you up a little," said Jenny.

"What's that?" I asked, managing to take a bite of pizza.

"Well. I would not be surprised if Bill hires a bodyguard to follow you around for the rest of your life."

"What?"

"Apparently—" Jenny started to laugh. Every time she started to talk, she cracked up again. Eventually I started to laugh too, it's impossible not to when someone's laughing like that, even when you have no idea what's funny and your heart is broken.

"Okay, so—" Jenny managed. "Word on the street—is that your Dad and Uncle are experienced at—disposing of bodies—"

I started to laugh again, I couldn't help it.

"And—cleaning crime scenes. And if—"

We both started to laugh.

"And if—anything. Anything. A single hair on your head, is ever touched again—they are coming back—"

Jenny was struggling to hold it together long enough to get the rest of the story out, and I was lying on my side on the couch, laughing so hard I couldn't sit up.

"They'll come back—and deal with him—permanently!"

"Oh my goodness," I managed to say. "I cannot believe those two!"

"Even—" Jenny said, "If Bill has nothing to do with it!"

We both laughed so hard, I thought I'd be sick.

It felt good to laugh. It helped to get out some of the emotions I'd been holding in. I wondered if Mom had any idea what her husband was capable of.

Jenny finally had her laughter under control so she could talk again.

"So, Anika. You not only have nothing to fear from Bill again, even after he's done serving his sentence, but none of the other guys in Cedar Oaks will be trying anything, either."

"Good!" I said.

We settled down to our pizza and chose a comedy to watch. I couldn't stand anything with romance or sentimentality, it would be my undoing.

We chatted while the movie played and got to know each other better.

"I had to delay college too," she said. "I've had to work hard, but I've got the money saved, and plan on starting next year."

"That's cool," I said. "You know what my family went through when Dad lost his job, and my sister was so sick. But I've been working towards the same thing."

"Would you be interested in sharing an apartment?" she asked. "It would cut down on expenses…"

"Yeah, I am most definitely interested in that," I said. I reached over to the small desk next to the couch, and picked up a letter.

"I got this today… I've been awarded a full scholarship from The Bannerman Foundation, to the university in Glen Haven. Polly and her grandson are so thankful that I found the proof of who really murdered the Bannerman brothers, and found the lost heirloom jewelry."

"I'm sure they are, it's amazing what you did," Jenny replied.

I looked at the paper in my hand.

"I do want to go to college… it might help me move forward. It helps to think we could be roommates, I'm looking forward to it more."

Jenny patted my arm sympathetically.

Conversation ceased temporarily, as we both focused on eating.

"You know… Nate is a really nice guy. I've known him a long time. He asked if you were seeing anyone," Jenny said. "I didn't know what to tell him…"

My eyes immediately filled with tears.

"Oh Anika, I'm so sorry. I am *so* sorry! I didn't realize, when you said your best friend… I'm so sorry, I wish I never said anything!"

I looked straight up, trying to keep the tears from spilling out, as she handed me a tissue.

"Um—yeah, just—I'm glad you can tell him—tell him I'm not up to seeing anyone. Probably ever," I sort of laughed, although absolutely nothing was funny at all. "My friend and I, we weren't... but if things had been different..."

I fought to stay in control and stop the well of tears that threatened to overwhelm me.

"It's crazy," I continued. "Polly keeps talking to me about her grandson. The hints she's dropping could crush a village."

"I'm so sorry, Anika. When it rains it pours, huh."

"No kidding." I sighed. "I love Polly... I do. But I'm dreading the day she comes back with her grandson. She keeps telling me how impressed he is with what I accomplished, and how he can't wait to meet me..."

I wondered what he'd think if he realized I turned in a recording that contributed to building a tighter case against Alfred Sullivan. I was so, so glad the PI kept my name out of it. If Polly knew, she would have our wedding invitations engraved already.

I groaned, and held my face in my hands. "And she's pressuring me to fly out there. Can you believe it? I can't do that. She has no idea how she's torturing me."

"I'm so sorry," Jenny said again, and handed me a king size Hershey's bar, which I accepted gratefully.

"He's going to college next year in Glen Haven, too."

If he didn't look like my Miles and have the same name, I wouldn't care. Although I still wouldn't appreciate Polly trying to set us up. I'm sure it's a disappointment to her that arranged marriages went out with the dark ages. It was unbelievable how pushy she was being. I had to remind myself, I do love Polly. I do. And in every other way, she is an incredibly sweet, wonderful lady.

Jenny and I finished our movie and she left me with a supply of chocolate and the rest of the pizza. It was late, so she went home, promising to call the next day and check on me.

I went to my room, where the dogs were totally sacked out.

273

"Move it, kids," I said, pushing Trixie closer to Chip so there would be room for me.

Was Miles ever right about her hair! Even with his warning, I had no idea one dog could shed this much. My bed was covered.

"You're pretty hard on the vacuum too, aren't you girl," I said, as I pet both her and Chip.

I crawled in bed and took Miles' picture out from under my pillow. I was so glad I had that, anyway. And the recording of him playing the piano. I picked up my iPhone and played it. Sometimes it helped me sleep. Usually I lay awake all night, but sometimes it helped.

I looked over at Trixie and Chip. Lucky for them, they still had each other. I wondered if Trixie chose, or if this time she had no choice.

I sighed. Miles should have had a choice. So should I. Good grief, why could Trixie choose to stay with him before, but I couldn't choose to stay with him now!

Chapter 21

"Anika, did you see the paper?" Mom was so excited, she didn't even say hello when I answered the phone.

"What paper?" I asked.

"Any paper! It's syndicated. The Cedar Oaks paper, the Glen Haven—have you? Evidently not, you'd know what I'm talking about. You have to get one, your story is in here! It's amazing, even though you've told us so many times what you were up to for the past year. Seeing it in print like this, you're a bit of a celebrity, honey. What you did, it really is amazing."

Yeah, well... I didn't do it alone. I couldn't have. No one but Miles could understand Sarah's poem, if nothing else. Everyone marveled at how I figured out the riddle note and found the cave, and wanted to know how I did it. I said I felt as though I was led there. It was the truth.

I picked up a copy of the Cedar Oaks newspaper, and it was quite an article. Everything we uncovered was sensationalized. Which wasn't hard to do, it really was pretty sensational. If only they knew who my detective partner was.

It was Sunday night, and Jenny showed up at my door. She was very good about making sure I went out at least once a week. I knew I needed to do that, and appreciated that she was diligent in encouraging me, because otherwise I'd just sit at home by myself.

I put Miles' picture under my pillow, and let her in.

"Come on," she said, taking charge. "Let's get you out of here for a while. I can tell you need somewhere else to be."

"You're probably right," I said dully.

We went to the coffee shop, but for coffee and socializing this time. No games. I draw the line there, my life is tortured enough without adding that horror to the mix.

I ordered a latte, about the only thing I felt like consuming these days, and sat at a table with Jenny and some of her friends, who I was trying hard to want to get to know. Not that there was anything wrong with them, it was just that everything was harder than it used to be.

"Hey, Nate!" one of the guys at our table said, waving as he came in the door.

Nate waved back. A few minutes later, coffee in hand, he sat in the empty chair next to me.

"Hi, Anika, how are you?" he asked.

"I'm great, Nate," I said, wondering if a bigger lie was ever told.

"Good, I'm glad to hear that. So what's been keeping you busy lately?"

Oh, let's see… the word "suffering" sums it up pretty well.

"The same old thing as usual," I said. "So what have you been up to, Nate?"

"Working, mostly. There's more work than my guys can handle, since adding the estate to our client list."

"I can imagine," I said, my head aching for so many reasons.

"My brother recently moved here, and he's joined the business as partner. That's allowing the business to grow to meet the demand. I'm excited about it, working with him is great, plus his wife is an excellent cook and I'm getting to spend time with my niece and nephew."

"That's awesome, Nate," I managed a smile, wondering which hurt worse—my heart or my head. "Family's important."

He talked some more, and I tried to be engaged and listen.

I don't think anyone but Jenny could tell how hard I was fighting to act normal, but I felt worse the longer I was there. Nate is a really nice guy, and I felt like by trying to listen and be friendly, I was leading him on. I don't know if I'd feel that way if Jenny didn't tell me he asked if I was seeing anyone. But she *did* tell me, and I did feel that way.

I finally begged Jenny to take me home. I had the worst migraine from holding in tears and keeping emotions under lock and key. Nate offered to take me, and I was so thankful that Jenny insisted she'd do it.

She apologized on the way, and said she wasn't trying to set me up. She told him I lost someone and wasn't up to dating, but guessed he was hoping to become friends and be there when I was ready.

I could understand if he was just trying to be friends... but he needed to find a girl who wasn't emotionally bankrupt, if he didn't want a lot of disappointment in the friend department as well as every other. He had no idea, and couldn't possibly understand that in every way, I was broken. I hoped I wouldn't always be, but... I was broken.

After the newspaper article, I was contacted by a television program, *History Detectives*. The host of the program, Josh McDaniel, read the article and wanted to devote an episode to Miles' story.

I was thrilled. Broadcasting Miles' innocence in hopes that anyone who ever heard the lies would now hear the truth, made me feel like I was still able to do something for him.

Josh had already approached Polly and received her okay to shoot video of the castle and the items I found that belonged to the estate. I confirmed that with her, then called him back.

Josh wanted more than to be shown around the estate, he wanted to interview me. It was really important to the guy, and I guessed it was because I tracked down all the info and no one could explain it like I could.

It was more than that, though. The tie between Sarah Williams and great-great-great granddaughter Anika Riley, was played up big time. The newscaster pointed out that I was the secret to solving the mystery. The proof wasn't located in the house, although supporting elements such as the death certificates and the evidence collected by Miles' Father, were. It took me, the great-great-great granddaughter of Sarah Williams Lawrence, to come along at exactly the right moment in history, believing in Miles' innocence, to track down what really happened to Sarah, and to hunt down her hatbox from the salvage company before it went up for auction, in order to discover the truth. If anyone looked too soon or too late, that opportunity to locate the hatbox would have been unavailable or gone forever. I was the mini celebrity of the day. They made as big a deal out of me as they did Miles, which I totally wasn't expecting.

The interview was very well done, I thought. Footage of the cave, the attic, the clearing, the castle, Miles' and Delevan's portraits, family photos, the hatbox and tin cases, the paper doll letter and the letter absolving Miles of guilt, Miles and Delevan's guns and death certificates, the diagram Miles' father drew, the salvage yard, the museum that is currently housing other artifacts salvaged from the Capricious... it was an hour-long program. A coroner was interviewed as well, and from what was written on the death certificates for Miles and Delevan, he confirmed that the original story was impossible. Miles couldn't murder his brother, then be shot twice by that already dead brother.

I have my suspicions that Sarah told the story the way she did in hopes that its validity would be questioned by someone other than Miles' parents. It just didn't work out that way, the Sheriff of the time was determined to be blind to the evidence.

Polly called every day to update me on her grandson's progress. She continued to encourage me to fly out to the hospital to meet Second-Miles, to the point of harassment. She told him all about me she said, and he saw the news articles and watched the program. Over and over.

"Miles is doing just wonderfully dear, physical therapy is going well. The doctors expect a full recovery. He is so looking forward to meeting you."

She had no idea how she twisted the knife in my heart every time she said that.

I was glad Second-Miles was getting better, but I was not looking forward to meeting him. I was afraid one look at him would destroy my carefully crafted composure. It was hard enough to talk normally and act normally around other people, especially my family. I didn't need such a visual reminder of who I lost, right in front of me.

Second-Miles' birthday came and went. Polly was relieved for so many reasons. Her grandson was awake to enjoy it, and the responsibility as trustee of the Bannerman estate was now out of her hands, and in his.

I was trying hard to be okay. I probably needed to give myself more time... it just seemed like after a month, why wasn't I starting to feel any better? At least a little? If anything, the further I got from the last time I saw Miles, the worse I felt. Depression was sapping the color out of life. Putting one foot in front of the other was becoming more and more difficult.

It was a struggle to hide it from those around me. I didn't know it was possible to miss someone this much. I *was* trying, so hard, to move forward, but being around other people was torture, and made me feel worse than I did if I sat alone staring at the photo Miles gave me, reliving every conversation we'd had... I wasn't suicidal by any means, but I was not looking forward to the rest of my life.

I watched through the window of the guest house until the last truck pulled out of the driveway and onto the road. Finally, Nate and his crew were gone for the day.

I stepped outside and closed the door behind me, leaving Chip and Trixie inside. I needed to be alone for this.

It was twilight in mid-May, and time stood still. The only sound was the water bubbling in the fountain, and my footsteps on the grass. I walked through the garden clutching a bouquet of roses as I made my way toward the path Nate mentioned last fall.

I found it, another cobbled path leading through the forest. My eyes ached from all the tears I cried, and the ones I held in. I hoped this would help... I was desperate to find a way out of this misery. It was supposed to get easier with time, not harder. I didn't know what else to do. Maybe this would bring that elusive closure people talk about.

The path made a gradual turn and the Bannerman family cemetery spread out before me.

I took a deep breath and moved forward, reading the inscriptions on the headstones.

I recognized the names from the portraits in the gallery. The first Delevan Bannerman, and so many others. This would have to be Miles' parents… Cynthia and her husband, Matthew. His younger brother James and his wife, and Delevan, and…

I dropped to my knees on Miles' grave.

MILES DELEVAN BANNERMAN
BELOVED SON AND BROTHER
APRIL 23, 1850 - APRIL 7, 1870

I traced his name with my fingers as I leaned against his headstone. I sat motionless except for the tears which spilled off my cheeks and onto his grave.

"I miss you—so much," I cried. "I know you wanted me to move on, but how? I don't know how…"

I sat huddled with my cheek against his headstone, hugging myself for warmth as the sun sank and the full moon rose.

"If I had it to do over again… I'd do the same thing. I'm glad you're at peace now. I wouldn't want you to ever be alone again, I would never want you to feel like I do. I love you too much for that. You were the best friend I could ever hope to have, and I'm so thankful for the time I knew you. I'll never forget you, not ever."

Sobs overtook me and I couldn't speak until they subsided.

"Trixie's doing okay. She misses you, but she's doing alright. I'm taking good care of her."

The limbs of the trees rustled in the breeze, and a cricket chirped in the distance.

"I—sometimes play the Go Vacation game that we used to play together. I find your Mii character, and invite you to join me, and we travel around the resort. I don't know if it makes me feel better, or worse… but for a little while it almost makes me feel like you're still here somehow."

An owl sounded mournfully from a nearby tree in the forest.

"I'm glad you're at peace… but I feel like I'm in pieces, and I don't know how to put myself back together. I'm trying, I really am. I know you'd be upset if you thought I wasn't. I go out with Jenny, I meet her friends, and I try to act like my heart isn't aching unbearably and give them a chance… I'm afraid I'm going to hurt this much for the rest of my life. I don't know how to fix it. When you left, all the happiness in the world went with you. I miss you so much. I miss talking to you, I miss listening to you, I miss the light in your eyes when you laugh, and I miss the sound of your laughter."

My tears fell silently as I thought dully that from now, on the scent of fresh cut grass and roses would remind me of misery.

"The longer you're gone, the harder it is, and the emptier I am. I hurt unbearably. I feel like I'm slowly dying…"

I spent the night talking to Miles and crying. In the cold, early morning hour before dawn, I rose and lay the crimson roses on his grave.

I slowly made my way back to the guest house, desolate and chilled to the bone, and convinced that there is no such thing as closure, after all.

April showers really do bring May flowers. The grounds of the estate were bursting with color. Lawncare Extraordinaire was worth their weight in gold, I'd never seen a more wonderful garden. The smooth lawn, the nicely trimmed shrubs and flowers. So many flowers. The roses were in bloom, and the air was heavy with their perfume.

The day finally came that Polly's grandson was scheduled to be released from the hospital. He was doing well, and was expected to have a full recovery, as she said. Evidently he had more than a brain injury from the fall though, and would require continued physical therapy for some time. Which made sense, the news program that announced he was awake and that Alfred had been arrested, also played footage showing the cliff he was pushed off of. I didn't know how he managed to survive at all.

There was so little for me to do anymore. I wondered if Polly really needed me at this point. Everything that could be fixed, repaired, cleaned, or updated, had been. The grounds were regularly maintained by Nate's company. Molly and her girls came like clockwork twice a week, and kept the inside of the castle sparkling.

It was nearing the end of May, and the months until college would begin stretched desolately ahead of me.

I dreaded the day that matchmaker Polly and Second-Miles would return to the estate. It would be soon, though I didn't know the actual day. With my scholarship, I didn't need a job to afford college anymore. I could move in with my family until school started in August. I felt a pang of guilt that after Polly had done so much for me, here I was wanting to pull a Jim and Patricia Henderson on her.

Everywhere I looked there were memories. Memories that were precious to me, but being here was a constant reminder that I would never see Miles again. For my sanity's sake, I needed to turn in my resignation. I couldn't leave Polly in the lurch like the last caretakers did, but I could give two weeks' notice.

I took my iPhone out of my pocket and called Polly. I tapped my foot anxiously, waiting for her to answer, but got her voicemail. She must be visiting Second-Miles. The hospital had the usual "no cell phone" rule, and she abided by it.

I disconnected the call without leaving a message, and sighed. I wanted to get that over with, having made the decision.

I felt so restless. I looked out the window of the guest house at the castle and at the windows of Mission Control. Then I looked above that to the room that was once Miles'.

There was one thing left for me to do.

I grabbed my keys and headed through the garden and up the stairs and through the front door. A pang struck me as it did every time I walked into the entryway... wanting so badly, but knowing I'd never again hear Miles say "Hi back," the way he always used to do when I greeted him.

I hurried up the many flights of stairs to the fourth floor and found his room.

I opened the door and stepped inside, softly closing it behind me. I looked around, wondering where to start. I guess it didn't matter where, what mattered was packing away Miles' things. Thanks to Sarah's letter, everyone knew Miles was innocent, and that was good. It also made him famous though, and there were people who had a macabre fascination with anything pertaining to him, now. The news station was flooded with letters, and some of them were pretty outrageous. There were women out there that wanted every last little detail about Miles, as if they had a crush on him or something. If I didn't know Miles, and love him, maybe I'd just think it was really, really weird. Maybe it wouldn't bother me so much... but it did!

Just in case Second-Miles wasn't as honorable as my Miles, and decided to turn the estate into a museum... I was determined Miles' things wouldn't be part of a display for people to gawk at.

I dropped to my knees next to his trunk. I opened it as I had on New Year's Day, a million years ago... and found Miles' bible lying where I'd left it. Miles' name was written inside, so that was one thing that definitely needed to be packed away. Maybe I should pack it away in the guest house. Miles would be glad for me to have it, but there was an heir to the estate now that had a say in everything. Maybe I could talk to Polly, surely she'd understand, after I worked so hard and solved the mystery. It seemed a very little thing to ask for.

I picked up Miles' bible and opened it, hoping to find that he'd written notes in the margins as so many people did, and instead found a sealed envelope that wasn't there before.

I turned it over. On it was written *to Anika Riley*.

I smiled, and my eyes filled with tears at the same time. I held that precious envelope in my hands and pressed it against my heart.

I wanted so much to know what Miles wrote to me, but once I read it, I wouldn't have it to look forward to any more. For a while I just sat and held it.

I took a tissue out of the pocket of my sweater and wiped the tears from my eyes, then rose from the floor and sat on a chair near the fireplace.

I carefully opened the envelope and took out a letter.

Dearest Anika,

Since you're reading this, I know you succeeded in what you promised to do. I know you're sad now, and hurting, missing me, and I wish there had been any other way. If I could have stayed with you, the all-me guy I used to be, I would have. I can't tell you how I prayed for that, but… that's an awfully big request, and just knowing you for the time that I did was more than I ever deserved. I know you dreaded the loss of our friendship as much as I did, but you wanted what was best for me, and that's what I want for you.

Since there are no tears in heaven, I know I'll see you there someday. When I do, I want you to tell me that you had a happy and full life. That's what I want for you, and that's why I was willing to give up our friendship for the time being, so that you would have it. I knew you wouldn't, if I stayed. Anika, I would have gladly stayed and been alone again someday, just to have more time with you. The thought of leaving you is unbearable, I can only imagine how hard it was to actually say goodbye. I did this for you, so please, I don't want you wasting the life you have missing me.

You are truly my best friend, and you matter to me more than anyone. Until I see you again, I'll play over every memory we made since the day you stood there glaring at me, demanding to know if I was Miles. How indignant you were, I felt sorry for Second-

Miles, not realizing at first that you were talking to me. But I'm so glad you were. I have a lifetime's worth of wonderful memories with you, and it was worth spending one-hundred and forty years alone to have them.

You are so special. You're funny, and fun, you're smart, you think in such creative ways and are always a surprise. You're kind-hearted, and deserve every good thing in life. You are absolutely beautiful, too. The longer we were together the harder it was to remember we could only be friends, and that I shouldn't wish for more. Don't ever doubt your worth, and don't ever let anyone else make you doubt it. If you ever do, then just remember what your friend Miles, who you always thought was so smart, had to say about it.

Don't stay alone. Make friends, life is worth living if you can find the right ones, and very hard if you don't. If you go out with a guy and he doesn't convince you that you're the most beautiful girl in the world, and treat you like you're priceless… then he isn't good enough for you. You deserve the very best, don't ever settle for anyone that doesn't believe that, and make you believe it, too. Go to college as you've always wanted, and do great things. Laugh, and be happy, and don't ever feel you're dishonoring our friendship if you aren't grieving. You'll honor the sacrifice I made in leaving you by living the best life you can and having all of the things you wouldn't, if I stayed.

Until I see you again, with all my love, your friend,

Miles

I held the letter to my heart and furiously wiped away tears, determined to protect what was now my most precious possession.

I sat and cried, reading it over and over, cherishing every word.

Chapter 22

I was so thankful to have Miles' letter. I missed everything about him, and what I wouldn't give to be able to talk to him again, even for a few minutes. The letter was as close as I could get, and I read it over and over that night after I finished packing his things, and returned to the guest house.

I wanted to do what he asked. I didn't want to hurt this much for the rest of my life. I hoped moving back in with my family would help, and that when college started it would give me something new to focus on. I wanted to move forward.

I wondered how to do that though, when my heart refused to come with me. An important part of me was missing, and I was afraid it was impossible to ever get it back. If I didn't, I'd never move forward. I would remain stuck in my own half-way existence.

Late that night I lay in bed in the dark, staring at the wall, wishing sleep would come and give me a reprieve. I heard the quiet purr of a car as it pulled into the driveway and past the guest house, on its way to the castle. I got up and looked out the window.

It was a taxi. I had a feeling I knew who it was… I dreaded meeting Polly's grandson, and what that would do to me. I couldn't bring myself to think of him as Miles… that name belonged to my friend, my Miles.

I left the lights out, hoping Polly would think I was asleep and wouldn't get any bright ideas about introducing me to her grandson right away. Although with that persistent little woman, it was anybody's guess if that would stop her.

Polly and her grandson got out of the taxi, and the taxi driver removed their bags from the trunk and carried them to the front door. Polly's grandson wore a knee brace on his right leg and limped slightly. Polly said something to him, and he looked towards the guest house.

It felt like the shattered pieces of my heart were being ground into my chest. He looked just like my Miles. I sank to the floor and pressed my hands over my heart, trying to hold it together, as tears welled in my eyes and I choked back first one sob, then another.

I was so glad the lights were out, and Polly didn't try to interrupt my pretend sleep. If only I'd been smart enough not to look out the window and spared myself that, as well.

I didn't sleep that night. I lay on the bed staring at Miles' photo, losing hope that it would ever get easier and dreading the morning and the rest of my life without him.

Painfully early, Polly came knocking. I slid Miles' photo under my pillow with his letter, ran my hands through my hair, and dragged myself to the door.

"Oh my dear, I'm so glad to see you!" Polly said as she gave me a hug, but then she held me back and looked alarmed. "Goodness, I don't remember you being so thin, you're positively wasting away. You're just a shadow. We need to do something about that immediately."

Polly saw Trixie. Her eyes narrowed and she gave Trixie a shrewd look. Then she looked at me, then back at Trixie.

"Trixie was homeless, and she and Chip made friends... I hope it's okay that she lives here," I said.

If it wasn't, I'd move out today. No way was I giving up Miles' dog.

Polly recovered.

"Of course, dear! She is more than welcome. Funny, the Miles Bannerman whose name you cleared had a dog named Trixie, who disappeared when he was murdered." She gave me a piercing look, and I did not say a word.

Polly didn't dwell on whatever thought was going through her mind. I didn't have to borrow her distraction technique and point out a squirrel after all.

"I can't wait for you to meet Miles," she said. "He is the most wonderful young man. Kind, considerate, and caring..."

She leaned in conspiratorially. "Miles always wants to hear all about you after we talk, and he's watched your news program a million times on his iPhone."

I felt sick.

"You can't do better than Miles, my dear," she said. "And he can't do better than you."

She smiled, patted my arm, and walked back to the castle.

I shut the door and leaned against it, dreading the rest of the day.

Well, forget that!

I wasn't going to hang around waiting to have my broken heart dug out with a dull spoon, I was running away. Well, not entirely, but I could drive into town and kill time, or just—drive. Anything other than wait here for the inevitable.

I dumped food in Chip's and Trixie's bowls, which they inhaled in record time. I let them outside, then hurriedly showered and threw on jeans and a t-shirt. I grabbed my keys and flung open the door, locking it behind me, intending to call the dogs and flee. I forgot my purse, but I wasn't going back for it. If a cop wanted to arrest me for not having my driver's license that was just fine, as long as Polly and her grandson didn't come bail me out!

I whirled around and collided with someone.

It was Polly's grandson. I jumped backwards as though I'd been electrocuted, my back hitting the door and my keys falling to the ground.

I stared at him in panic, and fought to keep the memories from flooding in.

"Hi," I stammered.

"Hi back," he smiled.

Too late.

I knew this would happen eventually. I couldn't avoid him forever. It was just—hard enough to overcome the grief of losing my friend without his double right in front of me, a reminder of what I lost. Add the injustice that they share the same name, and it just did not put me in a good mental place. It would put me in a medical mental place, at this rate.

As soon as Miles and I found proof and he was gone, I should have gone, too. I shouldn't have stayed here. And next year Polly's grandson would be at the same college I was, and—

He startled me when he reached out and grabbed me by the shoulders. I fought and tried to pull away, but my back was against the door, and he wouldn't let go. He had no idea how lucky he was that I wasn't packing pepper spray!

"Anika, snap out of it and listen!" he said urgently. "It's me, Miles. I'm not Second-Miles."

I stopped struggling and stared at him, my mind thick.

"Anika, it's me. It's really me. I'm not Second-Miles, Anika... it's me, Miles."

I stared at him, trying to comprehend the incomprehensible. No one knew that's what I called Polly's grandson, except—Miles. *My* Miles.

"M-miles?"

Miles smiled.

I burst into tears and threw my arms around him.

He hugged me tightly while I cried as I never had before. In spite of how many tears I'd shed, there were so many more that I hadn't. I'd held in so much, putting on an Oscar winning performance in front of everyone, hoping they wouldn't guess that my heart was hopelessly broken. But somehow, impossibly, Miles was here. He was ALL here, solid, I could feel the steady beat of his heart as I stood there and held onto him for dear life, overwhelmed by uncontrollable emotion and soaking his t-shirt with my tears, while he held me and told me over and over that it was okay, that everything was okay now.

Eventually my hysterical sobbing settled down to a somewhat manageable level. Miles held me back and looked at me, gently brushing back the side-swept bangs that I hadn't taken the time to try and tame with hairspray in my haste to run away, and which insisted on falling across my face. I looked into his gorgeous brown and green flecked eyes, even more amazing now that he was here, all the way here. Hesitantly at first, I touched his face, ran my fingers through his hair, felt of his shoulders, his chest, reassuring myself. It was too good to be true, but it *was* true! I traced the faint scar on his jaw. I wasn't dreaming, somehow he'd come back to me, all the way back. The happy tears continued to rain down, and I wiped them away so I could see him better, knowing that the scent of the aftershave he wore, would always remind me of the happiest day of my life.

Miles' eyes were laughing as he cradled my cheek in his hand and brushed away more tears with his thumb.

"So I take it you're not glad to see me?"

I laughed through the tears, lightly slapping his very solid chest with the back of my hand.

"Careful," he smiled. "I bruise now. And I'm pretty sure you've already cracked some ribs."

I put my arms around him again and squeezed even tighter, just for that. Miles laughed softly, and hugged me back just as tightly.

"I love you, Anika," he said.

"I love you too, Miles," I said, as a few more happy tears joined all the others on his very damp t-shirt.

The sky was never more beautiful than it was today, and the roses never smelled so sweet. The birds sang their trilling songs as if they, too, understood that now, everything was right with the world.

Several days later—okay, probably more like an hour later, I finally ran out of tears, and Miles loosened the vice-like grip I had on him and held me back again.

"Do you mind if we sit down? I'm not sure how much longer my knee can hold up."

"Of course," I said, looking down at the brace on his leg and keeping an arm around him, tightly clutching the side of his t-shirt in one hand, and the front of his entirely soaked shirt with the other. "I hope you know I'm never letting you go again."

Miles laughed, his arm around me also.

"That's just fine. You won't hear me complain."

We walked towards the fountain and the swing that was conveniently built for two.

As we sat down, Trixie bounded up and barreled into Miles' chest. He winced and hugged her at the same time. Chip had to get in on the attention. He was thrilled to find that this friend who only talked and threw sticks to him before, was now able to touch him. I felt the same way, minus the stick part. I begrudgingly gave them a minute, then pretended to throw a ball and the attention hogs—I mean, dogs—took off.

Miles turned to face me. He looked so amazing, so healthy, so solid, that happy light shining in his eyes.

"I can't believe you're here," I said, gripping his hand, the tears threatening to start again. "I missed you so much it was unbearable."

"I missed you, too," Miles said. "So what did you decide to do, go on a hunger strike? If you were any thinner, you'd be semi-transparent yourself."

I laughed at that, as Miles continued.

"Grandma Polly was right, you are wasting away. It's a good thing I'm back, or you might have pulled a Romeo and Juliet. Only that would make me Juliet and you Romeo, so never mind that analogy."

I laughed again, but the look in Miles' eyes told me he was genuinely concerned.

"I admit, I was wasting away. Inside, anyway. I wasn't trying to hurt myself, but I was unbearably depressed after you left. To do anything—it took too much effort. I couldn't eat, I couldn't sleep... about all I could do was cry, and miss you," my voice trembled, and I barely kept more tears from escaping.

Miles looked at me softly, then hugged me.

"If I thought I'd never see you again... I wouldn't have done any better."

"I'll be fine, now that you're here," I reassured him.

Miles sat back, but kept his arm around me.

"You have no idea how I hounded Grandma Polly about you. I wanted to be sure you were alright, that you were taking care of yourself. You sure had her fooled, by the way. She was shocked when she saw you this morning, she's in the kitchen right now giving orders to the chef to cook a carb-laden breakfast, lunch, and dinner. Plus snacks in between."

I laughed. Funny Polly. That was fine with me though, for the first time since Miles left, I actually felt hungry again.

"I wanted to know way more than Grandma Polly was ever able to tell me, though. She couldn't tell me if you were dating, or if you'd fallen in love with another guy in my absence, and believe me that thought was unbearable. It was bad enough when I was semi-transparent, even though I didn't want you wasting your life on me then. But once I was all me again, all I wanted was to get back to you before you moved on so far, I'd never be able to reach you. I nearly went crazy waiting for the doctors to decide to release me. I can't tell you how I regretted all the encouragement I gave you to move on, move forward, to find someone else."

"As if I could possibly do that," I said, holding his hand with both of mine. "When you left... my heart went with you, and I couldn't move on without it."

"I know," he said softly. "When I saw you, I knew. I couldn't move on, either."

"I'm so glad you didn't, I'm so glad you're here," I said, master of the understatement.

"I'm glad to be here," he smiled, and I smiled back, using his completely soggy t-shirt to wipe fresh tears, which made him laugh.

"You're proving that the human body really is made up mostly of water. You're going to vanish entirely, if you keep this up."

I laughed.

"So... what happened to you, after you vanished?" I wondered.

"It was the craziest thing. I went from sitting beside you in the parlor reading the letter, to an episode of ER. Doctors and nurses were frantic. I was in a lot of pain, I think I may have passed out.

"The next thing I knew, people were ordering me to wake up. I didn't remember falling asleep, and I was so tired, too tired to think straight. It sort of dawned on me I hadn't been tired in an awfully long time, but I was now, with a vengeance. I just wanted to sleep, so I pretended I was, hoping they would give up and leave me alone. It didn't work, they were extremely persistent, and tried even harder to wake me.

"As I became more alert, I started to wonder who these people were, and where I was. Not in heaven, that much was obvious, and the realization was more than a little alarming. So I opened my eyes and discovered I was in a surgical recovery room. Not that I knew that's what it was, at first."

"You must have been so... surprised, and confused," I said, as I tried to imagine what that was like for him.

"Bewildered is probably the best word to describe what I felt. I was lying in a hospital bed in a small curtained room, hooked up to an IV, and a heart monitor, and I'm not sure what else. I was still in pain, though not as excruciating. My shoulder was bandaged, and my right leg immobilized. There were several people in scrubs crammed into the room with me, and they all knew my name. I asked where I was, and some of them got kind of emotional, which at the time, confused me even more. None of it made sense. It wasn't until later when I saw the detective, that I realized who they thought I was.

"One of the nurses answered my question though, and told me I'd just come out of surgery and was in recovery. I somehow sustained life-threatening injuries to my shoulder and knee, and if they hadn't started a blood transfusion when they did, I wouldn't have made it. But they did, and she assured me I was in stable condition. The surgeries went well, and I'll need a lot of physical therapy, but the doctors expect me to recover completely."

"Oh my goodness, that makes me sick to think of you coming back and then almost dying all over again!" I felt the blood run out of my face at the horrifying thought.

"That didn't happen though," Miles said in the same tone he might use to talk someone off a ledge. "The doctors and nurses jumped into action and saved my life. Don't get stuck in that moment, it's over, and I'm here."

"Okay," I said, closing my eyes and taking a deep breath. "This is the moment I want to be stuck in, here with you now. And you *are* all you."

I traced the faint scar on his jawline with my fingers again.

"Yes, all me. No brain injury like Polly's grandson suffered. He was brain-dead, Anika. He was gone a long time ago, months before we even met. The doctors removed the ventilator to perform an apnea test to confirm that, right before they got the shock of their lives. Suddenly I was there, the person they thought they'd been treating all along, awake and with massive bleeding from gunshot wounds. No one will ever be able to explain that. No one's asked me about it, I'm the least likely to know. I was in a coma since I hit the ground, they think. They're referring to the injuries as having been sustained during the fall. You haven't heard about it in the news, and I don't expect you ever will. Unless someone wants to try and pin an alien abduction spin on it, years from now. You know, person speaking from behind a screen, 'I was working at the hospital when the strangest thing happened…'"

"So… is that why Polly said there was no change, when I called her the next afternoon, after you left? They hadn't told her?"

"Right. They were probably too freaked out by the whole thing to know what to say. Just imagine it, 'We've got good news and bad news, ma'am. He's awake and breathing on his own, but removing the respirator resulted in multiple gunshot wounds.' I was through surgery, out of recovery, and talking to a detective, before they contacted Grandma Polly."

"Wow," I said, resting against his uninjured shoulder. "But what about Alfred, and the attempted murder charges?"

"Somehow, I was given that memory. I remember it like I was there, seeing everything happen. Alfred tried to kill him. He was willing to commit murder, to get his hands on the estate. As large as my family was once, the only relations left at that time were Second-Miles and Alfred. He followed Second-Miles, and intentionally 'bumped into' and invited Second-Miles to join him on a hike. Second-Miles remembered him as a distant relation, and agreed. Alfred took Second-Miles by surprise, and pushed him over the edge of the cliff. Then he took Second-Miles' identification and disposed of his car, so there would be nothing to indicate Second-Miles' identity."

"How horrible!" I exclaimed, unable to imagine how callous a person would have to be to do that. Trying to kill him was bad enough, but then to take his identification as he lay there injured, and his life slipping away, and to have no compassion... it was incomprehensible.

"Yeah. It really is," agreed Miles. "It's a slight consolation that because his injuries were so severe, he was unconscious and didn't feel pain. Somehow he lived until another hiker found him and the paramedics got him to the hospital, but no one could survive that fall, not with the injuries Second-Miles sustained. If it weren't for the machines that were breathing for him, his body wouldn't have survived that long."

"You ended up in Second-Miles' hospital bed... what happened to him?" I wondered.

"I do not know," said Miles. "I've wondered that myself."

"Maybe... he took your place?"

"Maybe so."

"Wow. Just—wow."

We sat for several long minutes in silence and processed it all. Tried to process it, anyway.

"I am just so glad you're here, all the way here," I said as Miles kissed the back of my hand, and I squeezed his bicep with the other. "You've been working out."

Miles laughed.

"Physical therapy, baby. They work you to death there. Nearly."

I took a deep breath, which was so much easier to do now that the heavy weight of loss was removed.

"I missed you so much," Miles said. "It was awful being forced to stay in the hospital for over a month. The food really is as bad as people say. Imagine, going without food for over a hundred and forty years, and that's what you wake up to. The worst thing was having to wait to see you, to tell you what happened. It was the longest month and a half I've ever spent, and that's saying something."

I groaned.

"It was for me, too. I should have flown up like Polly wanted. I just—didn't know *you'd* be there, and I couldn't face seeing your double. She kept pressuring me to come meet you. She so obviously wanted to set us up, and made it clear you'd be all for that."

"I couldn't hide how I felt about you, and didn't really try. Grandma Polly never questioned it. I guess she thought after being at an all-male prep academy for several years, and then in a coma for most of one, it was only natural I'd fall hard and fast as soon as I saw your photo. After all, you are the most beautiful girl in the world. Of course I was desperate to meet you, before some other guy could swoop in."

I blushed, and laughed.

"Yeah, like any other guy ever had a chance! I can't believe you worried about that. All I ever thought about was you, and if I'd known it *was* you there in that hospital, nothing could have stopped me from coming to you," I declared. Then I pushed Miles back slightly, and raised an eyebrow. "So I hear you have an iPhone. Why did you not call and tell me!"

"I couldn't, I didn't have your number. As much as I begged, and believe me I did, Grandma Polly wouldn't give it to me. She was a stickler for the 'no cell phone use' rule while in the hospital. For some reason using it to watch your video was okay with her, while calling wasn't. Believe me, I wracked my brain trying to think of ways to contact you. I even looked your parents up, hoping to convince them to give me your number. I wasn't sure how receptive they'd be to that, but I was desperate. I couldn't find a number for them, though. Either it's unlisted, or they don't have a landline."

"Well I want your number," I said, taking my iPhone out and snapping a picture of the cutest guy ever. "I don't want to ever lose touch with you again."

Miles gave me his number, and I gave him mine.

"Don't expect to have to use it much though," he said. "I don't plan on being very far from you ever again."

"That's just fine," I smiled. "You won't hear me complain."

Miles smiled back as we both put our iPhones in our pockets, then settled into the swing once more.

"So have you tried walking through any walls lately?" I joked.

Miles laughed.

"Yeah, I ran into a couple of them at the hospital. It's hard to get used to doing things the old-fashioned way, again. I got put through more tests, as a result. They were just sure my missing brain injury was reappearing. That probably contributed to the decision not to release me sooner. They must have thought I was a major Star Wars fanatic too, more than once I forgot and tried to use the 'force' to pick up things."

I laughed. It felt so good to have my best friend back, all the way back. Unless I was severely mistaken, my best friend, the most gorgeous guy in the whole world, was now my boyfriend, too.

"May nineteenth will always be my favorite day from now on," I said.

"Mine too," Miles smiled. "Things sure turned out differently than we expected they would, when you were trying so hard to free me."

"Oh my goodness. If I had any idea freeing you meant freeing you like *this,* I would have spent every minute of every day and night searching!" I said.

Miles laughed.

"I would have too. But all of that time gave us a chance to get to know each other and become best friends. And now we have that foundation to build on."

I liked the sound of that.

"So I hear we're going to the same college next year."

"That's right," Miles smiled. "I'm looking forward to it."

"I'll bet, as much as you love learning."

297

"I do love learning… but that's not what I'm looking forward to the most."

Miles suddenly grew serious.

He faced me, taking both my hands in his. He looked so intense… one of those looks that made my knees weak, and my insides melt. That was one superpower he hadn't lost, it had only grown stronger.

"I need to ask you something…"

I held my breath. What is he about to say? He's not on one knee, but he couldn't manage it with that brace on. What will my family think? It'll seem awfully sudden to them, we're so young, I'm only nineteen, although technically he is a *lot* older. Is he skipping right over dating, and going straight to—

"Anika Riley… will you teach me how to drive?"

It took me a minute to realize what he said.

"Uh—yeah, sure," I said.

"Okay, great," said Miles.

He smiled as he sat back and put his arm around me again.

"And when I ask you that other question… it will be after I meet your parents, and talk to your Dad, and buy a ring."

"I'll drive," I said.

Miles laughed, and my good-as-new heart beat faster as he gazed at me with that soft, melting look in his gorgeous hazel eyes. He brushed the hair away from my face again as I thought how fortunate it was we were sitting on that swing. I don't know about Miles' knee, but neither of mine were capable of supporting me when he looked at me that way. I breathed in the intoxicating combination of aftershave and fabric softener as he cradled my cheek in his hand and hesitantly leaned closer. I gripped the front of his soggy t-shirt as my breath caught in my throat and my heart pounded.

I finally whispered, "If you're waiting for permission, you have it."

Miles laughed softly, then he slowly kissed me, as I became aware that he had another superpower besides his ability to melt with a look. His touch could instantly liquefy.

Miles smiled, that happy light in his eyes as I collapsed against his shoulder, still clinging to his shirt, lightheaded and dizzy.

Then he said, "I'll get the keys."

About the Author

Melissa R. L. Simonin writes "good clean, feel good fiction with a sense of humor." Her books cover a variety of genres ranging from romance, mystery, suspense, supernatural, historical, inspirational, and Christian fiction.

Once named, Melissa's characters take on a life of their own. They have stories to tell, and it's a race to keep up and write it all down. She learned by experience not to name characters until she's ready to write, because once they have names the book is going to start whether she's ready or not.

Melissa's current series include The House of Bannerman, Mystery Lane, The Investigations of Jack Ryland, and Terms of Engagement.

Get the latest news on upcoming books and behind the scenes info you won't find anywhere else by visiting http://melissasimonin.com

Also by Melissa R. L. Simonin...
Miles, House of Bannerman book 1
House of Shadows, House of Bannerman book 2
Darkness Falls, House of Bannerman book 3
The Lodge at Whispering Pines, House of Bannerman book 4
Depart the Darkness, House of Bannerman book 5
Camp Emmaus
Stonecastle Inn
715 Mystery Lane, Mystery Lane book 1
601 Suspense Street, Mystery Lane book 2
Isle of the Crescent Moon
Hiding Treasure
Last Chance Inn, The Investigations of Jack Ryland book 1
Cottonwood Hotel, The Investigations of Jack Ryland book 2
Terms of Engagement, Terms of Engagement book 1
Failure to Engage, Terms of Engagement book 2
Lochlan Museum

Coming soon...
423 Apprehensive Avenue, Mystery Lane book 3
Ashes of Roses, House of Bannerman book 6
Disengaged, Terms of Engagement book 3

CPSIA information can be obtained
at www.ICGtesting.com
Printed in the USA
FSHW010651271118
54059FS